I0594866

REVERIES

OF AN HEIR

A. D. AELIN

"It is possible to commit no mistakes and still lose.
That is not a weakness. That is life."

— Captain Jean-Luc Picard

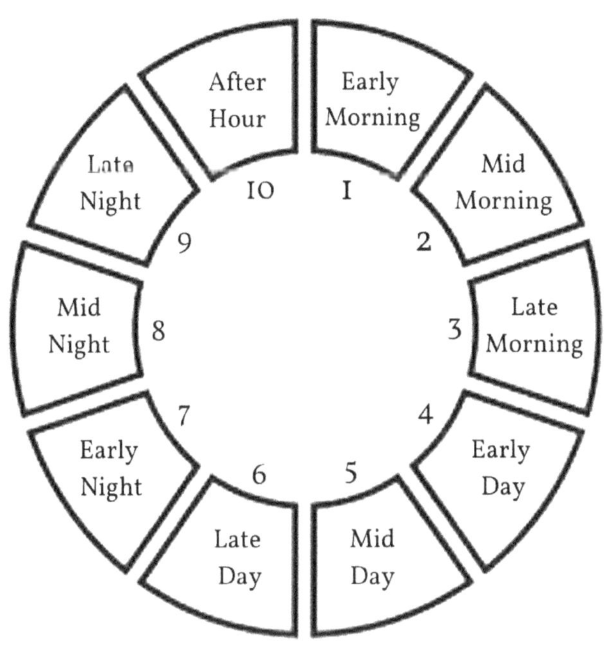

A Definitive Guide to Time
| Elysian and Universal |

100 Seconds	=	1 Minute
100 Minutes	=	1 Hour
10 Hours	=	1 Day
10 Days	=	1 Week
5 Weeks	=	1 Month
10 Months	=	1 Year
10 Years	=	1 Decade
10 Decades	=	1 Century
10 Centuries	=	1 Millennia
100 Millennia	=	1 Epoch
10 Epoch	=	1 Mya

*Each Era corresponds to its Empress
(E.g. Seventh Empress/Seventh Era)

Table of Contents

Chapter 1: Beginnings

We are the beginning and we are the end.

The Heir would arrive that night.

Trillions kept an anxious, eager vigil as the news was confirmed. For though the Empress' consort stood beside her even now.

He did not exist to be their Light.

At the core of their universe, where every hope was centered, Her Eternal Majesty labored in a calm and easy manner.

Most eventualities were inevitable, after all.

Especially when one is born with absolute power.

Dressed simply, her body hovered vertically in the birthing pod, her skin illuminating the otherwise dark room. That light ebbed and flowed slowly, never revealing the thoughts of the woman it surrounded. Her hands were relaxed, her golden hair neatly pinned back for the occasion.

With her eyes closed it was as if she slumbered.

By the morning, she would be going about her daily schedule.

If there was any anxiety in the room, it could all be attributed to her husband; who fluttered, paced, and generally made a nuisance of himself. Otherwise, she was attended only by her chosen physician and her Sentinels.

The laboring mother's mind drifted far away and over her domain, breathing with the hearts and lungs of her people, stabilizing an orbit or two of the worlds that found themselves protected by her love. Going over the endless steps, infinite was her patience. Infinite was her gaze.

In a flood of light and warmth, it was over.

From her body, a simmering serenity and clarity wove itself through the stars. Pulses of cool, soft calm radiated, its gentle touch bringing joy to those who understood and a brief chill to those who did not. Some awoke in their beds, certain that they had felt their ground shake. All felt an irresistible pull, and many turned themselves toward that all-consuming joy.

The stars themselves hesitated in their well-worn paths.

For a moment was all it took to begin a new era.

Cheers of jubilation rang out from every quadrant of their universe as the Empress dropped back down to her feet. The only sign of weakness was a slightly elevated color, her limbs not as graceful as they ought to be. A small noise escaped as her husband reached for her daughter.

One gesture brought the child to her.

□She was lighter than expected and did not cry. The infant's eyes were open and curious. It was obvious she had inherited all of the gifts entitled to her, and the Empress allowed herself a long perusal of this highly anticipated child. Did she feel the frenzied exuberance of her people? Nerves as her husband felt or the protectiveness of her Sentinels? Pulling back the cloth from around her head, a true trill of excitement gave her Eternal Majesty pause.

What seemed blonde under their moons, paled when lit by her Light and her husband's eager, fervent voice rose over the noise.

No one there paid him any mind.

Outside, celebrations were beginning that would last months.

Their new Heir was perfection incarnate.

And it was then her mother was certain.

You will not disappoint me.

Chapter 2: Admirations

"I'm sorry Mother."

After months of glowing praise and faultless performance, it was a shock to my academic commission when I stumbled over my cosmological geometry research project.

I was demonstrating my equations in real time on a hypothetical and it required all my concentration. This time, I was unable to hold the visual steady and before I could correct my mistakes, the model stabilized seemingly on its own.

It was the first time, since I left the nursery, that Mother was visiting me in the classroom. Behind me, the voices of my professors only magnified her silence.

When she beckoned, I ran to her. Despite my mistakes, Mother reached down to lift me up into her embrace. The Empress, ever gracious, smiled at my shyness; and though it wasn't good of me to cling to her clothing like this, I couldn't help but press my face against the cool folds of her overcoat.

"Saekonari is clearly struggling."

Embarrassed, I pressed myself tight against Mother's shoulder. I had no right to be sad or upset. My professors had resigned from their positions at the University and the Academy to oversee my education for the foreseeable future. Today, I had failed to meet their expectations just as much as I'd disappointed my mother.

"Being relaxed in your judgments is a mistake. Saekonari requires discipline. Look at the results of her ignorance and inexperience." The Empress's voice was soft, but so cold the air responded in kind. Her arms were even colder. "I recommend keeping to her fundamentals and theory for now."

"May I visit your study tonight?" I whispered. "I promise I'll be quiet. I won't make any noise." Mother was never wrong but next time... next time would be different. "I can do all of my assignments and maybe when we both finish our work, if you have time, we could—"

"Saekonari. You know better." She put me down.

Mother was gone before I could try to say anything more.

After just a second in time, the Empress could be anywhere.

A few minutes later, my footsteps echoed in the quiet of the Imperial Residence. Despite knowing my studies would occupy the rest of my daily schedule, it was possible I could finish in time to see more of my home. Perhaps I could find the medical observation rings or peek into the Academy's experimental accelerator research labs. I was already three years old. I needed to—

I was nearly knocked over as Esme threw herself at me from behind, her arms wrapped around my neck in such a way that I held us both upright. Her curly black hair sprung in every direction; her green eyes reminiscent of a sunlit spring.

"Sae! Hi! I can't believe they let you out already! Are you out of class!? Are you skipping!? Wanna see the baby lizards I found!?"

"Oh, we finished early, but I have homework. Hello Amie." I tried smiling, and Amie smiled back, always ready to be amused by her sister. The same black hair lay in loose waves on her head, her sharp gaze never failing to find me no matter the distance or crowded the room. Must come in handy.

My Sentinels.

We'd be together for eons. Birthmarked by a small white ring—Esme over her collarbone, Amie on her upper left arm—their family had been given gifts in exchange for their eternal loyalty. All Sentinels became advisors, protectors, and confidants of each Heir and eventual Empress.

They would stand beside me, even as the millennia passed.

"Who cares if you have homework!? Come on! The lizard babies are so scaly and cute! You haven't even been to the greenhouses!" She started spinning me, why the spinning? "They have really long tongues! You can't say no now!"

Esme began dragging me by the arm.

"It's okay Sae, go with your friends."

That voice had us all straightening our posture.

"Dad? I thought you had meetings off-world today."

Coliv Raajali was gone more and more these days from the palace. Today, his shoulders were slumped low and while his dark brown eyes could not be shadowed by exhaustion; I couldn't help but think he seemed sad again.

Slowly, I reached up to take his hand.

"Are you okay?" I was being serious, but he just chuckled.

Tugging at my ear affectionately, he encouraged me to go.

"Have fun. I'll talk to your mother." He knelt down to give me a hug and a piece of candy before Esme retook my arm.

Well, if Dad said it was okay...

Later that night, I hurried toward my dad's room. I'd drawn anatomically correct diagrams of the lizard babies, whose colorful bellies and silly smiles actually were very cute. I didn't know if Dad liked lizards, but I hoped he'd like my drawings.

"Never interfere with Saekonari again."

I shouldn't have stopped. The door was closed. Mother was angry. I knew I should have done my homework first. I wavered and took a step forward. This was my fault. Maybe if I told her I finished anyway, she wouldn't be mad anymore.

"Leti. For fuck's sake, does it have to be now!?"

I took another step forward, but then I ran out of courage and tried to leave as quietly as possible before I heard more. My limbs were too heavy, the floor underneath me was moving too fast. Dad never yelled. Mother never yelled.

"Yes. Now. Explain the note you left me."

I didn't want to hear them yell.

"I just wanted her to play for a little while.

"You know better. I told you to leave her alone."

It was like glass in my ears. Sharp. Brittle.

"She's my daughter Leti! I'm allowed to be around her!"

I tried covering my ears, but it didn't help me.

I shouldn't have been there.

"You're not acting like a father. You're being a nuisance."

Somehow Mother yelled without raising her voice.

"I told you not to fucking talk to me like that!"

And Dad yelled by screaming.

"Then stop acting like a fucking child—!"

Crash

I ran.

The northern orbital gardens were serene, idyllic under a perfectly cloudless sunset. The fuzzy pappus of nearby trees glowed silver in the fading sunlight. A light breeze made the fist-sized fluffs dance around their branches, stretching haphazardly across the sky. The grass below was long and flowing.

I couldn't help but stare at Esme's mismatched shoes.

"That's my favorite." She pointed to the left. "But I can't find the other one!"

They exchanged a look I had no hope of understanding. Sometimes, though they were my best friends, it felt as if there was no room for me. The silence stretched and I felt an overwhelming urge to braid the strands of grass surrounding us. Were they going to say something? You say something. Say anything.

"Amie, what's your shoe size?" Not that! "I just thought that—it's just an idea but—it's just—" I waved almost desperately at my shoes, which were not nearly as colorful as the pattern of red clouds on Amie's shoes. "—maybe we can exchange a shoe, and then Esme won't be the only one."

"That's hilarious. Here." Amie almost shoved her shoe at me, and a few seconds later... it didn't fit.

Of course it didn't fit, my foot was too big.

But Amie was laughing.

Suddenly, so was I.

"It wasn't that funny." Esme took off her shoes and took Amie's shoes, the one on her foot and the other from mine, and threw them into the bushes while proclaiming, "It's too hot for shoes anyway!" As soon as that was done, she rolled next to her sister on the grass and hugged her.

When Amie reached for me, I let her pull me down beside them too. "So, what's wrong?" She murmured in the ensuing quiet.

I didn't question how they knew. Thinking it over, I wondered if this was the kind of thing you spoke to your friends about.

Maybe they could help or I would feel better if they knew.

"I heard my parents arguing."

"So what!?" Esme scoffed. "Our parents fight all the time!"

"They always kiss and stuff after." Amie made a face and while they giggled, I felt a hard, twisting ache inside. It didn't seem right.

My mother and father...

"I wasn't supposed to be listening."

"Stop it, we hear stuff all the time we're not supposed to!"

"Oh? And just what were two eavesdropping on? Hmm?" Esme squealed as her mother dragged her by her ankles, blew kisses on her neck, and pulled her into a rolling hug.

"Let me assure you, darling." Their father followed her with a wide grin and a large case swung over one shoulder. "That I have no desire to know what these two have heard." Without missing a beat, he pulled Amie up with one arm and she clambered happily onto his shoulders.

Their father, Astral Esholitte, was a striking and devoted man who, according to reputation, could rip apart a small army single-handedly. Eluding numerous bounties in his youth, he'd made a notorious name for himself in the outer universe before capturing the heart of his last pursuer—his wife.

Anera Esholitte was my mother's Sentinel from birth. Willow slim and deceptively fragile looking, her deeply violet eyes were dramatically framed with lashes shades darker than the titan red curls on her head. Amie had inherited her eyes though the rest of her coloring was markedly different from her husband and children. Even so, no one could mistake her daughters' delicate noses and graceful mannerisms for anything else but hers.

"It's good to see you out of the nursery Sae." She held out her hands for me and I accepted after a brief hesitation. "I told Leti it was about damn time. Hungry?"

As the hour grew late, I was again entranced by their antics. When Anera wiped Amie's face clean before scattering kisses on her face or when Esme threw her arms around Astral's neck in a surprise cuddle, I had to remember not to stare. Their affection never lost its charm, each time as fascinating as the last.

"Girls, there's actually something we want to tell you."

Inexplicably, Anera reached for me again, pulling me onto her lap. "Sae, we wanted you to be here too because we're family and we love you." Her arms came around me in a hug. "I know we haven't been able to see you as often as we'd like, but I've been with your mother forever... Leti said she would try and make it tonight, but I suppose she's busy."

"Can I say it now?" Astral took back his wife's hand.

Anera brought Amie and Esme closer and nodded.

"We're having a baby!" Astral announced gleefully.

"A baby!?" Esme shrieked. "A baby!" She jumped between me and her mother, putting her hands on either side of Anera's face; smushing it slightly and erupting with questions. "Mom! You're having a baby!? When? How? Are we getting another sister? Can we name her? Can they sleep in my room!?"

"Esme darling!" Anera laughed, "I'm only a few years along." I moved off her lap as Esme waved her arms about in excitement.

Amie was more restrained but it was obvious how excited they all were. It was incredibly rare a Sentinel gave birth more than once. As Anera and Astral answered question after question, their children climbed all over them.

They didn't seem to mind at all.

Soon enough, it was past our bedtimes. Amie took my hand without a word as we headed back, their earnest chatter enveloping me in serene domesticity.

What could I say that would add to their joy?

They were all so very happy.

I wondered if I'd ever felt the same.

Chapter 3: Disappointments

I held my head high and walked carefully beside Mother into the Central Nexus. Original to the inner palace, it was an ancient structure of woven wood and stained glass forged in soft, swirling colors. I was all of ten years old and I needed to succeed tonight.

"Are you listening to me, Saekonari?"

"Yes Mother," I assured her quickly. A nation had petitioned to place themselves under the Empress' care after their home system was made uninhabitable by a stellar collision. They'd been unable to build the infrastructure necessary for evacuation; their leaders had refused our help; and endangered their people to preserve a veneer of control. Having made it to the border, their chosen representatives now filled this room. Only a few billion had survived.

"Did you pick out your clothes?"

"Is something wrong?"

"It's a bit... much."

Much? What did that mean? My clothes were in the same cut and style as the Empress'. Maybe the little birds were a bit childish?

"What did you do to your hair? I told you it looks best down."

My defining feature. So white the strands refracted light into rainbows, exactly matching the greatest of us. My face was hers. One of my names, Nicaristae, proudly proclaimed I was born from Aristae, youngest of the founders, first of the Raajali. No one could mistake me for anyone, anything, else.

"I'm sorry Mother." I had really liked it. "I can t-take it down."

"No. It's too late." Her attention shifted to Anera and Astral. "Where's Coliv?" Anera simply raised a hand and gave Mother a look that clearly said *I don't know, don't look at me.* "He's late." Even if Mother was worried, not a single sliver of discontent showed on her face.

There was no time to give another thought to my father. These people needed Mother and they were scared but there was no need to be so frightened.

We were nothing like where they had come from.

All we wanted was to love them as our own.

So, I made them laugh. I spoke to their young about the education systems waiting for them and to their parents about restarting their agricultural and industrial endeavors. The support now available to their families and communities. I made sure to give attention to their elderly, who told fascinating stories about the outer universe, answered any questions as succinctly as I could, and danced with whoever had the courage to ask me. All while knowing I was being watched from every angle from afar. Billions of eyes seeing the Heir for the very first time.

As the hour grew late, Anera signaled and I returned to Mother's side. The Empress' protection only extended to our own people. The legal documentation had already been completed in the weeks preceding this ceremony. Now, every sentient being who sought sanctuary in Elysia swore loyalty to the Empress; a ring of light appeared over their torsos that sealed their oath.

The light flickered out as quickly as it had appeared. Mother and I felt the vow repeated by their fellow refugees as she spoke of their new rights and protections.

Mother would never fail them. She would never forsake them for as long as she lived. Every day of my life, I'd watched her effortlessly uphold her daunting burdens alone and wished with all my might

I would one day be just as strong. Just as incredible. Just as eternal as the Empress who had raised me.

"Come with me, Saekonari."

Her hand dug into my shoulder.

It was a long walk back to the imperial wing. The warmth vanished from our surroundings the further we walked in silence. Everything I could have possibly done wrong rose to swarm my mind in deafening alarms; I had not done enough.

That much was perfectly clear.

"I'm sorry Mother."

"For once, I wish you had more to say." Mother walked quickly and while I was taller than average for my age group, every two of my steps was one of her long strides. "First your father and then you embarrass yourself in front of our people. Do you enjoy making things difficult?"

"It didn't affect the introduction," I said quietly.

"Saekonari. Everything you do wrong affects us."

"I know I wasn't my best but I think I did okay—" She stopped abruptly and I nearly stepped on the heels of her shoes. In my haste to backpedal, I tripped over my own feet. It was my own fault for walking so closely behind her.

She was so disappointed in me and I shouldn't have argued. I wanted to apologize again but it wasn't what she wanted to hear. Panicking, I tried to think of something to say but nothing would surface in my mind.

Mother walked away and left me there.

Though the halls of the palace were cavernous, the walls were shrinking down on me; the ground was no longer so solid underneath my feet. Trying to rationalize and make it stop did nothing. I didn't want to be alone right now. Amie and Esme wouldn't mind. They were probably still awake, but I didn't want them to know how angry Mother was. How badly I'd fumbled again.

I willed myself to get a grip.

Standing up, I began to walk toward Dad's room. I listened carefully, just in case Mother had gone in that direction, but all I heard was my own footsteps. He was away a lot of the time now, but he always tried to see me when he was home.

He would understand.

As I approached, I saw the door was ever so slightly ajar.

The inner door to his bedroom was also open and he was obviously asleep. I was going to leave, but something stopped me. I slid the door wider and went inside. "Hello? Dad? Um, I'm sorry it's so late. You must be tired, but I was hoping I could talk to... you..."

Something was wrong.

Turning on the lights, at first I thought it was another man lying in my father's bed. Silver markings were wrapped all along his arms, neck, face, and feet. Their intricate patterns were familiar to me, but my mind refused to take them in; his clothes were white, and his eyes were open. They were also flat and white like someone had dipped them in paint.

"Dad!?" I tried to rub out the pattern on his arm with my fingers.

"Dad!?" I started shaking and then I started shaking him.

I called out for my father over and over.

Why wouldn't he get up!? Why didn't he—

I froze. Someone was pulling my arms back.

Amie was holding me back. Esme was sobbing.

Why was she crying? Why were people shouting?

I'd never seen Mother in night clothes before.

"Amie. Let go."

I knew what was happening.

It was difficult for us to die. Not just anything would do it. We weren't sure if we could die of old age or disease. When one did, it was because of the overpowering urge to complete the cycle. Those markings told their own story. I had seen them in books and recordings, but no Raajali had ever passed so young. Before the next generation was prepared to take their place.

Before their daughter was ready to let them go.

Listening to my mother sob, letting Esme hug me and cry on my shoulder until it grew wet, not understanding what Anera was saying—I couldn't take it anymore. Esme almost fell over when I started walking. I could hear her begin to argue with her twin. I suppose she wanted to follow, and Amie stopped her.

I walked out of my father's rooms.

Through the crowd I couldn't really see.

Away from the sound of my mother's weeping.

Minutes—perhaps hours later—I stared up at one of our moons. It was unseasonably warm. Small, pink lit beetles flew about in lazy circles. Tucked away behind the imperial wing, you had to navigate through several more impressive gardens before finding this one. The centerpiece was a tree that provided a curtain of moss-like leaves. Huddled at the base, with its twisted branches surrounding me, it was difficult to say why I had fallen to my knees here.

I had felt like crying when I'd gone looking for my dad.

Now I pinched my dry cheeks, hoping I could cry now.

So I didn't cry at an embarrassing time. A bad time.

A small rustling had me jolting around, flinching when I saw eyes watching me from up in the tree—I knew the correct thing to do was to get to my feet, apologize, and leave—it had been too much to expect to be left alone.

They had obviously been here first.

My legs wouldn't move.

Why!? I buried my face against my knees as my body refused to listen. Hoping against all odds that they would have the decency and good sense to just leave me alone... all I wanted was a minute longer. Just one hundred more seconds to see if I could cry before I had to go back and fix my mistakes.

"You're a Raajali. Can't you just bring him back?"

What did he just—I felt heat coming back to my face.

"Maybe not you specifically, cause you're still a baby and all."

For the first time since I walked into my dad's bedroom, my body felt warm. I was shaking but not from fear or grief or shock. I stood. We were exactly the same height. His didn't even have the grace to back down as I opened my mouth and... closed it again.

Of course it just had to be now.

Turning away, I leaned on the smooth bark of the tree and felt sick from the effort of staying upright. Before I could even try to pull myself together, I felt his arms wrap around my shoulders and I couldn't stop. A single sob worked its way out and I let this stranger hug me against him on the ground while I cried into his clothes. I buried my howls against this boy's heartbeat. I felt the strength in the arms around me and it hurt so much.

Everything that had happened.

All that I had done wrong.

Everything that could have led my dad to leave me.

Eventually, I had to run out of tears and I finally, mercifully, did; I pulled out from my trembling, devastated core and into the firm grip of the present.

"I'm sorry." I fumbled away and he didn't stop me. "I am so s—"

"Don't apologize. I was trying to piss you off." The boy spoke to me with a soft murmur and a damp shirt. "It was all I could come up with." He slowly pulled out a handkerchief. "I know this is late, but I didn't want to move you."

He pressed the cool cloth against my face, and I inexplicably placed my hand over his on my cheek. No one ever touched me so cavalierly anymore. For a passing heartbeat, we stared at each other and there was an unexplored part of me that felt... odd.

I stood up from the ground and took a few, large steps back.

Carefully, he regained his feet like he expected me to flee. When he saw that I didn't, he spoke again. "Zarek Deutreax Trace." He reached out his hand towards me and out of deeply ingrained politeness, I took it. Instead of gripping or moving my hand in the form of greeting, he laced his fingers with mine.

"Saekonari Raajali." My whisper was barely audible.

He smiled and the markings of an excellent bone structure became evident. His face was impressively symmetrical. His hair, which at first glance seemed black, was actually several shades of dark, dark blue. It was his eyes that were a true black and marvelously full of what seemed like immeasurable warmth.

He was the only one to offer me comfort tonight.

Mother already had so much to deal with now and no one else had dared. Where Esme had cried helplessly, Amie had shut down, too stunned to act. Every time I closed my eyes, the image of my father's corpse rose up to the forefront.

This was inappropriate.

"I'm sorry. I'm not handling myself very well and—"

"You don't have to." His hand gently squeezed my own.

"I-I need to find my mother. She'll be looking for me." If he asked me to stay—I dreaded going back—I just might have, but he didn't. He let go of my hand and, knowing what the responsible choice was, I held out the handkerchief.

"Why don't you keep it?" He nodded towards the tree. "I'm only visiting but I'll be here if you need anything."

It wasn't right to think of him when my father laid cold upstairs. I shoved the handkerchief into a pocket, but I didn't let it go.

Walking down the halls to my mother's study, where she likely waited for my return, my dread only grew.

I heard raised voices.

"Leti. I am your best friend. Talk to me!" It was Anera.

"I loved him. I unified with him." My mother didn't sound sad or weepy, just annoyed. "But Coliv was nothing but a disappointment, and you know it."

My dad, who'd loved me so much.

Nothing but a disappointment.

It was the day after my father's memorial, which signaled the end of an entire week of strict observation. Meetings with mental health professionals, public appearances, and assisting my mother had taken all of my time. I didn't cry again, but Mother had done so publicly a number of times.

Raajali were not impervious to ourselves.

Mental health had been the cause of my father's passing. He had always struggled with it, according to Mother, and while he had lost the struggle, we would remember only the best of him. Mother had said this and a lot more yesterday; just before she obliterated his remains into open space. Trillions of incoming condolence messages had necessitated a temporary expansion of our personal correspondence and communications departments.

I dressed soberly in dark grey and completed all of my upcoming assignments ahead of time, even as my professors urged me to take leave from my academic work. I stayed close to Mother's side when she called for me and allowed Amie and Esme to keep me company at night so they didn't worry. I comforted anyone who approached me with their commiserations and turned down Astral and Anera's offer to take me away from the palace for a few days.

They wouldn't have been able to persuade Mother anyway.

That night, I finally convinced Esme that I would be fine by myself. Amie had accepted it a few nights ago when I first spoke up, but Esme was harder to shake. I was finally alone for the first time since my father's passing; I was ashamed to say I felt relief. My own aching sadness was constant but with a soft melody in the background, I comforted myself with work.

My rooms in Aristae's tower consisted of several levels of exquisitely crafted architecture and design. High, arched windows and doors gave astonishing views from every direction. Tonight, the palace and capital were obscured by a dense fog below. The only indication that my room didn't float above a frothy sea was in the polychromatic lights dotting the blanket of mist.

I paused just as the hour struck nine.

She was awake and I yawned with her as she stretched her limbs.

A gentle light enveloped my arm and swirled up to take shape. Sleepy tilted eyes, a delicate snout accented in shimmering blue leading down a slender neck, and wings veined in an intricate, gossamer membrane. A graceful tail wrapped itself around my arm in hello. We had been together since we were born. She was more beautiful than anything, my Yuki, and she was just a baby.

Ryunaga viewed only the Raajali as equals. The first sentient beings in all of creation, their civilization had fallen during my grandmother's reign. Yuki's ancestor and mine had forged a bond that continued to this day. When they were young, they slept on our bodies, taking in our strength over time. No one else but Mother and I could sustain them otherwise.

Mother's companion had been searching for a mate these past millennia but Mio promised to return to mentor Yuki once she could stay awake a bit longer.

Go see the boy. She could verbalize, but she preferred not to.

"I cried in front of—I cried *on* him, Yuki."

He was a stranger. He had most likely already left the palace. I couldn't tell Amie and Esme and if I couldn't tell them then it wasn't okay to sneak out behind their backs to see him. No matter how much I wanted to distract myself, I needed to process my grief in a healthy manner and not allow my thoughts to be ruled by a boy I barely knew. I had assignments that needed my attention and projects I hoped would convince Mother I was ready for more responsibility. I was fine.

You want him.

I made an involuntary noise, clapping my hands over my mouth.

That was not dignified and now Yuki was laughing.

"I can't have everything I want." I sighed as she nuzzled my cheek. "How do you feel about going over your linguistic syntax?" When she pouted, I pretended not to see and opened the appropriate texts on the screens around my desk.

You can have some. Yuki did not give up.

"Yuki." I weakly tried to scold her as she climbed from my shoulders onto the top of my head. "It's been a week. It's late. He's not going to be there."

He's there. Now.

"Is he really?" I couldn't help but look up.

Yuki was staring intently at me, upside down, only a few centimeters away from my face. Having thoroughly undermined my plans, she became far too pleased with herself. Gleeful in victory, she helped me put away my work.

This was a terrible idea. I couldn't help overthinking my every step as I walked down the halls and into the gardens. I felt so guilty for no apparent reason, straining my senses for any sign of another living soul. This was such a bad idea.

He's just a boy. Yuki yawned again.

I didn't even know if Mother—

She's not here.

"Yuki, your commentary is not appreciated right now." No one ever spoke to me unless it was about something official, logistical, or academic. It was either "what are your thoughts on the collapse of the Valee trade agreement" or "your application of particle conjecture in your axiomatic property paper was well-reasoned." Amie and Esme did all the talking when I was with them.

"I'm a coward, aren't I?"

Now? Yes.

"Thank you, Yuki. How supportive of you."

I had to stop thinking about doing it because I'd done it. I turned the corner, and I saw the tree and my feet would move no further. He was there. I could see him through the branches. The beetles were elsewhere tonight. There was no wind. It was too quiet. This was a horrible— "Gah!"

Go on.

"You bit me!" I couldn't believe she had bitten my shoulder. Besides being able to hurt myself, I had no idea that Yuki cause me pain. "Why would you do that?"

Then I heard footsteps. Oh no.

"Hello, Sae." Oh no.

"Hello." I didn't know what to do with my hands. I forced myself to look at him and not at the ground, but it was close as he stopped an arm's length away.

"You're beautiful, Your Grace."

He wasn't talking to me.

Oh, I like him.

"T-this is Yuki." She was usually shy with new people, but I could hear a low hum coming from her, a sign she was pleased with the compliment even if she hadn't been persuaded entirely.

"I didn't think you'd pay me a visit again."

What did he mean by that? What had I been thinking?

"Um, I..." I was panicking. Panicking was not good.

The low, calm cadence of his voice broke the tangle. I found myself staring as he moved even closer. Though I was well into my adolescence, as it seemed he was too, this was the first time I'd ever been so close to anyone other than my family.

"You don't have to do anything if you don't want to. Alright?"

Trying to give a response of some kind, I nodded my head.

"Good. You're doing great." His thumbs were stroking the backs of my hands and it was becoming difficult to concentrate on anything but that. "Come here."

The fog had grown even thicker since I'd left my room. The dark crept farther under the thick canopy, obscuring even the brightest of light sources in the distance. The night was unusually quiet, but perhaps with the palace in mourning, it shouldn't come as a surprise. We were moving past the summer now. Much of the landscape was curling into itself in preparation for the cold.

Luckily, the tree before us was untouched by the abscission that had robbed its fellows of their coats. Its blue-green leaves were as fluffy as I presumed they would be next summer... Yuki was falling asleep. I helped her into my pocket so there was no danger of her dozing and falling.

"Were you waiting for me?" The words just tumbled out. I knew better than to ask questions no one would answer honestly. When he turned back around, I tried to salvage the situation. "I'm sorry. That was rude and uncalled for. You don't need to answer."

"Yes. I thought it was obvious."

"What?" Apparently he found my reaction funny. "Why?"

"You might not need one, but I thought you could use a friend."

A friend. Other than the people who were born to be, he was my very first. He continued on without trying to convince me one way or another and I admired him for it. Perhaps it was because very few ever gave me the time or space to decide for myself.

I caught up to him at the foot of the tree. With one, smooth motion, he vaulted up onto one of the sturdy branches and reached back down toward me.

I took Zarek's hand without hesitation.

Seven days later, any residual unease had been replaced by joy. With my schedule filled with mourning, only the nights kept my days afloat anymore. I knew this guilty pleasure would end eventually yet I couldn't seem to stop myself from hanging onto his every touch. His every kindness.

"That's conquest." I captured his final pieces with a flourish.

"You have to admit, I was close that time." Zarek stretched back and grinned at me, showing no signs of distress at losing yet again. "What is it, fifteen to none?"

"Sixteen." I managed to keep a straight face as I said it.

"They're amber." He laughed. "Is it because you won?"

"It's not related to how I feel," I explained as I reset the board.

"Pink when you're embarrassed. Brown when you're sad." Our lightheartedness all but evaporated as somehow, I knew exactly what he was preparing himself to say. "Sae, I need to tell you I'm leaving the palace tomorrow."

I suppressed my first instinct. It wasn't my place to ask him to stay. Every day, I had put off asking him when and it shouldn't have been a shock. It shouldn't have felt like an unspeakable concept.

Zarek had his own life to live.

As did I, obviously.

What did I know of Zarek's life? I knew his favorite books and games; I knew the bite of his humor and the sensation of his hand on my own. Zarek knew I was attending University courses and about all of the things I was trying to learn to be a good Heir. I knew he could draw just as well as I could and that he had no siblings, but I didn't know anything about where he'd come from or if he would ever come back. He had successfully won over Yuki, who had fallen back asleep four days ago, but neither of us knew if he'd ever see her again.

In truth, we didn't really know each other.

"Do you live in Elysia?" He wasn't Elysian, but it was possible.

"No." Zarek closed the game. "Are you going to miss me?"

I couldn't call or keep in contact if he lived outside our borders. Mother and I were not to interfere or interact with the outer universe. There was no chance that Mother would petition the outer council on my behalf for this. To her, it would be a massive waste of time... and perhaps it was.

"Do you know when your next visit will be?"

"I don't," he admitted quietly. "Sae... let's play one more game."

Was he getting closer? He was. Zarek caught my hands and tilted his head down toward me. "Try and run. If you make it out of the gardens, you win. If I catch you, I win." The rush of cold air filling the space where he once stood was dizzying. "I'll give you a head start." When I didn't move, a grin stretched across his face. "Five..."

I bolted. I was already faster than all other species and I knew the way better than he did. It wasn't really fair, but it felt amazing. My thoughts were rarely this focused on one single goal. I was being too impulsive. Irresponsible even.

If Mother caught me running in the middle of the night...

Only she wouldn't because there was the nearest entry point, and I hadn't heard a single sign of pursuit the entire way. I slowed to a walk as I neared the palace walls and disappointment kicked in. Now that my head was clearer, I wanted to say goodbye properly.

"Caught you."

I crashed into him and he actually caught me. *Physically* caught me. For a brief moment, his arm wrapped around and I gripped his shoulders for balance. I let go, but he was slower to act. In fact, Zarek was still holding onto me.

"Do I get a prize?"

"We didn't agree to a prize."

"Can I have a prize?"

"W-what do you want?"

"How about a kiss?"

I think I was screaming inside.

No one would know. For a second, I thought Yuki had woken up again but that voice inside my head was all my own. Zarek waited, he didn't ask again, and he didn't try to persuade me. I felt the pounding of my heart in my ears.

I'm allowed to have some of the things I want.

"Yes."

Something rose in Zarek's expression that was almost unbearable to look at. I suddenly saw a hint of what this boy would look like as a man, and it was thrilling. Yes. I wanted this. I closed my eyes and waited, my heart threatening to riot.

He kissed my hand.

Dumbfounded, I opened my eyes to see him still watching me,

"Look at me," Zarek said against my palm. "Don't close your eyes." His lips brushed lightly against mine. It was sweet. Soft. Warm. My wide eyes took in everything, not even daring to blink. Something vibrant and primal flared from deep inside. Was this how everyone felt? As if pieces of them were miraculously falling perfectly into place? As if the universe itself stopped in its infinite step, cast its eye upon us, and paused to witness?

It was over far too quickly. He pulled back and I couldn't help but reach up and touch my mouth with my fingertips. My first kiss was mere seconds long, but the feeling lingered. I wondered how long this spark of awareness lasted. How long would this simmering warmth stay?

Hopefully forever.

"They're sky blue when you're happy." Zarek whispered, still so close to me... if I wanted, could I steal another? Would he let me?

The sound of bickering breaking into what was most likely the greatest day of my life had me whirling around. Amongst the thick shrubbery that lined the palace walls, two people had tumbled out, one clearly trying to silence the other.

"Amie!? Esme!?"

"Sae!" Amie kept her hand over her twin's mouth as they stood up. They were still in their night clothes. What were they doing here!? How long were they there? How much had they seen? "I tried to stop her," she groaned, "I really did."

"Forget that! Way to go Sae!" Esme shoved her sister off and would have probably cheered if Amie wasn't trying to stop her. "He was so cute!" She grabbed my hands, giggling, and started twirling me in a fast, uneven circle.

I desperately tried to find even a glimpse, but it was no use.

Zarek was gone and I hadn't been able to say goodbye.

"We were worried!" Esme laughed, "So we followed you."

"You followed her. I tried to stop you." Amie groaned.

"Please don't tell anyone."

Amie was surprised, but Esme was immediately upset.

"Why would you say that!?" Esme demanded. "Why would you even think that!? We were worried about you! I can't believe you never said anything! We're your best friends!" Esme looked like she was going to cry, she was so upset. "Everything that happens to you, it happens to us!"

"Not for me. I'm good. Esme can carry the bloodline."

"That's not the point!" Esme shoved at her twin's face.

Esme's words stirred up guilt. I hadn't meant to lie or accuse them of anything. I didn't think they'd be angry—I apologized.

They walked me back to my room and to my great interest, told me of their first kisses. Esme had kissed an ambassador's son for fun and Amie had kissed a boy who lived in the capital in the name of curiosity. Esme's had been nice, and Amie's was kind of gross. I couldn't imagine how I would have felt if kissing Zarek had been gross, but Amie saw it as funny.

I knew they were telling me in hopes that I would talk to them, but I didn't feel ready. I was still processing the experience myself. How did I feel? As I walked into my room, I knew it would be impossible to think of anything else.

Once alone, I doublechecked my doors before pulling out the small piece of paper I'd discovered in my pocket. I didn't dare look at it in front of anyone but now I carefully unfolded the triangle to find a few short sentences.

Just in case I don't get to say goodbye.
I'll write to you.
Zarek

Chapter 4: Expectations

It was just days after my fifteenth birthday and Mother had rejected my proposal to travel for the third time. I had completed all of my recommended courses at the University a month prior with highest honors and Mother was suggesting that I take up additional programs to fill my time. Specialties in exobiological technologies, speculative theology, and interplanetary sociology were recommended in her memo to me in order to boost my diplomatic prowess.

The problem was that I could continue my studies remotely. All of my professors as well as various University deans had given their approval for independent research and examination. Never had an Heir been so isolated from the universe. I could count on one hand the number of off-planet trips I had been allowed.

Even University sponsored events were declined on my behalf.

My Sentinels were entering the University themselves now, but Anera and Astral were more than willing to chaperone. Astral's ship, the *Redemption*, was a flagship of our fleet and there was nothing even remotely exciting about my plans.

If Mother would just allow me a project of some kind. I knew I was younger than most Heirs when they first took interest in governance... maybe Mother had felt this way when she was young.

As I sorted through my mail, I spared a thought to the clerical staff I should have recruited by now, but the next letter I picked up reminded me of why I hadn't.

Zarek, as it turned out, traveled extensively for his studies. I could never be sure if my letters would reach him and had to take several measures for both security and paranoia's sake. I never mailed or received anything in the palace itself but from a self-service postal office in the Capital. I never signed them and made sure to send them as soon as I got a new address.

So far, I had yet to be caught.

I wasn't allowed to send anything outside our borders. Not even a letter. If Mother ever discovered my correspondence, I would be forced to stop. Anyone was allowed to send me mail; although it went through an extensive screening process, and not many bothered with the ancient method of communication anymore except in cases of formal procedure. So, his handwriting always stood out among the carefully crafted, heavily ornate missives.

Hello from the third system of the Floreres Cluster. After a mere five days in this lovely frozen hellhole, I don't believe I'll ever feel all of my fingers ever again. Have you ever tasted the boiled blood of a giant, hibernating invertebrate? It's actually not bad if you don't mind the iron overdose.

The glacier cities encased in ice nine months out of ten are incredible. Sometimes, between the storms and unpredictable meteor showers, the stars come out and it seems like I could walk on them. Sometimes, when I'm surrounded by these burly scientists who whistle in their sleep, I think about you...

He never failed to make me laugh. With every letter, it became harder to stop writing back. This letter continued with both witty and sincere observations, descriptions of his fellow rough-and-tumble students, and several vivid sketches of the research base and surrounding landscape. Sprinkled here and there was a statement that was meant to make me think of him at inopportune moments. I don't know which one of us started flirting first, but he was much better at it. In the five years since we started writing, Zarek had never once come back to visit.

I hope you can travel to the border planets like you planned. On your second stop, I'll be nearby. ~~Maybe I could see you.~~ *Scratch that. If you do come, I'll already be there waiting for you. Look for the pile of walking fur. If you somehow miss me, just follow the smell of frostbitten acidic decontaminate.*

Zarek's letter was not the reason I was going to ask in person. I had already scheduled the meeting with Mother, but it didn't stop me from feeling exponentially more nervous. I checked my clothing one last time and when her door slid open, I made sure to stand as straight as possible.

"Hello Mother. Thank you for agreeing to—"

"Is it time for our meeting already Saekonari?" Mother continued going over the various holographic figures flying around her. "You're here to discuss which specialties you'll be taking on next I assume? I believe Amie is considering a systemic corrections route. It deals with several ongoing issues outside Elysia such as poverty, corrupt resource management, organized patterns of oppression, and other topics I'm sure you'll find enlightening. This should help supplement the other fields I've recommended." She sent the information over to me. "Now if that's all, Amie and Esme should be going to attend registration soon. You should coordinate your schedule with them on your own time."

Without making my argument, I had been dismissed.

I had actually turned to go out of habit but stopped myself.

"Mother?" I stepped closer, moving a few of the reports aside.

"Is there something else?" She moved them back in place.

"Yes. About my proposal for independent study…"

Mother's silence was as telling as anything she could have said, but I had come this far and this was the first time I had ever requested something from her that I really wanted. If I could just make some reasonable arguments, I was sure she would feel more confident in letting me go. It wasn't as if I was going alone. I would have a full escort at all times. I had a perfectly acceptable schedule planned and I was willing to compromise on a lot of the details.

"I-I was really looking forward to independent study. If taking official University courses is important to you, then I'm willing to take remote classes on top of my proposed workload. Anera and Astral have already agreed to accompany me for the initial half-year and my budget is well under my annual discretionary income. If you have any specific concerns—"

"My current concern is that I already told you no."

"I was hoping that if we talked more about it, you'd feel better about my plans." I sat down in a chair across the desk from her and pulled up a few screens of my own. "If you look to your left, I highlighted the regions where I've already established relations with academics in the field. They're really quite open to hosting me and have sent in some proposed—"

"We're finished talking about this."

The room was colder than when I had arrived, and I suddenly understood what Zarek had said about never being warm again. Mother wasn't even looking at my proposal and I was rapidly losing my nerve. "Would it be more acceptable if I organized the trip into shorter excursions? I'm sure that I c-could spend a month here at the palace or even alternating weeks would—"

"You're not leaving at all except to leave this room."

"But w-why?" I had worked for months, even years to put this proposal together. Zarek aside, it wasn't as if I was traveling for leisure or recreation. All Heirs travelled. I had been ready for

Mother to place additional rules or protections but she was refusing to even consider any part of my plans.

"I don't need a reason Saekonari. All this has proved is that you will make a spectacle of yourself. You are ill-prepared. Immature. And undisciplined. You can't even control yourself and you want the rest of the universe to know it as well? Is that what you want? To embarrass yourself? The answer is no."

A hard lump formed in the pit of my stomach.

My professors were no longer under mandate to report to Mother and I'd thought I had hidden it well. My Light was easily controlled in large concentrations, but it had always been difficult to wield on a smaller scale. I could effortlessly move planetary objects in open space, easily terraform small to midsized worlds, but my ability to pour liquid from one cup to another was dubious. It was a puzzle to all of my professors and myself that I sailed through expert exercises but struggled on simple tasks.

"What if I p-promise not to use them at all for this trip?"

"No."

"I believe that this change will be beneficial—"

"No."

"If you could please allow me to s-show—"

"No."

Mother's chair thumped into the wall as she stood, and I flinched at the sound. I stood up too, although slower; I was not going to get upset and prove her point.

"Mother." I tilted my chin back up and looked at the space between her eyes. "I-I think that I should be able to make some of my own choices. I understand that I am still legally underage, but I have p-passed many of the milestones for maturity in our family and I should be allowed s-some personal autonomy. I really think my requests aren't unreasonable."

"This is the last time I am going to repeat myself." Her speech pattern was clipped and sharp. With one hand, she closed all of the screens around her. The room darkened considerably as the sky outside decided a storm was better suited for the occasion. Only the lights behind the Empress remained as she placed her hands on her desk and leaned toward me. "No."

I opened my mouth, not knowing where my audacity came from, but nothing came out. I cleared my throat and tried once more and knew then that I was going to be silent until Mother decided otherwise. There was no use fighting back.

Mother was the Empress.

Her door beeped, interrupting whatever she was about to say.

"Sit down." I didn't want to, but found myself doing so anyway.

"Your Eternal Majesty!" One of my mother's aides burst into the room, looking frightened. I wondered how we looked to him. Mother standing over me, tension clouding the room, but it seemed he was too preoccupied to pay much attention. Either way, his next words would postpone my plans indefinitely.

"The *Redemption* is missing."

Chapter 5: Resentments

Today marked my majority.

Two decades and a year stood as a universal threshold for adulthood. Most sentient beings in Elysia averaged around one to two thousand years per lifecycle. In the outer universe, I'd heard it was more commonly around one to two hundred but one could never be sure. While I was still considered young, especially in the Empress' eyes, today I was not a child anymore.

After this week's celebrations, I would inform Mother of my plans to travel. Even now, I watched hordes of visitors entering the palace from my vantage point of Aristae's tower. Spread throughout their delegations were eligible individuals with impeccable credentials. The fact that nearly all past consorts had been "undistinguished" was not taken into account; nations of the outer universe insisted on sending them regardless.

Mother expected me to play host.

I wasn't expected to actually choose. Nevertheless, this was one of the rare times the outer universe overcame their fears and sent emissaries en masse. Otherwise, exceptions were only made when something catastrophic happened.

If it weren't for their intentions, I would have been more than excited to meet new people. If it weren't for their ambitions, perhaps we could have been friends.

"Sae, are you sure we can't go with you?"

Aoi and his brothers were crowding my bedroom door, each face more forlorn than the next. Anera Esholitte had given birth to not one, but three boys. It was an unheard-of feat for a Sentinel to have so many children. Two were identical and the youngest was fraternal. Aoi and Sil had inherited the same thick ebony locks their father had passed down to their sisters. Vis was the only one to lay claim to their mother's titan curls and her temperament.

When the *Redemption* and their parents had disappeared, the Empress had taken on the role of properly raising and educating them. Nevertheless, it had been their sisters who'd shown them the kind of family they should have been a part of. Though a touch wilder than my own mother preferred, all three had grown up secure in the knowledge that they were loved.

"You still have a bit of growing up to do, unfortunately."

"We can do that with you!" Aoi insisted.

"It's only for a few months, alright? We'll be back before you know it." I ruffled Aoi's hair affectionately. "I need you all here to take care of Mother. I know she won't be happy with me away but she'll be all alone without—"

"But she's always alone anyway!"

"To be honest Vis, I don't know if Mother gets lonely." I knelt down to look them in the eye. "But I know I would be if my family decided to leave all at once." Vis looked more than ready to continue arguing. "Besides, if your mathematics scores don't pick up by midterm, Amie will have both our heads."

At that, a bit of their bluster deflated.

Amie was much scarier than I was.

"Give it up already." Aoi put his arms around his brothers' necks and whispered theatrically. "Just think! Without them around, we can do whatever we want. We can steal a ship. We can kill each other with Amie's gear. Even go in Esme's room!"

Knowing they'd never risk their status at the Shipyard as early enrollments, I laughed. In the end, it seemed that was all they were really after. One more round of hugs later, I waved them off to their classes and returned to my balcony.

Later, as I finished my preparations, I wished I had taken Yuki up on her offer to come back early. She was awake most of the time now and Mio had returned to take her under his wing as promised.

Both of them would meet me there soon enough.

Systematically, my mind went through the long list of names I'd read a few weeks ago and the short summaries attached. Thousands of delegations had arrived and it was well documented that many had lived and died of old age in the palace before, hoping to be chosen by an Heir.

It all seemed excessively melodramatic.

Every Heir and eventual Empress had held a single, lifelong love or obsession according to who you asked. It was supposedly an intense, all-consuming experience and I was scared. Mother had loved my father and vice-versa, but some days, it seemed like it was against their own will. It was something only she could explain, but did I want to hear what she had to say?

Would she think I was foolish for asking in the first place?

"Yuki and Mio are running a bit late," Amie murmured to me.

Oh good, just what I needed to hear to feel even worse. I needed to be calm, I reminded myself. None of us had time for my nerves. Everything would be alright. I wasn't going to ruin this for myself. Mother would understand. The doors opened before I felt ready, but I straightened my shoulders and glided in with years of practice behind me; ignoring their stares was difficult but manageable.

Climbing the dais, I stood a little ways behind the Empress as she addressed our visitors. With the Circlet of Aristae hovering above the crown her head, she was a golden vision from head to toe and I knew there was no one in the universe more beautiful than my mother. Her voice never faltered. Her every move was graceful, ethereal. Her wisdom and kindness unmatched.

"Welcome to Elysia."

"When the universe was new, our ancestors evolved from a plane of pure energy into the physical. Peace reigned supreme. Great libraries and gardens, enclaves of community, prosperity, and introspection rose. Our people lived closely to the natural universe. Inherently logical and utterly pacifist; from the beginning, they could hear the murmurs of our shared existence.

The universe began to breathe through them.

Even so, their strength was limited. The Ryunaga had been the true inheritors of creation. They had come to our people, charmed by their friendliness, and helped them to develop their fledgling Light.

It seemed as though their paradise would last an eternity.

It was not to be. Developing nations in a young, fragile universe invaded what would one day become Elysia. A brutal conflict raged to possess this planet and the surrounding systems at the very core of our existence. For years, they laid waste; exploiting the riches within. The original Elysians were overwhelmed. No matter their individual gifts they were crushed under the superior technological advances and strategic abilities of those who had come prepared for war.

The Ryunaga fled. They had no desire to involve themselves in the conflict of lesser beings. Almost all remnants of our culture and history were destroyed. While there had been small pockets of resistance, once the invaders discovered our Light, our people were hunted to near extinction. Our species was so very nearly wiped from the face of the newly born universe.

The first of our family, Aristae Raajali was born in chaos.

Asheron, her elder brother, was a natural leader. Confident. Pragmatic. Brilliant. Jiaya, his second in command, was quick to anger and quick to act, decisive and passionate about her people. Eun-hye, whose aptitude for technology and invention had been unrivaled, held wisdom just as carefully honed. Tsuki, whose hands were of a healer. Uncompromisingly patient and focused. Her brother Taiyo; reckless where she was methodical, fearless and eager to protect those he loved. The last was gentle Yana, the ideal soldier; a poet and peacemaker at heart.

Children who barely remembered a time before the war. Children raised on fear and suspicion. They wielded enormous cunning and strength, gathered the remnants of our people, and began what seemed like an unbelievable campaign to regain the home world. Their enemies were blindsided.

Just as the tide was turning, Aristae vanished.

Without their heart, the six argued bitterly, each blaming the other for their loss. It was said that the very ground they stood upon trembled as they fractured, unable to handle the weight of their ambitions without her.

In those long, bleak years, the war raged ever more cruel.

Aristae's return not only signaled the end of hostilities.

She carried with her the dawn of a new era.

Though they kept Aristae's secrets until their deaths, the founders drove from this galaxy all other nations, established the borders far beyond Elysia's original purview, and laid the foundation for our protection to stretch to the farthest corners of our universe. A universe that responded happily to their Light.

A universe that ceased its expansion the day Elysia was established.

And Aristae Raajali had sacrificed herself for us all.

Yana and Tsuki, who loved her more than their own lives, left with her. Asheron and Eun-hye were the first to rule after their unification. Jiaya and Taiyo would uphold the mantle after as they too found love in each other.

All to ensure the happiness of our people.

Hundreds of thousands of years passed before the third Empress was conceived to Eun-hye. Jiaya would give birth herself not days later, to a son and a stillborn daughter. Their children, Kitome and Dante Raajali, would fall in love and begin the single bloodline that has carried down nine generations, over half the known universe, and twenty-three million years."

As Mother spoke of Elysia's beginning and accomplishments, summarizing all that had come before us, those who beheld her were drawn irresistibly to the light and serenity of her visage. A power unrivalled in our universe. I had seen it so many times before, but the Empress' will never failed to surprise or awe.

"As per universal treaties, we welcome you to our home. The Heir has reached her majority and thus possesses the right to choose a consort. Please enjoy our hospitality for as long as you wish. Abuse your privileges and you will be expelled from Elysia. Please enjoy the festivities."

When she turned back to me, I knew I'd already missed my cue.

Looking around as discreetly as I could, I wondered where in the Empress' name was I supposed to start. Amie and Esme followed me down the stairs only to find ourselves standing in the center of a wide semi-circle with everyone's eyes boring into me. Elysians never stared at Mother and I like this.

I hated it when people stared.

"Hello. Saekonari Raajali." I chose the fellow on the far left because I liked the iridescent material his vest was made of. It was a pretty green and I knew of his species. Good enough. I took a few steps toward him and offered my hand in his people's favored greeting. He just stared at me, so I dropped my hand before it got even worse. "Are you Prince Caillio or Felguri?"

"Felguri Dominin!" He burst into apologies for yelling.

Less than a minute later, I knew it had been a mistake to be friendly. My ears took in every individual voice as they clamored to speak over each other. An acute sensation of claustrophobia was manifesting. Esme had disappeared somewhere, and I envied her as Amie and I were slowly back into a corner.

This was suffocating.

Amie's voice suddenly cut through the noise.

"Excuse me. I have to attend to nature. Now."

Why would she announce that?

Then I looked at her face, oh! Right.

"I'll come with you. If you'll excuse us." I took the flimsy excuse to force a path to appear through the crowd. Amie grabbed Esme on our way out; she'd been roped into a conversation with a crowd of admiring diplomats; and as soon as we left through a side door, Amie barricaded it.

As soon as she did, I sterilized my lower arms and hands.

"Can we leave tonight?" Amie was ticked off. More than once, someone had tried touching her to get to me and it had not gone well for them. She tore off the mask she wore and tucked it back into her coat. Ancestral to their family, the masks she and her sister wore were stark and elegant in design; a scaled texture was carved into the bone for Amie and feathered for Esme; and they really only came out for public events or official purposes.

Esme shrugged. "Sae could do some damage if she—"

"Stop it!" Amie lightly smacked Esme's shoulder in rebuke.

"I just think we could have some fun with this while we're still here!" She argued back. "Just because Sae isn't interested—some of them were hot! Why can't I enjoy things!? You always do this!"

"If you didn't notice. It wasn't exactly fun in there!"

While they quarreled, I leaned against the cool stone wall and ran a hand through my hair. I felt like I had been locked in an airless glass tube and steamrolled. I knew I was expected soon for the optical spectrum display in the southern gardens, but all I wanted was to go back to my room and finish my budgetary reports. It would be so much more productive to try and finish what work I was allowed to do instead of being paraded around like this.

"I actually need to go." Amie admitted, waving us on.

Truth be told, Esme was always the easier one to be around. Her cheerful chatter meant it required no effort on my part to keep the conversation going. It was quite funny to hear her thoughts on all of the people we had encountered. I was laughing at her description of a woman who had tossed aside several others to get to the front and turned a corner without looking.

I hadn't noticed the presence of anyone else around us.

I rammed into a person and an arm shot out to catch me.

Unexpectedly, an intense feeling of déjà vu stole my composure away. I found myself staring at a perfectly tailored, dark blue coat collar that rested just below a sharply defined jawline. That was strange, even if I wasn't completely upright, there was almost no one I had to look up to see anymore.

"Caught you." The voice was unfamiliar.

It was lower and deeper, but I knew.

Look who I found! Yuki's head popped out of the coat in front of me. The sight of her so comfortable was, in and of itself, disarming. She was so excited that she squeaked when I removed her and had her reappear in my arms.

It only took a hint of resistance to be freed. I knew I sounded more than a bit hysterical as I muttered under my breath. "No. No. No. Not today. Not tonight. Not right now!" I walked away from this new problem and heard Esme behind me now trying to address the problem. Great, let her handle it. It'll be fine.

Did I care that Yuki was vocally protesting, not at all!

What I should have done was rejoin the festivities and did I? Of course I did. I walked to the southern gardens, exceptionally late as I took an even longer route.

Around my sixteenth year, he had stopped writing without any explanation. My eyes stung at the memory of writing with no hope of a reply. I had possessed no ability to find him in the outer universe but he had known exactly where I was.

There was a part of me that thought perhaps something had happened to him. To know now that he was alive and well brought all of that uncertainty and shame back to the forefront. I had spent so much time and energy trying to find answers. I thought I had left it all behind. The last three years had been spent purposefully putting him away with all of my other childhood things.

I had other priorities and plans for myself.

Zarek Deutreax Trace was not allowed to ruin them.

It had been five excruciating days of failing to ignore him.

Just a few more days. I repeated the words to myself as I spoke endless platitudes and faces began to blur together. Many of my guests were perfectly interesting and amiable but I struggled to give them my attention. His mere existence was enough. It was as if my every atom was being disturbed.

Yuki did not agree. For years, he had written little messages to her as well; had sent little treats and toys and so she had been quick to forgive. Amie refused to state an opinion. What made her silence pronounced was that I knew she'd spoken to him.

On the other hand, Esme—

Esme grabbed my arm.

"Sae, I think Yuki's sick." She whispered.

Fear sliced through the last of my equilibrium.

I was just with her, how could Yuki be sick?

Too many things were happening, too fast.

Excusing myself from my conversation, I didn't hesitate to follow her down the halls to a door that led out to an upper terrace. I didn't think to question why Yuki would be waiting for me here and not in our room. I simply walked over the threshold and into the cool, starlit evening.

The buzz of conversation and music could still be heard from below. A wild tumble of climbing flowers spread up the wall and along half of the railing. Stone benches were placed here and there, but otherwise, this part of my home was left fairly undisturbed.

"Yuki?" The door closed behind me. I didn't think much of it until I heard the lock sliding in place. "Esme?" My disbelief grew when the door refused to open.

Suddenly, the prickly awareness I'd felt for days returned with vengeance in mind. Heat threaded over my skin down to my fingertips. I would have broken the handle, but knew it wouldn't open the door. "Esme. Open the door. Esme!"

"I'm guessing this wasn't your idea after all."

It would be the height of indignity to put my hands over my ears and pretend to not hear him but Universe help me, I was tempted. I was now considering breaking down the door itself but knew how ridiculous that would look. The past few days had stretched my nerves taut and frayed.

"Sae, I just want to talk."

"You stopped writing." I didn't turn around. "Five years ago."

"No, I didn't. I stopped writing a year after you did."

"I stopped writing two years after your last letter."

"Do you see where I'm going with this?"

The laughter in his voice hurt.

The last thing I felt like doing was laughing. Two years I kept writing, eventually becoming desperate enough to write to the address he'd given for his affiliated school.

My recklessness had been inexcusable.

It had hurt to stop when I realized it had become unhealthy.

I was so sure something terrible had happened.

To have confirmation that he was *alive*. My relief was untenable. I moved away from the door and to the nearest bench. Sitting down, I tried to force myself to be calm because I believed him. Of course, I believed him.

I knew what it sounded like when people told me the truth.

"I'm leaving the palace in a few days. You're not invited."

"I know. And I didn't expect to be."

"Then why are you here!?" I pressed my hands against my mouth as I heard my own uneven breath. I didn't even need to breathe. Yet every time I panicked it felt as if I were drowning. I was shaking. I couldn't think. I couldn't do anything right. No matter what I did, it was always wrong, and I could never fix it.

Everything was spiraling out of control.

"Sae... sweetness, I'm right here. Listen to my voice."

My head was screaming. I couldn't.

Heirs did not have panic attacks. They did not cry over failures that should never have occurred in the first place. Every time it happened, I self-isolated until the feeling went away, and I never told anyone... the pain eased eventually.

I started to hear him.

His voice told me I was okay, I was safe, and that he was here.

All at once, the situation hit me. Hard. My hands were gripping the front of his clothes as I climbed out of the most humiliating episode of my life. Just as he had when we were children, he held me against him, his heartbeat the only steady star in a universe that had overwhelmed me one again.

"I'm sorry." I let go of his clothes. "I am so sorry—"

"Sae. Look at me."

I never thought I'd feel like such a child again. I had refused to speak to Zarek for days and had tried my very best to ignore him. I'd had a full-blown breakdown in front of him when all he wanted was a conversation. The least I owed him was to act like a reasonable, rational... I looked.

Dammit, I knew it.

Zarek was gorgeous. As a boy, he'd been beautiful, and nature had only chosen to sharpen his allure to a fine edge over the years we'd been apart. There was something dangerous in looking right at him. He looked as if he could take a bite out of me—I was not going to examine that thought.

"What happens now?" I asked quietly.

"That's up to you."

"If I ask you to leave?"

"I'll leave."

Secretly, I had considered him my best friend for years.

Amie and Esme were always there, but they'd also always had each other. Neither knew I liked studying ship tailpipes, poisonous herbs, nonresidential construction zoning, tertiary migration patterns, primitive jewelry design, or a thousand other obscure topics. It was always difficult for us to play knowing that I'd win. Zarek had played with me regardless if he won or lost and had even indulged in a few months of writing completely in convoluted ciphers for me to decode. Besides Yuki, he was the only one who ever seemed to take me as I was.

What would it be like to know this man and try again?

The next night felt fundamentally different.

All three moons were out and bathed everything in a soft glow as one of Elysia's most elite symphonies performed. Having been trained at the Conservatory on palace grounds, I knew how excited each of them had been to play for my coming of age ceremonies and again here before the outer universe. I wish I could have enjoyed their recital without having to divide my attention.

Though I now had the option of speaking to Zarek, it wasn't fair to the others. My partners, whether in conversation or otherwise, deserved my consideration.

Besides, the Empress was in attendance.

One moment I was listening to a pair of guests trying to outdo the other in naming their every achievement. The next, I was quite literally pulled away into one of the set patterns. Muscle memory kept me gliding through the motions instinctively even if my mind fumbled to keep pace.

"Zarek." I failed to stifle a laugh, "I was talking to someone."

"It didn't seem like you were doing much talking."

"I don't want to make it seem like I've singled you out."

He held me just a bit closer. "Would that be so bad?"

Before I could think of a response, a young woman with ash blonde hair and intensely shaded brown eyes stepped into our path. Before we could correct course, she grabbed my hand and I was caught off guard by a sudden, solid wave of hostility; not from her, but from Zarek.

"Cira. What are you doing here?"

"I had nothing better to do and I thought, why not go and meet Your Eternal Grace!?" She pulled me into the rotation and away from Zarek just as the music changed. I had the choice of either going along or causing a scene.

With Mother present, it wasn't much of a choice.

"Zarek's been busy... I suppose I should introduce myself."

"Cira Kyrian, correct?" Her name had been on the significant arrivals list today. "Of the Kingdom of Rateer." Her country had brutally expanded into neighboring nations in recent years under her father's rule. Due to the precedent of Elysia remaining neutral to all having to do with the outer universe, she had equal access. If the outer council didn't condemn them, neither could we.

Mother would know if she were a threat.

"You're smart and beautiful. It's not surprising. All of Zarek's girls are." When I didn't answer, her grin grew wider. "My father paid for his education so you'd think he'd know the importance of keeping his family nearby! But enough about him. What about you? The light of the universe. Heir of Elysia. Aren't you curious about where he's been?" She spoke so fast, she barely kept from stumbling over her own words. "What he's done since he left you?"

"I have higher concerns and you've made your opinions clear." Whatever Cira Kyrian wanted to insinuate, unless she found the bravery to speak candidly, I knew better than to listen. "I'd think we both have better things to—"

"I'm going to give you some advice. You'll both thank me for it."

"Please refrain." The dance was over. "I don't need it."

"How about a warning? You're not the one he wants."

Cira didn't let go of me. I tried to take a step back, but she just stepped with me. People were beginning to notice. Her emotions were a jumbled mess, but I didn't care about her internal struggles at the moment. Something flickered in her face as if she were seconds from saying something she was bound to regret.

"I'm only going to say this once." The threat was clipped and clear as glass. "Let go of her or I will break your hand."

As if summoned, Amie materialized out of thin air; her mask only adding to the implied menace. Nearly stepping between us, she gripped one of Cira's wrists and glared down into the woman's face. Right as I was sure Amie would go through with her threat, Cira let go and instead lifted Amie's hand to her lips.

I wasn't sure who was more surprised, me or Amie.

"So sorry." Cira stared at Amie through her eyelashes. "I was so mesmerized by her Eternal Grace, I simply forgot myself. Your reputation precedes you as well, Amythesia. Such a loyal friend you must be. I have never been more starstruck in my entire life. Would you like to dance?"

"No." Amie almost slapped Cira's hands off of hers and then marched me off of the dance floor. Amie was not happy and everyone knew it as they made way. "What did she say to you?" Amie demanded once we were in a less public space.

"It doesn't matter." So much for not making a scene.

"Of course it matters! The way she looked at you made my skin crawl." Amie and I both were taken aback at Esme's seemingly instant dislike for the woman. It was unusual for her to care about something so trivial. "What did she tell you!?" Esme demanded. "Whatever it was, she must be crazy to go up to you like that! Do you want me to go after her? You shouldn't listen to her!"

"And where were you?" Amie demanded at Zarek arrival.

"Stop," I said as firmly as I could. "I am fine. Cira made baseless claims about Zarek. I didn't believe her and even if I did, I can make up my own mind." I held up a hand before Esme could ask. "No, I am not going to go over what she said. I'm fine. Do not go after her. Whatever happened is not worth more interaction."

I spend the rest of the night fulfilling my responsibilities, putting the incident out of mind, and avoiding my friends. I didn't see Cira again and hoped she had concluded whatever business she was here for. Mother retired early and it was easy to go through the motions until it was late enough to leave myself.

I was so close to escaping that I cringed when I heard my name.

"Saekonari. I would like to speak to you."

Chapter 6: Rebellions

The Empress' anger was not something to be roused cavalierly.

"Of course, Mother. Is something wrong?"

"Don't feign ignorance."

I followed the Empress back to her offices as was expected of me. As we walked in silence, I tried to think of what I had possibly done wrong. Amie assured me earlier that Mother had left the proceedings before the fiasco with Zarek and Cira.

It couldn't have been that.

It was. All the color in my face drained out as I spotted Zarek in one of the chairs opposite Mother's desk. To see him so relaxed in such a hostile setting was bizarre. He even nodded to the Empress as she passed as if she weren't radiating cold like the south wind.

"Saekonari, sit down," Mother ordered and I obeyed.

"Saekonari. Why don't you introduce me to your lover?"

That accusation would have made a mockery of anything I could have said. Stupefied, I fought to think past the rush of shame. It didn't matter that I was no longer a child when Mother could so easily reduce me to one.

I struggled to hold my gaze steady and failed.

"Mother. T-this is Zarek Deutreax Trace. My friend."

A file box appeared and tipped its contents out on the desk.

Letters. Dozens of unopened letters and inside, I had known all along. Mother was the only one who could have stopped my correspondence. I had known, but I had not wanted to confront the reality. Now here it was being shoved in my face.

"You're lying. You've been lying for years. Undermining my authority and universal precedents of noninterference. You claim to want responsibility and yet take no accountability for your actions. You've done nothing for years but shirk your obligations and bring Amythesia and Esmeralda into your schemes. You have been flaunting yourself for days thinking I wouldn't notice. There are consequences when you decide to act in such a disgusting, disgraceful manner."

When I could not force words out, Mother turned to Zarek.

"I regret to inform you that my daughter, though of age, has yet to prove her ability to make informed decisions. She has clearly made choices based on her own selfish whims and I would appreciate it if you would no longer encourage her."

Hollowed out with shame, there was nothing left for me to say that would make this humiliation better. *Disgusting. Disgraceful.* Mother's words echoed inside, tearing apart everything I thought was innocent and harmless. Had I been so selfish? So delusional I'd justified doing thoughtless and stupid things?

"With all due respect, Your Eternal Majesty. Bite me."

What did he just say?

Stunned completely out of my thoughts, my shock was nothing compared to the pure astonishment on Mother's face. I pinched my cheek discreetly as, for the first time, I realized the Empress was not the only one in the room who was angry.

Zarek was *furious*.

"Why would you ever talk to her like that?" Though quiet, the words he spoke seemed to act as their own warning. "Sae hasn't done anything wrong. I am her friend, and even if I was more..." Zarek looked at me then and his voice got even softer. "It's none of your damn business."

"I can see where the source of her bad habits—"

"What bad habits?" Zarek actually laughed in her face. He stood and placed his hands on my mother's desk, bracing himself against it. "Sae has done nothing but try and live up to your expectations since the day she was born. She's never, not once stepped over the line and she absolutely should. Saekonari could use a few bad habits, and I'd *love* to be one of them."

The Empress stood up then and that was when I got afraid.

So afraid that I stood up too and I had no idea what to do.

"Mother. Please. We're all upset, b-but—"

"Be quiet!" I flinched at her rebuke.

"Sae? What's going on?"

Vis and his brothers peered around the doorway. The sight of their rumpled pajamas and wide eyes seemed to bring Mother's usual equanimity to the forefront. Zarek eased back from the desk and Aoi's jaw dropped as he straightened to full height beside me... dear universe please let them not have heard anything.

Sil pushed past his brothers to tug at my sleeve, yawning. "Sae, will you tell us a bedtime story?" It had been years since they'd last asked for a story and I seized the weak excuse to end this night before things further deteriorated.

"Of course. Mother, may we be excused?"

A few seconds ticked by before the Empress allowed it. Zarek closed the door behind us and I waited until we were well out of earshot before speaking.

"Let's get you back to bed. I'm sure I can find a story."

"I can do it." Zarek volunteered. "You've had a long day."

Aoi, who had never been shy and was obviously dying to interrogate Zarek immediately, agreed on behalf of his younger brothers. "You really don't have to," I whispered to him as the boys began to ask a million questions.

None of them were very polite.

"I got them. Do you want to talk about what happened?" He dropped the subject as soon as I shook my head no. "Then I'll see you tomorrow." Zarek brushed a kiss against the forehead and left with the boys clamoring around him; their voices overlapping as they wished me good night.

I couldn't hold off any longer. It was the last day before we left and I needed to tell Mother of my plans. We hadn't spoken since that night in her study and we had never gone so long without speaking. The state of affairs between us made me feel unbearably guilty. All of my requests to see her had been rejected. So, I shored up my courage and went without an appointment.

I didn't even get the chance to ring.

Mother sat at her desk and made it painfully clear that she could not be bothered at the moment to acknowledge my presence. While I still desperately wanted her approval, I didn't need it to go ahead with my plans. I had to keep reminding myself of the fact, but I wouldn't forget it.

"Mother. We need to talk."

"If this is about the trip you've planned behind my back. You're not going."

"How did you—?" I bit back the rest of the question.

The Empress knew the thoughts and fates of hundreds of trillions... all but for those closely tied to the bloodline. It's why she couldn't predict my father's death. It's why she didn't know what happened to Astral or Anera. We were the only ones, besides the Naga, hidden from her gaze.

I thought we'd been careful enough to be safe, but no.

"I don't know where you learned to behave this way. I've provided you with everything the universe had to offer and yet here you stand having proven yourself ungrateful." Mother's tone was more baffled than angry, which somehow cut even deeper. "You've become a disappointment to me Saekonari. Perhaps the biggest disappointment of my life."

I didn't want to be a disappointment. Mother had always been the greatest inspiration of my life. She was all I ever wanted be. I knew we disagreed now but all I wanted was to prove I could handle myself. That no matter where I may go, I took my position and my life seriously. I wanted to be a good Heir.

I just wanted her to be proud of me.

"Mother. I'm going. I-I don't need your permission."

Her only answer was to slide over one of the screens to me. I looked and saw a list of names, all of the contacts and places I had been planning to visit. A soft touch from the Empress opened one of the messages.

I regret to inform you and your esteemed institution that the Heir will be forgoing any interplanetary excursions in the near future due to recent indiscretions. Until further notice, this is a direct request to deny her participation in any prearranged activities and endeavors. A mandated report is now under effect if or when Saekonari Ioraeyln Nicaristae Raajali is found on your premises.

Contact this code directly to report any such breach of conduct.

11th Empress of Elysia
Deletii Mirona Corias Arget Raajali

Deny participation? This wasn't a school field trip. *Mandated report?* I wasn't a criminal. *Recent indiscretions?* The thought of these people, whom I'd formed professional relationships with, reading this—how could I ever show my face?

"Mother. Y-you can't do this."

"Oh?" The sarcasm was new. "Exactly why can't I, Saekonari?"

"Because it's w-wrong. I-I haven't done anything to warrant—"

"You have done everything to warrant these measures." Mother stood and I took a step back even though there was a substantial piece of furniture between us. "Do you really have such a low opinion of me Saekonari? That I haven't noticed your behavior as of late? I know why you're really doing this."

The door slammed behind me and I knew the sound barriers had also been raised. Mother had ensured that no one would interrupt us this time. Panic began to pool, but now was not the time for that. "Mother. I'm doing t-this because I think it's an appropriate time for me to—"

"You're lying to me because of a man and it is unacceptable."

'I'm not l-lying. Zarek isn't even coming!"

"I hope you can travel to the border planets like you planned. On your second stop, I'll be nearby. If you do come, I'll be waiting there for you." Mother pulled out yet another stack of letters, one that had been much more handled over the years and that I thought was securely locked in my room. "Disgusting drivel."

The letters in her hand dissolved into dust.

It was then I knew she wouldn't listen.

Those letters had been important to me.

This trip was important to me.

The Empress didn't care.

"You have n-no right to go through my things."

Her eyes narrowed and she moved around her desk to stand in front of me. I was shaking again, but stood my ground before her.

"Yes I do."

"What I choose to do in private is none of your business."

"Yes it is."

"And I am going w-whether or not you approve!"

Slap

There was a ringing in my ears. Where was it coming from? I raised shaking fingers to my face. It stung. My mother's hand glowed a dull white and that told me what had just happened. It took quite a bit of power to inflict pain on us.

My mother had used that power to hit me.

Incredibly, it was as if nothing out of the ordinary had just occurred. Without even looking at me, Mother waved a hand in dismissal, the door sliding open behind me. "It's become obvious I've been too lenient with you. For at least the next few weeks, I'm confining you to the tower. If you choose to disobey me, the consequences will become more severe. There is nowhere in Elysia you can go that I cannot find you, Saekonari and you only have yourself to blame."

"I'm sorry M-Mother."

I don't know why I said it. I only knew that I needed to leave and it was easier to say that than anything else. Even before I left the room, any pain was gone. I began to question if it had even happened. It couldn't have.

Mother had never hit me before.

Mother would never hurt me.

"Sae!" Amie was mad and I was really tired of people being angry. "Your mom confiscated the ship. Our payment's been returned and apparently, there's no other suitable replacements in the entire fucking system!" Amie began to pace back and forth. She always did that when she got really upset.

"Give me time to think." I didn't wait for their response.

I left them in the hall and went to lock myself in Aristae's tower.

Yuki was the only person I saw for the next few days.

She left the tower for long stretches with Mio and often came back too tired to do anything but sleep. She knew I wasn't allowed to leave my room, but she didn't understand why. I had tried to explain but she knew something else was wrong that I couldn't bring myself to tell her. She wouldn't understand.

Honestly, I was beginning to think I imagined it.

On my balcony, I gazed down at the bustling streets and lights of the Capital and knew Mother would revoke my privileges to even visit there. How long would I have to stay here? Five more years? A decade? A century? Ten centuries?

Yuki came into view just as I was working into another panic.

While I knew she was hidden from most, it worried me that I couldn't go to her if she got into trouble. She was just a baby. One who hated that I wouldn't go with her around the palace anymore. She landed less gracefully than usual, taking a few extra steps to orient herself—something was off. I picked her up when she reached for me and walked back into our bedroom. Yuki was so upset she was turning into a darker hue.

I want to bring him here.

Without specifying, I knew who she meant.

"Yuki, I'm in enough trouble as it is."

No one will know. He's not trouble.

"No."

Too late.

"Sae?" Kalla plums!

"You can't be here." Why did no one ever listen to me!?

Zarek paused mid-step. "I'll just go jump off the balcony then."

"This isn't funny," I mumbled in response to Yuki's giggling.

"Sae, there's something you need to know."

Yuki made a beseeching noise at his words that I couldn't disregard. Aristae's tower was a relatively safe place to talk and while

Yuki wasn't afraid of Mother, it had to be important for her to so readily break my confinement.

In the end, I begrudgingly agreed to the unavoidable.

"Are you okay? Do you need anything?" Zarek's eyes swept me up and down as if to check that I was still here. "Do you want to tell me what happened?"

It was so hard not to tell him everything.

"I'm still processing, to be honest... what is it?"

"Sae. I'm going to tell you because you deserve to know but it isn't pretty." His face was suspiciously blank. "Your trip went public. People think you did something to goad the Empress into canceling it. Elysians are adverse to gossip on principle, but the outer universe doesn't follow the same moral code. They're saying with all the visitors, you've been sampling the field. Which is a more polite way of saying you've been indulging in some of the contenders on the sly."

"I'm sorry," I said when he didn't elaborate. "I'm unfamiliar with your slang."

"They think you're being overly promiscuous with strangers."

"... Do people know I've been sent to my room?"

"No. She made a copy. It's walking around here somewhere."

It was like he was speaking gibberish. His words made no sense. I sat down on my bed and everything that had happened began to tumble around me. I wasn't a prude. I knew better than to care about the words of people I barely knew. "Everyone thinks it's true. Don't they? After all, w-why would Mother do this if it wasn't true? Why would I be here if it isn't true?"

This was such a stupid reason to cry.□

"You think I believe it. Is that what you think Sae?"

Zarek's hands wrapped around my upper arms.

"No don't look away. Look at me." His tone gentled once I did as he requested. "I know you Sae. I know it's fucking bullshit, and your mother is an ice-cold b—tyrant." I tried to defend her, but Zarek just shook his head. "I also know you haven't even been kissed since—"

"You can't know that!" I had stopped crying, thank the Empress.

"Yes, I can. You have the most transparent face in the galaxy."

"You have no idea what I've been doing while you were gone!"

"So you're saying you do have more experience now."

"Yes! No! Maybe!" I fumbled as Zarek's amusement only grew.

"You're an abysmal liar, sweetness."

How did the conversation even get here? What was he doing? Zarek's hands slid down my arms and onto the bed on either side of me. The ground seemed very far away. The air was suddenly loud in my ears. I knew Yuki was watching us intently but somehow I doubted she would intervene.

It was very difficult to think when he looked at me like that.

"Would you like more experience Sae?"

"You're just trying to distract me."

A grin split his face. "Is it working?"

Yes it was. Empress help me.

"This isn't a good time for this."

"Alright."

A sharp pang of frustration sliced through me as Zarek moved to give me the space I'd thought I wanted; but my face truly must have been as transparent as he'd said because he stopped short of leaving my bed entirely.

"M-maybe it is—never mind!"

I didn't know what I was doing. I hastily turned my face away and so I didn't see him close the space between us. I didn't know until I felt his lips on the curve of my left shoulder.

"Saekonari." I was blushing and it was unfair that his voice alone could do that. "I want to give you everything you want. Anything you want, sweetness but I need you to tell me what that is."

Anything I wanted.

"C-can you close your eyes?"

I waited a second before peeking... I'd never had an opportunity to look at him like this. Now that he wasn't looking at me, I couldn't help but stare. Leaning forward, perhaps I was trying to assure myself there was nothing remarkable in my reaction to him.

"Sae?"

I jumped, not expecting him to speak.

"Yes?" To my relief, his eyes were still closed.

"Are you planning on asking for anything else?"

I didn't know how to answer. The events of the last few weeks churned inside me. Zarek's return, my mother's ambush, Zarek defending me, how angry Mother was, how all of my carefully laid plans had been dashed as if they were nothing. The rumors, the accusations, the shame. I touched my cheek and finally admitted to myself that yes, the Empress had hit me. She had sent me to my room and had threatened severe consequences for disobedience.

What was it that I wanted?

He was the only one who ever asked me.

This was crazy.

I stared at the face that wasn't my face in the mirror. A short, plain girl of dark brown hair and eyes, it was vital I blend in if this was going to work. Although it was the most common coloring combination in the universe, it had also been my father's. Unre-markable in every way, a change in appearance had always been an option, but one I hadn't even considered before now.

Yuki assured me that Mother was in another section of the palace entirely before flickering away into an intricate marking around my wrist. She insisted on coming, no arguments had swayed her. Finally, I made sure the last of my work was neatly filed away before leaving the tower.

The palace seemed enormous at this height.

"Over here!" I jumped at Esme's call, but quickly slipped through the door and out into the side courtyard where we'd agreed to meet. She and Amie didn't have to hide their appearances. They wouldn't be instantly recognized everywhere they went, but I hadn't realized how far I'd have to look up to see their faces now.

It was unnerving.

"Let's go!" Esme grabbed my hand. She enthusiastically approved of our new plans and though Amie had her doubts, their support had gone a long way in assuaging my own misgivings.

"This is going to be great!" She was overestimating how far these legs stretched. "We are finally getting out of this place!"

"Slow down." Amie set our pace so I wasn't running to keep up.

Zarek had arrived on his own ship. Once I explained what I was going to do, he'd offered it to me. So now all we had to do was get there. All of the palace visitors kept their ships at the piers hanging off the eastern cliffs outside the capital. There were over a thousand of them that could be folded back into the false cliffside.

Most were in use right now.

Mother and I exclusively used our own private vessels at the Shipyard. Having only seen the piers at a distance, the sheer size of the operation up close was overwhelming. The majority of it was automated and the main gates themselves were incredibly busy, even at this hour.

Soaring metal ribs spread out overhead, mimicking wings arched high over the main terminal. The structure itself was enormous. The night sky on the winter solstice was inlaid over the highly polished, dark blue floor and while the piers were just as scrumptiously clean, ornate, modern, and beautiful as the rest of Elysia; I had never been in a place so chaotic.

The eighth pier to the far right of the central terminal. That was where Zarek said he would meet us. I was hoping that it would somehow be obvious which was his ship, but the dizzying array of vessels gave me no indication whatsoever.

As I took it all in, Amie pulled me to one side from where I had been blocking the thoroughfare. Several polite couriers were there waiting for me to move.

I apologized profusely. Walking down the center of pathways was expected of real me, but new me needed to do better at blending. It didn't help that I was wearing heavy veils, but I started moving as if I knew where I was going.

This was crazy. This was absolutely—

Found him. He was looking into an open hatch on a sleek black ship, an excellent color for camouflage in open space. It was larger than I had expected from his vague descriptions, but my only concern was that it was here.

"I don't know why, but I remember you being taller."

"Are you sure about this? It's okay to change your mind."

"Are you kidding? This is the most fun I've had in years." He closed the hatch and took a small ring out of his pocket. The cargo door slid open. "After you."

This may be a bad idea, but I didn't think I'd regret it.

"Sae." Amie caught my hand. "Are *you* sure about this?"

Her concern was genuine and I knew this wasn't like me at all. Amie could feel that I was scared and I squeezed her hand, trying to reassure her. Yes, this was impulsive, I wasn't denying that but I'd wanted this for a long time. Careful planning hadn't worked. Persuasion hadn't worked.

Negotiations had been a complete disaster.

"I am, Amie. I really am."

"Stop being such a killjoy!" Esme nearly shoved Amie and I apart. "This is a great idea. Don't listen to her!" She startled me by grabbing my arm and trying to haul me forward. "You already dragged us all the way out here! You can't back out now! You put us through so much trouble Sae and I am not—"

"Esme, I know you're excited but—"

"Sae's already made up her mind!"

"I'm just saying we could talk this out a bit more!"

This really wasn't a good place or time for them to argue. Esme took offense at her sister's words but before I could try to deescalate, I was plucked from the ground. Zarek casually started walking up the ramp with me in his arms; Amie and Esme left sputtering in our wake.

"What do you think you're doing!?" Amie demanded.

"What was that?" He said without looking back. "I'm in the middle of a kidnapping, maybe try again later!" He was grinning madly down at me and I couldn't help but do the same.

"I'm being kidnapped. Bye!" I waved over Zarek's shoulder.

One moment, I'm reveling in a reckless kind of euphoria. The next, I was tossed like a child's toy back to Amie. She shoved me behind her and my veils were so tangled at that point that I couldn't do anything but wrestle with them.

"Oh, is this a bad time?" It was Cira. She sat atop a pile of stacked containers, her legs hanging off the edge. There, in one of her hands, she tossed a ball up and down.

"What the fuck do you want!?" Amie was not having this.

"Can't a girl visit her future in-laws?"

"Don't screw with me Cira."

I'd never heard that tone from Zarek before.

Amie tried to shove me further behind her.

"Oh I know who that is Amythesia." Her voice sickly sweet. "And I can't believe she didn't listen to my warning! I thought she was so much smarter than this. Doesn't she know how fickle you are? I mean, look what happened to poor, innocent Alexi!" She hopped off her perch and headed toward us as if it wasn't exactly the kind of excuse Amie was hoping for.

Cira found herself pinned, Amie's hand at her throat.

"Leave. Before I throw you out."

"Promises, promises." Cira grabbed Amie by the hair and kissed her. Amie's shock allowed Cira to reverse their positions.

She nearly straddled her before the Sentinel came to her senses.

Being thrown into the far wall looked like it hurt.

"Amie, stop. She has diplomatic protections here."

"Who cares!?"

"I do. We can't just do whatever we want."

"Is she always this... nice?" Cira asked Zarek, who didn't respond. "I almost feel bad about this." Cira twisted the sphere in her hand a few times, and threw it at Zarek; whose hand flew up to catch it before it hit his face.

A searing light came out of it and while Amie and Esme shielded their eyes, I could see the sphere being broken into several smaller marbles. Once a matte black, they now gleamed maliciously. An odd mechanical clicking filled the air.

What in the ever-loving Empress!? Before I could even think of how to respond, Cira grabbed the marbles, shoved Zarek out over the side of the ramp, and sprinted deeper into the ship. I let go of Amie, who went after Cira like a shot, and ran to where he'd gone over. Before I could jump down, Esme grabbed me.

"Sae! Don't go running off without me!" She tried to pull me back into the ship but I shook her off. Falling to my knees beside Zarek. I checked for a pulse and it was only when I found it, regular and strong, could I think again.

"Sae. Stop it. We have to get Amie and get out of here!"

Cira shoved Esme aside to grab at me herself.

Why did people suddenly feel free to grab at me?

I yanked myself out of Cira's grasp, but she just danced me around so that I was directly between her and Amie, who was stalking out of the ship with fury leaking from her pores. We were now attracting far too much attention.

"Help! Your Eternal Grace! She's so scary!" Cira sang in my ear.

"You haven't fucking seen scary yet." Amie unholstered her favorite weapon. It was her fathers and it would have been illegal to carry if she wasn't a Sentinel.

"What did you do to Zarek?" I held up a hand to stop Amie.

"Is that asshole still out? Weird. I thought it would be quicker."

Enough. I grabbed hold of her arm before she could run off again. She struggled to pull free but soon realized it was futile. "I don't know what it is you have against any of us. I don't care. I want you to leave us alone."

Surprisingly, fear was all Cira felt; an all-consuming terror. If it was me she was afraid of, then she'd done a remarkable job of hiding it. Otherwise, I couldn't help but wonder what had frightened this woman so badly.

"Of course. If you let me go, I'll leave immediately."

"I say you let me shoot her." Amie said through her teeth.

There were too many people, too many eyes here and all of them were Mother's. So, against my better judgment, I let Cira go. Whatever was happening, it would only make things worse if Mother saw me holding someone like that.

A groan had my attention shifting elsewhere.

"Zarek?" I knelt back on the ground beside him.

His eyes opened and a small smirk appeared on his face.

"What? Did I accidently fall at your feet?"

I should have been relieved, but he wasn't looking at me.

"Zarek, are you okay? How do you feel?"

He was looking at Esme. Zarek propped himself up on his elbows and glanced at me only briefly. He ignored my question and dismissed me just as quickly.

"Where the fuck am I?"

"You're at the Capital Piers. Of Elysia." Esme added when he didn't respond.

"Great. So why am I here?" He wouldn't look at me.

Cira, though she'd been so determined to run off not a second ago, seemed frozen to the ground. I could feel myself growing colder as I walked toward her. Cira opened her mouth, but nothing came out. Was I doing that?

Was this how Mother felt when she got angry?

Boom

Zarek's ship exploded. I instinctively pushed back against the enormous force that rocked the piers beneath our feet. It was easy to pull the explosion back into itself. Inside the large space I'd contained the ship inside, whatever chemical reaction had been set off was still raging.

Cira disappeared into thin air.

She was no longer on world.

She wasn't inside the borders.

How could she leave Elysia!? What was I going to do!? I didn't even know what had been done to Zarek, much less what to do about it! If I tried to do anything to Zarek's brain, I could end up irreparably damaging him. There were skilled medical professionals in the Academy who could probably help, but all of them would report this to Mother. Should I beg her to help him anyway!?

She would never listen to me.

She wouldn't even let me see him.

Mother had finally noticed I was gone.

Her Light sank into my flesh and for the first time in my life, I resisted. I wasn't able to ignite a candle, but apparently I was strong enough to fight the Empress for as long as she held back. If she used any more of her influence, people would begin to notice. This was the worst possible outcome to an already bad crisis.

What was I doing!? What was I supposed to do!?

I needed to work fast. I woke Yuki up and forcibly sent her to Mio. Thank the Empress he was still at the palace even as Yuki desperately struggled against me. She wanted to come and she was not happy that I wouldn't let her. I couldn't fight both of them. It was either escape Mother's hold or keep Yuki in place but before I could choose a battle, the resistance from Yuki stopped.

Mio had noticed our struggle and had taken custody of her.

Saekonari!

I had to make a decision. I had to decide. Right now.

"Come on!" I grabbed Amie and reached for Zarek's hand. Amie grabbed her sister and Esme was yelling something, but with the shouting of the now frantic crowd and Mother's anger ringing in my ears, I couldn't hear her.

I could see the crowd parting like a wave.

I could feel her fury silencing them all.

But it was too late.

We were gone.

Chapter 7: Intentions

Above our heads fluttered a canopy of orange foliage. With trees spaced too uniformly to be natural, this orchard we'd landed on concealed plump pods of a cylindrical shape, growing heavy on ashen branches. I could hear the songs of birds and other small animals slowly resume around us. We may have interrupted their daily schedule, but the order of the universe regained its momentum before long. As I laid there, flat on my back in a sea of citron-shaded grass, all I could think was that the Empress of Elysia was going to murder me in cold blood.

The force of the sudden transport of billions of light-years over the border had knocked out the others. It wasn't safe for me to wield my influence directly on people. I'd been unable to prepare them, I'd never done anything like this, and I was deeply afraid I'd already hurt them.

Their vitals seemed fine. For now.

What had I done? The border separated the two halves of our universe. Elysia on the inside, the outer universe on the other. Our Light was contained inside that border. Outside, we needed to keep ourselves on a tight leash so as to not break one of the many amendments included in the noninterference agreements. The outer universe relied on our promises. I had the responsibility of upholding those promises and principle as there was no way for them to be enforced otherwise.

But who was I kidding?

I had stepped way, *way* over the line. I was outside the borders for the first time in my life. Without permission. I had already skipped over the shards of what had to be thousands of universal laws. I didn't even know if I could be detected like Mother would be. I'd never gotten even close to the border until now. I felt that horrible pressure in my chest again.

I needed to calm down.

With the border between us, she couldn't find me.

Maybe. This was all untested theory at this point.

I needed more information to fully assess the situation.

"Sae, where are we?" Amie blocked out the sun over me.

"Outside."

These were the times I truly loved Amie. She simply nodded, understanding without needing to ask further questions. She walked away to wake up her sister and I turned to look at Zarek. He looked exactly the same as he was before but the man I knew was likely gone all the same. He hadn't recognized my voice.

He didn't know who I was.

"I'll make this right," I whispered.

Raajali always kept their promises.

"What do you mean we're outside!?"

Esme was awake.

"This isn't right! Sae do something! This is insane!" She yanked me to my feet and babbled inconsolably. "This was not the plan!" Esme, who had been vehemently supportive of sneaking out, had completely changed her tune. "He doesn't even remember who you are! This was not the plan! We need to go back right now! Right now! This was not the—"

"I know. I know Esme. Please lower your voice." There wasn't anyone nearby, but that didn't mean we wouldn't be detected somehow. "I know I shouldn't have taken you without your permission and if you want to go back that's okay! I'm really sorry but I can't go back right now."

"And you think I can go back without you!?" Esme did not lower her voice. "Do you know how much trouble I'd be in if I did that!? This isn't the plan! Why can't you think of anyone but yourself for once!?"

Amie stepped between us and I wish she hadn't. Esme had the right to say what she wanted to say to me. I had pulled them into this without even asking for their input and it was painfully clear that I had made some shockingly bad decisions. Esme glared accusingly at me, her eyes brimming over.

"Amie? Are you really going with her?"

"You know I am," she said firmly.

Esme dissolved into tears. Very loud tears.

Amie and I tried to soothe her but Esme seemed inconsolable. Guilt racked me for having forced her to come along. She was right, she couldn't go back without me. Sighing, I glanced over at Zarek and jumped when I saw he was awake.

Amie blocked me, her hand going back to her thigh holster.

Zarek was completely unfazed. In fact, he gave Amie a dazzling smile as he stood up and dusted off his clothing. He didn't seem to care that he was once again in alien territory. "Well hello to you too. Mind telling me where I am now?"

"Who knows!" Esme threw up her hands and continued to cry. "I didn't ask to be here that's for sure! But do we ever do what Esme wants? Noooo!" I often admired Esme's ability to be so open with her emotions but at the moment, she was crying very loudly, and we still weren't sure of our surroundings. I tried reaching out to her, but she batted my hands away.

Zarek walked up to our little group and Esme threw herself at him. I wasn't quite sure if she'd mistaken him for Amie or if Zarek was going to be okay with it, but he allowed Esme to sob on his shoulder. I saw Amie taking a step forward and stopped her. No. They both had to be overwhelmed by the situation, Esme needed some sympathy, and separating them right now was not a priority.

"We need to talk strategy," I whispered and while she didn't look happy, Amie nodded. We kept them in view but I didn't think either could hear very much over Esme's misery anyways. We could hopefully talk more once she calmed.

Amie put the safety back on her weapon as we walked.

"Were you going to tell me you were bringing that?"

"Eventually." She shrugged. "It'll come in handy."

"What do you—never mind. I don't want to know. Do you think we should go after Cira?" Rateer was a nation in turmoil with no established diplomatic ties with Elysia. Mother had never travelled there herself and I doubted I would be welcome. It was one thing if I were discovered outside in a friendly nation, it was another matter entirely to go after Cira on her home turf.

"Can't you just bring her here?" It was a reasonable assumption.

"If I do something like that, someone might notice. Can you find her?" While Mother and I could mask to a certain extent, our very presence tended to create ripples. It had been drilled into my head that I could not and should not do anything to attract attention if I ever went outside the borders. This planet was barely outside, and I was afraid I'd already used too much.

"Let me try." Her eyes stared ahead, I could see the stars flickering past, and a flood of gratitude filled me at her easy acceptance.

"She's already in Rateer. But we don't need to go there." One look told me Amie and I had come to the same conclusion. Whatever Cira had done, they were now scattered elsewhere. If they weren't on her, where did that lead us? Experimental technology was notoriously detrimental to brain function.

"This is obviously a trap." Amie and I took a moment to think of the implications. Cira had proven herself to be a manipulative liar with a grudge. I had already taken us beyond the pale. It would be the height of idiocy to go along with this… and yet no matter how much I thought it over, going back to face Mother seemed like the worse option. "You can find them?"

Amie nodded.

I took from my pocket what I'd been holding in a death grip; a worn, faded handkerchief; and brushed my fingers over the childish embroidery of a small flower in the corner. I'd discovered the detail when I first washed it. It was all I had left after Mother destroyed my letters.

Esme's crying had resolved into quiet sniffles by the time we rejoined them but it was only when Amie cleared her throat did Esme let go of Zarek. The man was obviously waiting for one of them to speak, but Amie just kept looking pointedly in my direction until he finally faced me.

"So you're in charge?"

"For the m-moment. Do you recognize this?"

I held out the handkerchief in question and found myself wrestling to keep possession of it.

"Where did you get this!?" Zarek had never looked at me like that. "Give it back you little thief." It wasn't the accusation, but the sound of tearing that made me let go. He stuffed it back into his pocket and I watched it disappear.

"You gave it to me."

Zarek didn't believe me.

Things I was sure about when I left home was thrown into question. Mother had accused me of doing this all for a man and wasn't that what I was doing?

I couldn't go back without anything to show for it.

What awaited me back home was certain. Mother was enraged that I'd left my room. She would never accept any justification for crossing over to the outer universe. I had already made my decision. No matter what came, I had disobeyed Mother for him.

I'd broken interstellar law for him.

I didn't have the option of changing my mind anymore.

I had to at least get him to trust me. Just a little bit.

"Zarek. Do you know how old you are?"

I pleaded silently for him to answer as the seconds passed.

"Ten." Just before he'd met me. A teenager.

"You've passed your second decade already."

"That explains the growth spurt." Did nothing phase him?

"Cira Kyrian—" He held up his hand to stop me.

"I get the gist. Nice meeting you, pixie."

He was walking away. Wait! What!? I didn't think. I lunged forward to block his path. Amazingly, he stopped but he also looked as if he couldn't believe I was stopping him.

Well, neither could I at the moment.

"Can I suggest reading to the blind as an alternative to—"

"Let me help you." I had to reorganize my priorities. I had to be decisive. "Zarek. I'm going to find your memories. I can't make you go with me. But I assure you we'll get to them before you do."

"I'll just tag along then, shall I?"

Was he being sarcastic? Sincere? I couldn't tell.

"I would appreciate it if we could have a conversation... please. Just talk to me." I reached out cautiously for his hand.

There must be some part of him that knew me, but ultimately, my hopes were dashed as I barely grazed his knuckles with my fingertips before he pulled away.

As if I'd burned him.

"Tell me pixie, why are we friends?"

"W-why? You were kind when—"

"I was nice to you? Is that all it takes?"

"Zarek. I am your friend." Even if he now laughed at my expense. "I am going to help you whether or not you want my help. So please just talk to—"

How in the Empress' name did he move so fast? If Zarek thought I was going to be intimidated... he was right, but I wasn't going to show it. He wasn't touching me, but he was close enough that I could clearly hear his pulse and wondered if he could hear the racing of my own.

"One condition pixie."

Relief coursed through me.

"You need to do a better job at hiding your little crush."

Oh... I'm ashamed to say I backed down. There was nowhere for me to go. If I turned away, Amie and Esme were right there, and my pride refused to let them see my face. Their shock bore into my back, and it was all I could do to wordlessly nod my head in agreement because what else could I do?

"Good. You're not exactly what I would call my type."

In the silence that followed, I knew I was going to have to be the one to take charge. Not just now, but for the foreseeable future.

"Amie. Could you find us the nearest port? We're going to have to catch a ride." I forced my eyes up and looked at Zarek with as flat an expression as I could muster. "If it's all the same to you, I'm quite done arguing at the moment."

Ten minutes later, we arrived at another bustling terminal.

While much less crowded than back home, this one was not nearly as well kept. Amie and I went looking for a ship and left Esme with Zarek with the promise they would not move from where we had left them.

As we passed customs, Amie couldn't hold it in anymore.

"Sae. I don't like this. I don't like him. Are you sure?"

I nodded, not trusting myself to speak. Several public channels were being broadcast all over the terminal and I let my mind wander while I tried to rebuild my conviction. All of them were reporting an incursion into Isbulian territory by Rateer.

Isbul was the second largest nation in the universe in terms of territory at nearly two percent of occupied space. Unlike Elysia, power had changed hands there thousands of times. More often than not, that exchange of power was marked with bloodshed. With expansion efforts due to overpopulation and other nation states constantly nipping at their borders, they were almost always engaged in some kind of external or internal conflict. Nevertheless, they'd been at peace for the past few centuries and poised as they were at a major intersection of the universe, their trade was also stable as of late. So, this new conflict was a surprise.

They were also more than triple Rateer's size and from what was known of their military capabilities... it was an incredibly unwise decision. I wasn't even sure if Zarek was an official citizen of Rateer. Cira had said it was her father who funded his education, but I couldn't take her word for it. Isbul was dead center between Elysia and Rateer. If a war broke out, Mother would be processing billions of refugees very soon. It would be best for us to avoid both.

"Sae." Amie pulled me to the side. "His memories are in Isbul."

The universe was glorious no matter your choice in companions.

Passing through Isbul's borders had been surprisingly easy. We'd snuck onto a larger cargo ship; a rotund, dark green vessel; and once we'd come in proximity of their checkpoints, Amie and Esme took us the rest of the way. The jump was a smooth one and it had been a quiet trip up until this very moment.

If I had any illusions of discretion, they were dashed.

I hadn't realized how much attention Amie and Esme gathered.

We all knew it was a taboo in the outer universe to distribute images or information about the Raajali without approval from the outer council. Not to mention that, up to this point, their faces had been hidden behind their masks for public broadcasts. I went over these facts as people turned to look our way. The universe was a big place. It was unlikely they would be identified no matter how striking they were walking down the street together.

It was Zarek who was the real problem.

Never had I seen someone cut through a crowd like Mother could. He walked as if he breathed life into the galaxy and everyone owed him for his efforts. It was, admittedly, a useful skill to have. This was a grittier, more hectic city than I'd ever encountered and yet people still walked wide from Zarek's path.

With its status as a border planet, bipedal species of all kinds abounded. A beautiful mosaic of appendages and facial configurations streamed past us, reminding me of home. We took in more immigrants per capita than any other nation, but it was fascinating to see the minute differences in interaction.

Legal and illegal transactions were taking place despite the relatively early hour, and I spotted a line of slave vessels openly selling on this main thoroughfare. I stopped in my tracks. While it would have been easier for me to look away, this was my first time witnessing the practice.

Elysia, on the day of its founding, had been the first to ban the ownership of a higher order of sentient beings. It had taken millions of more years for other nations to begin doing so. To this day, no other government in the outer universe had been able to uphold the same promises.

The list of protected species within our borders was far longer than the unprotected, but it wasn't as if we could force the universe to follow our example. It was the exact opposite. Everything they were today; they had chosen for themselves.

We were not to interfere at all.

To my eyes, some of the slaves looked decently nourished and clothed but others were marked with brutal injuries or naked to the flesh. Their limbs were immobilized, and each stood on a small hovering platform.

The lack of innate dignity was chilling.

Especially for the handful of children who stood unblinking.

Averting my eyes seemed wrong even as one of the more well-tended slaves was having her ownership transferred. She was obviously newly branded; her code stamp was fresh and her expression defiant. She spit in the auctioneer's face and was backhanded for her efforts. I flinched as she hit the ground. I finally tore my gaze away and silently reminded myself of the laws that restricted Mother and me.

This was not my place. These were not my people.

To my relief, it wasn't too much further. Amie stopped at the corner of a busy hub. Huge advertising screens took up most of every visible surface and music pumped out from several different directions. The neon lights were oddly pretty even in the bright sunlight, and I marveled at the complex traffic patterns piled up one on top of the other. Large field barriers of all colors separated each lane of dangerously fast vehicles. What I assumed was a public transport line ran high above our heads with what should have been a loud clamor, but instead blended seamlessly into its landscape. The people themselves seemed tired and irritable.

Even wonders must seem mundane in the midst of the everyday.

"In there." Amie nodded at the building in the opposite corner.

In appearance, it didn't stand out in any way. Tall double doors stood in triplicate behind pillars shading their color a rich hue of red. Although several bright advertisements appeared above and around the entrance, it was impossible to tell if any belonged to the establishment itself. Although people flooded in and out of its neighbors, the corner building was oddly neglected by the crowd that flowed in front of it, passing by without a second glance.

"Can you get it from here?" I asked and Amie hesitated.

Instead of waiting for us to come up with a plan, Zarek seemed to recognize a signal that none of us noticed. He joined a wave of people crossing the hub at designated intersections going a dozen different ways. Without thinking, I went after him and was immediately overwhelmed.

I heard Amie shout my name, but was lost in the nonstop shuffle of a crowd determined to get to their destinations with little regard for if they were going to step on a confused foreigner. I moved forward as to not get trampled and as soon as I saw a break in the tide, I hurried to stand behind the small obstruction. Looking around, I cursed my decision to be so short.

There he was. In front of the building Amie had pointed out, leaning back against a pillar, Zarek was watching me.

He raised one of his eyebrows when I peeked out at him.

Somehow the act itself was vexing, as if he'd taunted me.

Before I could dive into the crowd again, Amie and Esme appeared next to him. They still hadn't spotted me; but when Zarek turned his back to me, I realized he wasn't going to tell them where I was. What was he doing? Cautiously I rejoined the crowd and kept as close as I could to the walls. It wasn't too far to the corner and I couldn't help but overhear just a bit as I got closer.

"She's never been away from home alone!" Esme was frantic. "Sae's mother is going to kill us if anything happens to her! Oh my Empress how could you let this happen!?" She turned on Amie who was trying her best to shush her. "You know I'm right! Look at what happened! You lost her, Amie! Why couldn't you listen to me!? I knew this was a bad idea! I knew it! I knew it! I knew it!"

"She's fine." As if on cue, Zarek stepped aside just as I arrived.

"Sae!" Esme grabbed my arm and spun me around as if to check if I was missing any pieces. "Don't do that! You scared Amie! And me!" It was only when Amie put her hand on her twin's shoulder did Esme allow me to stand on my own.

"We need a plan. Zarek do you have any identification codes?"

The three of us had no such markers allowing us to travel legally. I wasn't quite sure yet if any of us had access to money and we needed to gauge how strict the outer universe was with facial recognition and other means of detecting people who were not supposed to be there.

"Probably in my ship. Which I'm guessing is the one you blew up." Before I could refute him, Zarek opened one of the deep crimson doors to the building, and disappeared inside.

I followed before Amie and Esme could stop me.

Adjusting my vision for the darkness—I didn't want him to get too far ahead and I wasn't going to let him lose us—I dodged Esme just in time to keep her from catching my arm.

"Sae!" Esme yelled after me.

I sped up and pretended not to hear.

At her exclamation, however; Zarek glanced behind him and gave me what I was sure was another taunting expression before going up what looked like a central staircase, two or three at a time. I was not going to lose him. Reaching the foot of the stairs myself, my luck ran out as Amie and Esme dashed to block me.

"We know you like him Sae, but you can't just keep doing things without our permission!" Esme hissed, grabbing my arm again.

They'd done so before as we'd grown up and perhaps it was because I was so small in stature now but I wanted people to stop grabbing me.

"Speaking of permission. I don't recall giving anyone permission to wander my club after hours." An angry voice had me spinning around, but I should have known all I would see was Amie's back as she stepped between me and whoever it was that had caught us. I tried to move around her, but Esme held me back.

I whispered for her to let go, but she wouldn't.

"Who are you!?" Amie demanded.

"I'm the owner sweetheart. Who the fuck are you?"

The owner was average height and slender. His dark red formal wear gave him an air of elegance, despite his obvious anger. I caught a glimpse of auburn hair and equally bright amber eyes before Esme pulled me back behind Amie again.

"I'm crushed Fane. Can't you recognize an old friend?"

Zarek was back and I could hear him coming down the stairs, but with Esme in the way I couldn't look to see. Amie and Esme were slowly backing me into the banister and there was little I could do without causing a scene.

To all of our astonishment, Fane lunged at Zarek.

Zarek sidestepped, allowing him to tumble into the stairs.

He was up again and tried to have another go while the three of us stood by. Zarek easily pinned the struggling man to the nearest wall, which was actually a geometric partition much stronger than it looked... should we intervene?

"You fucking asshole! Let me the fuck up!" Failing to get himself free, he made what I assumed was an incredibly rude hand gesture with both hands.

Amie again tried to hide the vulgarity from my sight.

It was just one step too far.

"Zarek. Do not leave the building."

I grabbed Esme and Amie and marched them up the stairs. I didn't check to see if Zarek agreed with me because we were not going to get anything done like this. The nearest door led to a smaller lounge. Amie closed the door behind us and they immediately began to scold me and argue with each other.

"Let me talk. Please." I didn't want to make this an order. I'd never given them any like this and I didn't plan to start. "I know this is a difficult situation, but the way you're treating me is already suspicious and it's only been a day. We can't go on like this."

Amie put her hand over Esme's mouth to talk first.

"It's dangerous out here."

"It's dangerous out here for everyone."

"If your mother were here, oh my Empress, Sae. I just can't—"

"Mother's not here Esme. I am. This is my choice. Going forward with all of this is my choice. Whether or not you come with me is your choice, but if you do I need to be treated as a normal, sentient being who cannot be shielded from the entire outer universe. I understand I've been sheltered until now. I understand I know very little about what's out here. I need to learn. I want to learn." They did not look happy. "Just think about it for a little bit and let me know. Okay?"

I left them to stew over it and somehow was unsurprised to see Zarek and Fane had gotten over their differences in the meantime. They sat beside each other in one of the round booths, Zarek's legs stretched out on the low table in front of them, Fane laughing at something he'd said. They were sharing what I assume was an intoxicating liquid of dubious origins.

"Hey! You! Why're with this asshole anyway!?" Fane shoved Zarek's shoulder in a much friendlier manner than his earlier demeanor would have suggested, but I found myself wary of his quick change in tune. "I guess I do owe you one... hey! Can either of the twins dance? I got a fuck of a gig for them if they can!"

Fanelius Akon, somewhere in the higher twenties for the inheritance of the Isbulian throne, held no modern title. No major political affiliations. Owner of a string of nightclubs, refurbished from a long line of aristocratic social clubs founded in Isbul during the eighth era, his family name was ancient. Having successfully transformed the family business within his short stewardship, he enjoyed a scrumptiously luxurious lifestyle and a surprisingly private life. Father still alive but retired on an exclusive planet on the other side of the galaxy. No siblings or close friends on the public radar. Either way, the Inferno name and brand was praised even amongst the high echelons of society in the outer universe.

Which was why I was definitely going to take a look around.

Amie and Esme were exhausted and although Amie had given me a look, she didn't say anything when I left the room without them. Dressed in the club's metallic uniform, it was understood by all parties that this would be a test.

Staying close to the walls to avoid the crush, I marveled at the provocative clothing and colorful accessories that adorned every twisting body. At home, clothing was elegant, practical, and suitable for most weather conditions. I loved the glitter and sparkle of their ensembles, the boldness and flair. The color and music that beat against the skin in similar fashion.

Whoever said that was the universe was a quieter place than could ever be imagined had obviously never been there. The universe was noise and light and movement. I was absolutely enthralled. This was a universe I had no idea had existed beyond the palace and it was glorious.

Trying to keep as inconspicuous as possible, I couldn't keep from noticing Zarek. The solitary star on whom everything was revolving. Center floor, he held the crowd captivated with effortless style and aplomb. What had happened in our time apart for him to so easily dominate a room?

I watched Zarek whisper something into a beautiful woman's ear and how she could hear him was a mystery as they were closer to the source of music than I thought could be healthy for their auditory systems. All of a sudden, the knot I'd tied my hair in felt tight and I reached up to struggle with it. After a few seconds; however, I felt a hand move my hands out of the way. The loosening of my hair told me whoever it was had done me a favor.

"You're Sae. Right?" It was Fanelius. Of course it was.

It was strange having someone other than the Esholittes call me that name. I had wondered if using the shortened version was too big of a risk, but it was a fantastical abnormality for me to be here. The Empresses rarely stepped foot outside the border. A hundred thousand years could go by without such an event occurring. No one would connect the nickname back to the Heir.

As for Zarek's friend, where he once was hostile, there now was only charm.

"It's alright. You don't need to pretend."

I was afraid the music would drown me out, but his false smile dropped and he looked away. Our eyes were, of course, led back to Zarek and we shared the view for a short time before he motioned to follow him deeper into the club.

Down a nondescript door and a quiet hallway, he led me to what I was sure was not his office, but perhaps the office of one of his staff? It was small and cramped, but he seemed as comfortable here as he would have anywhere else in his club.

"Want a drink?" He seemed surprised when I accepted.

"Why offer if you didn't think I'd want it?" I took the glass he offered and had a sip of the green liquid. "Wow, that's actually terrible!" And I couldn't help but be absolutely delighted by it. "What is it? Does the general public enjoy it? How quickly do the effects of intoxication set in?"

I couldn't get intoxicated, but he didn't need to know that.

"What in fuck's sake are you doing with Zarek?" Fane put away the bottle after pouring another healthy amount in another glass. "No offense, I'm going to assume Sae's your actual name and that you're just as nice as you seem. He told me you were a friend. A friend. Seriously?"

"We are friends," I confirmed, peering into the cabinet of other alcohols. Would he mind if I tried some other ones? He had to have some kind of curation system so did he know anything about where they were manufactured?

"Zarek doesn't have friends. He has marks, people he hates, people who hate him, and people who think they like him, but actually hate him. He hasn't changed since we were kids."

Fascinating. "You knew him as a child? What was he like?"

Fane sighed and fiddled with his ear, which I now saw had a cybernetic implant of sorts. A small projection came out that showed a group of children. Zarek was in the back row and obviously trying to avoid the camera altogether. Fane was right beside him; smiling widely. They all wore a militaristic uniform with formal marks to distinguish their nation of origin. Zarek was the only one who didn't have one. The image was time-stamped.

"I met him not too long after this, were you always close?"

"We went to school together for a while, sure. I would get beat up, Zarek got there one day raring for a fight. Beat the crap out of them so bad they never came after me again. I worshiped him for it. Then he sold me out. That's Zarek."

"Sold you out?" I repeated, hoping he would elaborate.

"One day a bunch of skulls came out of the closet. Took down half the class. I haven't spoken to my own father since. The only person who could have known my dirty deeds was Zarek. He skipped out and I never saw him again. Until today."

Fane took a moment to take a drink and in doing so, broke eye contact with me. He shook his head as if trying to clear it and I remembered that I needed to be better about controlling myself. People tended to… say things to me without meaning to, but I couldn't exactly warn him.

"You don't know for sure that Zarek did anything."

"Yes I do and he didn't deny it today either."

"Fane. Are you still going on about that?" The voice coming from behind me belonged to a man just under Fane's height. He had dark skin and beautiful dark green eyes; it was the affection in those eyes that kept him from austerity. "Now, I told you to make nice with your friend."

"He is not my friend!" Fane snapped.

"Fane, you know you can't keep this grudge. Zarek will kill you!"

"I dare him to try it." Fane's features softened when the man came over to put a hand against his shoulder. "Dylis. I thought we agreed you'd stay upstairs tonight."

Dylis touched his forehead to Fane's and whispered something that was not discreet. I tried to play deaf and dumb, but I could feel my ears heating up from listening to those intimate words being exchanged. I was just about to try reciting chemistry formulas when, in a louder voice, Dylis began to reprimand him.

"You know I never believed it. Zarek wouldn't do that to us."

"And I'm telling you he's a backstabbing asshole. He doesn't give a shit about anyone but himself." Fane eyed me before adding, "and maybe Alexi." There was that name again.

"Why not give him the benefit of doubt?"

"Do you know what he does for a living!?"

No, but I wasn't about to admit I didn't know.

"He's a fucking freelancer."

It sounded innocuous enough.

"So he works for himself, what's wrong with that?"

"Everything. He'll kill your father for the right price and for a bonus, frame your mother. He's so good he's never been caught but people know his name for a reason. He's dangerous."

Dangerous? Zarek?

Sure he was abrasive, and a bit grumpier now, but he'd never even raised his voice to me. I couldn't reconcile this image of Zarek with the one that I knew. He'd never mentioned anything that came near the reality of Fane's words.

Had so much changed in the years we'd lost contact?

Why did he come back for me if this was all true?

"Who is Alexi?" I couldn't leave without knowing that.

"My guess?" Fane and Dylis exchanged a look. "The woman Zarek actually loves. He talked about her sometimes like she molded and hung the stars."

Did it even matter that Fane's words rang true?

"Is any of that bullshit about losing his memory real?"

Fane stood to allow Dylis to take his chair. I realized then that I'd just seen the man out on the floor. He must have had a long night on his feet. I looked back at Fane and saw the concern he was trying not to show... well, if Zarek was being honest with him, I again nodded a confirmation.

"Then you're in deep shit. There are a lot of people in the universe gunning for him. Trust me when I say you don't want to be caught in the crossfire."

I couldn't go back on the things I'd already sacrificed.

I could only work with the information in front of me.

If only I knew what information to trust.

"I'm going back to my room. Goodnight Fane. Dylis."

Chapter 8: Disclosures

Despite what I may have said, I wasn't ready to head back to my room. The office door closed behind me and I was alone. It was quiet. The walls must be completely soundproof to block out the music coming from the central areas of the club.

I wandered aimlessly.

Every once in a while, a person dressed like I was zipped by without even glancing my way. This was a well-run operation, with everyone seeming to know what to do and where they should be. I envied their certainty of what the next hour would bring.

Turning the corner, I caught sight of Zarek. He stood beside one of the professional dancers who performed at the Inferno, their sparkly outfit fit snugly around them, leaving their midsection bare. Bristly hair texture and glowing paint all over. I immediately leapt back to press myself out of sight.

They were having what looked like an intense discussion.

"Haven't seen anything but I can help you look after my shift…"

It was clear Zarek was going about this another way, but I had no interest in hearing the details. Before I could discreetly turn tail, I was very neatly caught.

"You can come out now. They're gone."

Wishing that I would just melt into the ground was not productive, I told myself before walking back into view. As soon as I did, Zarek's eyes flickered over my body. A hot lick of sensation crept down my skin, following his gaze down.

"Found a new job, pixie?" He'd just noticed my change in attire. There was no reason for a spike in heart rate. None at all.

"I just wanted to see Fane's club, how is your night going?"

"You just got an eyeful. How do you think it's going?"

I didn't answer. He was trying to get a reaction and I wasn't going to walk into his trap no matter how many times it was presented. When I let the silence stretch, his lips curved into what I now knew was a smirk rather than a smile.

"You're jealous. It's not a good look on you."

Outraged, but determined to stay calm, I quietly recited basic astronomical equations to regain my composure. "I am not jealous Zarek. I know you still don't believe me, but I just want to help you and I don't care what you decide to do with your free time. That has nothing to do with me whatever your suspicions. I was actually just speaking with Fane and Dylis and—"

"What did they say to you?"

"N-nothing, we just talked about how you knew each other."

"And I am sure Fane had a lot to say." His voice had gone quiet.

"Why do you care so much? Are you embarrassed?"

His eyes darkened. "I am not embarrassed, pixie."

"W-well you need to do a better job at hiding it then."

"You hold yourself pretty high up, don't you?" He was too close. "Watching you play innocent is starting to get old and watching the twins run to play along is—"

"I am not playing anything."

"You're lying."

It hurt. More than I thought possible. I moved sideways to get some breathing room before I said something I would regret. Zarek looked so angry. I didn't know what to do. I opened my mouth to try and de-escalate, but then he moved his hand up in a quick, unexpected movement.

I threw my arms up over my head, flailing back to land awkwardly on one hip. I cringed so fast I wasn't able to stop myself and when I finally lowered my arms, I saw that Zarek had moved his hand to drag his fingers through his hair,

It was just a gesture of frustration.

Why!? Why was every moment alone with him so humiliating!? What was that?! Of course, my legs chose that moment to be shaky. "I don't know why I did that. I'm just tired, that's all and I-I don't know what I'm doing. I'm so—"

"Who hit you?" He looked even angrier and I flinched when he took another step toward me. He froze and I told myself to stop it, but I couldn't help myself.

I knew he *literally* couldn't hurt me. I logically knew it.

"No one hit me. That's ridiculous!" I tried to laugh it off.

"You are the worst liar I have ever met." He swore viciously under his breath.

"No one hit me." I swallowed hard to keep from babbling.

"Do you think I would hit you?"

Before I could answer, doors down the far end of the hall burst open and a wave of screaming, blaring horns, and panicked people emerged. Their distress was apparent as uniformed and armored law enforcement streamed in alongside them, using what I considered to be excessive and unnecessary force. Colored gas sprayed fitfully out of their cases, those who seemed especially susceptible were clutching at their breathing apparatuses and collapsing; paralyzed; only to be overwhelmed by the mob. Stunned, it took me a second to realize that Zarek was no longer beside me but sprinting down the halls deeper into the building.

When I caught up, I was rewarded with a wide grin.

"You're faster than you look, pixie."

"I didn't think you would wait for me."

"I didn't think you needed me to."

Amie or Esme would have grabbed me and, as I was now, likely would have carried me away. Why was it that I felt so light from his words? We slid into a dark stairwell, lit only by the undersides of the steps themselves. Zarek moved to go down just as I moved to go up. Comically, we paused at the exact moment to look at each other, both halfway along our chosen flight.

"There's an exit this way."

"Amie and Esme are upstairs. I can't leave them."

"They can fend for themselves. They don't need you."

"That's not the point. Go, we'll catch up later."

Surprisingly, Zarek decided to accompany me.

I hadn't expected him to and I hoped it was a newly discovered sign of trust. In silence we bounded up the stairs and made it to our room without issue. It dawned on me then that Zarek's movements were completely silent despite his speed, but I didn't have time to analyze further.

A quick touch to the shoulder was all I needed to wake Amie.

Esme was a different story. She'd always been a deep sleeper and it would take quite a few more millennia before she and her sister would be able to put sleep behind them. Try as we might, she resisted reentering the waking world.

Finally, Zarek scooped her up, blankets and all, and impatiently left the room with her. Amie quickly picked up what little possessions we'd scattered and wiped what residue or trace we may have left behind. It didn't escape me the level at which I'd be reliant on them for as long as we were outside. If it wasn't for their help, there would be no way to help Zarek at all.

"Thank you." I said sincerely as we ran back for the stairs.

"... You're welcome." She wasn't wearing her thigh holster for once. I wondered if it was because she was trying her best not to intensify the situation or if she had packed it by accident, either way I was glad to have it hidden away for now.

My mind raced with the various variables involved with getting down the stairwell and outside safely; but Zarek wasn't leading us back the way we came; instead going toward the lifts at the far end of the hall. He stopped in front of the lift.

"Where are you going!?" Amie demanded as he pressed the request button.

"Out for a stroll in the garden. Where do you think I'm going?"

"The wrong way. Why the fuck would we take the lifts!?"

"Do people where you come from flee to the lifts during a raid?"

Amie couldn't argue with his logic, although she looked like she wanted to. We needed her and Esme to preserve their energy. They were still adjusting to being outside and, mercifully, the lift arrived to stop whatever argument was brewing.

Zarek inexplicably chose the top floor.

"What. The. Actual. Fuck."

Amie turned to me, but I was too busy looking at the controls.

The top floor button hadn't appeared until Zarek slid his thumb over the round impression. His actions answered the question of whether he remembered if he had any innate ability. Zarek had written about his studies; his options had been limited in the outer universe; but with his condition, it was unclear what he knew.

"There's nothing on the top floor except for Fane's living quarters," I explained when I finally noticed Amie was staring at me. "He thinks that Fane has a convenient exit or escape. Relying on the variables we know of, I agree with his reasoning."

Instead of being reassured, she just looked more troubled.

I was beginning to prove ineffective at comforting people.

"Why would he have an exit?" Esme's voice was confused and blurry with sleep. A few errant curls popped up and she looked around with half-open eyes.

"He has one." Zarek dropped her now that she was awake.

She remained wrapped in the cocoon and seemed disgruntled to be standing instead of sleeping at such a late hour of the night. Esme looked like she was about to say something to Zarek, but the lift doors slid open and there was no time to wait for or to fully brief her. The three of us sprinted out, leaving Esme to unwrap herself from her blanket enclosure in the small entry hall.

There were over ten rooms to search. It was an opulent nest with floor-to-ceiling windows pointed in every direction, providing a bird's eye view of a stunning neon metropolis. What it had been during the day was a pale comparison to its dark, outrageous night. Colors splashed through the panes over expensive textiles in forms of fur, silks, and leather. Low-slung furniture, sculptural pieces, and soaring artworks mixed in an eclectic and disorienting style.

I wasn't even sure what I was looking for, but as Zarek tore through the residence with determination rather than finesse, it was clear that anything would suffice. I ran my fingers through the inside of any possible seam or particularly unusual nook. Under, over, behind any movable furniture piece. It was accidental that I was the first to search a guest room, but providential. A flaw in the mirror, undetectable to most species' visual processors, split the mirror against its right edge.

It wasn't an exit, but a computer. Decryption wouldn't be possible without at least some basic tools, but something struck me as extremely odd. With such an advanced system atop his desk, it was curious that Fane would hide another. This was a separate network; I had checked his main one not minutes before. Mundane business proceedings littered the screens there, but this one... I tried a few simple scans, but even the most basic functions were locked behind asymmetric ciphers. I so desperately curious, but this was obviously one I couldn't indulge in.

"Try this." Zarek reached over my shoulder to insert a small universal serial bulb into one of the ports and instantly the screen rebooted. Manual controls appeared in multiple pop ups as it did.

I turned to look at him incredulously.

"Do you just keep that on you all the time?"

"Never. Unless I am." Was he being serious or humorous?

I chose not to answer as, in front of our eyes, layers of programming fell away only to reveal more business documentation... for weapons manufacturing and distribution.

What in the universe was all this?

"Fane is a criminal." Amie came from behind us. "You led us into an illegal operation!? You son of a bitch!" With one look between them, Esme grabbed and yanked me away from Zarek; who didn't look at all ruffled hearing the insult toward his parentage.

"Makes sense. I thought this place was a bit out of his league."

"Wait! This doesn't mean he does it illegally!"

"Actually it does," Zarek admitted quite readily. He glanced over some of the accounting files and waved in that general direction, as if to highlight a particularly interesting point in a lecture series. "Here's where he bribes people into ignoring the taxes."□

Okay. That was bad.

I tried to discreetly scoot away to freedom, but Esme was having none of it. She looked just as cranky as Amie and probably meant it more at the moment.

"I also found the exit. It's this way."

Zarek strolled off as if Amie's eyes weren't burning holes through his skull. I saw her dominant hand twitch, was once again relieved that she didn't have a weapon handy, and heard the deep breaths she took before she could unclench her teeth.

"Sae. Was he like this when we were kids?"

"... No."

"Good. If he was, I should have shot him that night."

The exit hatch was a metal staircase. It spiraled downwards in a tight circular weave and Zarek didn't wait before starting the descent without a light source.

The journey down stretched the seconds into a winding string and seemed never-ending. After sealing the door behind us, there was no more conversation. Unsure if there were other access points or of what awaited, we were all in agreement for the first time; chatter was unwelcome.

The stairs ended at what seemed like a bare wall, but the door at the top had sealed in a similar manner. Zarek ran his fingers along the bottom and there was a quiet click. The seams of the door appeared and popped inwards ever so slightly.

Light poured through the seams and on the other side was the largest collection of land vehicles I'd ever seen. I couldn't begin to identify them and their mechanics hadn't yet entered my studies. I was familiar with the design and engineering of our own vessels, but no one had thought to prioritize machinery in the outer universe. If an Heir had ever been inside one before this very moment, no one had ever mentioned it to me.

Zarek went straight for the control panels. It wasn't long before the protective shielding was lowered, and an entire array of activation keys appeared to his right. "Fane hasn't been here," He muttered, his fingers sweeping over the panels.

"Who cares!?" Amie grabbed the keys from him.

"He let us stay here Amie and he's in trouble,"

"Because he's a criminal!" She emphasized like I didn't know.

"They're holding him at the central authority." Zarek stepped away from the panels, his face curiously blank. "Let's go."

I knew Fane wouldn't mind us borrowing the unit; a small but sturdy-looking vehicle; but I still felt uneasy taking something without the owner's permission.

The controls themselves looked simple, the surface void of obvious identifying marks, and it was a discreet choice all things considered. Its floors began at higher than knee high in my current form and I was about to clamber in by gripping a strategically placed handle when Zarek offered his hand.

It was the first time he'd reached out. The first time he would touch me since he'd forgotten everything and I wished wearing gloves was more in fashion on this planet as I took it. It was a mistake. I let go of his hand as soon as I could, but it felt as if he'd marked my skin. Knowing the last thing he wanted to see right now was signs of infatuation, I stared down at my hands and I didn't see Zarek and my Sentinels glancing at each other until it was too late.

"What are you doing?" I asked as Amie slid into the driver's seat.

Amie didn't answer. She just slid the key into its slot, and sealed the doors. Zarek was striding away, toward the other end of the warehouse. Where was he—there was only room for three people in this vehicle. Neither of them would look at me.

"Let me out. Amie. Let me out."

"We'll meet with him later."

"He's going after Fane is that it?" Her silence was an affirmation. "Then we can't just let him go alone. Amie, are you listening to me? Esme let me get to the door." Instead, Esme's arm shot out to stop me from getting to it.

Shut in again, I felt a spurt of panic.

"We talked about this. You need to let me make my own—"

"No, we need to protect you." Amie refused to meet my eyes.

"I can protect myself!" I sounded panicked even to my own ears.

"No!" Esme was crying, her tears soaked into my clothes as she tried to physically hold back. "Do you know how many laws we've broken in the last day!?" I knew Esme wasn't in the best state of mind but the way she was trying to force me back into my seat was making my panic worse. "You can't keep being so selfish!"

Zarek was leaving. He'd stolen a bike; one built on austere lines and low safety protocols. The far wall was rising to reveal the city streets and he'd changed into a form fitting riding suit, The material rippled under the sharp light and he did not once look our way as he slipped on protective gloves and headgear.

"You can't stop him." Amie said as if that changed anything.

"How do you know? You won't even let me try—"

A beam of light arched past as Zarek accelerated outside and blended into the florescent landscape. Frustration pumped as if injected forcibly into my veins. With slow, deliberate motions I grabbed the key, broke the surrounding port, and saw how brute force worked where persuasion had failed. The safety protocols fell and I had to resist slamming the key back into the panel to smash it as well. Amie and Esme voices bounced into both ears with objections. Without looking at either of them, I placed the broken parts gently back onto the dash.

"Okay. This is what I am going to do."

An hour later I found myself sitting quietly with Esme inside the central authority building. Built in the shape of an icosahedron partially sunk into the ground, the trip by public transportation had been an experience. I had never been out in public at such an hour and the trains had been filled with the sleeping, the intoxicated, and those who seemed bent on disturbing the peace.

I wish I could admit to Esme that it had been exhilarating.

Backless rows of seats curved in a semicircle and provided a view of the few workers inside of the front desk's pale-yellow force field. The floor and walls were a harsh grey. It was not a long wait, but it was marred by awkwardness. Esme had refused to talk to me ever since Amie had agreed to my plan. I knew her feelings were hurt and I was the cause; I just wasn't sure what to say anymore. At least we sat in the front, which discouraged hashing it out just then.

"Miss? He'll be out in just a second."

"Thank you!" I wondered if Amie's mission was going well.

It must be common to wear veils around the city; not one of the employees had given so much as a second glance when we'd come in and they certainly didn't care now that we'd transferred a large sum to their accounts.

To our right, a door appeared to reveal Fane, who looked awful. His eyes were oddly swollen, and he looked like all the life had been drained out of him. Had something happened to him in captivity?

I began to lead him toward the front entrance.

Waiting at the edges of the plaza in front of the building were Zarek and Amie, who stood stubbornly ignoring each other. Amie had managed to find him after all. It was a relief to know Zarek hadn't planned anything drastic, or at least had been stopped before doing so. There was a slight tang in the air as we walked out. The sky above was not only darkened by the night but also by boiling clouds. We would soon need to find shelter from the rain.

Nobody moved or said anything as I led Fane to a bench under the tree-lined promenade. He was shivering, perhaps from the cold. I could withstand a far wider temperature spectrum than most other species before growing uncomfortable. I offered my jacket but was rebuffed.

"Do you need us to call anyone?" I tried soothing. "Dylis—"

"Dylis did this!" Fane exploded, as if he'd just been waiting to hear the name. He pushed away from the bench and angrily wiped at his face, his breath was fast and audible. "He turned me in! He just stood there and let it happen! After everything we'd been through, after everything I ever did for him. It wasn't enough for him. I wasn't enough for him!"

"Maybe if you weren't a criminal," Amie muttered.

"It was his idea!" Fane snapped before kicking a pole. "It was his idea, and I gave him the funding to start it. It grew too big, too fast!'" He hit the pole and would have hit it again if Zarek hadn't stopped his fist on the back swing.

"Let go!" Still, he didn't resist when Zarek swung an arm over his shoulder and only gave token resistance to being dragged off.

"Come on, there's got to be an indecent place to drink somewhere around here."

"I don't want a drink. I want to strangle Dylis."

Fane sounded utterly defeated.

No matter what he'd said, a quarter of an hour later found him venting about Dylis and their life together, intoxicated further than I thought healthy.

Also, cheap liquor tasted horrendous. Amazing.

"Dylis gave me this ring, right? I love that ring! I'll never be able to look at it again! Half of my wardrobe just gone!" He let his head fall down into his folded arms, which was good as the table was sticky to the touch. Esme and Amie were in the booth adjacent, Esme having ordered a whole bottle of for herself.

It was bordering on early morning. There weren't too many clientele occupying seats at this hour, and only one person available to tend to them. The headroom was low and the walls were alight with several neon signs and screens showing various publicly streamed networks. Their volume was muted so as to not interfere with the questionable music pumping through the ceiling vents. The air smelled stale and yet held the humidity of a swamp.

Secretly, I found it all wonderful.

Now, would the bartender mind if I asked a few questions...

"You paid his bail."

Zarek acknowledged me for the first time since we'd regrouped. Fane was sitting between us and had acted as a buffer until this point, but he'd finally succumbed to the natural conclusion of consuming sedatives in excess and fell asleep.

"Why did you pay Fane's bail?"

I wasn't sure how to answer that question. It had cost well over a fortune to pay it. For years I had hidden away credits, simply to have a sense of financial independence from my normal monthly income. I'd had the freedom to invest it as I saw fit and it had turned into a substantial amount. This was yet something else I'd anxiously kept from Mother. I'd never had any real plans to use the credits; that was how I'd justified myself; but it had cost me something to let it go now.

When I had so drastically set on this path with Zarek, some part of me had thought I could rely on it to smooth our path and that was no longer an option as most of it was gone. Yes, my choices lately were certainly questionable.

"Fane means something to you and he was kind to me."

"This can't be just a crush. You want something from me. What is it?" I couldn't understand his mood. His voice was carefully measured and left me feeling as if I'd done something wrong. His body was relaxed, but it now felt to me as if the storm outside was looming over us. Heavy and electric.

"I don't understand why you're upset."

"I'm not upset, pixie but I can't be bought either."

"I'm not trying to buy your trust. I'm trying to earn it."

Something flickered in his eyes and my throat felt like I'd swallowed a stone. Fane's earlier words reappeared clearly between us. *He's dangerous.* I could see it now; how ruthless he could appear when he wanted to be. How his dark eyes, so warm when he'd looked at me before, could inspire fear. His relaxed form now felt like a deliberate subterfuge. Had he hurt people?

I didn't want to believe it.

When he spoke again it was smooth and mocking, as if daring me to do things I shouldn't ever consider. "You want me to trust you? Tell me something you're ashamed to tell anyone, even your precious friends... why don't you let me see what's under all that control you wrap yourself in."

He was always taunting me these days.

Needless to say, there were things in the past I felt embarrassed about but most were witnessed firsthand by other people. In private I'd always done everything correctly; it was especially easier to perform when the Empress wasn't watching. I'd never purposefully done anything shocking until just the few days prior. I didn't participate in any typical vices. Until recently, Yuki had always been around. I knew who I wanted to be and how that person needed to act. I wanted my people to be proud of me...

"My mother was the one who hit me. I-I disappointed her."

My voice hitched at the end, shame painting me in uncertainty.

Even though I had come to accept what had happened, it was still a difficult admission. More than anything, I wanted Zarek to know who I was and why I cared so much for his opinions and for him. He was the only person who had ever crossed mother on my behalf. How would he have reacted before all of this? If I had only told him when he'd visited Aristae's tower.

I braced myself for ridicule, but it never came.

"It wasn't your fault, pixie."

And just like that, I knew I had made the right choice.

I let his words roll over me and smiled for the first time that night. All night I had been harboring doubts and he'd been able to silence them all with just a few words. Guilt didn't have to be acknowledged to leave behind wounds and Zarek, no matter if he knew me or not, had never once—

"Sae. We need to leave." Amie grabbed me when I was slow in processing the interruption. Zarek hauled Fane up out of his seat, Fane mumbling objections as he was forced to stumble beside Zarek's long stride.

Esme was already at the door.

We plunged into a torrent of rain. The illuminated cityscape turned surreal under its fuzzy curtain of precipitation. Amie didn't stop, not bothering to keep the rain off us and almost dragging me along as we made our way to a covered alleyway nearby. No one sane would be outside in this weather, but Esme was scanning our surroundings in jerky, nervous movements.

Reflections pooled on every surface, blurring the city's hard edges and running down in energetic waterfalls only to crash into the numerous grates that lined the streets. Dark rivers clung closely to the walkways and carried with them refuse and residues. I had always loved the smell of a storm, but had never thought I'd be outside in public during one.

The alleyway, once one had gone in deep enough, shielded us from the worst of the rain; however, we weren't the only ones seeking shelter. A small form huddled not too far from us, their head rising from their knees as we approached.

It was one of the slaves I'd seen earlier. The girl. Before any of us could react to her presence, she threw herself back, failing for the nearest wall. Her actions brought along only half of her body; the other half, dangling by a few wires, flopped uselessly.

She wasn't fully organic, but I could see greenish blood coming from one of her arms. So, she was at least partially composed of biological material. Either an android or a cyborg; her status as a sentient being was questionable. Elysia had laws regarding both and although it was rare to find them inside our borders, we had given refuge to many over the eons as their status fluctuated wildly; all depending on the time and their locations outside.

"Hello. Do you need help?" Amie wouldn't let me closer and her reasoning was sound. Especially as my answer came in the form of a piece of metal rubbish thrown in our direction.

"We have other problems to deal with." Amie turned her back to the girl and pulled me into a tight circle with the rest of our group. I couldn't help but feel awful as I could hear her trying to collect herself, literally, from the ground.

"Sae! Focus!" Esme hissed.

"There was a news broadcast on one of the screens at the bar." Amie explained in a whisper. "They found evidence of treason against the state in his building. Interplanetary missiles were sent to Rateer. We can't help him anymore. His charges have gone up and they're looking for him."

As soon as Amie finished her sentence, Zarek grabbed Fane's right arm and slammed it into the nearby wall with enough force to revive him out of his drunken stupor. Fane yelped in pain, tried to pull away, but Zarek held fast to him. With one hand holding Fane's arm to the wall, he ripped a thin metal cuff off that hadn't been visible just seconds before. He then proceeded to cook it with his fingertips until it blackened, and he could smash it to bits against the ground.

"Tracker," he said grimly. "Won't be long before a cop uses their department's collective brain cell and scans the public areas. Fane needs to get off-world."

Esme disagreed. "We are not bringing him with us!"

As Esme and Amie tried arguing with Zarek, I crept away.

The girl had managed to gather all of her errant parts under her cloak again, with only a few pieces still scattered around. She eyed me warily from under her hood, but she didn't make any moves to stop me from coming closer. One of her eyes was cybernetic and it had stopped operating at some point. Her other eye and the left of her face seemed organic, inflamed from blunt force trauma.

I had never been around such an injured person before.

"What's your name? Can I call someone for you?"

"No!" She was hysterical. "I ain't... fixed again!"

"I can help you. Take you somewhere else and—"

"Don't want need your... fucking help!" Her speech was slurred and disjointed. "Make me into bottlecaps... useful... nothing ain't helping me... trash...fuck off!" When she saw that I didn't move away, she just got angrier. "I said fuck off!"

Despite her words, she looked scared. Carefully, I dropped to my knees on the cold, wet ground and sat with her. I could tell that her operating systems were shutting down and her blood loss was at a critical stage. I tried asking her for her name again, but she either couldn't or wouldn't tell me. If I had my status or abilities or anything of worth, I could remedy this. Powerless, I sat with her.

She struggled in the end, but not once did she ask for my help.

"Could one of you please remove her brand?" It was the first time I ever watched someone die. As she faded, her head lolled to one side and the code stamp on her neck came into stark relief. It was still raw, stark against her dull pink skin. My friends had stopped arguing during the last few minutes of this girl's life.

"It's illegal to mess with the outer universe's slaves."

Amie did not argue with her sister's assessment.

I wanted to argue, but I had already asked so much from them already. I couldn't. So, I reached out to close her eye. As I did, another hand came into my field of vision, and I watched as the brand faded away.

There was no trace of it left when Zarek lifted his fingers away.

Right there and then, I made yet another decision. "Fane is coming with us." I held up my hand to stop Amie and Esme before they could begin. "We need money. Unless you two have some I'm unaware of, we need Fane's money."

"He doesn't have any if he's a defector!" Amie argued.

"I have money in hidden accounts," Fane argued. He'd come to grips with his new situation fairly quickly, considering that he was still somewhat inebriated. "And I may be an asshole but I'm not a traitor. I wouldn't be caught dead selling shit to Rateer, much less interstellar weapons."

He was telling the truth and Amie knew it.

"Whatever! I don't care anymore. We need to leave." Amie tried to get to me, but I circled around Zarek to put him between us.

I couldn't think when other people grabbed at me.

"We can't leave until we find Zarek's memory."

"No," Amie hissed. "That damn club is crawling with police."

"Um, yeah... about that..." Fane reached into his back coat pockets and pulled out a small, black sphere.

"You had it all along?" His deceit, though somewhat understandable, stung.

Fane gave me a sheepish look. "Sorry, I was hoping to use it for leverage, but in light of recent events..." He handed it over to me.

It felt—there was no other way to say this—weird.

This was the first chance we'd had to look over the thing. It was black but cybernetics wrapped over the smooth surface. Amie tried a few quick scans but came up empty as to what it was made of. We'd never seen anything quite like it but I vetoed the option of dissecting it. We had no idea if we could break it but I wasn't taking that chance. In the end, I just held it out to Zarek.

As soon as it hit his palm, its faint glow vanished.

Apprehensively, I waited for some sign that it had worked.

The sphere disintegrated in his hand.

"Well, Did it work?" Fane asked.

"It worked." Zarek confirmed.

That told me nothing. I ached to question him, but Amie was right. We'd done what we'd set out to accomplish and now we had to leave. We'd have to make our jump from here. Right now we couldn't risk going to any of the city's ports where they would be looking actively for Fane. Amie prepared to make the leap while Esme hid any sign of us. It didn't take long.

As dawn broke over the city, and people began their lives anew, there was only a small woman's corpse to be found in that alleyway. Her face was etched into a death mask of pain. Her body would not be picked up for several hours as the city was busy searching for a high-level fugitive. It would not be a dignified event as her body was thrown into a bin for recycling parts.

Chapter 9: Nowhere

"Pixie, it's time to wake up now."

I jolted upright, almost slamming my head into Zarek's in the process. He'd moved back only just in time to prevent a collision. What? Where were we? Why had I been asleep? I almost never slept anymore and never involuntarily.

The world around us was murky. Barren.

The dark sky hung low in the atmosphere, blocking any natural light from reaching us. I looked at my hands and saw that they were cast into monochrome hues. Everything seemed to have adopted the same color palate. Even the slightest hint of blue was washed out of Zarek's hair, leaving only the darkest greys behind.

We were alone. Esme, Amie, and Fane were nowhere in sight. Had something gone wrong with the jump and separated us? Although the ground was hard beneath, dust centimeters deep covered it and now my clothing. The air smelled dry and heavy, like an old tome gone to ruin over time. When I stood, dust billowed around me as high as my knees.

"Are you alright?"

He didn't bother to answer me as he scanned the distant horizon. There was nothing in sight for kilometers but hardened earth. There was no sign of civilization, no sound, no wind. The ground was almost the exact same shade as the sky, which gave the disorienting feeling of floating.

"Zarek, I—are those piercings?"

When he'd turned his head to look at me, I saw them. Three studs in his left ear and two in his right; black, like his eyes. I had gotten used to many kinds of body modifications over my years of diplomacy and ears were a common place for such decorations. They followed the upper ridge of his ears, and they looked... good.

I had to remind myself not to stare.

"Oh no. I forgot to hide them this morning."

His voice was drier than the dust.

"N-no, I really—I think they're lovely."

It wasn't a joke, but he laughed anyway.

Just as quickly, his smile faded as his eyes locked on something over my shoulder. I turned and saw exactly what it was that had caught his attention.

It was a low building in the distance, close enough to see that it had a single door centered in the middle with no windows. Just like everything else, it was painted with the same muted grey brush.

It hadn't been there when I looked seconds earlier.

Without speaking, we began to walk in the direction of the building. As we drew closer, we began to spot lines in the ground here and there, as if a person had run a stick through the dust. There seemed to be a pattern to the marks, but if Zarek recognized them, he didn't say a word. I tried to keep a distance between us, but by the time we neared the building, we stood side by side.

Every once in a while, I was tempted to look behind us, but I was afraid the building or Zarek would disappear if I did. I didn't want to be left alone here. I'd never been in a place so empty of life. Every bit of me was gritty with dust by the time we reached the structure.

"Do you think the others are okay?" I said in a hushed voice.

Zarek didn't answer but the question was largely rhetorical.

Wherever they were, I just hoped they were together and safe.

Its door was ajar, swung ever so slightly inwards to create a thin gap. The building had that unmistakable quality of abandonment;

the pitched roof sagging in the middle and its frame leaned forward toward us. Beckoning. The lines in the dust had come closer and closer to form a circular pattern around it. It looked to be two stories high judging by the size of the door.

"Do you want to stay here?"

"No, I'm coming with you."

Zarek nodded, but instead of going inside, he moved to go around the right corner. I made to follow, but almost stumbled.

Whipping my head around, there was nothing there.

I could have sworn I felt fingers wrap around my wrist.

"What is it?" Zarek appeared so quickly, I jumped.

"I felt a hand on my arm," I admitted, knowing how it sounded.

Instead of dismissing it or trying to reassure me, Zarek gestured for me to take the lead. I rubbed my wrist absently and nodded. We made a quick round around the building and saw that there were no other doorways or windows inside.

There was nothing around the building.

There was nothing else here.

Plants dared not to break the monotony of the landscape, and no shadows lay in the distance that may indicate life. The marks went all around the building, some tiny scratches while others made complete circles around the place. There were no distinguishing marks on the building itself.

The door was completely flat. It lacked any kind of obvious handle or switch, and a corner was partially obscured by a gathering of dark grey dust. From this distance, we could see the dust had settled inside as well. I still couldn't check myself right now, but I trusted Zarek to have looked for any obvious dangers.

Something leaped at us the moment the door swung inwards, it came all at once from the ceiling as a dark blur of movement and a nauseating snap sound. I ducked instinctively to the right, my heart shoved in my throat, and watched its spindly limbs jangle unnaturally in the doorway before settling.

It was a life-sized doll of some kind, its arms and legs triple-jointed and discolored. The head was on too loose, and it was naked. The worst detail was the thin cord that was wrapped around its neck. Whatever its outer skin was made of was soft as the thin cord had left a deep impression behind.

It had no face, the head bent at an unnatural angle. The doll now swung from side to side in the doorway like a metronome.

Also, Zarek had a knife.

It looked wickedly sharp, its grip molded seamlessly against his hand and the blade followed the curve perfectly into a jagged edge. As soon as he stopped applying pressure to the handle, the blade rescinded smoothly back into its sheath.

"Why do you have a knife?"

"I like to chop my own vegetables," he said with a straight face. "Roots and tubers react especially badly to dull knives. Why be so cruel as to butcher the poor things? Bringing my own along reduces needless pain and waste on all sides."

"Do you have only one?"

"Wanna search me pixie?" Zarek stretched out his arms.

"Actually, I mean—I meant can I have one?"

Another handle appeared in his free hand. He held it out and I took it. Blades slid out both ends to create a circular-shaped weapon. The edges were smooth rather than serrated, but I had no doubt they were expertly sharpened. A locking mechanism kept the weapon open without having to apply pressure. It was also much lighter than it looked and made me feel better.

"Thank you."

Zarek moved to slice the cord hanging the doll up. Once tossed aside, we could finally peer into the narrow hallway beyond it. There were three doors on either side. None of the doors had handles, but all stood ajar. A steep staircase at the other end extended upwards into the darkness.

There were footsteps everywhere.

A thick layer of dust was disturbed by prints leading in every direction. Not just one shape, but many. Some doubling back on each other and others were replicated going in circles or stopping at a wall or door. They looked recent, as if a crowd could appear at any time to claim them. I could see them making their way up the staircase, but saw none going down.

Zarek motioned for me to wait and I watched quietly as he grabbed the doll and threw it down the hallway, where it rolled and bounced before crashing at the foot of the stairs. Some of the limbs detached in the process and hit the walls.

The sound was horrible, but the silence afterwards was worse.

Taking the initiative, I took the first step inside. The floor for badly warped, but unless there was a hollow space for the floor to fall into, it was safe enough. Looking back, I watched Zarek take one last precaution before joining me. He ripped the door off its hinges and propped it neatly outside against the house.

Even with light from the front door streaming into the building, shadows clung relentlessly to every corner. Zarek stood at my back as I opened the first door to the right. Having braced myself for the worst, it was relief to find the room empty but for a few pieces of broken furniture.

One in particular caught my eye, it was a small desk for a child and it was laid on its side due to a broken leg. It looked like a desk I would have used during my earlier studies. Cautiously, I bent down to get a better look.

Nothing out of the ordinary, but...

The footsteps seemed to grow smaller in this room and looked as if a child had been pacing back and forth. I used to pace during my studies; before I realized it was undignified. Leaving the door open, I turned and nodded to Zarek to open the one directly opposite.

Glassy eyes stared right at back us.

Although I had kept from jumping when the stuffed creature was unveiled, I couldn't help it when Zarek slammed the door back shut. The large, taxidermied animal had been stuffed in a closet no bigger than it was. With long ears, a pointed snout, patchy fur, and a wide ghoulish grin, I couldn't blame Zarek for not liking the look of it. But something else was wrong.

Zarek had one arm braced against the door and he was unnervingly still. In the growing quiet, I reached out to touch his hand. It was coiled up so tight that it looked like his fingers were cutting off circulation.

My fingers brushed against Zarek's.

He moved so fast that I almost was pinned to the wall by my throat. I ducked just in time, and looked up to meet Zarek's eyes. They were flat and dull; nothing was there and it was as if I could see right through them to the back of his skull. I wanted to shiver. Dust and small pieces of debris fell into my hair, his hand had pierced through the rotting wall. Zarek's knife was extended again and from my curled-up position on the floor, it was only millimeters from my face. I waited as the cold left his gaze and it seemed to dawn on him what he'd just done.

"Zarek. It's just me. Sae."

He broke eye contact first.

Stepping back, Zarek pulled his hand away only to cause more dust to fall. I don't think I'd ever been this dirty in my entire life. Dirt coated my skin in a thick layer and my hair felt matted and grimy to the touch. I pretended to dust myself off for a moment, even though I knew it was futile, to give Zarek some time.

"I'm sorry pixie."

"No harm done. I'm on edge too."

I didn't want him to feel guilty about it. About me. I tried to give what I thought was a reassuring smile, but it only seemed to make Zarek more tense. He nodded and we carried on. I opened the next door to find an expansive room, the walls and floor were white and bare; completely empty but for a small black cloth bag placed directly in the center.

Warier than ever, I picked up one of the doll's dislocated arms from the floor and threw it at the bag. It smacked against the fabric before rolling away.

Nothing happened.

Stepping closer, I nudged the bag with my foot and opened it enough to look inside. The bag was filled with sweets. There were sugar sticks and squares, small pieces wrapped in paper twists, and rounds made from the sweetened pods of a rare flower. My father had given me such things once in a while in my childhood. As had Anera and Astral when I was still in the nursery.

The fourth door opened to a room riddled with small holes and grooves dug into the walls and floor. Many of the holes had a burnt ring around them and the grooves looked as if a wild animal had gone and dug their claws in, scratching at things over and over. This door was the only one with a working lock.

The fifth room held another doll, one nailed into the ground.

My skin crawled the longer I looked at it, so I stopped.

Finally, the last door on this level.

This one was markedly different than the other doors. It had a small X carved into it. The other doors had been blank. Zarek and I took up positions on either side of it, I on the side closer to the staircase. I waited for him to nod before opening the door myself and letting it swing inwards.

"Alexi!?"

The next thing I knew, Zarek had entered the room and grabbed the arm of what looked like a young woman in a dress with long, dark hair. She sat faced away from us, in a recessed nook. Like a window alcove without the window.

The instant Zarek touched her, her head fell off.

It was just another doll.

The most gruesome doll we'd seen so far.

Hundreds of black eyes had been glued to her face, one on top of the other in a way that, at first glance, seemed like a rancid skin condition. Dust plumed upwards from where it landed on the ground. It rolled toward me, but stopped short as Zarek pinned it by the hair with his boot.

Standing there, watching him, I didn't know what to do. With each moment we spent in here, Zarek seemed to go further and further into himself in a way I didn't fully understand.

Walking around the doll's head, I stopped an arm's length away.

"I'd like to get some air. Will you come with me?"

There was still another door at the top of the stairs.

It didn't matter right now.

"You're not going to ask?"

"Ask about what?"

My reward was a small smile, wry yet sincere.

We moved to exit the room and I was careful to keep a wide berth from the doll head. It was frightening to look at, even though I knew that it could do me no harm. There was just something in that bumpy texture that disturbed me. On that note, I should have closed the door opposite. The doll nailed to the ground was just as unnerving. It lay in a perfect circle untouched by the footprints

It was almost ritualistic.

Then, just as I stepped out into the hallway, at all went dark.

Doorways disappeared and where the entrance had been providing light was now a long corridor ending in a black void. The walls tilted and the floor came out from under me as what felt like dozens of hands wrapped around my legs and *yanked*. My head bounced off of the floor, sending a dust cloud up to obscure my vision. I instinctively tried to dig my fingers into the floor, scrambling for purchase as what looked like shadows wrapped around my feet and legs. I used one hand to shove one half circle of my knife into the floor, but it was no use as the blade sunk into the floor like sand until I was left holding nothing at all.

Zarek grabbed onto my arms and I gratefully clung to him, he pulled me closer and I tried to wrap my arms around his neck. Before I could, the shadows rallied and pulled me almost out of Zarek's grip. They swirled at a sickening pace around us and I couldn't seem to move my lower body anymore.

Zarek and I held on like that for what seemed like an eternity.

From behind the shadows lunged at Zarek, pulling at him from every angle. Zarek was forced to let go of one of my arms to slash at the long spindly fingers wrapping themselves around his limbs and torso. I could see the shadows trying to break Zarek's foothold before I was blinded by another hand gripping the top half of my head and another pulling me back by the hair.

Stop touching me! I wanted to scream. *Stop grabbing me!*

One moment I could feel Zarek's fingers being pried off my arm and the next I was flying back and up the stairs, I tried to grab at one of the steps only to find a smooth surface where the stairs ought to be. In desperation, I called out to Zarek.

I could hear him yelling my name as we were pulled in opposite directions. That was when I decided that this had gone far enough. I didn't care if I was caught out here, I was prepared to blow apart the entire building if I had to...

But my Light was gone.

Panic rose as I tried again and again with none of the familiar warmth filling my soul. I couldn't think, Hands were grabbing at me from all directions. No! Don't touch me! I tried to speak, to scream, but my voice had abandoned me.

Why couldn't I do anything right? It was my fault if Zarek got hurt. It was my fault that all of this had happened. I couldn't do anything right. I didn't want to be grabbed at anymore! Let go of me! I was such a failure...

That voice wasn't coming from inside my head.

It was coming from all around me.

Getting a grip took longer than I'd like to admit. I was crying. It felt so painful. It felt like I would always be in pain; like I would never surface from my fears ever again. Slowly, eventually, I stopped struggling and forced my panic down.

It was my voice coming from all directions.

Because this was a dream.

The two suns above were blindingly hot and barely tempered by their relatively low positions in the sky. Finding myself in the middle of a sweeping meadow would not usually be a cause for alarm; but I recognized the tall, bright yellow blooms, heavy with pollen on their long twisting stalks. A medicinal plant prized for its numerous uses in both general and regional anesthesia. Its roots were used in small doses for sedation, and its stem and leaves were both analgesic and a concentrated narcotic.

Its pollen was the most dangerous.

My friends and I were inside a giant, visible cloud of a powerful dissociative hallucinogen. Quickly, I checked on my friends. To my relief, Fane was still breathing, which meant I had only been under for a few seconds at most.

The fact that I'd been asleep at all was alarming.

The majority of beings couldn't survive this amount of the hallucinogen for very long. Workers who came in contact with the flower were usually equipped from head to toe in integrated safety equipment and individual breathing apparatuses. I needed to get everyone away from this field as soon as possible.

Amie and Esme would survive.

Zarek and Fane had seconds, not minutes.

The gravity was noticeably lower on this planet, but carrying them all out would be too unwieldy to work and one by one would be too slow. The stalks were too high for me to see over in my current form, and I had no idea what the nearest safe location would be to physically take them. There was a steep mountain range to my left that was heavily forested. If I could get them to a high enough altitude, the pollen wouldn't be able to reach them.

I had very few choices and none were favorable to our circumstances. I was shockingly inept at wielding my Light on a small scale, and I could certainly hurt the others by accident. But if I used too much I was afraid we'd be discovered, and this trip would come to a premature end.

Turning, I had to stifle a yelp as I saw Zarek struggling to sit up. I rushed over to help him, seeing that he was fighting to stay conscious. It was so improbable for him to be awake that I had to wonder if I was still suffering from the effects of the flower myself.

"Zarek can you get us up to the mountains?" I tried to convey the urgency of my request, but I wasn't sure if I was getting through to him. His eyes were unfocused and once I was within arm's reach, he pulled me down against him.

My next sentence was muffled by his clothing.

"Sae... you... okay?" He buried his face in my hair.

No, not a good time! I reminded myself, trying to push away. This was not the time for this but Zarek's grip only tightened when he felt me pulling back. "Zarek I need you to let go. Please let go. I'm okay, I promise. Let go." He let go.

"Where are...?" I could see him sinking.

"Zarek! Look at me! We need to get out." I waved my hands in front of his eyes, trying to keep him awake. "I need you to take us up the mountain. That one." I pointed and his head only slightly tilted in that direction. "Please, Zarek. Listen to my voice. We aren't safe here. I need you to help—"

If I wasn't already on my knees, my legs would have given out.

He'd done it. Zarek had succeeded in saving us all.

Braced against a large tree, the newly dappled light played gently against his features, softened by sleep. Just as Zarek's eyelids finally gave up the fight and closed, I heard Amie and Esme stir behind me. I wasn't surprised that whatever dreams they were having were not friendly ones.

Carefully, I stepped away from Zarek and went over to where the rest of my friends rested. The grass was curly and purplish green in color, watered generously by mountain springs and protected from direct sunlight by a luscious canopy. I checked Fane's pulse and was alarmed at how much slower than the universal average it had gotten in such a short time. This was not good.

"Amie." I went over and shook her arm. I didn't know how well their systems would resist inhaling so much of the hallucinogen, but physically they were as similar to me as possible for another sentient being to be. They could also purge themselves of the toxin, but one of them had to wake up first.

"Esme." I reached over to shake both of them at the same time.

I knew that their mother and father were immune to all but the most powerful drugs, even then one needed quite the quantity to affect them, but my Sentinels were still too young. They needed a few more millennia and Fane didn't have the time to spare.

Esme was the first to respond to my efforts. She batted my hand away and tried to feebly roll away from whatever was keeping her from her nap. I persisted, hissing her name into her ear and generally making a nuisance of myself. Finally, I pulled her into a somewhat sitting position.

"Sae stop, let me nap." Her head lolled to one side.

"Fane needs help. You were all exposed to a dissociative hallucinogen. That's why you're so tired. I don't think Fane's body can handle it for much longer. Esme stay awake." I held her up firmly so that she couldn't fall back down. "Esme I need you to help Fane before it's too late."

"Alright already," Esme snapped.

It wasn't pretty. Fane barely made it to his hands and knees before he heaved the contents of his stomach and lungs. Pollen made its way out of his eyes, ears, and nose; he would have collapsed face-first into his own mess if I hadn't grabbed him by the back of his shirt. I eased him away and back down onto a new patch of grass. He groaned as I checked his pulse, and it seemed to be back within a reasonable spectrum of speed. Esme was again out cold.

Hours would pass before any of them stirred again and I was able to assess our surroundings thoroughly. We were in a boreal forest with little to no signs of development. The flowers below were laid out in a grid pattern indicating planned agriculture. It was likely that we had landed on a nonresidential sector zoned only for cultivation. If automated, there would be little reason for anyone to check in unless it was planting or harvesting season.

We had left Elysia with little to no possessions. None of us had expected to go outside and we had packed light. More than that, Amie and I had both dropped our bags inside when Zarek's ship had blown off the face of the galaxy.

Fane and Zarek had nothing but what they were carrying on them, but at least Zarek had gotten himself new clothing while at Fane's club.

Finding myself still dressed in the Inferno uniform was not ideal, but I couldn't exactly rummage through Esme's bag without her permission. It was beginning to get dark and while a light source wasn't really a personal concern, I wanted to anticipate any possible difficulties when it came to Zarek and Fane.

Now, why was I so bad at making fire?

I had been under the impression that fire was an easy feat to accomplish. Fuel and oxygen were both abundant and I had constructed a small area of dirt to prevent unwanted expansion. I was pleased when friction yielded a quick flame but was discouraged to find that it did not spread readily across the wood. After trying several different kinds, I was at a loss.

A familiar prickling sensation gave me pause for long enough to kill my most recent attempt. I'd had high hopes for that one. I sighed over the lingering ashes before giving up and going to check on Zarek. He was gingerly getting to his feet, his eyes taking in that Amie, Esme, and Fane were all still asleep.

It occurred to me then that my time would have been better spent coming up with a plausible lie about why the hallucinogen hadn't worked on me.

"You need kindling to make a fire."

Zarek offered me a handful of dry grass. He walked around picking up small twigs and more grass until he'd made a decent pile next to my larger sticks and failed fire experiments. Next, he pulled yet another knife out of his coat and dug a groove down one of my pieces of wood. Taking another good-sized stick, he carved one end into a blunt point and gave it to me.

Following his instructions, I rapidly moved the stick up and down the groove, which created a small pile of coals. When a flame appeared, he fed it with grass and then with progressively larger pieces until the fire caught. Then after a bit of maneuvering, a respectable campfire appeared.

Something unspoken kept us from conversing above the bare minimum. Secrets that we knew each other was keeping, questions that neither of us wanted to ask, and words that would shatter the quiet companionship we were enjoying. Sitting next to each other under the brightening stars, a careful distance between us, I felt myself relaxing for the first time in days.

Firelight suited Zarek, who seemed just as comfortable here as he had been in the middle of the Inferno. I admired his confidence, the ease in which he moved about the universe no matter the circumstances. It was a trait I had tried emulating all my life.

"How long have we known each other?"

"Over a decade, we met as children."

"I still don't know who you are."

Well, at least that answered one of my questions. How many more fragments of Zarek's memories were out there? We had to be more strategic in how we gathered them. The first had run us into the authorities, the second had landed us in the middle of a major threat and it was supposedly still down in the fields.

Cira had done this for a reason, but why do it at all?

It didn't escape us that she could reveal my presence at any moment. However, besides having me face interstellar consequences, the only other motivation I could see is causing tensions between the Empress and Isbul. It didn't make any sense. Pulling Elysia into the conflict wouldn't change anything. We'd never interfered in a war before. All this could accomplish was to provide Isbul reason to demand aid in exchange for forgiving my trespasses.

Even that much would be a long shot.

It could be that her personal grudge against Zarek was overriding her common sense, but this all seemed too elaborate, too deliberately aimed at me. Cira couldn't have predicted I would defy my mother, break the law, and go along with her scheme. I was methodically going over what I knew of Rateer, when I realized a hand was being waved in front of my face.

"Be careful of where you drift away pixie." Zarek didn't look upset that I hadn't been paying attention, which was good. I knew better than to let my mind wander during a conversation. I waited to see if he was going to say anything else, but he just added more wood to the fire.

"I'm sorry for not paying attention, it's a bad habit of mine."

"No pixie, I'd say apologizing is your bad habit."

"An apology isn't bad; it signifies a person acknowledging their faults or mistakes in earnest and is an indicator of self-reflection and low egocentrism."

"If you say so."

"Your tone implies you don't agree."

"Apologies are a diversion to avoid either liability or guilt. Like all forms of self-pleasure, they leave people unsatisfied when done badly and others inclined to do it more often as if doing so would make the practice palatable."

I couldn't tell if he was joking. He sounded as if he were serious, but there was a look on his face that made me feel as though...

"A-are you teasing me?"

"What do you think?"

"So you don't ever apologize?"

"Not if I can avoid it."

"Then why did you apologize to me?"

Oops. As soon as I said it, I knew I had walked neatly into his snare. I had my suspicions that he and I had shared a delusion, but it had felt too intimate to talk about. To his credit, Zarek didn't dwell on it or ask any questions. I think we both knew it would only open the door to more confessions. More truths.

None of which we were ready for.

"You hesitated. When I asked if you thought I would hit you."

"I don't think you would ever hit me Zarek... do you?"

This time, he chose not to respond.

Nothing else was said that night.

It wasn't long until Amie woke up and purged herself of the rest of the drug. Once she checked the area and saw no immediate dangers to me, Amie went down to collect the memory hidden in the fields. Prepared for the pollen on this second trip, it was a simple matter for her and she returned quickly enough. We agreed to stay the night, but by the time the second sun peaked over the hills, there was nothing left but a small, cold pile of ashes.

Chapter 10: Players

A week later and money was running out. Amie and Esme were exhausted from multiple timespace jumps; which was further than they'd ever gone alone, much less with a group. In the interim, Fane had recovered from the hallucinogen and discovered Dylis had taken even his most hidden reserves.

Truthfully, I saw no reason to force him to leave as he hadn't asked any questions when we offered him no explanation. Fane treated me with an open friendliness that no one had ever shown me and, unexpectantly, I found a source of support I was reluctant to lose. Even now, he kept up a running commentary, requiring no input on my part as we weaved through the excited masses.

Among Isbul's most important cities, one had to admire the architectural feat that was Solaris. Massive, webbed domes encased the city and all the industries that supported it from the punishing heat of their star. It was a preplanned state with other satellite cities accessible by underground rail systems. While the planet itself was uninhabitable for most species outside the domes, this planet was rich in mined resources and Solaris proudly reflected that wealth.

Structures twisted from the bottom to the top of the dome, overflowing with chartreuse plant life and heavy with alabaster fruit this time of year. Large portions of Solaris were dedicated public parks with different biomes and ecosystems, with curved walkways carved out between them. Most people walked but there were free teleportation hubs scattered throughout the city.

It reminded me somewhat of the cities back home.

Until we discovered the lower decks.

There, a shocking underbelly of wealth disparity and a sub-standard quality of life was hidden away. The workers of Solaris could barely afford to house themselves inside the city their labor had created. We had found lodging near the bottom, but with my Sentinels only waking for brief periods, it was impossible to pin down who was carrying the memory. My dwindling resources wouldn't be able to pay for much more of our foray outside.

The city was in the middle of festivities to celebrate Solaris' founding; visitors had flocked here for the occasion and it would be another few weeks before those visitors would begin to trickle out. When Amie was able to give us a general location, Fane, Zarek, and I would attempt to narrow it down but each location would prove more crowded than the last.

During our search, the streets had been lined with temporary attractions and performances. I couldn't help but catch a glimpse of the masked and colorfully dressed keeping their audiences entertained. Although I knew Isbul still printed national bank notes; it seemed they were no longer widely circulated; I observed people funneling credits into a performer's personal code.

Fane tapped on my shoulder and I nodded nervously.

This would be a good time for me to come to my senses. The optimal time would have been before I bought the mask, but it was too late for that. No one paid any attention to us as Fane helped me up onto a wide ledge separating a building from the square below. It was still early. The nocturnal crowd was transitioning into the diurnal and this allowed a short lull for us to prepare.

I felt guilty about not telling the others.

Fane seemed like the only one who wouldn't talk me out of it.

Taking a deep breath, I brought myself back to my years of music theory and practice classes. All music was formulaic and could be broken down into foundational components. I possessed absolute pitch, was predisposed to be skilled in all intellectual ventures, and there was little to no chance of failure.

If I kept repeating it, I would eventually believe it.

Fane set up the hologram with his code prominently displayed.

I kept my hands gripped tightly in front of me as I began.

"Unprepared and unprovoked
Write their names on every wall
Out through these hazy streets
Hear me less
See no more
Shake me down.
To the core..."

After the first verse, I relaxed into the melody and rhythm. I had forgotten I liked singing. Music was a language and a life all of its own, made of long forgotten aspirations and newly discovered passions. I tried to project my voice as much as I physically could, paid close attention to the pacing, and as the song came to a close, it occurred to me that I may have miscalculated.

I had attracted too much attention.

The entire square was quiet.

During the course of the song, they had congregated in a way that gave me no room to exit. Seconds passed as my final note died away and the first person tried to grab me. I was forced back against the building behind me as they surged forward.

Their ardor screamed into my ears.

I should have picked a less accessible place.

I knew better than to try and attract attention.

Fane was yelling, everybody was yelling until I couldn't think past the sick, demanding sound. A man with a slack jaw grabbed my ankle with both hands. I tried to shake him off, but he seemed determined to pull me toward the grasping wall of hands.

"You don't touch people without their permission."

Zarek, contrary to his own words, grabbed the man's shoulder. In one decisive twist, he dislocated the arm and released me from the man's grip. The man was in obvious pain but was quickly swallowed up by the rabidly besotted throng.

It had been so smooth and effortless.

The ones close enough to witness backed away as Zarek turned his attention to them. This was enough to douse their enthusiasm. There were those in the back who tried to push forward as the crowd dispersed; they too were discouraged once they saw him.

Fane weaved his way back to us, looking very much worse for wear from his experience. His once pristine clothes were wrinkled and his shoes were stained.

"You can stop scaring the public Zarek, I think they get it."

"Did you wake up like that or do you work to look like shit?"

"At least I don't make children cry with just my fucking face."

"It's not just children, all beings weep at the sight of me."

Sitting down on the ledge with my feet dangling, I listened to their banter. It was nice to see Zarek baiting Fane and enjoying himself. As they talked, I quietly checked Fane's account and was gratified to see we had enough money for at least another few weeks in Solaris. This hadn't been for nothing and next time I would make sure to take more precautions.

"Hey, you! Girl!"

I gasped as I was grabbed around the waist unexpectedly and spun about by yet another stranger, this one with the sour scent of intoxicants all over him. He was incredibly unbalanced, and I was afraid if I struggled, he'd pull me down with him in a fall. He was dressed in a flamboyant fashion. If the materials weren't so fine, I would have mistaken him for an entertainer.

He only stopped spinning when Zarek put his hand on his arm.

"Zarek! Is that you!? Fuck me, I haven't seen you since that one ambassador's shindig, you remember right? Or maybe you don't cause I barely do! Ha-ha!" He stumbled a bit as Zarek hauled him upright. His smile remained wide and unbothered; between his clothing and muddled hazel eyes, he seemed harmless. "You went off with that gorgeous—"

Now that I could get a better look at him, I recognized who he was. The tattoos around his neck gave him away even if he hadn't been the spitting image of his father. Aaro Uride, the only child of the United Federation of Yiter's president. President Uride had been in power for over two thousand years now. Due to a combination of biological enhancements and a high approval rating, Yiter's presidency had not seen a serious challenger for generations. It was customary for the active president to sire no children as to not encourage a line of succession, but even the birth of Aaro a century ago had not dulled his popularity.

Aaro was kept from public circles, not much else was reported.

"I'm surprised to see you in daylight." Zarek discreetly lifted him up higher, forcing Aaro into straightening his posture. I was finally able to slip out of his grip as he did so. "What'd you do to the girl to get kicked out this early?"

The man almost tipped over from laughter, even though it hadn't been that funny. He swung his arm over my shoulder once again; I should have moved further away; and continued to laugh. Fane was semi-hiding himself away in some nearby foliage. "Zarek, I have this thing that's coming up! Since you're here, providence really, maybe you could help my friend...?"

"I'm busy at the moment, maybe next time."

"Your loss!" Aaro put his head on my shoulder, nuzzling his face against my neck. "Hey, what's your name?"

"My name is Sae and I—"

"It's your lucky day! You my darling are invited to perform as my guest to the Solaris Conference at the observatory. No need to thank me, come with me and I'll get you something better to wear. Do you know "No Regrets Tomorrow"? It's a favorite of mine. You don't really have the physique to pull it off though! Ha-ha!" He seemed not at all discouraged when I didn't budge. "You'll get paid of course! Name your price dear girl, I'll double it. Who knows, with a voice like that you could always buy a new face after finding a sponsor or two—"

"No, thank you." I tried to pull away discreetly with no success.

"You're funny too! Hey! Rayde! Look at what I found!"

So. Many. Diplomatic lines were being crossed right now.

Rayde Hion, representative of several pre-industrial, embryonic planets, was the latest secretary on the board of the Interstellar Trade Association. The organization was the only one able to directly negotiate trade terms with the Empress and held members from over eight hundred thousand systems.

I only knew him through my interstellar politics lessons. Gingery hair and brown eyes, his placid appearance was juxtaposed only with his ambition. One of the youngest secretaries to be appointed, it was reported that he was being groomed by the president of the ITA as a possible successor. I couldn't legally speak to him unless both sides had authorized councils present.

Visibly annoyed, he pried his friend off of me without even glancing in my direction. "Aaro, I have better things to do than spend time looking for you."

On one hand, I was relieved that he paid me no attention, on the other I was slightly put off by the disdain I felt from Rayde Hion. He nodded once at Zarek before hauling Aaro away to a private vehicle guarded by Solaris constabularies. Only the privileged few were authorized to have one within city limits and if I hadn't been watching them, I would have missed it.

Someone sitting inside was wearing Zarek's memory.

"Wait!" I rushed forward and then halted as their escort moved to block me. Not good. Interstellar incidents were not good. I saw Aaro peeking his head out to look, but I couldn't see past him to who was wearing the necklace.

New plan. I needed a new plan.

"Aaro!" Zarek called out from behind me. "We'll do it."

After five days, four of which were spent discussing the plan with Amie and Esme to their satisfaction, I donned the colors of Solaris in a gold and earthen toned dress. To my surprise, Esme had taken my side in attending the conference, which meant I had the majority vote to go even with Amie's objections.

Nevertheless, she had concerns and I listened to all of them.

Unfortunately for her arguments, the festivities were drawing to a close and we had no idea where that person would take the memory next. Zarek and I would attend the conference while Fane and Amie searched the place. Esme would be there to protect me, but as an unseen guest.

Amie was more worried than upset.

This was the first time we'd been left alone for a while, and I was grateful it hadn't been spent being lectured. No matter her objections were, it was clear she would support me. Her hands were gentle as she coaxed my hair into a formal style.

The dress itself was made in Isbul's current fashions with a wide collar that flared slightly over the shoulders and tight, lacy sleeves that ended at the wrists. Swaths of gold lace fabric layered with warm browns, the colors tumbling over each other to my knees where the dress ended. I quite liked it and hoped I would get more opportunities to wear the fashions of other nations.

Aaro had kept his promise to get me appropriate clothes and had insisted on repaying Zarek by getting him an outfit as well. For what? I didn't ask. Zarek had gone for his final fitting and I hoped he'd be here soon. I preferred being punctual.

Finally, I donned the matching hose in a darker brown and the golden shoes I insisted be flat at the bottom. I had never worn such colors before as Mother had always insisted on pale shades in cooler tones for my wardrobe.

Maybe once I was home, I'd try out more colors.

I'd always wanted to wear red.

My hair was still being pinned into submission when I heard the door open. I kept my head still and watched in the mirror as Esme twirled into the room in a dazzling green dress and dark orange curls piled on top of her head. I laughed, of course Esme wouldn't miss the chance to get dressed up and she looked amazing! We grinned at each other through the reflection.

"What did you do to your hair!?" Amie said, shocked.

"Relax, it's temporary!" Esme giggled, pulling her into a waltz.

Busy putting in the final pins in my hair, I only looked up when Fane swatted my hands out of the way to take over the task himself.

Apparently, we were meant to be a matching set tonight. Zarek's clothing was closely tailored in russet and cinnamon; his coat was embroidered with golden thread and a paludamentum was pinned over one of his shoulders. He'd left the coat unbuttoned to reveal a black vest and undershirt and, to my secret delight, Zarek was openly wearing his piercings again.

I pretended to fiddle with the objects in front of me while I went over the timetable again in my head. Maybe my friends would think it was silly, but this would be my first time ever attending a formal event of a foreign nation and outside the borders no less. I wanted to make a good impression. I would hold my own outside the mantle of my birth and I needed to succeed.

Empress, please. All I wanted was to prove I could do this myself.

"What do you think about pixie? When you drift away from us mortals?" His breath warmed the arch of my shoulder and I took my time putting the items in my hands down. I have never been so scatterbrained in my entire life.

"I'm thinking about the conference, that's all."

"You don't have to come." Zarek braced himself against the table and though I took the opportunity to stand, I still had to tilt my chin up to look at him. "The twins are raring to go and they might actually enjoy themselves."

"They won't let me go anywhere without them and it's taken me days to get their agreement to go at all, Zarek. I know I'm far from your first choice, but you don't have to accompany me the entire night. I can enjoy myself without you."

"Consider me chastised." Zarek did not look at all remorseful.

He was teasing me again and I wasn't sure if I liked it. He stood up before I could decide and reached into his coat for what at first glance looked like a stem of delicate black flowers but was actually an elaborate jeweled hair ornament.

"Aaro always forgets the details. Shall we call a truce, pixie?"

The observatory was undoubtedly the crown jewel of Solaris. Centered at the apex of the city's dome, the structure seemed to organically rise from its base where gardens grew in a wildly lush design. The telescopes themselves were built above the city's dome, keeping all of the light pollution from reaching its lenses.

We would regroup in a little over two hours.

Having already gone through two security checkpoints with no issues, this was where I felt Amie and Fane leave us. In reviewing the basic layout together, we'd discovered the majority of the visiting dignitaries were being housed under the observatory in the top five stories of the skyscraper.

"Good luck," Fane whispered to me before they left.

Zarek and I continued toward the conference, which I now knew was more of a social event than anything else. This party wasn't anything we hadn't faced before and though I couldn't see Esme, I could tell she was keeping close as always.

Another part of me wondered why Isbul's prime minister was attending tonight when they were all but officially at war with Rateer. Ch'Maja Dorj was an experienced politician with a military background. Surely he had better things to do.

Either way, Fane had given me permission to use his family's name tonight as a distant relation; the Akons were a prolific family, so it shouldn't raise any questions. We joined the steady stream of people entering the observatory with Esme keeping herself close to the walls to prevent jostling someone accidentally.

I made sure she was able to keep up before continuing.

The octagonal ballroom extended through four archways into several smaller rooms. Acrobats floated inside the central rotunda while masked waiters, guards, and other staff circled the room in pale cream uniforms. The guards seemed overly armed, but it could be custom in Isbul. A quick scan of the room told me that most of the guests held Isbulian citizenship as they wore the same fashions and colors that Zarek and I were sporting tonight.

Of course, Zarek, even here, caused a stir.

Although I knew nothing of Zarek's rank or status, I could see the recognition in peoples' eyes as they saw him. Quick nods of acknowledgement and excited whispers followed in his wake. I couldn't help but hear the open speculation about me. They didn't know I could hear them so well and I kept my expression neutral, but some of those unkind words lingered.

I refused to take it personally.

"Zarek, how are you darling?" A beautiful Crenoan approached with her hands out. Her species' characteristic antennae were folded back and down the length of her spine. The reds of her home world draped over her body perfectly, intricate painted patterns adorning her skull told me she was of a noble family.

Zarek smiled as he took her hands and brought them to his lips.

Feeling superfluous, I politely excused myself and set my sights on the group of De'Nahu standing stiffly next to one of the archways. Social events such as this were not a usual place to find their people. They were defined by their strength and intensely private lives. In addition, I knew that they saw eating and drinking as a private matter and the food and drink being passed around by the waiters was clearly uncomfortable for them to see. I had never met one in person before and admired their intricate braids. As I made my way toward them, I could see their eyes lock on to me and some of them seemed less than pleased.

I stopped at the appropriate distance and clapped my hands together and then to my elbows, never breaking eye contact. As no one could make my introductions, I needed to use a particular greeting. "It is my good fortune to behold your strength as I assure you your good fortune in facing mine." Their native language was a tricky one that required a rumbling of the throat. I was happy at the opportunity to try as I waited to see their response.

As one, they stomped their right foot, and I was thrilled to see the looks of approval they offered me. They were an androgenous species, and I was worried they would take issue with my gendered clothing. If I were meeting them back home, I would have prepared a more neutral outfit.

Even so, I found myself in a lively conversation about their home planet and culture as well as the prime minister's appearance tonight. Their territory was adjacent to Isbul near where their border touched Rateer's and the De'Nahu were concerned about the possible interception of their small, but growing shipping operations. I could now see why they'd made an appearance.

The conversation was held entirely in their language and the more I spoke to them, the more comfortable they became. In turn, I let it slip that Dorj's niece had energy resource interests near De'Nahu space and that it wouldn't hurt to remind him of that fact. While I was usually discouraged from engaging in outer universe politics, that didn't mean I wasn't fully versed with knowledge pertaining to every major player on the board. I knew mine was a privileged position, but I also believed knowledge was never wasted on those with good intentions.

I wished them success in their efforts to speak with the minister. De'Nahu culture discouraged an extended first contact and I moved on with the hope that we would speak again later. I soon found myself chatting with an Ech couple who had recently relocated to Solaris to pursue their careers in industrial terraforming and being presented to their colleagues who oversaw the mining operations in this sector of Isbul.

Over the next hour or so I was introduced to many people and was relieved that, despite my nerves, I was able to make genuine connections. I listened to a group of young graduates who were just beginning to enter society and spoke with an older diplomat who was disgruntled at the recent restrictions being placed on his nation's software exports. At one point I got into a lighthearted debate with a Kovsko about the finer points of his country's military exploits during the Ninth Empress Venetha Raajali's reign and I also found myself switching from language to language more frequently as people realized I could do so.

There was a universal translator in place, but I knew speaking in a native tongue was comforting when away from home.

There was one conversation in particular that stood out. As I joined a group of economic lobbyists, I caught the tail end of their discussion on the possibility that troops would have to be sent to blockade the border to Elysia. They were discussing the logistics of possible sanctions that would be held until the conflict with Rateer was over, but I couldn't understand why.

"Excuse me, but I find myself ignorant on this topic. Why is it that Isbul needs to send troops to the opposite border of where defenses are presently being gathered? Isbul can't possibly expect an attack. Historically, there is no precedent for such an event. Elysia has never held an external military presence."

My question seemed to make everyone uncomfortable.

"It isn't something we've had to deal with recently, so I suppose you're too young to remember." An elderly woman finally huffed. "During times of upheaval, disloyal citizens will flee to the Empire. If we don't blockade, they'll run. Traitors, every last one."

"I know that it's illegal for citizens to cross the border without the proper paperwork, but why not allow refugees to seek temporary shelter if necessary?"

"Because they will refuse to return." Another man snapped.

I burned to ask more questions, but I dropped the subject.

There was no use continuing on a topic when the other party was this unwilling to talk about it. I kept my ears open for more news or opinions about home, but nothing new would appear in my time socializing.

Once in a while, I found myself looking for Zarek and I always found him either laughing, dancing with, or whispering into the ear of one being or another. It was astonishing to see powerful figures of all ages and rank eagerly falling at his feet. Eventually, I found myself in close proximity... but something was off. I excused myself from an Al-Delian physicist with incredibly misguided views on molecular gravitational field capacities and managed to time my arrival to coincide with the end of Zarek's conversation.

"Hello pixie, enjoying yourself?"

It wasn't Zarek.

I chatted with his projection for a short while and then made a measured retreat to where I'd seen various waiters enter and exit. Just as I was about to discreetly slip away, Aaro Uride appeared in front of me. Once again smelling of intoxicants.

"I remember you! How's the party going sweetheart?"

Aaro reached out toward me and I quickly ducked under his arm and got through the door. Hopefully, he'd think I was a figment of his imagination or maybe something else would catch his attention. Alas, I heard him stumble after me and hurried to get some distance between us.

"Well fuck you too, princess."

Looking back, I wasn't sure why I stopped.

The words were angry, but there was no malice in them. Aaro had managed to prop himself up against a wall and was taking a long drink out of a flask. He was dressed like a colorblind jester and sounded so very sad.

"I'm looking for someone Aaro, do you want to come?"

"Yes!" Aaro got up too fast and his shoulder hit the wall as he tried to reorient himself. He tried again and almost fell back down. Impatient, I drew one of his arms over my shoulder and drove him forward. For a moment, it was like I surprised him out of his stupor. "You're stronger than you look!"

"Thank you. Now I've gone over the floor plans and I believe there's a library to our right correct?" I was going to take the turn regardless, but wanted to keep Aaro's mind on the task at hand. "Esme can you—" I stopped in my tracks.

Esme wasn't there.

Where did she go!?

I shook my head and briskly walked into the library.

One thing at a time.

The two men inside stood up as we entered. Aaro gleefully went forward to greet Rayde Hion and his companion. The library, although quite large, was built with nothing to block my line of sight from the entrance.

A quick glance told me that Zarek wasn't here either.

"Aaro. I'm busy." Rayde tried to pry Aaro off of him to no avail.

"But Sae's looking for someone, we should help her!"

"I am in no need of assistance, thank you."

Rayde's companion had looked familiar and I had figured out why. I had met his brother on the first night of my birthday celebrations back home. It seemed like such a long time ago, but it was only a few weeks and in the name of international relations I offered my hand in their traditional greeting.

Caillio Dominin was a much more robust version of his younger brother. As his mother was ailing, it would soon be time for him and his relatives to compete for the right of accension. He was a popular contender and had three wives if I remembered correctly; two of those wives had other spouses. They were an infamously polygamous species and any royal member who was of age would eligible. I had always wanted to witness the event, which could take anywhere from a few days to a few weeks' time. Chances were slim; however, that I would ever attend one.

Caillio grasped my hand and in the ensuing seconds tried to twist his wrist back. I was too competitive to let him win and successfully forced his hand forward. Although he looked a bit surprised, he smiled at me in a good-natured way.

"Are you looking for Deutreax?"

Rayde Hion's tone was insulting.

I held a small debate with myself before turning to face him.

"Your amendment to the recent bill on Tullre warp transistors is flawed. You should have levied section five's import tax on the purveyors rather than the producers with an annual gross profit cap based on inflation. You'd have better control over consumer pricing, reduce the time spent crossing border checkpoints, and gain support from those with investments in interstellar shipping. Additionally, secretary Wal has little to no intentions of backing your amendment even though he may have implied his agreement. He possesses shares in a competing company under his half cousin's name and has no desire to streamline the system nor lower the price of Tullre hardware for nonmedical purposes."

I turned back to Caillio to try and break the awkwardness I had created. "I actually met your brother Felguri recently and—"

"Let me guess, he didn't seem like he was a Dominin?"

His observation was an accurate one, his country's history indicated that the ruling family had always been athletic, bold and boisterous. Felguri had been someone who I'd describe as being uncomfortable with his body and shy in manner. Nevertheless, I remembered him as being truly interested in what I had to say and that he was eager to discuss his academic passions.

Why was Caillio suddenly angry?

"He was quite knowledgeable about the zero gravity hydroponic farms Elysia cultivates on nonterraformed satellites and I think he has a lot to offer to the Dominin name." I was bewildered to see the man relax, even smile at my words.

"I think so too. I'm glad you got to see some of his strengths."

Ah. I found it very sweet that he was protective of his brother. I spoke a bit more to Caillio while Rayde got Aaro to let go of him and then excused myself. Zarek and Esme were both still missing in action and there was only a little more than an hour left until we had to regroup.

To my chagrin, Aaro decided to keep clinging to my side.

"People underestimate you Aaro."

"Nah, they estimate me perfectly!"

"You're pretending to be intoxicated. Why?"

"So, you noticed." Aaro stopped stumbling and actually let go of my shoulders. He may have wanted me to pause in my search, but I was in a hurry, so I kept walking. Once Aaro realized I wasn't going to wait, he caught up to me.

"I know your type you know. You're going to give me an inspirational, heartfelt speech about how I have so much potential to do something with my life and how I have so much power to help people. That I can do better than being a clown."

There was more, but I wasn't sure if he was actually asking my opinion, so I just let him talk. I learned during my time in interpersonal relations lessons that many people were simply looking for a place where their inner voice could spend time as an outer voice. Aaro was also older than I was and I was sure he had far more experience about his problems than I did.

"Are you even listening to me!?"

"You have grievances against your relatives, you're estranged from your arranged fiancée, and you hate only being seen as your father's son. You find pleasure in offending your father who, as president, feels embarrassed by you. Your mother sounds nice."

Aaro shook his head as if to clear it and I felt a little guilty for not warning him. It varied from person to person and species to species. Most officials were briefed beforehand. However, I did get to check more rooms in silence as Aaro recovered from his daze.

"Don't you have anything to say to me? You may be an Akon, but I'll have you know that I am considered an excellent alliance candidate. I have both pedigree and credentials." I continued to walk, and he shouted in a louder voice behind me, "Credentials!"

"Thank you, but I'm not looking for a romantic partner."

"What is it about Zarek that appeals to you?"

"I never said anyone appealed to me."

"Is your species asexual?"

Hypothetically... well technically I could, in fact, reproduce asexually. It had only been done once before when a former Empress' consort was an androgynous queen. I had no idea how to go about the procedure, but there was the option.

"Only under very specific circumstances."

"... How did you know I wasn't drunk?"

"You change accents when you're drunk."

"Why did you help me then?"

Sigh. "Aaro, would you like to hear another lecture?"

"From you? I would absolutely love to hear it." Sarcasm ran rather than dripped from his words, but I decided to take them literally. Even if only to keep him quiet.

"It doesn't matter if you want to do anything with your life and it doesn't matter if you waste your "potential" or those "credentials" as you call them. Your life is incredibly limited, and you should do whatever you want to do, regardless of whether it seems meaningful or not."

"...That's shockingly cynical of you."

Really? It seemed to me Aaro was burdened by unwanted expectations. Most sentient beings were born to no destiny and with no bigger burden than to live as their own individual. So why not seize their opportunities for joy when possible?

"If you're happy, why should you care?"

Aaro finally fell silent as he contemplated my words. I opened and checked every door we came across until we reached the end of a hall with a door ajar.

Opening it, we went in...

And walked right into a homicide scene.

Chapter 11: Ceasefires

Prime minister Ch'Maja Dorj was most assuredly dead due to multiple stab wounds. A girl with tangled dark hair crouched in the corner like a wounded animal, murder weapon in hand. Aaro walked further in before I could stop him until he slid bonelessly to his knees in shock and, closing the door with my foot, I knew it was too late to hide Aaro's biological identifiers.

There was copper-toned blood everywhere.

The prime minister was not a small man, gaping slashes marred his once arrogant face, with his blood splattered up the walls and pooling quickly underneath his corpse.

The smell was already becoming fetid to my nose.

When the door snapped shut the woman's head jerked up. If I hadn't known, I would have recognized her then. Leah Dorj, formerly Leah Akon, had just killed her husband. This was a political disaster. The Akons and the Dorj had a dormant blood feud whose truce had always been tenuous at best. In recent generations, that feud had been tempered through strategic marriages and Leah may have just plunged the ruling families back into conflict.

My presence here couldn't be a coincidence.

Aaro opened his mouth, and I was forced to muffle him before he attracted attention. I could not be a witness to this. If Cira had brought us here, then there was a good chance that what I did next would determine whether or not I would be discovered. I kept my eyes averted from the body and although there was a part of me that was revolted and frightened, I needed to stay calm.

"Aaro. Please be quiet." I bent down so that we were eye to eye. I tried to radiate a cool, peaceful feeling, like when Mother had to settle a chaotic room. Aaro's eyes cleared, and it seemed like it worked. I let my hand drop from his face.

He didn't scream. Good.

"Leah Akon." I made sure to keep my distance from the minister as I approached her. We needed to act fast, but I needed more information. "Why did you murder Ch'Maja Dorj?" She was breathing too quickly, as I got closer, tears fell faster from her eyes.

"He was beating me; he was going to kill me."

Leah was lying.

Not all the way, but somewhat.

"Don't bother, Sis. She can see right through you." A small creak was the only warning before Cira Kyrian stepped into the room.

Leah Akon was now openly sobbing, hysterical. She held onto my dress and started shaking her head. "No! You swore I wouldn't have to go! You swore—"

Cira, instead of answering, pulled out a phaser and aimed it at Aaro's head. Now, whatever was happening here, I could not have two murders in the same room that I was in. The safety of her weapon was still on. I had some time.

"Is Cira your sister, Leah?" The blood that stained her hands and arms was now smeared all over me. I had been under the impression that Leah was an Isbulian citizen. If she was Cira's sister than someone at home had incomplete files.

Leah's tawny brown eyes were horribly swollen, and pieces of her dress were ripped off. It did look like she had been assaulted, that much rang true; but I couldn't piece together what my eyes were seeing and the lies I knew she had told me. There was undeniably a resemblance between the two women.

Leah seemed so unbearably young, her whimpers genuine.

"We happen to share the same daddy issues." Cira sighed and pushed Aaro a bit forward with the barrel end of her weapon. "And Daddy wants to have a little chat with both of us. So, how about a fair trade Your Eternal Grace? I'll give you your little princeling here and you hand over to me the spoiled little girl."

"Okay." If Cira was surprised by my capitulation, she didn't show it. Leah shrieked in fear as I made a show of prying her hands off of my dress. Honestly, I didn't try very hard as it gave me the opportunity to drag her to her sister myself.

It was Cira's mistake to let me.

I moved as fast as I was able. I pushed Leah into Aaro, seized the phaser, and shoved Cira away from them. I had to wipe some of the minister's blood off of my hands in order to get a better grip, but then I kept it aimed at the ground. Amie and Esme had much more training than I did in weapons handling. The last thing I wanted was to fire it accidentally or gain any unwanted attention.

"Aaro. You need to get Leah Dorj away from here. Now."

"What!? But what about the prime minister!?"

"I'll handle it. Aaro I'm trusting you with her safety."

"How do you know Cira Kyrian? Who are you!?"

So, he was quicker than he let on.

"Go. Now." I kept my eyes on Cira as they left.

"You'd save anyone, wouldn't you princess?"

I didn't answer her. The weapon I had taken from Cira had no weight to it. I could lift objects much heavier than my appearance would suggest with ease, but this one was weightless. I threw it back to Cira and turned my back to her. She couldn't harm anyone with it and there was no way for her to reach me because Cira Kyrian wasn't here in Isbul at all.

Had she ever been in Elysia in the first place?

Her projection, unlike Zarek's, had a technological basis.

It meant the entire observatory's security was compromised.

I needed to find the others. Right now.

Luckily, I ran into none of the employees as I dashed from room to room. It was maddening that I was reduced to trying to find my friends manually. Taking a detour into a small washroom, I took the time to rinse the blood off my neck and arms. Although the browns of my dress hid the blood decently, there were still too many suspicious stains to feel safe.

I couldn't understand why Esme hadn't already found me on her own. Amie thought I was with her, but Esme had no idea where I was at the moment. Something must have happened to keep her away at a time like this.

Splashing cold water on my face, I just took a moment to think.

The only abilities I had left to rely on were physical. With no idea of what events were unfolding, I couldn't risk setting off an alarm. So, I opened my ears and tried to ignore the partygoers above me, the fact that they had only gotten louder since I'd left didn't help.

Taking off my shoes and tights, I could tell by the vibrations that almost no one was on this level. Rifling through the images I'd seen of the layout, there were several people rushing around in the kitchen and surrounding areas, patterns of footsteps circled the ballroom and there was an odd, muffled shuffling coming from a far corner of the floor below me.

It was a residential floor below this one. The only people who should be down there were guards, servants, and Amie and Fane unless they'd already found the necklace. There was no way to get down there unless I went back up through the main floor and down one of the central lifts.

Walking barefoot, I threw my tights down a trash chute and carried my shoes. It was easier to pinpoint where the vibration was originating from without them and I headed there as quickly as I could without breaking into a run. My trail ended in a hallway with a floor to ceiling window. The shuffling came from just below my feet to the right and sounded like more than one person. I looked around for a moment before resigning myself to the unavoidable.

Wishing I'd kept my tights to wrap around my hand, I made sure no one was around before pressing my palm against the window.

To the architect's credit, the material warped rather than shattered under pressure. I slowly applied more and more force until eventually, the adhesive pulled away from the walls. I was then able to fold the bulky pane and pull it to one side of the hallway. The wind was petulant here, every surrounding structure only exacerbating existing wind tunnels, the oxygen recyclers creating a howl all its own as it worked to keep Solaris habitable.

The next minute consisted of arguing with myself about the optimal way to get to the floor below. My final conclusion was that I was overthinking this. Before I could take another shot at second-guessing, I lowered myself with my hands until my feet were braced against the top corner of the window below.

I used my legs to swing back.

It only took one attempt to tear through the window.

Several muffled voices were now muffled yelling as I bent their window and came in uninvited. I quietly apologized to the people I had landed on top of as I took in the room and tried to understand what I was looking at—sixteen people were restrained and gagged, sprawled against the walls and floor of this storage room. They were all wearing the same uniforms as the conference's waiters.

Some of them looked like they'd been accosted.

A few looked far more accosted than the others.

Their restraints wrapped entirely around their hands with several safeguards against tampering. The hands and forearms were made immobile as were their knees down... I decided to check on the one inching frantically toward me.

"If I remove this gag. You will whisper." She nodded, so I did so.

"Please help us, my lady!" It was barely a whisper, but I'd take it. "We're just doing our jobs! We didn't do anything!"

She was lying, so I put the gag back in.

Changing tactics, I walked over to a man who looked the angriest. This man was noticeably more injured than the others but he didn't say anything after I took off his gag. So, I just across from him quietly, letting him glare into my eyes.

"Did you know the mines are being automated?" he hissed. "My wife and I, my sister's family, we all work, and we can't afford to live anymore. Our kids won't grow up in the city that my great-grandmothers' hands built. We tried to strike, but they just brought in more machines. When our contracts were up, we had to take the cuts. They got their yearly bonuses doubled. We lost our pensions. They raised the price of water and food. We starve."

"Is that what you're doing here? Protesting?"

"We're beyond that now—"

One of his fellow workers, who had been trying to get his attention, threw herself forward to headbutt him. It wasn't a very good hit, but it was enough to tear his gaze away from me. I shoved the gag into his mouth again before he came to his senses entirely and stood back up, my eyes taken in one body after the other.

What now? What in the universe did I do now?

A raw, prickly shiver went down my spine.

Zarek was heading this way. Even with my shoes on, I knew it was him on the other side of the door. I slowly moved to the center of the room and heard a slight hesitation in his step. I guessed he'd heard my own footsteps even if he didn't recognize them. He knew someone was freely moving about and it didn't seem to surprise him in the slightest to find me here.

How were his clothes just as unruffled as the last I'd seen them?

Contradicting what my eyes were telling me, Zarek looked as if he were just completing a mundane chore. He didn't look caught out. Despite the blood running down the face of the man he was dragging and evidence of blood loss on the uniforms in the room, he was completely clean. I didn't understand.

Zarek could be used to getting blood off his clothes.

I wanted to reject the idea but I needed to know.

"Did you assassinate Isbul's prime minister?"

Zarek didn't answer right away. He cuffed and gagged his latest victim and sat him down next to the other unconscious workers. He was confident enough to leave the door wide open. Light from the hallway at his back cast his face in shadow, but I could feel his eyes roaming over me. "Is that where the blood's from pixie?"

"Yes."

"Didn't anyone ever teach you the truth is never the answer?"

"Zarek—" I bit down hard on my lip when I heard my voice break on his name. I felt so weak whenever he was around. I just wanted someone in this blasted city to give me a straight answer! I needed someone to act rationally! If I looked him in the eye maybe I could get the answers out of him, but even if I could I wanted him to tell me because he wanted to tell me.

"Did you assassinate prime minister Dorj?"

"Would you believe me if I said no?"

I nodded.

"Then no. I didn't kill Dorj."

Zarek was telling me the truth.

I let out a shaky sigh of relief. Thank the Empress he had told me the truth. Quickly, I restructured my options in my head and walked forward so we could talk in the hallway and not in front of an audience. I only came to a stop when Zarek remained stationary in the doorway. He'd unfolded his arms when I'd rushed forward, but now he seemed perturbed.

"Did you want something pixie?"

"To talk in the hallway?"

"Right." Was it my imagination or did his arms drop ever so slightly as he stepped back? Did he think I was going to faint?

Or throw myself at him...

I recalled the reactions he'd been subject to in the ballroom and decided it was a reasonable assumption to make.

"Why are you apprehending these people?"

"Apprehending?" He laughed. "If that's what we're calling it."

"You left a projection of yourself in the ballroom and left without saying anything. Cira appeared when I discovered minister's body claiming Leah Dorj was her sister and if I'm not mistaken, the safety procedures for this entire building has been compromised. None of the hidden security cameras I spotted were in operation, multiple emergency exits have been blocked for reasons unknown to me, and I have no idea where Esme, Amie, or Fane are."

"What's your point?"

"My point. Is that I can help. If you just tell me what is going—"

Heat bloomed from the pit of my stomach to the tips of my ears as Zarek was suddenly all around me. He'd trapped me against the wall with one hand pressed beside my head. Not one part of him was touching me, but his open coat created a kind of barrier from the rest of the world as Zarek leaned down. He smelled like a winter storm and oddly it reminded me of home. Like waking up in a familiar place. Whatever thoughts may have occupied my mind were scattered as I retreated as far back as I could.

Slowly, I looked up to meet his eyes.

"What if I'm here to slaughter everyone in that room?"

"I don't believe it. Or else they'd already be dead."

He didn't ask me anything else. Instead, we just looked at each other for what seemed like an eternity. Why did he always end up so close to me? Why did it feel like he was getting closer? Was he waiting for me to say something? Zarek's heartbeat had inexplicably increased. Mine wasn't operating properly anymore. He was far too close. What was I just thinking about?

Finally, I couldn't take it anymore and my eyes fluttered shut. Zarek stepped back.

As if a vacuum closed between us, I was left flailing for something to hold onto. I opened my eyes to see Zarek had not only taken a few steps back, but he'd turned away from me. It felt as though a line had been drawn in the distance between us. I wanted to slide down the wall onto the floor and disappear. Stupid.

What in the universe were you thinking? Stupid. Stupid.

"I'm doing a job for Hion and a favor for Aaro."

"What? Why?" I still felt slow in the head.

"You wanted to come, and I was bored."

"Will you tell me what the job is?"

"Labor's been gutted in Solaris and people are obviously pissed but no one cares. They've been getting aggressive and Dorj knew they were going to make a move tonight."

"But why not just arrest them if they had the evidence?"

"Think everyone has good intentions, don't you pixie?"

"That is not the question I asked you, Zarek."

"Dorj doesn't have the evidence. That's where I come in."

"These workers have rights under Isbul's current constitution."

"And you think Dorj gave a shit about their rights?"

"What now Zarek? These people are desperate."

"Exactly. Desperate enough to kill everyone who doesn't agree with them." Stunned, I searched his expression to see if he was somehow making fun of me. Zarek's words rang true, but... I thought back to what I had heard from one of the captive workers.

We're beyond that now.

"But it doesn't make any sense! They'll just lose the public's opinion." Terrorism was something I only learned about in my studies. The number of incidents of unrest in Elysia could be counted on one hand and none ended in violence.

"And here I was applauding them for their brilliant foresight."

This was not a time to be joking.

Although only about a third of all adult citizens chose to work in Elysia at any time, they held major legal safety nets, inalienable to their livelihoods. Food, water, housing, education; freedoms of dignity, equality, identity; they were the most basic of rights in Elysia. Work was not compulsory by any means as the Empress protected and cared for every single one of our people.

I had no training on how to handle such a situation. My University work had never covered the legalities of labor organizing in Isbul and had no idea of what was necessary to help these people. I couldn't think of anything I could do. I needed to talk to Fane or some kind of economic counsel. I needed time to help them. Wait no, I couldn't help them. It wasn't my place. I couldn't.

I couldn't leave them like this.

"Zarek. We need to help them."

"You have fun with that."

"Where are you going?"

"To finish what I started."

"Let me help you."

"Are you sure you're ready for more blood?"

"We can talk to them, Zarek. Get them to back down before people get hurt! If these workers are arrested, it'll just cause more unrest. This doesn't make any sense. None of this does. How did they even get in? How did they break through security? Why didn't prime minister Dorj have guards with him? Why was Leah Dorj alone? Something doesn't seem right." He didn't even spare me a glance as he kept walking. "Fine. I'm going to solve this on my own. Without violence."

"Do as you wish, pixie."

Chapter 12: Revelations

"Sae! Is that blood!?"

Amie and Fane were not hard to find in the end.

As soon as Amie felt me nearby and alone, she rushed to my side with Fane on her heels. Still no Esme. I gave them an abbreviated version of the last half an hour and as soon as I finished I launched into a preemptive argument against what I knew were going to be Amie's main concerns.

"If whatever their plan is succeeds, we'll be locked down in Solaris with no chance of escape while they hunt down the perpetrators. Prime minister Dorj's assassination will trigger an investigation, but the search will be much more targeted than if Solaris' workers are revealed to be behind an interstellar act of terrorism. We need to stop whatever's going to happen and we need to do it without violence. Cira appeared tonight, the memory's here right now, and those events are not coincidences."

"We saw her too. She told us to leave." Fane squeezed my arm reassuringly. "I don't know if she was lying but I'm with you, Sae. Ch'Maja was a dick anyway."

Amie, who was already openly wearing her thigh holster, pulled yet another weapon. This one was a standard issue. She maneuvered the specs to a hard stun and hesitated slightly before holding it out to Fane. "Can you shoot straight?"

"Luckily, it's the only thing I can do straight."

"Thank you, Amie. I know you'd rather we leave."

"It's because Kyrian suggested leaving that I'm going along with this." Amie was on board for now at least. She was pulling her hair back into a high tail as we walked and just as she tied it off, she asked "Where did you send Esme?"

"I don't know where Esme is."

I was actually hoping she was with them.

"Did she leave you alone!?" Amie took a moment to look for her and seemed even more confused. "She's in the ballroom, dancing with Zarek's projection."

"What's the plan?" Fane asked once we got to the storage room.

"I'm going to go in and threaten them," Amie said mildly.

Fane and I exchanged a flabbergasted look.

Apparently, she had been serious.

Amie insisted that we stay outside the room while she went in. As soon as the door closed behind her, I tried to hear what Amie was doing in there, but there was no sound at all. When I couldn't even hear the breathing or shifting of the captives inside, it dawned on me that she could easily soundproof the room.

"Fane. What do you know about Rayde Hion?"

"Hion's jackass but his reputation's spotless." Fane tapped his fingers on his thigh, his brow furrowing as he thought about his next words. "If he knew Zarek was going to be involved, then Hion has to be getting something big out of this."

Was there anything the Dorj had that I knew Rayde Hion might want? They ran in almost separate political circles. I had no knowledge of anything that connected them. Dorj represented an older generation of traditional values and conservative ideals in Isbul. Rayde's record with the Interstellar Trade Association so far would indicate that they would disagree over most, if not all issues.

So why would they be working together at all?

The door opened and Amie dragged out one of the workers. He was a small, thin man with a docile appearance. He looked very much like a sleepy great-grandfather who spent his days solving puzzles and drinking soup. Amie's grip on his arm alone looked like it would be enough to snap his bones and she made sure to keep him a good distance away from me.

"This is their leader."

This didn't make any sense. If he was their leader, then why hadn't Zarek been able to get that information? I doubted the answer was as easy as Zarek being inept at his work. Now that we had their "leader," what were we going to do with him? What were they planning? How was I supposed to respond?

My mind swam with endless questions. Outcome after outcome played out in my head with the limited facts I possessed. I could have spent hours ruminating over it all but when I caught Amie and Fane staring at me... I realized I didn't have time. I couldn't calculate the probability of a million possible paths.

I needed to choose one now.

"Fane can you show Amie what Rayde Hion looks like? We need to find him." He nodded yes and pulled up an official image of Hion from the implant he had embedded on top of his right ear.

Amie did a quick search of the floors above.

"Leah Dorj and two other men are with him."

"Lock down that room until we get there."

Nobody was in the halls or rooms that we passed. Just an hour ago, there were at least some people moving around the corridors, but now they were entirely deserted. Amie carried the old man easily under one arm and insisted on checking around every corner before letting me continue.

"Sae are you secretly a national treasure?" Fane joked in exasperation after Amie checked for the umpteenth time. When neither of us responded to his offhand comment, he went quiet and followed along with our staggered pace. Fane was no longer hidden from sight, but I didn't think it mattered at this point. I was just glad he'd been so supportive up to now.

We reached the correct door only to feel the walls shake slightly as something hit the door from the inside. Amie snort laughed when they did it again, only weaker this time. Lowering the old man to the ground, Amie waited until there was a calm moment and got in front of me before she let the door open.

Caillio Dominin was just about to take another crack with what looked like a heavy steel pole he'd procured from somewhere and was barely able to stop his next swing. He hadn't been able to see the energy field with the door closed, which explained the hitting. Rayde, Aaro, and Leah were standing at a distance, probably to give their friend some space to work.

Caillio, who'd removed his coat, was wearing Zarek's memory.

The faint glow of the field dropped and I nudged Amie forward while she glowered suspiciously at everyone. Leah, who wasn't crying when the door opened, resumed crying as soon as she caught sight of me. Fane pulled the old man in and shut the door.

"You! What did you do to Leah!?" Hion pulled her behind him.

"I told you Sae saved her from Cira Kyrian!" Aaro insisted.

"And I'm supposed to believe you!? You're never more than five fucking steps away from a hangover! We were locked in this room until they happened to arrive and I for one will not stand for it!" Rayde Hion, taking Leah by the hand, tried to get past me.

I blocked his path. His anger unnerved me, but I didn't care. This man was endangering my friends and couldn't just walk away.

"Why did you conspire with Dorj and hire Zarek?"

"What!? How dare you! I did no such thing—"

He was lying and I was getting tired of being lied to.

A few things happened simultaneously then. Amie tackled Rayde when he moved to shove me, causing him to let go of Leah; and I was caught off guard when the old man was suddenly out of his restraints, the key clanging on the floor. He dived to take hold of my arm and held something to the side of my neck. It was some kind of explosive I think, but I couldn't get a good enough look at it to tell what kind. I put up my hand to stop Amie before she did something I knew she'd regret later and gave myself a second to try and calm down a little bit.

"Sir. I am trying to help you."

"Take me to Dorj or I'll kill her!" he screamed right next to my ear. Fear rolled off of him in waves and I could feel his hands shaking as he held up the device. "I'll do it! I'm tired. I'm sick. I have nothing left to lose! Take me to Dorj!"

Amie was growing tenser every second that this man held onto me. We didn't have the time for this. We were in a race against Zarek to solve this before it got to the point of no return, and he had much more experience than we did at his disposal. No matter if he agreed with me or not, Zarek needed my help.

I didn't think I could take it if I failed.

People were going to be hurt.

Zarek was going to get hurt.

I grabbed the explosive device and shoved the old man away.

The device engaged as I forced it out of his fingers, emitting a high-pitched whine. Quickly, I enclosed it in my hands and the yelling coming from the others around me was drowned out by the soundwave I was unable to stop from escaping. The ground below me shook as some of the kinetic energy was released under my planted feet. I kept my hands firmly closed as I felt shrapnel bouncing inside the circle of my closed palms. As soon as I was sure it was safe, I opened my hands and let the pieces fall to the floor. My hands were dirty but unharmed.

"Sae? How did you do that?" Fane's awed question broke through the paralysis that had held everyone in the room.

Caillio Dominin took several large steps back from me.

The old man got off the ground and nearly hurt himself trying to run away. Amie made the strategic decision to grab him and leave Rayde, who was too shocked to react to his sudden freedom, on the floor. The man tried to bite Amie, and she was having none of that. She shoved him into a chair and locked the restraints he'd escaped back onto his legs and arms.

"You're lucky you're still breathing." Amie hissed at him.

"Listen to me." I tried to appeal to him once again. "Prime minister Dorj is dead. If you go through with your plan, you're only going to hurt yourself and your cause. There are better ways to protest. Appeal to a higher court of law if Solaris doesn't negotiate with you in good faith."

"Are you the ones who murdered Dorj?" Rayde Hion pulled the man's head back by his hair, causing him to cry out in pain. "If you are the cause of the crimes committed tonight, you will be persecuted to the fullest extent of the law!"

"Let go of him." When Rayde continued without letting go of his hair, I felt my patience wear thin. "I said let go of him!"

Rayde let go just as his fear finally found him.

"I don't take orders from you!" He sputtered, unconvincing.

Caillio pulled Rayde to the other end of the room and into a furious, whispered argument. Was I about to tell them I could hear them loud and clear? Not just yet I wasn't and it didn't matter how unethical that nondisclosure was.

"Rayde, this has gone way too far. This can't go on."

"Zarek has it under control, no one's getting hurt tonight."

"Dorj is fucking dead! Rayde, there are other options."

"Kiefer is here and I am not going to ruin this chance."

Kiefer… I had never heard the name before. There were no major political or social figures that I knew of with that moniker.

"Fane, who is Kiefer?" I didn't bother to lower my voice.

They stopped their whispering as soon as I said the name, their heads turning slowly to look back at me. Fane didn't answer right away, taken aback himself.

Unexpectedly, it was Aaro who answered me.

"Kiefer's the head of a group of radical insurrectionists. They've cost trillions of credits worth of damage to nations adjacent to the border. They say that every government is corrupt unless it's ruled by the Empress and so shouldn't exist."

"Are you the one working with Kiefer, Rayde Hion?" A fierce look came over his face and he charged forward until he was right in my face. He was angry, but almost a quarter of an hour had passed since Zarek and I had parted ways and he needed to give me answers now. "Was prime minister Dorj involved with Kiefer?"

"Who are you to question—"

"How do you benefit? Who is Kiefer to you?" I was shaking.

Leah, who had been silent up to this point, came up and put her hand on Rayde's chest. Even without words, it was clear they knew each other far better than I'd have guessed. Leah stepped between us and turned to face me; the blood that was now dried onto her skin and clothes was a grisly sight. She seemed as brittle as a sub-zero breeze. Her voice shook as she spoke.

"I already told them that I killed my husband. Rayde is just trying to protect me." She was still holding the very knife that would implicate her. "Kiefer went by a different name years ago when he was Rayde's mentor. He held the secretary title, but when he left the seat was scraped. Rayde managed to reinstate it last year but he's had a hard time gaining the trust of the others. In the time between, the ITA made a few questionable decisions that put embryonic planets at risk of exploitation. Rayde's doing his best. Please don't blame him for something he never asked for."

"That's why you needed Dorj!" Fane exclaimed "Dorj holds one of the primary ITA seats. You can't rescind a new provision before it gets enacted without prior authorization from a primary!" Fane looked very pleased with himself before he realized that he'd drawn attention to himself and that Rayde knew who he was.

"Fane Akon? Weren't you just arrested!?"

It must sting to be labeled a traitor to his own nation, but he'd explained to me earlier this week that he couldn't fight the accusations in court unless he had the funds. As Dylis had taken virtually all of his money, Fane was stuck in limbo.

"How did you and the others get into the observatory?" I turned to the old man, but when he refused to look at me, Amie took his chin in her hand and forced him to look. It didn't take long for his once flat eyes to regain their spark.

"My daughter left Solaris for the mining asteroid belt of Wlekka. She came back with money and told us that this was our chance. This was our only chance." His voice broke. "Is she dead? Is my daughter dead because of this? Empress have mercy, please."

Things were clicking into place.

Dorj knew Kiefer was going to be here tonight and Kiefer knew that Solaris' workers were desperate enough to follow his daughter's instructions. It made sense that he was their leader as his daughter was their only point of contact. Rayde, in exchange for Dorj's veto, hired Zarek for him to get rid of the workers and terrorists. Capturing Kiefer was the bonus that tipped the scales for him and convinced him it was a risk worth taking. And if something did happen tonight or if the plan failed then the workers would be here to take the blame.

"What's your name?" We had seconds, not minutes, to act.

"Roland." He deflated before our eyes, seemingly resigned.

"What were you planning? What was going to happen tonight?"

"W-we were going to hold them hostage temporarily." Tears were coming out of Roland's eyes and I felt his confusion as he continued to speak. "My daughter said we'd keep them inside so we could talk to Dorj. She said he'd listen if we had a public audience. We just wanted to talk."

"I'm going to help you, Roland. Listen to me. Your daughter went to the wrong people. I'm sure she's a good person, but Kiefer and Dorj both are using you and the others. You don't deserve that." Picking up the key from the floor, I undid his restraints. "You need to get everyone who came with you and wait somewhere safe until I come and get you. Can you do that for me?"

"But what about my daughter? I won't leave without her."

"I'll try and find her, but you and the others need to go. Now."

He was dazed, but steady on his feet as he went to follow my instructions. Hopefully, he would be enough to sway the others.

"You can't just let him leave!" Rayde's volume was excessive. "For all we know, he was lying!" Rayde tried to leave the room through the open door himself, but Amie's shielding slid down before he go even a few steps. The door was shut for good measure, the quick snap making its point known.

"You have no right to hold us here!"

"I need your help Rayde Hion."

"And why in the Empress' name should I help you!?"

"Come on Rayde, just listen to her. It couldn't hurt."

"You stay out of this Aaro!"

"Will you stop being such an ass!?"

"I will end you Dominin! Don't think I won't!"

The room erupted into a shouting match, with each player more tone-deaf than the last. Leah quickly raised her voice as well to try and mediate. Fane tried it too until Rayde insulted him and then it was all bets off. Even though it was three against one with Leah trying her best to intervene, Rayde argued for a living and was capable of dragging this out for far too long.

Just as I was going to enter the fray, Amie ran out of patience. "Shut the fuck up!" Her voice was filled with such a threat of violence that they stopped and I leaped at their momentary hesitation.

"Hion, all I want you to do is file a temporary injunction on behalf of Solaris and its workers. Solaris largest mining operations runs on the fuel crystals they import from Elysia. However; they will only export the crystals to places that adhere to a minimum of operating standards. It includes a clause that is enforceable if and when a group of workers file a formal complaint to the ITA. The Empress will send a delegation to the border and negotiations in good faith will be held if there is evidence of violations. Which there are. Peaceful settlements. Everyone gets to go home."

After a moment of stunned silence, Rayde *laughed.*

Secretary Hion laughed so hard that he had to brace himself on a nearby chair. Caillio and Aaro looked as if they too wanted to laugh while Fane actually looked pained at my suggestion. The rest of my arguments dried up as I found their disbelief was genuine, as was Hion's obvious hilarity.

A feather of embarrassment rose in me at their reactions.

"Are you serious!? Where the hell do you come from!?"

Rayde was still laughing.

"Sae, what do you think the ITA is for?" Fane asked curiously.

"The Interstellar Trade Association exists to foster free trade among its members and act as a mediator between Elysia and the outer universe on matters of commerce. Their duties include, but are not limited to: negotiations, bargaining on behalf of emerging warp societies, regulating market trends, enforcing—"

"Wow." Fane cleared his throat awkwardly. "Sae, the ITA limits communication with Elysia so that no one can trade directly with them. They'd give away resources if we let them. No one could compete with that. The ITA prevents Elysia from participating in the outer universe as much as possible. No one is going to support an inquiry to jeopardize that. Ever.”

“Why is it a competition at all?”

No one answered my question.

“It would destroy my career.” Rayde told me plainly. “No one would ever take me seriously if I filed an injunction against a primary seat. You’re delusional.”

“What if you file on behalf of my late husband?” Leah handed over her knife to Aaro, who held it gingerly with two fingers. “I took this from him before we left his corpse.” Leah pulled out a small rectangle carved from a gemstone. It was Dorj’s seal marker. If Rayde appeared with a document with Dorj’s seal, no one would be able to question the authenticity of it.

“Once they find it missing, they’ll know I committed fraud.” Despite his words, he took the seal when Leah offered it to him. “They’ll never believe Dorj filed against his own nation.”

“He can’t argue. I’ll put it back myself.” Leah urged.

“No.” Rayde said even as he pocketed the seal.

“Don’t you want to help these people?” I appealed to him

“What the fuck are you talking about? No!” Rayde vehemently denied. "What is wrong with you!? Are you serious!?"

“Isn’t that why you took on the ITA seat!? To help people!?”

“Why should I help them!? What the fuck is in it for me!?”

I couldn’t believe what I was hearing. I could feel it in my bones that Amie and I needed to leave. Right now. We had spent too much time here, but I had told Roland that I would try and help them. Did I stay and try to convince Rayde or go and help Zarek before it was too late!?

What could I give Rayde to convince him to help? I was nobody in this form. I had nothing to give him that would change his mind. No leverage of any kind to offer for negotiation. I looked over at

Amie, who didn't look at all surprised by Rayde's callousness. Was I so ill-equipped for being outside that I could do nothing?

How did mother handle the outer universe all these years? Or was our only real option to ignore everything that went on? Every sign along the way was leading me to believe the right choice was to step away. Turn away from it all.

I had one move left and I didn't like it.

"Leah. Aaro. Caillio. Rayde. And Fane. I need you to swear—"

"Sae no!" Amie all but carried me away from the others.

"Amie." I dug in my heels, "I know what I'm doing."

It was true. I did, I just didn't know if this was going to be the correct solution. I knew the stakes and the law, but I couldn't predict how this would go.

We were raised to believe that if it was right, it must be done.

When Fane tried to walk toward us, Amie got between me and everyone else. It was an unimaginable risk and Amie in particular felt that she was responsible for me out here... but I had to be responsible for myself. I had been taught all my life to never abandon those who needed me and I had to trust things were going to be alright as long as I did the right thing.

Helping these people was the right thing to do.

I stared at her until Amie stepped aside.

I wouldn't hear the end of this for a while.

"Fane, do you swear to not betray me or my secrets?"

"Yeah, of course I do Sae." Fane agreed instantly.

"I need you to promise." I went around the room and had each of them say it out loud. Caillio and Rayde seemed to think I was crazy. When I got to Leah, she hesitated even longer than Rayde did, but she too swore to me.

I really hoped this worked outside Elysia.

"I'll hold you to your promises."

A ring of light appeared around their wrists.

Leah's face had gone pale at the sight.

Thank the Empress it had worked.

They would never be able to break this promise. It was possible to find a loophole, but this held them to the spirit rather than the word, so it would hold.

Probably. This was my first time trying it.

"Sae? What just happened?" Fane asked nervously.

"Amie, I'm gonna need you to change me back."

"Change you back!? To what!?"

Aaro was even more freaked out than Fane.

Amie was not happy but her own lessons must have left an equally strong impression as she did as I asked; it felt like a taut elastic band snapping back into place as my body became familiar to me again. Funny how good my own skin felt once I spent some time away from it.

"Hello. My full name is Saekonari Raajali."

For a breathless second, no one moved or spoke. Then Aaro turned to Caillio and with a shaky voice said "You know, I think Rayde was right. I do drink too much."

Leah's knees gave out.

Chapter 13: Reassurances

Five minutes later, Rayde capitulated, and I was once again in my disguise. I had promised him a favor to be called in at the time of his choosing and that was incentive enough for him. Aaro, Leah, and Caillio were helping to draft the documents now and they would be off-world within the hour. Caillio had handed over the necklace with barely a word from me.

Understandably, Fane had a lot of questions.

"So, you know what everyone in the universe is thinking?"

"Mother does, but she doesn't do it to people outside Elysia."

"Is it true you turn into a Ryunaga to nurse their young?"

"They're not mammals so no. Yuki just slept on my body and used me like a battery until she was old enough to live on her own."

"So, you can consume stars and collapse black holes for fun?"

"The Empress can... I wouldn't call it consume, exactly."

"Uh-huh. And why can't we tell Zarek again?"

"Because I don't want him to know yet and you promised."

Amie signaled for quiet as we neared the ballroom, and I could see why. The guards that we hadn't run into until now were all congregated in front of the doors. I wonder if Dorj had given them orders to stay close in case something happened. It was no wonder they were so well-armed tonight.

With their masks on, it was hard to say what they thought of us; Amie and Fane who didn't have formal attire on, and me, who was splattered in blood. They didn't move from their positions as we walked up and I was unnerved at the lack of response. Shouldn't they be more concerned about why we were here?

They didn't even stop us from getting close to the door.

"We need to evacuate the observatory." Amie was signaling to me to be quiet, but we didn't have time to quibble over the details. "It's an emergency. I swear we aren't here to make trouble. Please let us in so we can help."

They looked at each other and one of them moved to open the door for us with a quick spin of the lock. As the sound and lights of the party appeared in the doorway, something felt wrong. This was too easy, but maybe I was just being paranoid after everything that had happened. Amie and Fane rushed forward, tugging at my arms and leading me inside before I could take a minute to think. I heard a buzzing noise then of the door being locked behind us.

Why would they lock the door after what we just said?

I was about to point it out to Amie when Esme appeared.

"There you are!" Esme was being escorted by Zarek's projection, actually more like the projection was the only thing keeping her steady. "One of the rooms is filled with gold clouds, it's really relaxing once you breathe it in!" She yawned before slouching more of her weight on the arm she held. "You should try it!"

"Esme! I thought you were going to watch Sae!" Amie threw Esme's arm over her shoulder and took over the role of keeping her twin steady. "You promised me you wouldn't get distracted."

Esme just kissed her on the cheek, giggling.

"Relax, she's fine! Everyone loves Sae, they can't help it."

"I left the ballroom an hour ago," I said as I scanned the crowd.

"Why did you do that!?" Esme finally looked a bit disgruntled. "You were supposed to stay! I thought since Zarek was here, you were here the whole time!"

"Zarek left before I did. That's just a projection." As if to emphasize my point, Amie waved her hand, and the projection dissolved. "A lot's happened and we—"

"What!?" Esme's voice was far too loud. People were beginning to look our way. "Where's Zarek!? Have you all been doing something without me? Where were you? I thought we agreed not to change the plan! Zarek was supposed to stay here! You were supposed to stay here!"

"Amie, could you fill her in? I have to find Zarek."

"I'll go with her," Fane added hastily.

Fane grabbed a mask off a waiter and we quickly searched every room. As we did so, I was forced to be rude to those I'd spoken to earlier and it was difficult to go against what I'd been taught all my life. Either way, it was to no avail.

Zarek was nowhere to be found.

Where could he have gone? The date was about to turn and this party would end shortly after. More importantly, we didn't even know how the attack would begin. Maybe Zarek had stopped them from getting to the ballroom at all? I needed to switch around my priorities and get everyone outside. It was the best way to help at the moment. I could see Amie and Esme making their way toward me and forced myself to wait until they caught up.

"We need to get everyone out. Do you have any ideas?"

"I do! I do!" Esme giggled. "This'll be fun!"

Before I could ask her what she meant, she ran off.

Seconds later, the first shouts and screams rang out and people rushed away from the blaze that was now fully engulfing the back wall. Glasses and platters of food tumbled onto the ground, trampled by the frightened hordes. I could see waiters abandoning their stations and melting into the masses, rank no longer holding significance in the wake of a visible threat.

Although there was some panic, I suppose it was faster and easier than drawing more attention to ourselves or explaining what we knew. Their formal coats and adornments were now impediments, some even discarding such clothing in the name of practicality. The rumble of a scared mob was ear-numbing.

What I hadn't counted on were the main doors being locked. While it made sense for some side doors to be locked in the name of security, there was no reason for the front doors to be barred.

Why weren't the guards letting people through?

Surely, they had heard the screaming from within the—

"It's the guards!" I yelled over the crackling fire at our backs.

As if they'd laid in wait for my cue, the crowd surged backward. While I couldn't see over them, I could hear the sickening sound of firearms. People scattered, shoving each other to try and get away from the barrage. The doors in every direction were locked, but even worse, the doors themselves were all flanked by people in cream masks hiding their identities.

All of whom were firing into the crowd without prejudice.

The events unfolded slow and surreal. The rush of people who flowed to either side were distortions of overwhelming fear. Amie jumped in front of me to block them from jostling me. Fane, who had taken position behind me, yelled something incoherent in my ear. The blaze of the fire cast everything in a hazy glow, the shadows elongated and blurred by smoke.

"Sae! Sae!" Fane was shaking me. "What do you want us to do!?"

Fane's question snapped me out of the fog.

That's right. I kept forgetting that I couldn't wait for someone else to tell me what to do. The Empress wasn't here to protect everyone. I didn't have forever to make my decisions. We were not in Elysia, I had to rely on my own decisions, and I couldn't panic; at least not right now. What did I want them to do?

"Esme!" I shouted over the noise as she appeared beside her sister. "Blow out the back wall and get as many people outside as you can! Fane go with her! Lead people out of the observatory to the southwestern exits! Amie, make cover for them so they have time. I'm going to stay with you. Don't try and cover everybody, we need it to last until everyone's out!"

So much for conserving energy.

Amie waited until the back wall was blown open before pulling up her fields. Even with people moving in tighter formation to get out, it was a strain to take on that much firepower all at once. Dozens of highly-charged weapons designed to neutralize most energy fields were not exactly what she or Esme had been prepared to take on without my help. Not to mention covering such a wide area and holding back the flames from blocking the only exit.

Lights went out as the fire climbed relentlessly up the building. The back wall fully collapsed, sending the flames shooting upwards toward the sky, rejuvenated by the high winds swirling around the top of Solaris' dome. The fire was the only light source now as the guests plunged gratefully into the night.

I could see Amie's feet physically sliding backward and she barred down to keep herself from faltering. All of her concentration was focused on the task as the fake guards began to congregate or else she would have noticed the three who'd been on the inside of the shielding when it went up. But I saw them. They ran toward us, realizing that we were the source of the fields. I grabbed Amie's weapon from her thigh holster as they raised their own.

It happened so quickly that I didn't see him make the slice. Blood spurted from the backs of their necks as their spinal cords were severed and they collapsed.

Behind them was Zarek.

Other than the blood now staining his boots, he was fine.

Zarek didn't even glance at the bodies as he stepped over them.

I now knew how Leah felt before she collapsed.

"Pixie. Now, what have you been up to?" Zarek asked me casually as he put a finger on the barrel of the weapon I still had aimed at him. I hadn't moved since I saw him appear and hastily pointed the phaser at the ground. He tasked at me. "You should know better than to lower your weapon in a fight."

"Where have you b-been?" I hated that I sounded so unsteady.

"They planted explosives. They were going to get rid of the evidence once they were done here. I was just about to deal with them when you set the place on fire." He pulled a small, broken trigger device out of one of his pockets. "Luckily I found their toy, but it's best we make an exit. After all, I would never be caught dead lingering past my welcome."

"Will you shut the fuck up and get Sae out of here!?" Amie said through her teeth. The remainder of the terrorists were now shooting at the same spot in front of Amie, and I could see a small crack widening. Amie couldn't hold forever.

"Wrap it around you and pixie."

"What!? No!" I held on as Zarek tried to take it from me.

"Don't you trust me?" Zarek laughed and I couldn't believe he could laugh right now, but Amie gave me no choice in the matter as she did what Zarek suggested. One moment I was holding onto the phaser for dear life and the next I saw Zarek flick the safety off and shoot the nearest man in the head with it. I couldn't tear my eyes away from the sight of Zarek expertly hitting vital organs while being shot at himself. Amie tried to yank me away and failed.

My feet were wet. Blood had soaked through the thin soles of my shoes. I could see the bodies of the innocent people the terrorists had shot. The sound of wet chunks of flesh and organs slapping the floor would haunt me. I didn't even have time to process before they were all dead. I'd never seen so many corpses.

It was like I couldn't feel the ground anymore.

If any of them were still alive, they would be dead in seconds from blood loss. Zarek pulled the safety back and offered the weapon back to Amie, who put it in her holster as if it just hadn't been used to kill people. Zarek strode over the group of corpses and turned a few of them over, taking off their masks one by one. I think I was going to be sick for the first time in my life. He found what he was looking for apparently and ripped a colorful patch of clothing off of one of them.

That must have been Kiefer.

Zarek had just completed his job.

In the end, many guests left the event with serious burns and injuries but there were less than twenty civilian casualties. The bodies of the terrorists were hauled off as we dodged the crowds and the next thing I knew, we were escorting the workers back down the city to their homes at the bottom.

I let Fane explain to them what Kiefer had planned for them and how "Dorj had agreed to petition the ITA on their behalf." We couldn't tell them the truth about Rayde Hion and everything that had occurred. Our words were clearly not the answer these people were searching for but there was nothing else I could do.

They were grim and subdued the rest of the walk back.

Luckily the bulk of Solaris' authorities were busy back at the observatory, and we didn't run into many people at this hour of the night. No one around to stare at our blood soaked clothes.

Every government is corrupt unless it's ruled by the Empress.

Looking at the haggard faces of the workers who'd been used by both sides, I didn't know if I disagreed with them. Mother would have never let this happen. If Mother had been there, she would have known exactly what to do to avoid violence. How could Solaris and Isbul let the situation get so dire for their citizens? How could Dorj wait until his peers were in danger before acting?

How could I call myself the Heir if I couldn't help people?

Roland was a broken man. I never found his daughter and was certain she was dead. After the group scattered and we led Roland back to his small home, he curled up in his bed and cried. Having nowhere else to go, we went and took over Roland's main room for the night. Exhausted, no one spoke.

Once I heard Roland's breath even out in the other room, I handed Zarek the necklace. He took it and again showed no sign that he remembered me. Numb, I sat on the ground beside Esme and Amie and leaned back against the wall. I still slept every once in a while but no matter how much I tried, I couldn't. As I sat huddled in a corner, I grew more and more agitated with every peaceful breath my friends took. I needed to distract myself.

We'd vacated the hotel room earlier, thinking we'd have moved on by now, but both Esme and Amie were drained. They needed at least a few hours of sleep before we went anywhere. I tried to look over our star maps as they slept.

It was impossible to think right now.

Each place we landed put us in more and more danger.

We had to be prepared for our next step.

I stared at those star maps for who knows how long as the movement of the galaxies and planets flew by faster. Faster until I felt sick looking at them. I couldn't breathe. The walls of this tiny room were shrinking.

I found myself on my feet and then out the front door.

Roland lived on a narrow street and the buildings were stacked closely, one over the other. I struggled to keep quiet. My friends were sleeping. Amie and Esme had never seen me like this. Fane was exhausted. They needed to sleep. I gripped the railing of Roland's porch, my fingers digging themselves into the metal. The anxiety and fear I'd been holding back decided to hit me all at once.

The weight of my failure was heavy on my chest.

The night outside was stuffy and airless. Thick and smothering. Just as I was beginning to hyperventilate as quietly as I possibly could, I felt a blanket fall over my shoulders. Its warmth was not what gave me pause, but the smell. Zarek.

Sure enough I turned to find him closing the front door that I'd left open. He'd changed into more relaxed clothing, but I'd seen the holes shot through his coat. I hadn't been thinking straight earlier; I hadn't thought to check; now I worried that he was seriously injured though he was moving just fine.

"Can't sleep pixie?"

"I-I'm sorry, did I wake you?"

"... Are you reconsidering your travel plans?"

He really did have issues answering my questions.

"No. I just can't—I wish I'd been able to help you more."

"Help me." Zarek sat down against the railing beside where I stood. While the rest of us smelled like soot, blood, and smoke, he was untouched by the madness that had singed everyone else. "I didn't need your help."

"I know! I know you didn't need my help."

"You didn't let me finish." Zarek was absently playing with the tails of the little ties holding my nightgown together. It was actually one of Amie's shirts, but in this form it fell modestly past my knees. "I didn't need your help but you minimized a lot of damage. Dorj's body was found and they blamed it on Kiefer rather than your precious workers. Who all got out somehow. Fane told me what you got Hion to do... and I still can't believe you got to the ballroom before I did. I'm impressed."

"I didn't know what I was doing. I couldn't—"

"You knew." The back of Zarek's hand grazed my own fingers, but this time, neither of us flinched away. I didn't know what to make of his mood and he seemed content not to question the sudden intimacy. "And you made it happen."

"Either way, it all ended in violence."

The hand that played with my shirt ties froze.

"Is that why you can't look at me, pixie?"

I immediately looked at him because that was not why. It was true that I was still coming to terms with what he'd done, but I didn't blame Zarek for his actions. I mostly blamed myself for not stopping it all together. They would have killed everyone. They would have killed him if given the chance and I would much rather my friends were safe than the alternative.

"Zarek, how much do you remember now?" Although I didn't blame him, it had scared me to see him so comfortable with what happened tonight. I was getting used to the idea that his past was more complicated than I was prepared for, but I needed to see in order to understand.

I needed something from him in order to accept.

"I want to know you, Zarek. Give me a chance."

He didn't answer right away, and I wasn't going to push him to answer me; I didn't have it in me to interrogate another person tonight. If he didn't want to talk to me, then so be it. His deft hands tied and untied the small knot of my shirt rapidly as he considered my words and yet I even found his distraction attractive. I cared too much about him. I could admit that much.

"It comes in bits and pieces," Zarek admitted gruffly as he continued to toy with the ties on my clothing. "They're not linear, but I remember enough to know not much has changed since I was a kid. Not worth the effort, really."

I waited, but he said no more.

"You acted like you remembered Aaro, but you didn't."

"You're too observant for your own good, pixie."

"Thank you. I'll take that as a compliment."

"You should, I don't give them out to just anyone."

He was teasing me again and I was beginning to like it.

"Do you believe me now? When I say I'm your friend?"

"Yes." His concession surprised us both. It was as if his honesty wound a thread between us, fragile and new. He didn't take it back. The thread grew. What could only be called a self-deprecating grin stole all the words I could have said from my lungs. "I'm starting to think I've got the better end of the deal, pixie."

I knew now that Fane and the others had told me the truth.

Zarek was a man who intimately danced with a darker universe than I was ever meant to know. I knew nothing of his life in the outer universe just as much as he did not remember mine... but there was no part of me that wanted to condemn him. He hadn't trusted me with the truth until now.

Even knowing the truth, I couldn't turn away from him.

"I'm sorry that you had to do it and I'm still processing what happened, but it didn't change anything, Zarek. I just wish I'd been able to stop it all. I wanted to do more for you." I reached down and stroked his cheek gently as a gesture of reassurance...

What was I doing?

I jumped back from him and consequently heard a small rip.

One of the ties was still caught in Zarek's fingers and had taken a part of the hemline, still attached, with it. We both stared in dismay at the now mutilated edge, and I bit my lip to try and keep from giggling, but the embellished woe on Zarek's face put me over the edge. We both had to stifle our undignified snickering and failed every time we tried to look at each other.

Chapter 14: Miracles

We left before the sun rose and traveled by underground train to reach the edge of Solaris where an off-world terminal was placed. It was built inside the shell of an ancient city, carved in the side of one of Solaris' many gorges; the distinct layers of lithosphere evident in every floor of the station. Zarek and Fane had gone to look for passage where they hopefully wouldn't ask too many questions like "what's your nationality?", "where's your home planet", or "do you have the necessary travel documents?".

Meanwhile, I stayed with Amie and Esme who dozed on either side of me; it was only natural after being overstretched again.

This early, there weren't too many people around. Ships were still arriving and departing, but they were mostly for cargo rather than people. I was mostly interested in the rough style that this city had originally been carved. Many of the original buildings were long gone, but the columns had an interesting convex shape to them. I wondered about the configuration of the material. It could be a more polished version of the surrounding stone or they could be made of a synthetic mixture. I wish I had been able to spend more time in Solaris' libraries.

The palace back home contained the largest collection of published literature in the universe, but we were rarely able to record locally traded books from outside our borders. They could have told me more about this terminal, for example, or why a group in billowing white robes was coming toward us.

"Good morning!" The man in front smiled in a friendly way.

"Oh! Good morning!" I told myself to stop being paranoid and smiled back. This was a good reminder. Just because the last few days had been stressful didn't mean that most people weren't inherently good and usually welcoming to travelers.

In any case, it was hard to stay wary as they began to chime hellos; more than one greeted with a hand gesture that I returned.

The idle chit-chat that followed was nice. Apparently, they had just arrived in Solaris and were excited to see the city. They were supposed to arrive last week, but their ship had been forced to take a stop for repairs that delayed their trip. I was giving them some recommendations for local food that I'd seen Fane eat when I saw him and Zarek coming back over their shoulders.

"We found a ride." Fane looked incredibly uncomfortable.

He and Zarek were obviously making a point of ignoring the entire group of people standing right in front of them. Seeing their reaction, I shifted Amie's bag back onto my shoulder just in case I'd made a mistake in being sociable.

"Hello, friend. Beautiful morning isn't it?"

The combination of Zarek's brusque demeanor and the look he gave the woman who'd spoken directly to him was deterrent enough. The group mumbled excuses and begin to shuffle away; like a school of fish faced with a predator.

The man who originally spoke to me gave me a piece of paper. "May your travels be blessed by the Empress and the One herself."

"What?" But he was already moving away with the rest of his group. I opened the folds of the paper to find my own face staring at me and I was so surprised that I almost dropped it. No, it wasn't my face. It was Aristae's face. She hadn't yet reached adulthood when she passed and her face held that strange, youthful other-worldliness I could never achieve.

My friends, it is not too late to devote yourself to the One.

For she has brought endless generations of happiness, justice, freedom, and peace to the universe. Rejoice for the Empresses shall one day free us from hate and greed, war and poverty, from sickness to the clutches of death itself. The day of reckoning will soon be upon us. The Ryunaga will return, the stars themselves will weep as reincarnated, a miracle walks among us again.

Nicaristae Raajali will be the bringer of a new era of love.

Pull away from your sorrows, your fears, for we have been fortunate enough to see the second coming of the One. *The Temple of Aristae will rise for all to witness. And when its Light appears on we who are forsaken, to my brothers and sisters unlucky enough to be born outside the Empress' embrace, may we find the wisdom to accept the gift of a higher existence.*

Join us as Apostles of Aristae.

I read it twice and then again. I glanced up at Amie and Esme, who were reading it over my shoulders. I wasn't sure if it was appropriate to laugh. The group was now standing by the side of the main walkway, trying to talk to people who didn't seem very happy to be spoken to—well, now we knew why.

"I'm guessing you've never run into the Apostles?" Fane asked.

"Is it a religion?" Why had I never learned about them? There were no major religions back home; in fact, the vast majority of Elysians were secular; but I had been briefed on many of them just in case I found myself in the position of offending someone. I now felt like I should have known about this one considering it was about me. What in the Empress' name...?

"Yeah," Fane rubbed the back of his neck and gave me an apologetic grin. "They're an old one too. After the third Empress agreed to absorb a neighboring system for the first time, they popped up everywhere. A lot of people think the Raajali are gods anyways, so it's not a huge leap."

"Is there a sect inside Elysia?" I'd never met one until now.

"One of their commandments says they can't cross the borders themselves until everywhere is under the Empress' domain. Don't get the wrong idea, they're mostly harmless—they're all pacifists—but, well they've gotten really pushy about it ever since uh... well ever since Nicaristae was born."

Amie made a disgusted noise before grabbing the paper, crumpling, and throwing it on the floor. It took a few more seconds before she huffed and went to pick it up from the ground again.

Littering was not in our nature.

The ship Zarek and Fane had found was another cargo ship. We needed to head to a fairly isolated system this time and Fane explained that this ship would take about a day to take us a little more than halfway there. That should be enough for Amie and Esme to take us the rest of the way.

It was a fully automated ship, and its captain was more than happy to make extra credits on the side without having to change his flight plan. He was a Givvh, meaning that fully grown he was only about 120 centimeters tall and possessed an agile tail almost twice the length of his body. It was the Givvh's strongest limb in fact and was used to signify rank and stature on his home world.

"I got two rules before you board," he said as Fane was transferring the credits to him, "Don't touch anything and don't go anywhere outside the pilot's compartment. I programmed her to take a short pause where you said, so I hope your ride's on time to take you." He bounced lightly on his tail as the payment cleared. "Else you'll be on til she lands and you'll 've wasted your credits."

"Thank you for the use of your vessel." I switched to what was most likely his native language. "Good voyages to you and yours. May you outlive your ancestors and your descendants the same."

He blinked. "Ah, you're welcome miss! Have a safe trip." His feet touched the ground, and he flipped his tail in salute. I wish I had a tail so I could do the same but, since I didn't, a hand salute have to do. He even waited until I was inside before going back down the ramp and closing the doors for takeoff.

"How do you know Givvhan?" Zarek asked me as he bent to avoid hitting his head on the short ceiling. The truce we'd declared was still in place to my delight and I got to tell him vaguely of some of the language tutors I'd had in the past.

"We get it, Sae. You know a million languages."

Esme was still grumpy from the early wake up, so she'd been unusually quiet until now. I think she was still upset at how the conference had ended last night and at the fact that she hadn't been able to wash the dye out of her hair yet.

The hum of the engine was audible even in the pilot's compartment; a dull brown inside with only two chairs; Amie went to go sleep against the starboard side while Fane got up from the chair he'd been sitting on to offer it to me.

I didn't take it. While I was resigned to Fane's temporary change in behavior and, Empress help me I hoped he'd grow out of it, it was best to ignore his antics.

Esme took it when I didn't.

The ride through Solaris' atmosphere was uneventful as was the jump to warp. There wasn't much to do but stare at the stars and search through Isbul's networks for entertainment. While there was a part of me itching to try flying the ship myself, cargo ships like these were limited in terms of manual navigation. The precaution was to make hijacking the vessel more difficult. Due to its programming, the ship would continue on its flight path unless destroyed entirely.

Instead, I found myself playing a strategy game with Zarek.

He had gotten better since we were kids.

The first four games ended in a tie until I spotted a flaw in his technique in the fifth round. I felt ludicrously smug as I surrounded his pieces, decimated his defenses, and claimed victory.

"I demand a rematch!" Zarek laughed as I was declared winner.

"I don't even know what happened," Fane mumbled as he munched on snacks. It looked as if he'd almost finished the box.

"Didn't we just buy those?"

"We skipped breakfast!" He was equally indignant when Zarek grabbed another box out of his bag to toss into my lap. "Hey! I was saving those for later!"

"I bought that one, Fane. Pixie hasn't eaten for days."

"Yes, I have! I uh, ate last night at the conference."

"You looked at food last night. You didn't eat the food unless you can absorb nutrients from across a room... can you do that, pixie?" His tone implied once again that I was a bad liar.

Flustered at being caught out, I nibbled at the small vitamin cookies. They were very bland and inoffensive; I ate the suggested serving and told myself to remember to eat and drink at regular, nonsuspicious intervals. If I had picked a more greenish skin tone, I could have lied and said I was photosynthetic, but I had to go for ordinary over practical. I wasn't nearly green enough to put up a convincing argument. I could have even been a chemosynthetic!

My overthinking led me to lose the next round.

I was going to demand a rematch of my own, but Esme wanted a turn, so I went to go look around the control panels. They looked simple enough, but I had never been allowed to fly anything so what did I know? I moved to look underneath, but a quiet thump made me smash the back of my head into the panel above. I stood up and started to look around "Did you hear that?"

"The sound of your head hitting the panel?" Esme knew I was unhurt, so she kept playing, but Fane and Zarek weren't paying attention to it anymore.

"I'm fine, um ouch." I patted my head absently in the place that I think I hit it. I couldn't hear anything out of the ordinary, but I had definitely heard a thump. I did a circle around the room with Zarek and Fane watching as I stopped and started randomly, putting my ears to the walls here and there. I eventually gained Esme's attention as she realized she was playing by herself.

"Sae what are you doing!?" Esme grabbed my hand. "Stop it!"

"I thought I heard a thump," I admitted. "Before I hit my head."

"Maybe the cargo wasn't secured properly." Fane shrugged

There it was again. Would I look sillier taking off my shoes or crawling on the ground? Another thump made up my mind. I dropped to my knees and pressed my ear against the floor. If I ignored the sound of the engine, I could swear something sounded like the murmur of people talking.

"I think there are people in the cargo hold."

Another two thumps, only louder.

Amie sighed as her nap was interrupted yet again.

"Let's go look!" Esme was already heading toward the hatch.

"Wait! We don't know why they're down there!" Fane beat her to the cargo hatch and blocked it with his body. "They could be dangerous or hiding for a good reason like we are!"

"Just looking isn't going to do anything!" Esme argued.

"Esme wait!" Amie swore as she very nearly cracked her head full force on the ceiling. Fane and I were the only ones who could stand upright in here. "Dammit, do not open that hatch. It has nothing to do with us. Leave it."

"Sae don't you want to take a look?" Esme pleaded with me.

"Not if the others aren't on board. Majority rules remember?"

"Does that make me the tie-breaker?" Zarek asked, he was the only person still sitting and was watching our little drama unfold with unabashed amusement.

"Yes! That means I get to open it!" Esme shimmied with glee, but she was destined to be disappointed as Zarek opted against opening the hatch. According to him, it had something to do with not pinching a Ryunaga's nose. Good idiom.

I missed Yuki.

Zarek's words only reminded me of my worries that she could be feeling abandoned or upset with me. It was harder than I thought it would be to be away from her and even though we had been spending more time apart as of late didn't mean I didn't feel her absence keenly. With the hatch now off the table, I spent some time thinking about how Yuki always hoped to find the remainder of her kind. Neither of us had ever met one besides Mio but it would be a long time before Mother let me out again.

Maybe Mio could take her someday soon.

Absently, I doodled a little Naga on my palm.

Yuki used to be able to fit in my hands when she was a hatchling. Her species aged quickly only for their aging process to slow to practically nothing once adulthood was reached. Mio was much older and his size spoke of the many millennia he'd spent with Mother. One day, Yuki would be that big too.

I heard Fane suck in his breath sharply behind me.

"What's wrong?" I turned to see Fane fiddling with his implant.

"Nothing." Fane was lying to me, and he was bad at it.

"Let her see Fane. She'll hear about it eventually." Zarek reached out and slid his finger along Fane's implant to show a projection of Solaris' local channels.

No. I read the words again, not wanting to accept it. The list of the dead stretched on until I saw a name that cemented it as reality.

Roland Toors.

"It's a common protest tool in Isbul," Fane explained to me. "Some labor groups have an old "escape clause" grandfathered in. It gives them the right to die rather than work and provides any of their living dependents with a monetary amount paid for by the company and state. All major labor disputes in Isbulian history have been marked with mass "escapes."

Nothing more was said of the matter.

As the hours went by, the thumping got more frequent. Esme didn't mention it again, but I think we were all relieved to get to the drop-off point. Fane, who'd been sitting on the hatch this entire time, finally got up to pack his snacks away.

We should have known better than to let our guard down.

Esme dived for the hatch and had the latches flipped open at record speed. The sound of the locks scraping against a rusty part instantly had Amie on her feet once more and this time she was unable to keep from hitting her head. As her twin swore viciously at her sore scalp, Esme grabbed the handle and, flush with triumph, pulled the hatch free. The door slammed against the floor, releasing a rolling white cloud of cold air. The cargo was evidently temperature sensitive and as Esme eagerly looked down, we could hear people rapidly trying to move away from the opening. As was Fane, who was now hiding behind me.

Esme screamed.

What!? What was it!? Esme flipped out even as her sister pulled her away from the hatch and shoved her toward me. Fane was dislodged as Esme took his place clinging to me in fear. Amie had her weapon out now, even though we all agreed that shooting inside a pressurized cabin was not a good idea, and approached the opening. We could see our breath now as the compartment rapidly chilled. The thumping continued, even more rapid than before.

A gnarled hand twisted with open sores plunged upwards out of the cloud, the cold raising its veins to the surface. "Don't shoot! Please don't shoot!" A voice with a heavy lisp called out.

Amie didn't shoot, but she also didn't lower her phaser either.

"Who are you!?" she demanded, putting the safety back on.

"We're no one! We're sorry! We'll keep her quiet, please! We mean you no harm!" The thumping noise was now constant and much louder with the hatch open. The hand tried to close the hatch again but was too weak to budge it.

"Wait!" I gave Esme to Fane and walked forward, realizing what I was looking at. The man was a Givvh, disfigured by large bubbling abscesses. The sore on his face had eaten away at his facial tissue, taken his nose and was eating into his eye on that side. You could see some of his teeth through the rotten flesh. "You need medical attention." I pushed Amie's weapon down and she begrudgingly put it away. "It can't be comfortable in there."

"It doesn't matter. Please close the hatch." The thumping was coming from a woman who was banging her head against an inner wall, Pieces of her scalp seemed to be scarred over from past attempts. From what little I could see; they were all similarly disfigured or seriously ill in some way.

"What's happened to you? Do you need help?"

"Please miss, all we want is to make it across the border safely." The man's one could eye clouded over with milky tears. "It's a viral, genetic condition. There nothing to be done unless I reach the Empire. Please have mercy on us."

"Why are you in a freezer?" Amie asked in a gentler tone.

"Patrol ships. They'll think we're part of the cargo ma'am."

They were hiding their life signs. If the hull was thick enough, as long as they kept their body heat down, it was possible to evade some of the measures taken by Isbul to stop ships at the border. I knew we took in a number of medical refugees each year, but I'd never met any of them.

I'd also never seen a being so debilitated before.

I'd rarely ever seen a superficial illness before.

Disabilities didn't exist in Elysia.

The central control panel beeped.

We were at the drop-off point.

"Esme, Amie, Zarek, can any of you spare anything?"

"We can't." Amie tsked. "Not if we're getting off here."

Zarek just shook his head.

"Are you in pain?"

"There is nothing you can do. Except close the hatch. Please."

Arguing with an ill man doing his best to protect himself seemed wrong. I knew nothing of their situation and could not make any decisions on their behalf. I had already interfered too much with the outside universe and if I tried to help them myself, they would surely be discovered. All I could do was respectfully close the hatch, even if the thumping was only getting more rapid.

In silence, we readied ourselves for the jump.

Amie was working out a few last-minute calculations while the rest of us stood around trying not to look in the direction of the hatch. Esme was curled up as far away from the hatch as possible, looking absolutely miserable.

"I can't take this!" She shouted out of the blue.

"Esme leave it." Amie said firmly, but Esme persisted.

"Sae can't you do something!? I can't believe you want to leave and do nothing to help them!" Esme had never shouted at me like this before. "If they die, it'll be your fault for not helping them! Sae, why aren't you doing anything!? Why—"

"Esme!" Amie shoved her things into her bag and stood.

"But Amie! It's not fair! Sae could do something if she—"

"Stop yelling at Sae!" Fane snapped

His defense of me only made Esme cry harder.

"Oh, have you fallen in love with her too!? Boo fucking hoo—"

"Esme!" Amie glared at Fane to back off.

"Why are you always taking her side!?" Esme was not good at whispering. "This time it really is Sae's fault! You know she could fix it if she really wanted to!"

I tried to tune out their arguing while I stood there.

Was Esme right? How had things gotten so convoluted? We couldn't help them get across the border without risk of being discovered and I couldn't do anything here without taking an even bigger risk. I couldn't keep revealing myself to people whenever a problem popped up. I couldn't even be sure that my Light could be wielded precisely enough to help them instead of killing them. We were almost out of time, Amie was still tired, and taking a jump at warp was much harder to do.

"I'm really sorry Esme." I hesitantly went over to my friends, who I'd never known to be so at odds before. I couldn't help but feel like it was my fault too. "I don't think we can do much to help them, but maybe we can ease their way."

"Oh yeah? How?" Esme sobbed even as she yelled at me.

I had to go over a few details with Zarek, not even sure if he'd be willing, but in the end, he was able to do as I requested.

Although Esme still wasn't completely happy about the situation, she accepted the fact that we had to leave when we did. I left a piece of my heart with those sick people, who would all sleep peacefully without dreams until they crossed the border into Elysian space.

CHAPTER 15: KINSHIPS

We were falling.

Tumbling all around me, ground over sky, we were in freefall tens of thousands of meters above the planet we'd come to. I caught a glimpse of Amie and Esme frantically trying to reach each other.

Fane was unconscious from the lack of oxygen at this height.

"Amie! What happened!"

The earsplitting whistle of the wind drowned out my voice.

"I don't know!" She yelled back. "It's not working!"

If I could get dizzy I would have started to feel really sick right about now. I tried to grab onto Esme's arm, but my limbs fell short of being able to reach them. They had managed to grab each other's arms and yet whatever they were trying to do yielded no results. Were they panicking? Were they drained from the jump? The ground was rapidly getting closer and while I didn't think Amie and Esme would die from such a fall, I wasn't sure what condition they'd be in if we hit the ground at max velocity. My skin was tingling, an unfamiliar force that felt like diving into warm soup disoriented me. If they couldn't stop our descent soon, I would have no choice but to step in.

"I've got you. You're okay."

I was glad no one could hear the squeak I made as I found myself pressed securely against Zarek, who'd been behind me this whole time. With one arm he anchored me to him and stretched out the other with his fingers spread wide.

Gradually, our descent slowed. Amie grabbed Fane, who was still unconscious, and we all held our breath as the ground crept closer to us. We were still falling, just not as quickly. Zarek's breathing got more ragged the longer we were in the air.

His head dropped against the crook of my shoulder.

"Zarek? What's wrong?" I tried to wiggle out of his grip but stopped when, to my horror, I realized he was unconscious. His hand dropped and the arm around my waist slackened. We were still too far off the surface for a safe landing. We were picking up speed again and I didn't have the luxury of second-guessing myself.

For the first time in weeks, I dug down deep and tried to pull only the smallest pinprick of energy. I felt the core of my being surge white hot, eager, and restless. I pushed away from Zarek, trying to get as far away from my friends as possible, and pulled the wind from its current.

Control. I had to have control. The wind was too fast, a sharp edge sliced into Fane's leg, and it wouldn't slow under my hands. I tried to spread the Light thinner, but it buckled fitfully, fighting me. The harder I pulled, the harder it pushed. Empress, why was I so incompetent?

□

□*I was two years old and no matter how much I wanted to please Mother; I couldn't make the light any smaller. It pulsed too bright and blinded my tutors. It was not the warm beacon of hope or the glow of a welcoming hearth an Heir should produce, but a searing failure in the eyes of the Empress.*

□*"Saekonari. This is a simple, basic exercise. You lack focus."*

□*"I'm sorry Mother, I'm trying really hard—"*

□*"Raajali do not need to try."*

□*"I-I'm really sorry, I'll p-practice and—"*

▢But she'd already turned her back to speak with my tutors. I just wanted Mother to be proud of me. I needed to try harder, do something good so that she would know I was going to be a good Heir.

A good Empress.

▢Left alone in the nursery, I tried again and again all night long to make the light smaller. It should have fit in the palm of my hand. It should have the soft glow of a late sunset. It should have listened to me. Why didn't it ever listen to me? I tried and failed; and as I failed over and over again, the light only got brighter.

Seconds later, we hit the ground. Hard.

I rolled onto my feet as soon as I could feel gravel against my body. The cyclone of wind I'd created to try and break our fall broke in all directions; a rusty pile of scrap metal to our left was sliced into ribbons by the impact. As quickly as I could, I took stock of the loose pile of debris we'd landed on. It was only one of many mountains of trash. Amie hadn't been able to detect any signs of intelligent life beforehand, but it was clear that this planet had been industrialized to death by its former inhabitants.

A sickly yellow miasma hung in the lower atmosphere of this planet. Crumbling urban sprawl stretched out for thousands of kilometers around us and garbage was piled in towering skyscrapers of rot. The smell was pungent and somehow wet as if it'd only been weeks instead of centuries that this world had been abandoned. There was a thick grimy quality to everything from years of negligence and irreversible pollution. The air should be just about breathable for the others, but if we stayed too long, we ran the risk of Fane or Zarek getting sick. Gravity was more than twice the average. Temperature was high but radiation, by the look of things, wasn't too much of a danger.

"Sae! You shouldn't have done that!" Esme gasped.

"Esme. Give it a rest." Amie effectively silenced the lecture I was sure to get sooner or later and went to check on the boys, who were still unconscious. After a quick check for any critical injuries and finding none, she pulled out ponchos from our bags. Their design meant they could double as air filters if the cowl was raised and drawn over the nose. I knew Amie had stocked up on supplies while in Solaris, but I hadn't realized how thorough she'd been.

What was that?

I felt another tug and whipped around.

Nothing was visibly there, but I knew.

"Amie? Something's here." I took a poncho and threw it on,

"What? What's there!?" Amie threw the remainder of the ponchos at Esme. "Get these on them." She pointed to Zarek and Fane before she came up to join me. Amie didn't question my instincts even once as we transversed across the uneven terrain of garbage.

We heard it before we saw it.

A small, sparkling ring was floating, spinning above a circle of bare earth. It was emitting a low frequency droning that vibrated against the teeth unless you clenched your jaw shut. I'd never felt anything like it before. It was startlingly white, the refuse around it only emphasized the stark nature of its design. I slid down a slope to get closer and Amie didn't stop me.

Nothing happened as I approached it.

"Amie. I have an odd urge to touch it."

"No." She was emphatic as she came down after me and usually I would take the time to hear her out, but there was something oddly compelling about the thought of touching it. I held up a hand to keep Amie from coming any closer and reached out my other to do just that.

The ring stopped spinning before I could even make contact, dropped, and burst into a cloud of powder as soon as it hit the ground. The tugging feeling was gone as abruptly as it appeared, and I was left staring down at my feet at all that remained of the ring. Everything about this trip was getting stranger by the second... yet it was all quite anticlimactic as nothing happened in the moments to follow. The universe was a weird place.

Eventually, Amie tugged at my arm, and we started to head back.

Amie had leaped back up to the crest of the slope; she'd knelt down and was about to give me a hand up; when someone we hadn't noticed wrapped their gloved hands around her eyes.

"Guess who!" The man's voice was distorted by the filtering mask he wore over his face. His clothes were stained with streaks of a dark, oily substance and he was wrapped in a long coat with bulging pockets of various tools and unidentifiable objects. Until now, no one had ever been able to sneak on Amie before.

Never had I ever seen her so caught off guard and she immediately lashed out at whoever dared to come at her from behind.

I heard them roll down the other side of the mountain of trash, both of them yelling very similar curses. The clamor of debris collapsing followed their descent. It didn't take me more than a few seconds to get over the top by myself and find them again, but it was enough time for them to regain their footing.

Amie was furious. The stranger, whoever they were, seemed very much unaware of the danger he'd just put himself in. He moved with a light step for a man of his size, his hands were tucked into his pockets as if he was on a casual stroll.

"Don't be like that darling, whatever did I do this time?"

The man should have had his feet swept out from under him as Amie moved to shatter his kneecap but instead, he was able to sidestep her kick and land elegantly on his feet beside her, again dodging her fist with ease.

What followed was a frustrating ordeal as the man weaved in and out of arm's length, never truly retreating, but never retaliating either. Probably what was even worse in Amie's mind was that the man refused to stop talking.

"Oh, almost got me that time! Can't I just kiss it to make it all better? You know I absolutely love our little chats, but isn't this a bit excessive? It's just like that one time in bed when—"

Amie almost screamed in frustration.

There was something familiar about him.

Just as I thought it, he was somehow able to grab Amie's hand and twirl her around. In what I would almost call a flirtatious manner, he tugged Amie's hood off her head and her heavy locks of her hair tumbled out. Amie wrenched herself away and the poncho ripped as the man had suddenly gone completely still, her hood gripped tight under his knuckles.

Amie shook her head to get her hair away from her eyes and turned back around to face him. It was then I noticed her thigh holster wasn't on her, but kicked to the side.

Whoever he was, he'd managed to disarm Amie.

"Who *are* you!?" The distortion couldn't hide his confusion.

The man didn't move fast enough this time and caught a foot directly in the solar plexus. He flew backward with a dull thud against a pile of construction pipes and Amie was about to leap after him when I hastily grabbed her arm.

Amie took one look at me and tore her weapon out of my grip.

Her already bright violet eyes were glowing with anger.

He wisely kept his distance from the one holding a phaser and raised both hands in the universal sign of surrender. Amie didn't look like she cared and was *this* close to shooting him anyway.

"Amie, I don't think—"

The man let out a strangled noise.

Reaching up, he tore the mask off his face and threw it aside, revealing deep green eyes and only the faintest hint of laugh lines. His nose showed signs of having been broken before, but it detracted nothing from his roguishly handsome face. The hair under his hood was black.

Just like Amie's.

No one moved. I couldn't stop staring at him long enough to see how Amie was taking this, but I could feel her shaking beside me.

Amie, who'd always been so strong. Amie, who had held everything together when her parents had disappeared; leaving behind not only her and Esme but their younger brothers who barely remembered the time before when their family was whole. Amie had never faltered, but now... now she was crying.

"Daddy!?"

Amie dropped her weapon as her father, Astral Esholitte, swept her up into a crushing hug. Amie cried uncontrollably into his shoulder and I moved to give them some space as they collapsed to their knees, clinging for dear life.

Astral and Anera Esholitte had been missing for over six years. No trace of them was ever found and considering that Mother had had endless resources to look for them, it had been a damning sign. The only beam of hope was the chance they'd disappeared in the outer universe where the Empress' reach could not go.

Mother had taken their loss badly.

Although the search had never been officially called off, it was presumed that they were dead. It was why Amie and Esme had taken on their roles so early in life as they were the only Sentinels left after their disappearance.

Esme had never given up thinking they would return.

Amie had chosen not to hold on to that hope.

"Amythesia! Empress' mercy, look at you! You're so big!" Astral held his daughter's face in his hands and was crying even harder than she was. Neither of them looked as if they could believe what they were seeing. "You can't have—You've grown up! You look just like your mother." Astral's face crumpled. "I am so sorry. I am so sorry Amie. We didn't want to. I swear we didn't mean to stay away, button. My beautiful girl."

Amie couldn't stop crying enough to form coherent words.

Feeling very much like an interloper, I stood a little ways off and politely pretended I was invisible. Had Astral been here the whole time? Was Anera alive? What had kept them here? Was this a trick—no. He was a Sentinel.

Every part of me was certain of that undeniable fact.

"Is your sister here!?" Amie nodded as she rubbed her eyes. "Who's this?" Astral said as he noticed me for the first time. He pulled a handkerchief from one of the many pockets of his coat to give to his daughter as he scrutinized me.

"I'm Saekonari, I'm just... in disguise at the moment."

It was going to be so difficult to explain this.

Astral's eyes widened. A strange expression was on his face already. It wasn't like I could revert back right now and prove it; he'd just have to take my word for it. Or Amie's word once she calmed down—Esme was going to be a wreck.

"It's good to see you Sae." Astral stood and helped his daughter up. As he did, he also lifted up Amie's weapon. "This is mine isn't it? I knew I'd left it behind somewhere." He wiped a tear off Amie's cheek, only causing more to fall. "Are your brothers here?" His face fell ever so slightly when Amie shook her head no.

"Is Mom...?"

"Your mother is fine. I just saw her a little while ago, after all didn't I just mistake you for her?" Astral brought a small laugh out of her. "Empress look at you! How did I miss how tall you got? Your mother always hoped you'd get my height." He sighed. "I know you have questions. So do I. Let's get your sister, find your mother, and we'll talk."

I took the lead to give them some room to breathe. Amie had stopped crying, but I'd never seen her so shy. They spoke softly to each other. The years gone by had predictably taken much of the familiarity away, but it was clear the love remained.

Esme had her back turned away from us as we approached. She'd done what Amie had asked and they were all covered by the ponchos now, but the cold shoulder she was giving us could be felt from a kilometer away.

Steam could have risen from her; she was so mad.

"Esme—" Amie started but Esme didn't give her the chance.

"No! Don't bother! It's perfectly fine that you just leave me here to babysit! No one cares what Esme wants! I mean I just love being dragged all over the universe and..."

Her voice died away mid-sentence as she turned and was greeted by the sight of her father, in the flesh.

Speechless, Astral moved to embrace his daughter but, to our shock, Esme flailed backward, her hands scrambling for purchase in her quest to move away from him as fast as possible. She almost barreled right over Fane as she did so.

"Amie! Who the fuck is that!? Where did he come from!?"

"It's Dad, Esme, don't you recognize him?" Amie said cautiously as her twin continued to back away. Any further and she'd run right into a stream of unknown sludge. Esme must as known it too because she stopped just short of it.

"Dad is dead!" Esme shouted. Her gaze flew in every direction like she was expecting to be ambushed. "Amie, Mom and Dad died six years ago! They left us behind and never came back!"

"Don't you get it? They didn't die!"

"Yes, they did! Or else they would have come back!"

"Esmeralda. Your mother and I didn't ever mean to leave you alone. We can explain if you just let us." Astral reached out his hand, but Esme was having none of it.

"My mother is dead. Don't touch me!"

Her father looked absolutely devastated.

"Esme what is the matter with you!?" Amie grabbed her twin's hand. "Can't you feel it? We know him." Amie's eyes narrowed as Esme tried to shake her off. "You always told me Mom and Dad were out there. That they'd never abandon us. That they'd come back one day because they love us."

"I was just saying that to make you feel better! I didn't actually believe it! There's no way that's Dad." Esme broke down sobbing. "No! No! No! It can't be Dad! It can't be! They're dead! You know they're dead! That's not him!"

It took a long time to calm Esme down.

By the time we had accomplished it, it was nearly dark.

Zarek remained asleep through it all.

"I'm surprised he didn't kill himself trying to stop your fall." Astral explained as he loaded them onto a hovering stretcher. Unfortunately, Fane had awakened to the pain of a few broken ribs, the increased gravity only making the situation worse.

Once we finally began moving to where Astral and Anera had set up a base camp, he revealed that the speed in which this planet's molten core moved and cooled created a magnetic field so strong it had kept my Sentinels from slowing down our fall. It also explained the abnormally heavy gravity wells everywhere.

She and Esme were exhausted.

They were only as strong as I could make them. With my inability to strengthen them combined with their age and inexperience... it was no wonder they'd been so susceptible. It also explained the soupy feeling I'd experienced as we fell.

"We caught a distress signal." Astral glanced at me for a split second before looking away again. They'd been on a diplomatic mission in the outer universe. Their last communication had been to tell the Empress they were on their way back home. It was assumed that they'd crossed the border due to their ship's frequency checks but apparently, they'd been waylaid after all.

"Your mother and I went to see if someone needed help. This planet wasn't marked on the star charts. It wasn't picked up by sensors. We put everything into preventing the crash when we should have focused on getting out without the ship. Anera nearly drained herself dry when—"

"Will Zarek have any lingering effects?" I interrupted.

"Not unless he decides to keep doing it while he's here." Astral led us into the mouth of a large tunnel of some kind. A path had been cleared along the side of it and soon, we reached a door. Esme hadn't said a single word this whole time and kept a healthy distance between herself and the rest of us.

Astral was visibly struggling to give her space.

The bunker barely showed signs of occupation, but as soon as I stepped inside I felt another odd feeling. Again, it was unlike anything I'd felt before. A tingling sensation at the base of my skull and the nape of my neck.

It wasn't unpleasant, but it was distracting.

"Sae! Are you coming!?" Amie and the others had moved forward without me, and I filed away the impression for later. I walked beside Astral awkwardly as Amie and Esme were now whispering furiously to each other behind us. Although I had technically known Astral all my life, there had never been any reason for me to engage him in a one-to-one conversation before.

"Sae, may I ask you a question?"

"Yes, of course," I said hastily, not wanting to offend him.

"It's not possible for the dampening to affect you. Correct?" I nodded, "So why don't you fix his ribs? I'm sure you could get it done faster than I can."

"We're outside the borders. It's a risk we're not willing to take lightly and..." I added in a quieter voice, "I'm still struggling to control things on a smaller scale. My Light is temperamental. I'm afraid I'll hurt him or worse if I try something now."

If Astral was disappointed in me, he hid it well.

Fane, who could barely move under the current gravity levels, loudly protested being left in the infirmary. "I'm dying!" he moaned, "Sae, you don't want me to die alone do you!? After everything that's happened between us—ow!" Fane, in the act of trying to sit up, hurt himself somehow. "Sae, my one true love! Don't leave me! I'm fragile! Like krill silk!"

I couldn't help but laugh as Fane tried to look helpless and meek.

After we dosed him with pain medication and realigned his ribs, we left Fane and Zarek both to rest in the makeshift infirmary. I tried not to feel too worried about leaving them when they were vulnerable, but I couldn't help but look over my shoulder at Zarek. Even after a couple weeks of travel, I couldn't remember a time where I'd caught him so unaware.

Following Astral through the labyrinth of tunnels, I was reminded of why I'd looked up to him as a child. Astral Esholitte was a man at ease with himself, full of charm and irrelevance. It was obvious how much he wanted to shower his daughters with affection; but he held it back, conscious of how Amie and Esme were trying to come to terms with him.

Finally, we entered a room where a behemoth of a ship rested on once gleaming haunches.

A hibernating storm locked in a makeshift hanger.

The *Redemption* was a vessel in a class all of its own, designed and built by Astral from scratch, it was renowned for its speed and maneuverability. Now; however, it lay slumbering with huge pieces of it mauled to tatters. An engine had been taken out and was in carefully organized pieces to our right. There were open wounds all along its port side and belly. A large pile of mismatched scrap metal and parts littered the back wall of the room.

There, on top of a large adjustable draft table, a beautiful woman carefully soldered a neat line on a propulsion disk. Titan red hair pinned up for the task, her lithe figure was graceful and deliberate as she circled the disk, paying us no attention while she worked. It wasn't until the seal was completed that she put her torch down and addressed her husband absently.

"Did you pick up those linking cuffs I saw over by section eight? I swear it's the only way we're going to be able to fix the pressure valve in the..." Anera's torch dropped to the ground where the automatic shut off went into effect. She pulled off her safety goggles and approached us in a careful, measured pace.

As she got closer, her eyes began to fill with tears.

The last few steps were taken at a run and she threw herself at her daughters, not giving Esme the chance to reject her. The next few moments were filled with tears, explanations, apologies, and the sheer joy of being together after so long. Esme broke down in her mother's arms and spoke no more of her anger.

Anera embraced me as well and it was just as a surprise now as it was back when I was a child. Unlike her husband, she had recognized me instantly as soon she'd gotten over the shock of seeing her grown daughters. She smelled exactly the same, like warm linens and sunny, summer days.

I returned the hug and it was like I was three years old again.

She used to pick me up when I was an infant, even when my nurses didn't dare, and had always been a source of unexpected comfort and acceptance. She had once sung me lullabies.

As Anera held me, an unknown man walked in.

Astral and Anera went silent as he leaned against the door frame and yawned. His light blue eyes were curiously taking us in, but he seemed in no way in a hurry to join us. He was quite beautiful. Tousled silvery blond hair and thickly lashed eyes gave him a dreamy quality, as if he were a trickster of ancient myth.

He looked as if he were half asleep, but perhaps it was all a ruse as his voice came out clear and authoritative when he chose to speak.

"Family reunion Anera?" His mouth curved into a lazy smile.

Instead of answering, she and Astral exchanged a glance.

Then they both looked at me and then back at him.

I did not like the direction this encounter was taking. There was already something odd about him, something that set my instincts thrumming, but their strange behavior solidified my discomfort.

They seemed to come to a conclusion as Anera broke away to go to the man in the doorway. Astral put his hand on my shoulder.

"Sae, would you mind going back to yourself?"

"In front of a stranger?" Baffled, I waited to hear his explanation, but it didn't seem forthcoming. "I don't think that's a good idea."

"Sae, I promise that I have a good reason to ask. Trust me?"

When he put it that way, I had no real reason not to trust Astral.

It was always easier to undo something than to change it from its original form, so it was a quick change. I was now taller than Astral by a noticeable margin, making me feel self-conscious all over again. Also, my clothes needed a refit.

My midriff and calves were bare now.

"So why do I need to look like myself?" I asked as I tugged on my poncho to cover my stomach. My hair was still pulled back in the braid I'd put it in, so it was simple to maneuver it outside of my clothing. The shoes were another matter—I had to kick them off—I blinked when Astral put both hands on my shoulders.

He turned me around to face the strange man who was now looking right at me with vibrant, glacier blue eyes. Eyes that, now that he was only an arm's length away, I could recognize were the exact same shade and shape as Mother's.

He stared at me.

I stared at him.

"Sae, meet Kelex Raajali." Anera slapped him on the back.

"Kelex, meet Saekonari Raajali!" Astral said at the same time as his wife. "Your granddaughter."

Chapter 16: Imperfections

What was the appropriate thing to say when faced with a long-dead relative? Nice to meet you? How was death? No. That would be stupid. Was there any kind of protocol I could fall back on? Was I letting the silence stretch on too long? I was. This man had raised Mother. Oh my good Empress why hadn't my lessons prepared me to introduce myself to my grandfather lost in the middle of nowhere with no prior warning? Should I wait for him to say something first? He wasn't saying anything so did that mean he was waiting for me to say something? But what did this man want me to say!? Should I apologize for not saying something sooner? Did he want an apology? Sometimes Mother didn't want one, was this one of those times? Should I not stare? No it was impolite not to look someone in the eye when in a conversation, but it wasn't really a conversation since neither of us had spoken yet.

"H-hello."

Was that really the best I could come up with!?

I could feel the Esholittes staring at us and to further my mortification, Kelex Raajali began to circle around me as if to peruse me from all angles. I could do nothing but stand there and contemplate exactly all the things I should have done before meeting him, like wash my hands and prepare a short but meaningful monologue. What must he think of me?

"Well, you look nothing like me. Lucky you!" He grinned and linked his arm with mine, leading me toward a small seating area in the corner. "Good thing I woke up from my nap today, eh? Astral wasn't kidding when he said you look just like her. Universe help us, Leti must have loved it when she saw this—" He tugged at my braid gently. "And I can imagine that's why it's so damn long. I tried long hair once, Shimi liked it but it was way too much work."

"Shimi is my grandmother? Is she here!?" Liashimi Direane Helios Raajali, 10th Empress of Elysia and possibly the youngest Empress ever to pass on. Maybe they were too young to pass, and they were here for some reason!?

No consort had ever outlived their Empress.

"No, your grandmother really did pass on."

Kelex collapsed on a settee, his limbs carelessly relaxed. I stood where I was until he patted the seat next to him. I sat down quickly, unsure if I had said or done something wrong already.

The Esholittes had discreetly made their exit, and I found myself alone with my grandfather and very, very scared.

I could feel his eyes on me as I stared down at my lap. I knew nothing about him. I had never seen any pictures or personal records of my grandparents. I knew he was waiting for me to speak and I forced myself to ask the obvious questions weighing down on us both. "I'm sorry, but why are you here? Why didn't you go with Grandmother?"

"I thought I did." Kelex sighed. "Somehow I screwed it all up and I woke up here. A few months later and Anera and Astral came to keep me company. A few days more and you appeared."

His explanation made no sense.

He was supposed to have died ages ago.

Anera and Astral had been missing for years, not days.

"I can see the planets turning in your head." He chuckled, "You want to know why I woke up from my nap today? I felt the time readjusting. Thought Astral finally cracked it, but I'm guessing it was you. Did you happen to stop a little spinning wheel?"

I nodded, mystified.

"It compressed time on-world. You should have seen their faces when they found me!" He went on to briefly explain how Anera identified it as an old Elysian time-space experiment. How it got there was anyone's guess.

"But why didn't you stop the wheel and leave?" He frowned and I instantly regretted questioning him. I didn't know my grandfather well enough to gauge his mood or predict his reactions.

"How much did your mother tell you about Shimi and I?"

Taken aback, I almost told him the truth.

That mother had never once talked about them.

Most of my studies on my bloodline were purely theoretical in nature. I studied their major legislative and cultural influences, their impact on Elysia, and the intricacies of their leadership styles. Besides the first and second Emperors, who were of the seven founders, emphasis was largely placed on the Empresses. The Tenth Empress had been among them but...

I had to be judicious with my words.

"I never asked her personally." I tried to relax my hands from their white-knuckled state. "But I'm sure she would have told me when she thought it was the right time. Mother must have—"

"You know, you're nothing like Leti."

My heart sank.

"I know Grandfather. I'm sorry."

"Why? You remind me of Shimi when she was young." His words floored me. "Shimi was shy too when I met her... and you sound just like she did." Kelex smiled wistfully and I was further shocked when he held his right hand out and allowed his unity mark to appear on his palm.

I'd never seen one before.

It was a private affair that was rarely seen by other people. Elysians permanently stained their palms with a pattern when they were certain that their partner was a life-long companion and it wasn't connected to any legal bonding ceremony. A person could go through several established relationships without, but the Raajali in particular had always been notoriously monogamous.

All Empresses and their consorts were thought to have one.

Each design was unique, but a normal Elysian marking was shaped into a triangle, to represent the past, present, and future. Only the Raajali ever used a circular pattern, as eternity only ever applied to our family. My grandfather's mark was stained with a rich, vibrant gold and was absolutely beautiful. It was a given that my grandmother's would have been on her left hand, so that when they walked together, their hands would hold their promise between them. Whenever they were apart, that promise would be carried until they met again.

"When I joined the family I gained extraordinary power in return. But my tie to the universe is through your grandmother, your mother, and now you. Here, outside the borders, with so much time having past, without Shimi... I'm really just a bad imitation of who I was with her. I should be apologizing to you."

□I had never felt grief like my grandfather's.

□A sadness and pain beyond reason.

Not knowing if he'd accept the gesture, I reached out tentatively for my grandfather's unmarked hand. Mother had never enjoyed physical affections, but Kelex Raajali not only accepted the comfort I offered, he smiled gratefully for it. For the first time, I saw what those eyes looked like when they warmed.

"When I first woke up here my grief was horrible. I simply didn't try to leave. I had been sleeping for who knows how long when Anera found me and woke me up. Leti had been so happy to be left in charge, I wasn't in the right state of mind, and I'm still not sure if I can take going home without..."

He reached into his coat and took out a projector disk, when activated it displayed a tall, black-skinned woman with thick, shoulder length curls. She was beautiful. As she walked and laughed, she emitted an aura of boundless energy and stunning grace.

Her smile was breathtaking.

"You miss her."

"With every dim flicker of my soul. I tried to die with her, but there was a part of me that didn't want to go. I wanted to live with Shimi, to be with her. I had doubts that we would be together after life, about leaving your mother alone, and for not waiting for you to be born. Those doubts just never went away."

My grandfather was preserved at peak health when he unified with my grandmother and joined the family. He looked barely older than I was, but now I could see the centuries falling down on his shoulders. The trace of eons that lived in his eyes. "For anyone in our family, I'd guess you have to want it. I suppose I didn't want to die enough for it to work... it still won't work."

"But why here? It can't be a coincidence."

"No, you're right. The universe circles around you, Saekonari. Raajali always end up where they're supposed to. "Fate slumbers in the Empress' pocket" and all that. You didn't even know I was here, but you found me anyway didn't you?"

Kelex closed the projector with a flick of his wrist and placed it carefully inside his coat, right over his heart; and it was in that moment I decided to inform my grandfather of all that had led up to this unlikely reunion.

Zarek's memories. Cira. How I disobeyed Mother. How I was afraid of all the laws I'd broken and how nervous I was that this trip would end prematurely or badly. He listened and I began to relax after it became apparent that he would not interrupt me; after I finished my summary of the last few weeks, Grandfather looked as if he had questions, which I expected.

"You like this boy? Zarek?"

I wasn't expecting that question.

"Of course I like him, but that's not the important part."

"The next Emperor of Elysia is always the important part."

Speechless, I watched as my grandfather; the former Emperor; waggled his eyebrows at me. Was he joking? Should I laugh?

He certainly was laughing now.

"I don't think I find this funny, Grandfather."

"Yeah, I didn't either when I found myself lying awake at night thinking about Shimi. You have no idea how horrible that was. I'm an Allusi for Empress' sake."

That would explain why he kept talking about naps.

Allusi spent as much time as possible asleep. They believed time spent in the unconscious world was far more valuable than time in the waking universe. I had no idea that my grandfather was an Allusi; they rarely ever left their home worlds and could spend days, weeks even, sleeping. Their biggest cultural exports were slumber parties and sedatives designed to invoke lucid dreaming.

"Don't I get a choice in the next Emperor?" If it were true, I would only have until the end of his lifetime to bind him to me. It was too soon. I wasn't even a single century old yet. I'd always believed I would have more time. I didn't want to be part of a pair before I fully experienced who I was individually.

"I'm just hoping I like this one. Coliv is a pain in the ass."

Did Anera and Astral not tell him about my father?

I wasn't about to be the one who told him.

"Listen to me, Sae." He gave my shoulder a gentle squeeze and I tried not to make too much of the small gesture of affection. "There's no reason to be worried. I never wanted to be an Emperor, but I wouldn't have any other fate; because it was the only path I could walk with Shimi."

"But what about Cira? How does she fit into all of this?"

"You know what? I'm not sure, but..." He stood up and patted down his pockets. "Ah-ha!" he said before pulling out a piece of Zarek's memories and dropping it into my lap with a flourish. "I found that when I woke up today. So if I were you, I would rethink why this girl would go through so much trouble in the first place."

"I still don't think this is a good idea." Esme said tearfully as she clung to her mom and dad. "Why can't you come with us? We can all go home together!"

It was early the next morning.

Grandfather and I had spoken well into the night. We had strolled through the corridors of the bunker, stopping briefly at the infirmary so he could fix Fane's bones and get a look at Zarek, whom he declared "just about as pretty as I am."

My grandfather was kind. He told me to call him by his first name and answered any question I asked. It overwhelmed me that Kelex genuinely seemed to like me. Mother must have felt their loss keenly to have never spoken about them.

She was going to be so happy to see him.

Maybe it would even change her mind about my own actions.

"We've talked about this sweetie," Anera gently wiped away Esme's tears. "If you girls are discovered, we can say you snuck out on a rebellious whim. There would be a bit of paperwork but if we're caught with you, it's a much more serious case. Especially as we've been missing for so long."

"But we just found you again!" Esme cried.

"We know, we know," Astral stroked her hair, now returned to its silky black color, soothingly. "But we've been away from home too long and we need to see your brothers." The man looked close to crying himself at the thought. "And Kelex is convinced Sae needs to finish this trip you've all started on."

Amie took her turn in the circle of her parents' arms.

"We are so proud of you for staying by her side."

Anera hugged Amie so tight, she squeaked.

"You're positive we won't get caught?" Amie asked again.

They'd explained I should feel free to do things as long as we weren't in heavily monitored locations or areas restricted to the public. Anera explained that when Elysians went outside the border, they voluntarily wore cuffs that tracked them as a gesture of goodwill, but none of us were restricted by one. There were ways to identify me, but no one would think to use them.

"But if you do trip an alarm. Run like hell." Kelex added dryly.

So here we were, with me about to interrupt the Empress of Elysia's schedule and rip a hole in spacetime into Mother's office.

The plan was simple enough.

I would inform Mother that I'd found Astral, Anera, and somehow her long-dead father. While she was preoccupied with shock and awe, I'd send them through and close the gap before anyone was the wiser. Astral would go through official channels to reclaim the Redemption. Grandfather would tell Mother why I should be allowed to stay outside for a little longer.

It was a good plan.

I couldn't seem to bring myself to do it.

I knew I needed to do it and change back into my disguise before Zarek woke up, but still, I procrastinated. It was about the right time for Mother to be in her study but I was afraid she was going to be angry—really, really angry.

"Saekonari? What is it, my girl?" Kelex asked quizzically.

"Nothing! Are we all ready?" I tried not to sound nervous.

It didn't work.

I stepped forward into the empty air hanger I'd just cleared out moments ago. Kelex moved to give me some space and I tried to think calm thoughts. Hand gestures weren't really necessary, but they helped to draw a visual as I wasn't just practicing with theory.

The area directly in front of me rippled and swirled like fabric.

The tunnel shot out and inwards into empty space, crumpling the distance in between. There was a slight disturbance when I bypassed the border, but it was nothing compared to the vastness of the universe. It felt good, like stretching your muscles leisurely after too much time spent in one position.

Mother was already standing and facing my direction when the other end stabilized. My pulse leapt into my eardrums. It was ridiculous to feel as if I were in danger all of sudden. It was just Mother; I had seen her almost every day of my entire life and loved her with all my heart.

I just hated it when she looked at me like that.

"Hello Mother, I—"

"Saekonari. Come back here. Now."

Oh yes.

She was unbelievably angry.

"You have been missing for over a month." The Empress' eyes were entirely iced over. "Do you think it's my responsibility to look for you all over Elysia? Do you know how embarrassing it would have been if anyone had noticed your absence? Now I know you left our borders. You ran away when you didn't get what you wanted. You are a shameful example of everything that I—"

"Mother, I'm sorry I left without your permission, but—"

"Do you know how humiliated I would be if you were found breaking interstellar treaties? Do you understand the sheer arrogance and stupidity that must have led you to act this way for a man? You have never been able to live up to your name and now I have doubts that you ever will. You have been—"

"Mother, please—" I flinched at the look on her face, my words drying up in my throat. I had been prepared to take on the consequences of my actions, but somehow the reality was even worse than anything I could imagine. Of course Mother was disappointed in me. I deserved it. When Mother spoke again, she sounded as if she was barely containing herself.

"I hope this unbelievably repulsive behavior of yours was worth it because you have forfeited all of the privileges that I have allowed you. It was a mistake to be so lenient in your upbringing. It was a mistake to put my trust in you. Amythesia and Esmeralda may have been pulled into your antics, but you have acted with the moral judgment of a lowborn, lying tramp—"

"Oh like hell am I going to let you slut-shame my granddaughter!" Mother and I were stunned into silence when Kelex appeared in front of me. His normally sleepy eyes were narrowed into familiar, frigid blue slits.

I'd forgotten he was in the room.

I had forgotten I had an audience at all, I felt so numb.

"Deletii Raajali. What in the ever-loving fuck!?" My grandfather's anger burned hot instead of cold. "I know exactly who died and made you Empress and she did not raise you to turn into—whatever it is you're trying to do! You act as if you didn't sneak off every other damn week!"

"Dad!?" Mother had gone pale. "How—"

"My granddaughter would have explained if you'd— "

"Saekonari. If this is some kind of joke I swear—"

"Uh-uh. Saekonari don't listen to your mother. Leti, we are going to have to have a serious talk and all I wanted to do was sleep in my own damn bed again. Do you know how wrong it is that I have had to sleep on a cot? Me! For months! Universe help us all. Astral! Say goodbye to your kids because we're going home. Leti, I've only been gone for what? A few millennia at best!? And you..."

He continued to lecture my mother as Astral and Anera stepped through to the other side. For a moment, The Empress seemed to soften at the sight of her Sentinels, but it was soon overtaken again by anger. It didn't seem like my grandfather's words were making much of a difference.

No matter who was present, she was still furious with me.

Once they were safely across, Grandfather paused in his monologue to ruffle my hair affectionately, as Amie did with her little brothers sometimes. "I'm glad I stuck around to meet you. Don't worry, I'll set Leti straight before you get back."

Mother's expression darkened even further.

It was going to be one hell of a talk.

Hours later, I sat in the infirmary waiting for Zarek to wake up. Amie had gone to show Fane the Redemption now that I could lower the gravity for him to move around freely. Esme and I sat in silence while I tried to lift small pieces of metal up and down off the floor. Unfortunately for me, it disintegrated.

Again. I put another piece of scrap on the floor.

"Sae, give it up. It isn't going to work." Esme grumbled.

"I'm hoping that practicing will make it work eventually."

I went through another two pieces before Esme spoke again.

"Look. I'm sorry if you think I've been giving you a hard time. You haven't even been trying to listen to me! You've been acting crazy for weeks and you really hurt me too! I'm sorry if I went too far. I just want what's best for you. Okay?"

"Esme, I know it's been stressful lately, I get it. It's alright."

"Sae!" Esme jumped up and hugged me, breaking my concentration and making another piece of scrap vaporize. "Don't you ever get tired of being so perfect?" She squeezed harder, so I hugged her back just as enthusiastically. It was good to know she supported me despite what I put her through.

The next few rounds of lifting the small object were a bust as Esme cheered me on out loud, but I was too happy that she was back to her cheerful self to care. There had to be some trick to it that I wasn't understanding.

I tried once again only to see it crumble into more dust.

"You're trying too hard, pixie."

Esme leaped up out of her chair at the sound of Zarek's voice. It was funny to see her try to take Zarek's temperature and test his reflexes to see if he was alright. She was the only one of us with official medical training so it was good of her to step in and I was grateful for the time to think.

Was this how Grandmother felt? How Mother felt?

I didn't understand how they could feel so out of control and still act rationally. I kept my back turned to Esme and Zarek as I tried to lift another piece.

It exploded into dust.

Zarek took a small piece from my pile and placed it on the ground. One of his hands was braced on the back of my chair. I dared not move a centimeter. "Don't give it so much of your attention. Be strict with it." His voice was low and encouraging. "That'll teach it to behave."

There was no way this could work; my brain was like gelatin.

The scrap metal lifted off the ground and *then* exploded.

"Well, no one's perfect," Zarek laughed.

Empress help me.

Chapter 17: Bitter Colds

When one encounters meteorological phenomena of an extreme variety, it is often accompanied by the reasonable expectation of being able to separate oneself from said event if desired.

In other words, we should have checked the weather.

The sudden transition into pelting ice and snow gave the impression of blindness. Amie had chosen a place far from any signs of life and now we knew why that was. The landscape loomed menacingly; jagged spikes propelled themselves upwards into the dark sky. Much of the surrounding tundra was carved into such gravity defying sculptures and yet they blocked none of the screaming wind from cutting through my friends' skin and freezing the moisture from their eyes.

Zarek and Fane wouldn't last long in this climate. Although I could sense civilization in several directions, it was too risky to simply appear in what would be heavily isolated settlements. Especially dressed so lightly as we were. I didn't have to experience it firsthand to know the subzero temperatures must be painful for my friends, including Amie and Esme.

I melted a small hole in which I could carve out a suitable temporary refuge. Not too far beneath the surface were empty cavities in the permafrost, making it easy to melt out a decent shelter. Soon we were out of the wind, but I hadn't considered that the wind was not the worst of it. We were soon drenched from the melting snow and ice, making our clothes stiff with frost.

My Sentinels were truly tapped out.

They couldn't even warm themselves.

Even so, I didn't dare try and warm the others directly.

"Too cold. So c-cold. F-freezing!" Fane's skin was pale, which I assumed was not a good sign. A fire would eat up the limited oxygen as I sealed the entrance, so instead I searched underneath for some sort of rock bed. Finding one less than a few kilometers below, I dragged a piece of it upwards until it cracked through the center of our little refuge. I heated the rock until it began to steam but was still bearable enough for Fane to rest against it.

Until the blizzard slowed down, we'd stay and regroup.

"Sae, just say the word and we can get married."

Fane slid down to the ground, hugging a piece of the rock.

"Get in line." I bumped my shoulder playfully against his.

"Hey, I only need another ten or so people out of the way before I can't be prosecuted for my crimes, I could be a prince any day now!" He managed to pry an arm away from the rock long enough to pick up my hand, his own fingers still shivering, and place exaggerated kisses all over it.

I laughed. "Even if you don't get your name cleared, you can always come home with me Fane." He managed to smile with chattering teeth, and I noticed his flesh was still cold. So I scooted over so I was sitting back-to-back with him. Fane made a dramatic groaning noise as my body heat sank into him.

I'd need to locate suitable clothes for him before we moved on.

Esme had burrowed herself against Amie, her entire body wracked in shivers. Esme hated the cold. She had found a particularly flat piece of rock and was curled up on of it with Zarek at her back. It was pitch dark in our little cavern with only the heated rock giving off a soft glow.

In the ensuing quiet, I looked over to check on the others.

I caught Zarek staring at me and couldn't help but jump.

"You've been holding out on me, pixie."

Zarek wasn't impressed by my confusion. "You melted and refroze a cave to a length and width of over five meters. Lifted over three tons of rock out of the ice and heated it from subzero. You've been holding out on me."

I'd gone too far. I should have been more conservative or acted more tired. The corners were all exactly ninety degrees and I should have been less exact. With everything that had just happened with Grandfather and the Esholittes, I'd forgotten that Zarek hadn't seen me do anything until now. I had been in a hurry because of the weather and now seemed suspicious.

"I'm sorry Zarek, I didn't think—"

"Didn't think what, exactly?" Zarek's tone froze the words in my throat more effectively than any amount of ice could have. "That I wouldn't notice? That it wouldn't matter? A lot of things aren't adding up and you know why."

"Just because you didn't know doesn't mean I'm a liar."

"No. Lying to me makes you a liar, pixie."

A surge of anger caught me off guard. My nerves, already frayed from seeing Mother, felt rough and irritated. There was a voice inside that I didn't want to listen to, that said the Empress was right and I was wrong and that everything I was doing wrong was for the wrong reasons. He was catching me at a bad time.

I just needed a minute to myself to calm down.

"Zarek, I have many of the same questions that you—"

"What else are you hiding? What's in this for you!?"

I was standing and so was he all of a sudden.

Forget the cold, I was boiling.

"Nothing. Okay? There's nothing I'm getting out of this!" I raised my voice and I never raised my voice. "I don't even know why I'm here Zarek! You obviously don't want me here. Everyone keeps telling me this is all a bad idea, including you and maybe I'm starting to think so too—!"

"Woah, woah!" Fane abandoned his warm rock to get between us. He put his hands on my shoulders to try and deescalate the situation, but for once I didn't want to deescalate. He tried to take me to the side, but I didn't budge as Zarek and I glared at each other over his shoulder. "Let's all just take a second here."

My anger was heating the air. When a drop of water fell on my head from the warming ceiling, I tried to take Fane's advice and let him throw a shivering arm around my shoulders.

An incredibly threatening sound came out of Zarek.

It was almost a snarl.

"Fane. I swear if you don't take your hands off of her—"

"Don't tell Fane what to do! He can do whatever he wants!"

"Well if that's how you like it, pixie."

Whatever he was insinuating, I hated it.

"That is not my name!"

Had he ever used my name this whole trip? Even once?

At that point, Amie jumped in between us with Fane, very clearly sending Zarek the message to back off.

For some reason that made me even angrier.

"Amie. I am not a child and I didn't ask for help."

It took a second, but Amie begrudgingly grabbed Fane's arm and dragged him back to the rock where Esme was sitting up now, watching Zarek and I with wide eyes.

I put a sound barrier between us.

If Zarek was going to yell at me, I'd rather he do it privately.

"Why do they listen to you?" Zarek demanded. "Why should I?"

"You don't need to! I'm not trying to make you do anything!"

"Do you know where Alexi is? Answer me."

That name again.

"I don't even know who she is!" I was sick of hearing her name.

"Do you know where she is?" He asked me again as if I was somehow magically going to pull her out of my pockets. As if I had her stashed away and was keeping him from going to look for her himself since he didn't seem to care whether or not I meant anything to him—Empress no, that was so unfair of me. I couldn't blame him for not knowing how much he meant to me.

"Do you know where Alexi is!?"

"No!" I was so tired of yelling already. How did people do this on a regular basis? "I don't. I don't know who she is or where she is or even why you think I would know! Not one of us—" I gestured wildly to myself and the others, "—knows a-anything!"

My voice broke on the last word and I immediately turned around, crossing my arms to try and make my hands stop shaking. I was not going to fall apart. My clothes were still stiff from the cold and I knew it was even more suspicious that I took a few steps away from the rock to get away from the others, but I didn't care right now how it looked to Zarek.

I wasn't cold and I wasn't going to pretend I was.

The ice was singing.

As I got closer to the walls, I could hear the eerie moaning vibrate through hundreds of kilometers of frozen water. Although there were no signs of temperature fluctuations, there were rivers that ran in the underbelly of the tundra at breakneck speeds. Something in the water must lower its melting point so some of it froze when approaching the surface. This cycle of the water melting and freezing over and over was the source of the music.

I had never been to such a cold biome. Listening to the frozen song, it reminded me that Zarek hadn't been the only reason why I wanted to leave home. I had wanted to see the universe and now every day was so different from the day before. When was the last time an Heir had been able to freely move outside Elysia? I lightly ran my fingers across the ice, appreciating the crystalized patterns.

It was a shame I couldn't bring samples of the ice back home to the Academy to analyze further.

Brekekekex, koax, koax.

One of the oddest sounds I'd ever heard raced toward us; a strange clicking accompanied the noise and the ice beneath our feet rumbled. A visible crack broke under my left foot and I was forced to retreat away from the rest of the group.

I heard Amie yell my name.

Brekekekex, koax, koax

Rows upon rows of carnassial teeth burst through the ground, encased in the open jaw of an annelida invertebrate of gargantuan proportions. Engorged red feelers gyrated all over its body as a gelatinous fluid sprayed out of its open maw. It had no visible eyes or nose; the body had already stretched the height of the cavern, yet an unknown amount of mass still remained tunneled under the ice. The head was a grotesque amalgamation of dark burgundy skin and clicking tusks. This creature of pulsating flesh writhed as more and more of the tail slithered into view, forcing me to move even further away from my friends.

I could see Amie yelling, trying to get the thing's attention as it turned in my direction. She was fumbling in our bags to find her weapons; I couldn't see Fane or Esme and I didn't have the luxury of worrying about them. I dove to the right as the head struck into the ice where I'd just been standing, its teeth smashing through meters of solid ice easily. If I could circle around, I could leap over a section of the tail and get to the others, but I was forced backward as the head took a hairpin turn toward me once again.

It was fixated on me, I realized in horror.

The thing was obviously carnivorous, so it was hungry. I didn't want to kill it just for going after a possible meal, but I also did not want to be digested today. I was about to try a different route when I ran straight into Zarek.

He shoved something into my hand.

How many weapons could one man carry on him!? This one was longer than my forearm with pointed teeth and almost no curve. He carried an identical on in his other hand. Before either of us could say anything, the worm made a screeching sound that didn't seem very friendly and lunged at us.

We dove to opposite sides of the head and I tried to stab what looked like a nonvital spot noting that Zarek stabbed a similar spot on the other side of the worm's body. What I hadn't been expecting was the knife to stick into the animal as hard as it did and it was wrenched out of my grip. The head flailed upwards, the knife still lodged in its flesh, and then redirected, diving back into the ground and causing the ice beneath us to cave inwards.

Amie had gotten close enough to us that she was swept up into the avalanche. The worm's tail broke through the ice and whipped us down into a newly unearthed crevasse. Zarek, Amie, and I were plunged down a steep, jagged chute and into a current of water so strong that Amie didn't get the chance to orient herself before her head slammed into a chuck of ice and she went limp.

Amie! I swam over to where she was and grabbed her arm, I tried to swim away from the bottom, but it was quickly apparent that the current had dragged us away from our entry point. Amie could survive longer than most without oxygen, but I wasn't sure if that meant forever. Zarek appeared on Amie's other side. He wrapped one arm around her waist and grabbed my hand before swimming at an impressive rate in a direction I wouldn't have chosen myself.

I didn't know if Zarek could see in such darkness, but eventually, he changed directions and we swam up into an air pocket. It couldn't have been more than five minutes underwater, but I had to remind myself to gasp for breath.

Normal people needed to breathe and I needed to be normal.

To my relief, as soon as we emerged, Amie awoke and violently coughed up water. Zarek pulled her all the way out, but let go once Amie pushed at his arm.

She took a moment to herself before asking if I was alright.

Amie tried to hide it from me, but she was freezing. I didn't want to expend any more energy in front of Zarek, but I had little else in terms of available alternatives. Amie wouldn't die from hypothermia, but Zarek could.

So, in the end, I raised another rock and heated it.

I knew I ran the risk of Zarek questioning me again and I honestly didn't know how to respond if he did. Was it time to tell him the whole truth? Would he even believe me? No matter how I thought he would react, I just didn't feel ready to tell him; I dreaded every second that passed until he finally spoke.

"Pixie. Now I don't mind lending you my toys but it's rude not to return them." He lounged against the warm rock like an overgrown *felid* while Amie lay next to him belly-side down. Their clothes were steaming from the heat.

The way the rock was shaped, I could either lay down next to Zarek or, as far as he knew, I could freeze to death.

I should have made the dumb rock bigger.

"You have an exact copy. It couldn't have been a significant loss."

"It's a tragedy of epic proportions, they're meant to be a pair." Zarek opened one eye to see me sitting as far away as I could get. "Pixie. If you don't lay down and relax, you'll hurt my feelings and make it unreasonably difficult to grovel."

"Am I groveling or are you?" I laid down as he chuckled.

"That was me groveling. It's your turn now."

I knew he was joking, but...

"I shouldn't have raised my voice at you Zarek, I'm sorry."

"I see you're better at groveling than I am." I held very still as Zarek's hand hovered over my forehead, pushing wet strands of hair from my face. "And I can see why Fane enjoyed your fondling. You're as warm as a summer on Okniuse."

"I've never fondled anyone in my life."

"Oh? What a waste of perfectly clever hands."

"You two know I'm still here, right?" Amie sounded annoyed but I knew she was embarrassed; this was just her way of hiding it; and it occurred to me I'd gotten to understand Amie more in the last few weeks than in an entire childhood.

Esme had always done most of the talking.

We'd rarely ever spent time together without her.

"Didn't I just save you from a particularly gruesome death?" A grin flashed on his face when Amie didn't reply and I couldn't help but grin back. "You'd think she'd be more grateful," Zarek mock-whispered to me and I had to hold back from laughing at Amie's indignant huff.

"We need to get back to the others." Amie sat up and I saw that she'd rolled over at some point so both sides of her clothing were now practically dry. "Stay here." Weapon in hand, Amie went to scout the path ahead and left us alone.

Although she had left a sizable portion of the rock empty, Zarek did not move to allow more room for me. I doggedly stared up at the darkness and ignored the feeling of my insides twisting themselves into nervous knots. I could see him looking at me in my peripheral line of sight and continued to stare straight ahead.

"Sae..." I nearly missed the rest of his sentence.

"... do you want me to stop calling you pixie?"

"Why do you?" He'd never called me it before we left Elysia.

"Thought it was obvious." His voice was oddly rough. "You're tiny." I opened my mouth to disagree and then closed it when I remembered he was correct. In this form, I was quite small.

"I don't mind." I swallowed before whispering. "I like your nicknames. They're very... endearing."

We both went quiet at my admission.

"I shouldn't have called you a liar."

"You had every right to be suspicious—"

He shushed me, laughing quietly. "I'm not netting for an apology, pixie. I'm trying to give one. Now say you forgive me so we can stop this melodrama. Empress knows I've had enough for one day." Zarek had come closer as he spoke, so much so that I could tell his clothes had dried.

"I forgive you."

Zarek ran his fingers through my hair as he gently untangled my braid. The slight brush of his fingertips on my scalp was causing a physical reaction I had no hope of controlling. No one had ever treated me so informally and I was suddenly afraid he would stop if he knew the truth. His next whisper was right beside my ear.

"You should have made me work a bit harder."

"Okay." I made another decision. "Who is Alexi?" I turned my head when his hands stilled in my hair. His expression was guarded once more but I knew she was important to him. I had to know if I was going to cross an invisible line somewhere along the way. How he felt mattered just as much as how I felt.

"Not many people know my secrets, pixie."

"I promise I won't ever betray you or your secrets, Zarek."

He laughed again, but this time it held the bitter tint of cynicism. Zarek let go of my hair so that he could take a turn staring up at the ceiling. "Why is it so damn easy to believe you? You might mean it now, but you'll change your mind about me eventually."

"It won't matter if my opinion of you changes." Seeing him now, I could pick his eyes out of a billion worlds. "I keep my promises."

He didn't answer right away and I didn't expect him to. So I turned my head to look up again and give him time. The faintest flicker of something moved across the ceiling as I did so, and I didn't have to ask to know that Zarek had seen it too. I allowed the light floating above us to dim and fade out. As it did so, a web of red light stretched across the once-dark crevices of the ice above.

One by one, the lights seemed to run along in all directions, revealing a swirling pattern being repeated over and over again in an ever-expanding fractal. Strands of light would move along the tubes, overlapping each other in a rapid sequence.

"It's some kind of biological system," I said in awe. It was a kind of chemiluminescence fauna that I'd never come across in my studies. "Do you think it's some kind of fungus? Oh, maybe it's a kind of slime mold! Or a bacterium that only propagates in sub-zero temperatures. The rock we're lying on is heavy in calcium; it could be a key component that lends itself to the... I'm sorry. This can't be very interesting to you." It was a bad habit I needed to suppress.

Mother hated it when I went on a tangent.

"Actually, I was just thinking about the adenosine triphosphate that could be coming into play. Too bad we don't have any optical biosensors... oh wait. I do."

Against my usual protocols of decorum, I made an excited grab for the device he held, only for him to pull back at the last second.

"Patience pixie." He laughed as I reached for it again, only to have him raise it out of arm's length. If only I had my real arms, I could make a decent play for it.

"Why show me the biosensor if you're going to monopolize it?"

"We can share, that's why. Come here."

Come where? I was right next to him. Any closer and I'd be lying on his outstretched arm... oh. "I'm fine where I am, thank you."

No biosensor was worth moving even a bit closer.

"Oh? Why not?" I just shook my head vehemently.

"You know why not, Zarek."

"Enlighten me."

"You're taunting me."

"But you make it so easy." I actually yelped out loud as Zarek snaked his arm around my waist and effortlessly tugged me closer so that we could both view the biosensor. "This isn't so bad, is it?" He said against the hair right above my ear.

Great universe above, what had I done to get myself here?

Whatever peril my brain had gone into frenzied alarm for proved to be unfounded. The minutes passed and Zarek quietly narrated some of the initial findings in real time. The arm that was pressed against me after the first tug was in no way constricting and I knew I could escape if I wanted to. I soon discovered that lying with another being was surprisingly comfortable.

It was only once I settled in his arms did he tell me.

"Alexi Deutreax is my sister."

"... You told me you were an only child." I tried to keep as still as possible, but so much about him now made sense. When we were children, I'd asked him if he had any siblings or close family members. He'd told me no.

Apparently, I should have checked if it was the truth.

"I tell everyone I'm an only child. It's easier that way."

"But you're looking for her?"

"Yes."

I'd grown up knowing that the possibility of a sibling was impossible, but the Esholittes were fiercely loyal to each other, and I knew how protective Amie was of her younger brothers. It was no wonder Zarek had been so upset if he'd suspected I was involved. I didn't dare voice any of the questions that now bounced inside, but I needed to give him something in return for his confidence. I had a feeling that telling me had not come easily.

"Zarek, after we find all your memories, I'll help you find her."

"If we manage to keep breathing until then, I just might let you."

I tried my hand at bantering. "Who's going to stop me? You?"

"Yes me, no one else could even hope to stop you." I felt a trill of exhilaration as I felt his arm squeeze me ever so slightly against him. I couldn't stop smiling at him... that is of course, until I heard someone clear their throat from behind Zarek. A light fell over us, and the soft glow from the ceiling was instantly dark once more in the wake of the light in Amie's hand.

"*Ahem.*" Amie pointedly looked at anywhere but where I was lying on Zarek's arm and I could swear she was holding back a grin as I buried my face in my hands. I would never hear the end of this if Amie ever told Esme.

If it were only possible to die of embarrassment.

"We found slime mold," Zarek said innocently

He did not help as I moved to disengage myself.

Amie raised her eyebrows but didn't respond.

"I found a route back up."

"Great!" My voice was too loud. "Let's get going."

As I walked past, she couldn't resist.

"Slime mold?"

"Don't ask."

Chapter 18: Slaves

We were being followed.

Underneath the icy ground of this planet was a labyrinth of passageways, carved by centuries of crashing, freezing, and melting water. Some of the tunnels forced us to proceed one by one. Others were so short Amie and Zarek doubled over in order to get through. We passed several waterfalls and were forced at one point to wade through a stream that, while it only reached my friends' knees, was hip-deep for me. Some caverns with thinner ceilings were lit by the light of the upper world and others were pitch dark. Either way, we quickly made our way to higher ground, dodging icicles and sheer cliffs along the way.

My sense of direction was inhibited by the constant drum of the ice. The song was no longer as wonderous and much more of a nuisance when trying to navigate an exit strategy. It was possible Esme would go looking for us, but it was equally likely she would choose to wait with Fane until we returned. The creature that'd attacked us had made a hasty exit after being wounded and we could only hope that it didn't get hungry enough to return.

From the start of our ascent, I heard someone's footsteps. I had hoped it was just a natural sound echoing in the ice, but I couldn't ignore it once I saw them. Just as we'd scaled a slope of jagged ice, their shadow creeped into view directly below us. They most likely believed that we wouldn't be able to see far out of the circle of light we were in, but they were wrong.

Amie and Zarek had both seen it too, I confirmed with a glance.

Whoever they were, their footsteps were as quiet as our own. They moved without a light and at a speed only those familiar with the terrain could possess. As confrontation was the last thing we needed right now, we increased our speed until it was clear that whoever they were had fallen behind. The corridor we now found ourselves in was riddled with holes large and small and we had to focus on our footing to ensure we didn't slip into a pit accidentally.

Amie's light floated in front of her by a meter or so. We were close to where we'd been sent tumbling down and the humidity was rapidly dropping as we approached the surface. We didn't anticipate any more issues.

We should have.

A head popped out of one of the holes in the ceiling and was almost brained by Amie's light before she pulled it back. Their skin was dark blue, highlighted by milky eyes framed under thick, bushy hair. Its white hair grew wildly around their head and face so thickly that, at first, I thought they were some kind of primitive primate, but I could see an intricate tattoo on their shoulder as well as a glove wrapping one of its hands.

They were of an intelligent species.

Amie demanded they identify themselves.

In answer, they bared their teeth, complete with pronounced canines, and hissed. That was all it took to inspire Amie to reach for her weapon, but as soon as it clicked out of its holster the being ducked back up and disappeared.

Amie kept her hand on it the rest of the way back.

An entire section of ice had been destroyed, leaving a mound of sharp ice chunks between us and where we had taken shelter. We could only hope it hadn't fully collapsed. Amie started to call out for her twin while Zarek and I started melting the ice. I was more prepared to answer his questions about my capabilities but, for now, it didn't seem as if he was going to ask.

Neither Esme nor Fane answered Amie's calls.

Zarek managed to break through first and we were met by the sight of our things thrown around everywhere and abandoned. In the twenty or so minutes it took to hike back, there had been a struggle, and our friends had vanished. Amie's light had been flickering out the last few minutes and was totally gone now.

She must be so tired.

"Any chance you can you find them?" Amie called out as she gathered our scattered possessions.

"Are you talking to me or Zarek?" I answered from across the room. I was looking into markings left behind by the worm, the smooth sides of its tunneling reminded me of some of the passageways we'd used to get back here. One could theorize we were in the midst of a giant burrow that could be attributed to this species... which would be absolutely fascinating. I wondered if they used some kind of sonar to navigate and if the specimen we'd seen was average-sized or even fully grown. A sample size of the larvae would help, but how to find such a nest?

"Sae!"

I hurried back to where Amie was calling me, guilty of being distracted and not listening to what she'd been saying. She was sitting on the heated rock, angrily knitting up a rip on the side of her bag. She'd laid out our things neatly and it was now easy to see that much of our supplies had been taken. All of the food, water, and several pieces of clothing were gone. We didn't have anything sentimental, but it did look like Fane's things were mostly here, while Esme's was gone entirely. As I got closer, Amie reached out her hand and dropped a small, clear vial with a black powder inside. I opened it slightly and a bitter scent hit my nose.

"A medication?" I guessed.

It was clear Amie didn't approve of the substance.

"Technically, yes." Zarek took the vial from me and stashed it in his coat. "It's more commonly known as Nitro Venom, Flashbang, Burnout, Warp Speed... do none of those sound familiar at all?" I shook my head, about as bewildered as Zarek was at my lack of recognition. "Nitro is used as a recreational drug."

"So?" There were plenty of drugs that were legal in Elysia, all of them were regulated and well-incorporated into our recreational systems. Addiction was supremely rare as to be nonexistent under the eye of the Empress.

"Sae. Nitro Venom is a bad drug to take for recreation." Amie explained. "It causes long-term damage in users, it's highly addictive, the withdrawal symptoms are often lethal, and it's a Class A felony to carry or distribute it." Amie looked at Zarek then. "Which is why we do not just put it in our pockets."

Zarek pretended not to hear her.

"So whoever took Esme and Fane must have been carrying this substance and dropped it in the struggle." I deduced. "Also, why do you know what Nitro Venom is?" Amie had recognized the drug on sight and had understood why it was bad. In fact, looking back, there were several times where it seemed like Amie or Esme knew more about the outer universe than I did.

Amie threw a pointed glance at Zarek before choosing her words to be as vague as possible. "Our parents wanted us to be taught the more unsavory parts of the outer universe. So we got a different education than you did Sae. There were just some things you didn't need to know right away."

I disagreed.

When I went back to the palace, I promised myself that I would take control of my education and stop sending my schedules to Mother for approval. It was spineless of me, but I secretly hoped my grandfather would also take my side and help me make my case. If Amie was able to learn these things, then so should I.

"We have a few options here," Amie said, finishing the repairs on her bag. "Sae, you can try to boost my signal so I can look for Esme without getting used up. I can tell Zarek how to look for Esme. Or you can try to look for Esme yourself."

None of those options were very good.

It would be a short radius to cover as they couldn't have gotten very far, but whenever I tried to lend my reserves to Amie or Esme, it hurt them. If I looked for her and Fane myself, there was also a high probability of hurting them.

Now if Zarek could learn how to—

Why was Zarek hugging me? As I was thinking, he'd snuck up behind me and had his arms around my shoulders. My train of thought had derailed and was falling off an unmapped precipice. This was not a proper place or time for this.

"Try and find your friends, pixie."

"What? Right now? Why?"

"Don't think about it too hard, go on."

I found them. One second I didn't know where they were, and now an image came clearly to mind. They were with a group of people in a caravan of large vehicles travelling away from us at a pace we could easily keep up with. Esme was at the front of the procession and Fane was near the back. They were on the surface, heading directly toward a sizable city to the north.

In the next second, a surge of some kind wiped the image away, like I'd grabbed hold of a live electrical current. I leaped away from Zarek just as he did the same away from me. I looked down at my hands where my fingers were still tingling and wondered if Zarek felt the same thing I did. It was bizarre.

Amie looked even more tired of our antics.

"Um, I found them," I told her sheepishly.

Amie took the lead as soon as I explained where they'd gone. We followed her but kept a healthy distance between us. As we got closer to the surface, the awkward silence was filled with the howl of the wind, which had not calmed in the slightest since our initial descent. We went as far as we could underground, but we soon reached a predictable dead end.

I pushed a bubble of heated air upwards and melted the snow off the rim of the surface, so Amie had a ledge to grab onto. She jumped and hauled herself out before reaching down a hand for me. Zarek followed and soon we were trudging through the snow.

This was a terrible way to travel.

The shifting slush slowed even my ability to walk and that was barring the fear I'd fall through a loose pile of snow. I adjusted the bubble to provide a platform, allowing us to step above the snow and making things much easier.

It only took a few minutes for Zarek to look at me and ask "Do you need me to take over?" We both knew I had held the field for too long, so either I admitted to being tired or I kept my charade, as he called it, going for a while longer. There had to be a better way. I gave it some thought and while I wasn't sure if he'd be willing to listen right now, I had to try.

Soon, we were zipping forward as I held the bubble, and he propelled us forward over the icy slopes of this planet. I had found myself pleasantly surprised when Zarek had agreed with my ideas, even if he did have some constructive feedback. It made much more sense to limit the amount of time we had to hold up the bubble for our own comfort and this was much quicker than if we'd walked the entire way. Also, the sensation of his touch around my own was... nice.

Almost pleasurable really.

While I kicked that notion very far down inside, I signaled Zarek to slow our speed. We could see the convoy now that held our friends inside. There were about thirty vehicles, and each looked like a squat grey mushroom. A wide tread system underneath kept them from sinking into the snow, but it was the insignia on the sides of the machines that gave us pause.

A ten-pointed star with interlocking lines was painted on them. That symbol represented the largest slavery racket in the universe. Billions, maybe trillions were bought and sold through the Ring's established trade routes over the eons and there were records of their business going back to the very beginning under one name or another. They'd weathered regime changes, war, and laws to continue their trade. For the first few million years of Elysia's existence, Taiyo Raajali had been an unyielding force against the entire practice. His influence still held strong and any slave that made it to the border was instantly freed.

The Ring was one of the few organizations that the Empress openly condemned and any government that officially dealt with the Ring were barred from association with us. I was taught from an early age that while the Elysians had never accepted slavery as a requirement of a civilization, we could not interfere. We could not meddle in the affairs of the outside universe or inflict our own moral standards on others. Each system, planet, and species needed to build upon themselves without the Raajali unless they collectively chose to accept our rule. That is how our territory had gotten so large over time. Yet, the very existence of the Ring was a warning that our Light was limited.

Even if those limitations were only self-inflicted.

"Esme's in there?" Amie's voice shook from fury.

"You should be more worried about Fane." Zarek said as he stopped us from going any further. "Esme's too beautiful for them to try and damage the goods. Fane, as much as we like him, isn't."

We needed a plan and fast.

Being thrown headfirst into the worst smelling room I'd ever been inside of was… disorienting. I expected it due to Zarek's warnings, but somehow I'd underestimated even their most dire descriptions of a slave transport vessel.

There was a dull strip of light lining the walls close to the floor, but it was blocked by the mass of bodies huddled in front of them. Many of these beings were soiled in their own waste and all of them were malnourished. Several had missing limbs, including a Tarren whose ridges had been cut off her back.

Without them, she was half-blinded.

After waiting until I heard the locks shut behind me, I broke through my restraints and stood, noting there were about a hundred people in this space too small to be regulation. "Hello? Fane?" I called out, "Are you in here? Fane?"

"Oh my Empress, Sae! Over here!" Fane burst into what I hoped were happy tears as I approached. "I am so fucking glad to see you. They suckerpunched me. I didn't stand a chance but can I please shoot at least one of them before we go?"

"I might just do it for you," I muttered, breaking his restraints once I got my fingers between his skin and the metal. He looked awful. His right eye was swollen shut and a huge bruise spread over one of his upper arms. Fane's shirt, shoes, and coat had been taken from him so he was only clothed in his trousers. The sight of his bare feet infuriated me. He could get frostbite!

None of this was legal in Isbul; surely the Akons checked once in a while to see if these people were being treated correctly. Before I could think twice, I heated the cold metal floor under us and there were audible whimpers as they huddled as close to the ground as possible. I swallowed, but the hard lump in my throat refused to go down. No one would look at us. They shuffled and cowered away when I broke through Fane's restraints and set him free.

"Fane. How much would these people go for on the market?" There were several ways one could become a slave, but all of them were a result of poverty, cruelty, a condition of birth, or some mixture of the three. One didn't need to be in shackles to understand this violation of their innate dignity was indefensible.

"Sae..." He rubbed his cold feet, "two, maybe three million."

"That's it!?" Had the value always been so low that I could buy this entire fleet with less than a few minutes of my private allotment? What kind of individual would be able to buy a sentient being for such a low price?

Who in the universe would be able to stomach it?

"We need to go." I moved to follow Zarek's instructions.

First crawling through a ventilation funnel to a place where I could turn off their monitoring system, allowing me to pry open an outer panel. The funnel itself was disgusting as it seemed no one ever cared enough to clean it. Once outside I launched myself up and over the mushroom top, nearly clearing the other side accidentally. The hatch was around the back, easily found, and the lock broke under minimal stress. I reached in to give Fane a hand up and put him under a large protective bubble to keep him warm.

All I had to do now was to close the hatch and go.

"Do any of you want to come with us!?" I stuck my head in but none of them said anything. I asked again, this time louder.

Nothing.

"Sae, the penalty for running away is... really bad." Fane put his hand on my arm to try and comfort me. I appreciated the gesture, really I did, but it was just so wrong. So incredibly painful. How far had these people been pushed to get to this point? They were so scared they couldn't even imagine taking the risk.

"They're waiting for us." I closed the hatch.

Amie and I had gotten "captured" by the slavers and while we were reasonably sure Amie would get put with Esme once they saw her face, it was a gamble whether or not I'd be put with Fane.

Even so, Zarek didn't seem surprised at all when I returned first.

We'd chosen a midway point in the convoy for Zarek to set up a base in the space between a vehicle and its treads. It was tricky to time our entry, but between us, we were able to give Fane a much needed hand up into the hidden pocket.

As a greeting, Zarek threw Fane some of his clothes to borrow.

While Fane got dressed, I peppered him with questions about the people we left behind. Where were they headed? Were they more or less likely to be sold off-world and how often are families kept together in Isbul? Do the Akons do regular checks on the slave trade? How many of them are freed each year versus how many enslaved? Are unsold slaves microchipped?

Zarek spoke at my last question.

"I know where this is going. Don't."

"Wherever you think I'm going, it's not. We are looking at different maps." I had to speak past the pit in my stomach, but I managed. "I have no safe haven to offer them. No way to keep them from being prosecuted. I could be endangering the workers who may be slaves themselves and even if we let them go, they would most likely die before reaching s-shelter." I took a breath to center myself. "It doesn't mean I should stay ignorant of what exactly is going to happen to those people if I don't interfere."

Fane, now fully dressed, hugged me and almost bowled us both over when the ground shook from a shockwave coming from the front of the convoy.

Oh dwarf star. What now!?

A profane word escaped Zarek as I shot past, before running after me himself. Fane was left floundering, but I was too preoccupied with the scene in front of us to worry. Chemical flames invisible to most engulfed the first and second vehicles. Fuel had made contact with oxygen and was rapidly spreading to the third.

Particles of burning debris rained down and while they wouldn't hurt me, I sent most of them off to our far right so they wouldn't hurt anyone else. Up ahead, Esme and Amie were back-to-back, in very thin clothing, surrounded by men with guns.

Neither of them had their weapons and I hadn't thought to bring any along with me. I sped up and leaped so that when I landed, my feet would knock over the one poking Esme's face with the barrel of his phaser. The damn thing went off anyway and shot one of his coworkers in the upper leg.

That was all the distraction that Amie and Esme needed.

They'd spent years preparing for a situation such as this one and disarmed several of them with minimal damage. I'd seen them spar at the Shipyard quite a few times and it was good to know they'd become so proficient.

Zarek walked up next to me, eyeing the two of them as they disarmed the inexperienced group trying not to shoot each other.

"Why does she carry when she's enjoying this so much?"

"Esme's the fighter in the family. Amie's a better shot."

"Hey!" Amie shouted at Zarek. "Get Sae out of here!"

He looked at me and I just shrugged in response.

"But we're having so much fun!" Zarek yelled back.

It really wasn't a fair fight.

The storm had sped up to whiteout conditions and none of them could see through it better than we could. Esme was crying when we caught up to them and threw herself onto me. She must have been so scared, and she hated physical altercations.

She sobbed into my shoulder while Amie and I tried to work out a decent plan of what to do next. In the meanwhile, Zarek put out the fires while I kept the snow off of everyone.

"We're in the thirty-second quadrant right?" Fane interjected.

"Yes, why?" I patted Esme soothingly, her cries fading to sniffles.

"Ugh. Can I get a map or something?" Amie dug out his extra implant and Fane scrolled for a bit before he found where we were. "I have a great aunt on my mother's side. She might not give us up if we offer her some contraband slaves."

"Might?" Amie looked closely at the map over his shoulder.

"She's old school. Complains about how the prices keep going up. If we give them to her wholesale, fake a bill of sale, bribe and threaten the guards, and compliment her complexion... we may be able to prevent my untimely incarceration."

Fane marked a place on the map.

"Is that all?" Amie said sarcastically. "We don't need to give her an extra organ... that's nearby!" She took over the map, "and it's where the memory is."

Chapter 19: Idols

In the end, we couldn't abandon them.

We did steal the guards' spare uniforms, although none were short or small enough to fit my current frame. The one-piece thermal suit was like a tent, encumbering all limbs and obscuring one's senses inside its voluminous folds.

I was forced to pull the visor all the way down to see.

The mushrooms were designed to follow the lead of the primary vehicle. So it was a logistical nightmare to evacuate the first two, redistribute people among the vessels, and reprogram the third as the head vessel. This caravan had been heading for the exact same city that we wanted to go.

It made Amie especially twitchy, but she didn't say anything.

After restraining the guards, we stashed them wherever we could find room. Esme seemed to take issue with the last task and silently stood in place while we hauled the guards by her. Once we were inside the foremost vehicle's cabin; however, she made her stance abundantly clear.

"Why are we taking them with us? They tried to sell me!"

"You didn't seem too concerned about it when you went with them." Fane said brusquely as he and Zarek entered, closing the door behind them. "You were happy to let them fawn over you while they beat the shit out of me—"

"I didn't know they were doing that!" Esme's eyes filled with tears. "I am so sorry Fane that they did that to you, but they were just so nice and they said they'd help us find Sae! They tricked me! Please believe me." She pleaded.

"You know what? I don't believe you." Fane snapped. "I wasn't exactly fucking shy about screaming for help. Are you deaf and blind!? Why the fuck didn't you recognize the Ring's logo?"

"It was snowing and I was freezing! So I didn't see it!"

"They're painted like ten meters tall!"

"I said I didn't see it! What happened wasn't my fault!"

"For the love of the fucking Empress, stop crying! I don't feel bad for you. Can you please just act like a—"

"You're lucky you're even here!" Esme exploded, "I told Sae it was a bad idea to take you out of jail! Why are you so mean to me!?"

Zarek pulled Fane away before he could say anything else.

Esme turned away to cry into Amie's shoulder. The first few minutes of travel were punctuated by her tears and the air noticeably relaxed once she fell asleep. Amie covered her sister with a blanket and joined me at the main navigation panel.

"What caused the explosion?" I asked quietly.

"I explained and Esme lost her temper." Amie sighed.

"She could have killed someone."

Fane did not back down at Amie's glare.

"Esme really isn't used to so much stress," I quickly interjected to try and prevent another argument. "We were raised to hate the practice. It's just been a bad day for everyone. Just give things a while to settle. We're alright now."

The subject was dropped and soon enough, we approached our destination. Each mushroom vehicle had a predesignated code on the sides that was scanned upon retrieval. The dock was completely automated and required the full shut down of the vehicles as a conveyer belt unfolded from below and the treads were clamped down for transport. I was uneasy that we'd be discovered at any moment, but there was no one around to question us.

The city was a tiny blip offshore of a soaring glacier the arched outwards, its shadow almost swallowing the scattering of dark metallic towers. The tide was minimal here. This inlet sported high ice walls blocking the wind from three sides and protection from the rough waves of an open ocean. This planet had at least sixteen moons, so it wouldn't be a surprise for the tide to be especially fickle. All in all, the city planners had chosen well.

As we approached the shore, the tracks seemed to stop at the waterline where a steep drop off submerged the convoy. Sinking deep underwater, the tracks dragged us down onto the seabed where I realized I had grossly miscalculated the size of the settlement.

It was a haphazard conglomeration of tanks and tubes that spread out to either side of the inlet and bolted even deeper down a second drop off into an inky abyss. Exposed tracks ran all over the outer walls of the city alongside massive anthozoa species latched on and branching out from the city's hull. I had never seen such a mismatched mess of metal before.

And it was beautiful.

The current swirled around the structure, causing the anthozoa to dance in a mesmerizing pattern; the dark red and blue tentacles were thicker than an average tree trunk and triple the length. A forest of the anthozoa's cohorts spread out in on either side of us; brilliant white tetracorallia, iridescent sea anemones with mouths large enough to swallow me whole, scleractinia in every imaginable shape and size, and other coral-like structures whose names I wished I had to assign to them. Cataloging the images to look up later would take hours.

I pressed my face against the windows, darting from one side to the other, trying not to miss a single detail. It'd read all about oceanic life, but had never been inside an artic ocean until now. Such a diverse assortment of marine life was rare in cold waters and I was absolutely thrilled to get the chance to observe this environment in person.

"First time, pixie?" Laughter infused Zarek's voice.

Nodding, not at all discouraged, I ran back to the other side.

"Look closer at the cliffside." How had he gotten so close to my ear? Obediently, I looked and gasped when I realized the bumpy texture along the cliff walls were breathing. Zarek tapped on the glass next to my shoulder to emphasize the fringe of feelers along their spines. "*Gigantus Orectolobidae*, one of the only artic nesting grounds in the universe."

They were glorious. Just as glorious as the feeder species nesting in their folds. I nearly cried in excitement as I described their known migration patterns... then I shut up when I realized who I was talking to. I muttered a quick apology before returning back to the front observation window where Amie waited for me.

Looking out, I couldn't help but gawk some more.

Schools of fish and larger predators swam around the city, A vibrantly yellow spotted mammalian glided lazily on its back nearby. An entire herd of crustaceans scuttled across the underbelly of one of the sea anemones, which closed with incredible speed to secure a midday meal. There were strange, spindly creatures that feasted on a furry growth of moss, revealing a broken passenger tank thickly coated in rust. A group of flat faced fish pushed forward with their anchor-shaped, barbed tails right next to a species that spun itself like a torpedo to dive into deeper waters. Much of the reef itself was bioluminescent, casting a greenish glow on the lower half of the walls that were quickly rising up to obscure our view.

A tunnel unbolted before us that was also filled with sea water. The transfer from the sea floor to the dock was bumpy and woke up Esme from her slumber. The tracks themselves rounded off inside to create a carrousel of mushrooms and once everything was inside, the room sealed shut and the water rapidly drained out. Soon enough, the main bay doors themselves opened.

Fane, who was most familiar with this kind of transaction, hid his hair and face under his uniform's hood to speak with the person approaching our stolen fleet.

Zarek went with him just in case something went awry, leaving the three of us alone for the first time in a while. Esme seized upon this lull as soon as the door closed behind them, grabbing my arm and motioning for Amie to come closer.

"Sae. I don't think we should keep Fane anymore." Esme put her hand on my mouth before I could say anything. "Just listen. He's too fragile and gets into danger wherever we go. It's for his own good and it would be cruel of us to keep bringing him along with us. You know? I think his aunt could take him off our hands and we should let her. We'd be doing everyone a favor."

"Esme, Fane is in trouble, we can't just abandon him."

"We wouldn't be abandoning him! He doesn't belong with us!"

"It's his choice either way and I think Fane wants to stay."

"Amie, back me up. You know I'm right don't you?" When Amie disagreed, Esme's eyebrows shot down in an angry pout. "Fine! Majority rules! Whatever." She poked me in the shoulder. "But it's going to be your fault when he gets hurt."

Esme clammed up then and refused to talk it out. Even though Amie and I tried several times to appeal to her, it was no use. Zarek and Fane returned with the falsified documents without issue and the slaves and guards were quickly unloaded in the next half an hour. We had gagged the guards and they barely resisted being inventoried; but it was soon clear why they didn't.

One of the guards had been tortured and killed.

The man's frontal lobe was caved inwards with a dull object, his appendages were bent at unnatural angles, and his teeth had been broken out of his mouth. Blood splattered all over the floor, speckled with fecal and brain matter. We didn't bother to ask who had been responsible, as the way the slaves simply stepped over his corpse told us all we needed to know.

They wouldn't be willing to talk about the incident without being tortured themselves. The dock worker that had found the body assured Fane the mess would be cleaned before the vessels were sent back to the Ring's satellite office.

The slaves themselves were packed into narrow, suspended animation units that would keep them alive until they reached their final destination. We discovered then that some of the slaves had already been sold and they were taken out of our hands. The majority would be kept in a numbered warehouse until they too, were sold. It made me sick to think of how we'd been thrown into this position of engaging with the Ring and their horrific trade. My only hope at this point was that Fane's aunt would be a merciful and compassionate woman.

The inside of the city itself was gloomy, with every window to the outside world tinted to a muddled grey. The muted clothing we wore was colorful in comparison to the clothes of the average citizen; who overwhelmingly were covered, head to foot, in black.

Sun lamps high overhead cast a cold, bluish atmosphere and an endless parade of shadows within. We were repeatedly jostled as we navigated through the crowd in the poorer levels of this structure. Although Isbul had long abandoned its formal caste system, Fane explained to me in hushed tones that those status barriers still prevailed in areas like these to the modern day. There were ten castes with one being the highest. Anyone who was born in the eighth to tenth tiers were almost never able to escape their caste and were often shunned for trying.

Water of unidentifiable origin ran through the dips in the streets, the skeletons of half-finished buildings were rusted and bent toward the walkways, and there was a distinct air of hostility here that I had never encountered before. While our group stuck out, it wasn't just because we were foreigners, I realized, but that all we saw were a monolith in appearance.

Everyone we passed were thin and had incredibly sharp bone structures. Their hair either black or dark grey with skin tones ranging from smoke to charcoal. Although all of us wore hoods, I could feel their stares turn to our backs as soon as we passed by. It must be unusual for them to get any visitors at all, which was a shame. I found their home riveting.

We had almost crossed the platform to the hydraulic interior train when I felt something tug on my tunic. It was a little boy whose clothes were little more than rags. He gestured to his mouth and then held out his hand. Assuming he was nonverbal and hungry, I dug out one of the fruits we'd found in with the guards' quarters and handed it to him. He dashed off.

Suddenly, I was surrounded by what looked like children of all ages with their hands out. I hastily handed out the rest of the food I had on me, but soon ran out. Although I tried to convey that I had nothing else for them, they refused to let go of me. I tried to gently maneuver myself away, calmly explaining to them that I needed to find my friends and that it was irrational to ask for something from a stranger who had nothing to give them. It didn't seem to help.

I tried several other regional languages that I knew, but that did not deter them. They also did not speak, simply pointing at their mouths. I was about to try to negotiate about visiting at a later time when someone stepped beside me.

One look at Zarek, who wore a very stern expression, had the children melting back into the crowd. It seemed quite rude, but effective. Perhaps I should try adopting a similarly unfriendly demeanor for dealing with insistent crowds.

"I was handling it," I told Amie when she rushed back to me.

"They were twice your size," Zarek said before Amie could.

"They were children, and they were hungry," I insisted. "It's not their fault. I would have been fine on my own."

Zarek looked like he really wanted to say something else, but Esme pulled him back and Amie kept me in front of her the rest of the way. To keep the peace, I didn't argue and just chatted with Fane about his aunt and what to expect.

Nileanna Akon was born a member of the first caste and enjoyed lording it over others according to Fane. She knew every obscure branch of the Akon bloodline so I couldn't masquerade as one to get into her good graces. She'd had two sons, both of whom were deceased, and one grandson who she was grooming to take over her house and business. She also adhered to the most fastidious of formal rituals and was generally seen as tolerably xenophobic.

Approaching the oversized, solid diamond doors, I pulled my upper garment down and wrapped it into draping pattern similar to a skirt. It left my arms exposed but covered the state of my shoes. I also carefully wrapped my hair up into an elaborate fabric twist. Zarek saw where I was going with this, and I could swear he was barely holding back a smile.

Fane took his hood off to speak with someone on the side screen and we waited at least another five minutes for the door to open. As I suspected, we were greeted in foyer encrusted with patterns of precious minerals and lined with servants in pressed uniforms.

In the center of the foyer was Aunt Nileanna. A long, narrow nose met with arching cheekbones to create a face made to frown. Her dark gray hair was cropped closely to her scalp with little in terms of personal ornamentation. She was razor-thin with sharp eyes and equally sharp ears. Her complexion was not only flawless, but a magnificent color of dark sapphire.

Fane went first to formally give her the informal greeting between family members. Zarek went next and gave an equally formal greeting, which shockingly was returned by a smile that even Fane did not get. Then it was my turn.

I walked forward and snapped into the initial curtsey.

Nileanna's eyes narrowed, but she thrust herself into the first position. In a tempo that defied her age, we circled into a star pattern with each motion stopping for just half a second into another. It was not a flowing ritual, but one of dexterity and core strength. By the end Nileanna's breath had grown deeper, but each movement was just as controlled as we finished the ritual.

"I am Sae Dominin." Quietly, I hoped Caillio wouldn't mind me borrowing his family name. "These are my attendants." My hand snapped into the correct gesture. "And it is with both fortune and reverence that I enter your great house."

"Well done! Good show!" Nileanna's eyes had warmed, losing much of her earlier disdain and ire. "That was one of the most accomplished examples of the first reception sacrament I've seen since I was a young girl myself."

"Such praise is humbling my lady; may I compliment you on the early second era carvings on your columns encrusted with geran rubies? Thirty carat gems of such clarity are so difficult to source. You have impeccable taste."

She beamed and offered me her arm.

I graciously accepted the offer of calling her auntie and entertained her lengthy descriptions of jewel acquisition. In turn, I complimented the Akon name; her incredible sense of generosity to her family for allowing us to enter her home considering her nephew's unfortunate situation; and yes, her flawless complexion.

"Fanelius Raquel Akon, where did you find such a refined creature? Why, she is almost worthy of the Akon name herself!" Nileanna trilled "I have not had such a stimulating conversation since your grandmother was still alive. Such an impressive result of her upbringing and lineage."

We had reached the end of the involuntary house tour not a moment too soon as I was running out of adjectives in her chosen language to praise her house with. Also, she was heavily implying that Fane should consider an alliance with my family, and it was just a matter of time before Auntie Nileanna caught him rolling his eyes back into his head.

While Amie and Esme stood by, the rest of us were invited to join Nileanna for a short meal. As we waited for refreshments, I turned and pleaded silently with Fane to please ask her about the favor we needed before she talked again.

Fane nodded and knocked on the table to get her attention.

"Fanelius your posture is atrocious." Fane uncrossed his ankles and sat up straighter. It still wasn't good enough.

"Just look at the examples your friends are making. Sae is near perfection in her visage and why this handsome young man absolutely oozes virality and good breeding."

If I didn't know better, I'd think she was flirting with Zarek. I also got the feeling that Zarek was distinctly uncomfortable even though he showed no sign of it. Nileanna turned her attention to the correct positioning of the cutlery, and I excused myself to view an original second-wave, post-nyloon surrealist artwork. I volunteered Zarek to accompany me.

"What's wrong Zarek?" I whispered, keeping my eyes on the art.

"You think something's wrong?" Zarek too didn't look at me.

"It seems like you don't want to be around Nileanna, that's all."

Zarek broke protocol and looked away from the painting to instead look at me. I didn't understand why, but it suddenly felt as though we'd spoken far more than we had. He didn't want to be here but he didn't really care about his own comfort and...

He trusted my judgment.

"I don't know how you do it, pixie. You surprise me every time."

"We can find another place or solution for those people." I didn't want Zarek to do anything he wasn't comfortable with. His opinions mattered, and I hoped he could understand me just as I did him. "It's a big city. We don't need to stay."

"No. Let's just get this over with, shall we?"

Luckily, Fane had opened the topic and he and his aunt were talking about the finer points of the business all through the brief midday meal. Apparently, her hands were quite full at the moment in preparations for her birthday, but in the end she agreed to look over the "cargo" and have an answer for us in a few days.

A few days was longer than we expected to stay, but even at such short notice we couldn't reject her hospitality. We were given a suite of rooms in her guest wing with views of the ocean on the other side of the city. Instead of a bright reef forest, the ocean on this side was cold and dark with only glaciers and the occasional fish to break the monotony.

Here was where we ran into a bit of contention when Nileanna's chief servants attempted to take Amie and Esme to where the servants stayed. I clarified that I wanted my attendants with me at all times before Esme could lash out at somebody and had to anxiously watch Esme almost lose her temper again when the servants brought in rough floor cots for them to sleep in.

"Esme you know I don't sleep. You and Amie can just take my bedroom," I said as soon as the door closed behind them and their footsteps faded away.

"Why didn't you say we were your sisters or something!?" She kicked a cot so violently, she nearly knocked over a chair.

"I'm sorry, I didn't think you knew the introduction ritual."

"Is sorry all you have to say!?" Esme hissed. "I can't believe you!"

"I-I should have asked first, I thought it was the obvious—"

"Obvious!? I—" Esme stopped when Fane and Zarek came in.

A third person also entered the room with them who could only be Nileanna's grandson and successor, Onitneir Akon. If his grandmother was thin, then he was emancipated in stature. His garments draped in what should have been a regal style but fell short on narrow shoulders. Overall, along with his slender features and pronounced nose, it gave him the unfortunate impression of a drowned bird; the image only becoming more pronounced as I came forward and gave the appropriate formal greeting.

"Don't bother. I don't follow my aunt's shitty rules."

I straightened to catch him looking at me up and down, so I did the same to him. With a swish of his arm, he snubbed me and went to go look at Amie and Esme. He circled them and got his hand slapped when he tried to touch Amie's hair.

His other hand shot out toward her face.

Amie grabbed his arm and twisted, bringing him to his knees before any of us could register what was happening. Onitneir cried out, his expression twisting into a cruel mask of disdain and fury.

"How dare you touch me you presumptuous bitch! Let go of me this instant before I report you!"

Amie was not impressed. She did let him go but shoved him backward so that he landed on his ass in a heap of tangled robes. His shoulder made contact with a side table on the way down, knocking it over. I hurried to get between them before he really provoked them. Not that I cared if her grandson liked us or not, but we still needed Nileanna to help us.

"If she were mine, I'd have her beaten for insubordination."

"Well, she isn't. Amie belongs to herself." I snapped at him.

Onitneir sneered at us. "I came to see if I could buy the pair of them. But obviously they're not worth the trouble. You pamper your servants. Disgusting." He swept past without waiting for a response. Fane held the door for him, but he paused and mumbled something to Fane before leaving.

I could see that whatever he said had greatly distressed Fane, who almost slammed the door behind his cousin.

"He hasn't changed since we were kids," Fane grumbled.

Zarek had taken up residence at the corner of the sectional in the center of the room and Esme went over to join him while Fane apologized profusely to Amie.

I went to go pick up the table Onitneir had knocked over, when I noticed an odd little circle underneath one of the joints. I turned over the table to look at the other five joints and saw that the little circle was only on the one. I ran my finger over the circle and it was so thin that it almost felt like a part of the table.

It made a very slight noise at a low frequency.

"It's an audio bug." Zarek identified it as he approached.

"How do you always manage to sneak up on me?"

"Because you make it so easy." Zarek reached around me, and instead of trying to peel off the device, he simply ripped the joint piece out bug and all. "I'll just return this to its owner. Try and get some rest, pixie. It's good for you." He lightly touched the tip of my nose with one of his fingers and swiftly left the room before I could come up with a coherent reply.

My nose tingled where he'd touched me.

"Do you always have to be the fucking center of attention!?"

Esme was curled up on the chaise, staring furiously at my general direction. I was tempted to look over my shoulder to see if she was speaking to someone else. No matter how stressful our circumstances, I'd never heard her talk like that.

"Esme, are you okay?"

I was getting concerned about her behavior.

"Am I fucking okay? Is that all you want to say to me!?"

"Esme! What is wrong with you?"

"What's wrong with me!?" Esme stood and so did Amie. She shoved her twin aggressively in the shoulder. "I've had enough!

That's what's wrong with me! It's always about what Sae wants! Oh, she's putting herself in danger again we better clean up after her! Oh, Sae's putting us in danger, well that doesn't matter! Sae doesn't care if we're cold or sleepy or—"

"Oh. My. Empress. Why are you even here!?" Fane interrupted.

"You stay out of this! This has nothing to do with you!"

Amie held back her twin from getting to Fane and tried to speak in a calm manner. "Esme, if you're unhappy, why don't you go home? It's alright if you want to go home without us. Mom and Dad would understand and you can check how Aoi, Sil, and Vis are holding up."

Esme burst into tears.

Ear-piercing, wailing tears.

Amie quickly raised sound barriers the moment they began as the metal walls of this residence were in no way insulated enough to hide them. Only then did she try to comfort her sister.

"I don't fucking want to go home! Stop telling me to go home! Why do you keep taking their side, Amie? It's not fair! You've changed and I! Want! My! Sister! Back!" Esme pushed Amie away and openly sobbed into the frigid air.

I slowly approached, not knowing if her mood would abruptly change again. Amie looked like she was at an absolute loss. I didn't know if she wanted to hear from me right now, but I gently patted Esme's arm and tried to calm her.

"Esme, I'm sorry I haven't taken your concerns seriously—"

"This is such bullshit." Fane minimized his news screen and stood up too. "Sae, whatever is actually bothering her has jack shit to do with you! I can't fucking believe this. Am I really the only one who thinks she's milking this—"

"You don't know anything about me!" This time both Amie and I held her back as she tried lunging at Fane. "No one cares about how Esme feels! Or what Esme wants! No one ever asks Esme!" She stopped struggling and collapsed, crying louder than ever.

"Oh, for fuck's sake, I can't listen to this anymore." Fane ignored Amie's warning and yelled over Esme. "I'll bite, okay!? What is it!? What is it that Esme wants!?"

"I want Zarek!" She screamed.

As if she shocked herself, Esme went quiet.

"You want Zarek." Fane said with an excessively slow speech pattern, as if he couldn't believe his own ears.

"I want Zarek." Esme confirmed, looking at me. "I love him."

"You love him!? What do you mean you love Zarek!?" Amie pulled her sister to her feet and I was left staring at the ground while they began to argue. Loudly.

Fane came over and quietly stood beside me.

Was I really that obvious?

"You've never even had a conversation with him!"

"It doesn't matter! I love him Amie, don't you get it?"

"No. I don't! When did this happen? How? Why him?"

"Back when we were kids. I saw him and I fell in love right away! It was love at first sight! He kissed Sae and I didn't like it. So I pushed you out on purpose." Esme stared unnervingly down at me. "When I saw him again, I thought Sae would reject him so I could have a chance... but there's no way I can compete with a Raajali!" Esme wailed, crying again. "I love him so much and I can't make him fall in love with me if Sae keeps leading him on!"

Shoving her sister aside, Esme grabbed me.

"He makes me feel so good Sae. I don't know if you can feel this way, but I feel beautiful when he looks at me. I feel *aroused*. Do you understand that word at all? You probably don't." Esme's fingers were digging into my clothes. "Zarek is absolutely gorgeous and he's perfect for me. We're meant to be together. I can feel it. And

I'm sure he loves me too! I deserve him! And I know you don't love him! You don't, right!? So can't you just let me have him!?"

"Esme, I don't think that's how love works…"

"That's because you're you! You can literally have anyone in the universe!" Esme angrily shook me, her nails dug into my clothes. "Everyone loves you Sae! Why can't you just give me this one man. Just one! That's all I'm asking for! This isn't fair! You're not being fair! Why can't you just let me have him! How can you be so selfish!? You don't want him, so let me have him!"

"Zarek is his own person, Esme. I can't—"

"Yes, you can!" Esme screamed in my face. "Zarek doesn't even like you Sae, but it's a freak law of nature that! Everyone! Loves! You! It's not fair to me! It's not fair!"

"He doesn't have all his memories back yet, I don't—"

"But if he remembers who you are, then he'll never fall in love with me! I have to get him to love me before he remembers who you really are! No one can compete with you! Not a single being in this universe can complete! Raajali were born better than everyone! It's not fair! It's not fair! It's not fair! It's not fair! It's not fair! It's not fair! It's not fair! It's not—!"

"Esme. Stop." Amie tried to pry her hands off me.

"Look at Fane! He loves you and he's a fucking homosexual!"

Fane joined in Amie's attempts to separate us from each other.

Esme shoved at them both with one hand and kept hold of me with the other. "Can you tell me that you love Zarek? You can't right!?" Esme cried. "This isn't fair! It's not fair! It's not fair! It's not fair to take him just because you want the best! What about me!? Don't I deserve—you'll just end up making him fucking miserable! Just like your dad!"

Amie gagged her twin and that was what finally made her stop. Esme let go and curled up into a sobbing ball on the floor. Fane and

Amie were speaking to me, but who could hear anything when a sharp wall of misery and grief insulated you from the inside out.

"Esme. I-I... I..."

I turned away and left.

I couldn't yell and scream like Esme did. I couldn't argue with her about this. *Just like your dad.* Those words were like a dull blade slicing through parchment; a blunt instrument that left only jagged pieces behind. I couldn't think.

My tattered composure trailed behind me in ribbons.

I blindly fumbled at the door, opened it, and...

Of course, there he was.

"Didn't I wisely advise you to—what's wrong pixie?"

"Nothing's wrong." I sounded wrong. "I just need some air."

Opening the door wider, I tried to move around him without saying more. I got a few steps away before I felt his hand gently brush against mine. I whirled around and whatever Zarek saw in my face made him take a step closer.

No. I would fall apart.

I saw a hand reach toward me.

I flinched back.

Zarek froze and so did I.

I moved as fast as I could without breaking into a run. I could hear someone following me, but all I knew was that it wasn't Zarek. So I didn't care. I kept going until I felt the air cool noticeably around me. Nileanna was frugal enough to keep the unoccupied parts of her house unheated. My steps slowed as I finally reached a dark dead end where the only illumination came from a small window on the ceiling. I looked up for any trace of life but found no ne.

Fane took his time walking to my side and he didn't say a word.

"She was right you know. My father was unhappy."

"So what?" Fane bumped his shoulder against mine, the point of contact helping to ground me back to where I was. "My father's a miserable bastard too. You don't see me blaming anyone but him for his own sorry existence."

"I just need some time to think, that's all."

"What you need, is a change of scenery. Come on. It's been a while since my last visit with Nileanna, but I bet I can still show a girl a good time." Fane offered his arm, and I took it.

It would be good to spend some time away from the others.

"Shouldn't you cover your hair?" I asked once we were outside.

"Nah, let the locals see what real fashion is for once."

"But we still need to keep you from being recognized."

"Not anymore we don't." Fane and I hopped onto one of the raised trams that circled the city before he elaborated, handing me the news screen he was looking at earlier. "The crown prince and his sons were caught in an accident. Along with his brother and niece. That means I'm less than ten spots away from the throne." He didn't sound happy about it.

I read the articles Fane had pulled up and several others to understand what the underlying message was. Although journalists were not allowed to speculate unless they openly published an opinion piece, there was enough inuendo to see that they had all landed on the same conclusion.

"Everybody thinks this was revenge for Dorj's death."

"Exactly." Fane's face was grim. "I was never meant to be this close in line of succession, but now that I am, I have immunity from all but Class A felonies."

"You don't need to stay with us then..."

"You're not getting rid of me that easy." We hopped off onto an actually busy platform. This city had seemed so quiet at first, even this moderate amount of noise was a welcome change. "I'm safer with you if the Dorj is really targeting us again," Fane said as we exited the station. "I am not dying for family honor. No ma'am. I am perfectly happy being a sniveling coward if it means I get to live." He draped a long black scarf over both our shoulders. "Black is so not your color Sae."

"It isn't yours either." Not actually knowing if that was true.

"I know." Fane sighed dramatically. "But I live my life in hope."

No more was said of serious matters. Fane led me through the market district, not giving a flip that his vibrant coloring attracted all sorts of attention and telling me that I was there to protect him, so he had nothing to worry about. He'd swiped Onitneir's credit slip and was not shy in spending it all on food. I found myself being handed all sorts of concoctions and confections, almost all of which Fane claimed were his favorite food.

I had to admit that I had a grand time trying all these new dishes. There were crunchy things on sticks and soft things in cups. There was an especially spicy stew boiled inside a fish and something with leafy tentacles candied into a hard shell and stuffed with sauce. For a city in a tundra, there was quite a sizable variety of cheap meat available. Mother and I were essentially vegetarians as there was no real need for physical substances. So why eat meat unnecessarily? I took a bite of a few meat dishes anyway to please Fane. Some were better than others in quality, yet I still didn't fully understand why it was so prized as a food source.

As the sunlamps were dimmed, smaller blue and purple lights were spread over the low canopies of the market. Shops that closed were quickly replaced by stalls and the crowd grew thicker and louder with the end of a work day. The center of the market was a large circular space built in a corkscrew pattern. The metal floor was textured to provide traction and the dark storefronts, normally showcasing goods during the day, reflected light back onto the crowd in an ambiguous blur of color. Somewhere Fane had gotten me a fuzzy hat with pom poms mimicking ears and he had gained an even fuzzier jacket to combat the cold.

We followed the flow of the crowd and held hands to make sure we weren't separated. I could see there was a stage platform up ahead at the center of the corkscrew and wondered if there would be a performance held tonight.

Fane and I were stopped by a garment seller as we neared the center of the market. The man had checks drooped with age and carried a basket on his stooped back full of black veils. "A ceremonial hood for the lady?" He beseeched "Only the finest of lace for such a pretty couple!"

"Ceremonial?" Fane bit into a pastry. "What's the occasion?"

"Visitors to our humble town!" He smiled and I saw that all of his teeth had been filled in with metal replacements. Fascinating. "An old tradition of the sea you see. We wear black. Our chosen queen wears white. A lot of girls vie for the title each decade and she brings good luck and prosperity to our world. She's being crowned tonight on her last night as queen!" He held out his wares "Join in the revelry! Half price just for you and your lady!"

"Why not?" Fane picked out two and pinned the veils to our fuzzy hats. "I guess that explains why everyone looks like they got a dress code!" Fane gestured with the remainder of his pastry. He almost tripped over a small child, and I had to brace myself to keep us both standing.

"I think you've had too much to drink!" My voice was almost drowned out by the crowd. Fane disagreed with me, laughing that he was perfectly sober, but also wisely stopped imbuing anyway. We should head back soon as the hour was getting fairly late, but I just wasn't ready to face the others. Fane and I could stay out a little while longer, I decided. We could see some of the pageantry of the event and be home before Amie got too worried.

It was standing room only inside this public amphitheater. The platform was raised high in the center and was covered with a white cloth. Fane and I were packed tightly against the crowd as more and more people shoved inside for a view of the stage. The ground here was sticky from spilled beverages and children were being hoisted on shoulders as prevention from being crushed by the weight of a stranger. Just as I was getting uncomfortable enough to suggest heading back, the sunlamp above the square darkened entirely and the crowd fell silent.

A familiar voice boomed over us then.

"Welcome one and all to our final night of darkness! May our queen bring us into the light of a new dawn!" The crowd gave a loud roar of approval as Onitneir stepped onto the platform.

Fane made a sound of disgust once he realized his cousin was on stage, finishing his candy and grabbing my hand.

"If he's here, I am out!" However; there was no chance of reversing our steps as the crowd would not move out of our way. There were simply too many people. Fane tried for a few minutes while Onitneir expounded upon the history of this millennia-old tradition and how a sacrifice had to be made in order to preserve the peace and fortunes of the many.

It was at that point that Fane seemed to realize something.

"Sae. Get us out of here! Right now!" He yelled over the cheers.

"Why? The crowd will thin out eventually!"

"No! Trust me! You do not want to see this!"

"If I take both of us, I might hurt you!"

"Then go! I'll catch up later! Just go!"

"I'm not going to just leave you here!"

Fane's response was drowned out by the crowd as once more they screamed their approval. A figure rose up inside the center of the white cloth from the platform. The cloth draped over the curves of the woman's body as she rose up, sticking to odd places on her form. Perhaps she'd been painted or dipped into ceremonial ink of some kind as dark stains appeared on the fabric.

Onitneir introduced the "queen" and ripped the fabric away.

Time seemed to break. Fane was screaming something into my ear, but I couldn't separate his voice from the gleeful cries of the crowd as the woman was revealed to the public. A wig of long white hair had been placed on her head as well as a paper crown. If you were to guess she was dressed similarly in white, you would be wrong, because she was naked.

And openly, gruesomely tortured.

It should have been impossible for her to be alive. If not for the slight shaking of the mutilated body tied to a post, I would have thought she already was. Her lower legs had been amputated and what was left of her upper leg muscles were ripped to shreds with both femurs sticking down out of the infected red meat.

The rest of her body had been flayed.

There was no visible skin left on it.

Her jaw had been broken open into a macabre grin, and if she once had teeth, tongue or appendages at all inside her mouth, they were all gone. The interior of her mouth itself looked as if it were melted by an acid or poison of some kind. Her arms and upper body were pitted with holes and her hands had been crushed into shapeless lumps. I couldn't look away from her.

Onitneir slapped her and an animalistic cry came from the mangled throat. It was depraved. A crime against the living soul.

"Stop!" I screamed and for a brief moment, everything did.

The crowd stopped cheering and Onitneir's hand stopped midair as his head snapped in my direction. To my horror, cameras that I hadn't noticed before also turned my way. Fane had the wherewithal to yank me back behind him as the crowd collectively shook off the intensity of my order.

"Ha-ha! Welcome cousin! I didn't know you were man enough to want to watch!" Onitneir took a bow. "My cousin there has brought his little girlfriend to celebrate with us tonight!"

A half-hearted applause was his response.

"Be kind to them now! They don't know our customs! They don't know that she asked for this!" Onitneir yanked on the wig and revealed the burnt scalp underneath. I could see bone under the flaking flesh. "This girl competed for the honor of being queen. They sacrifice themselves for the happiness of others! Isn't that right!? I said isn't that right!?" He kicked the girl in the abdomen. "We left you an ear! Now tell them!"

The body slowly, but visibly nodded.

"I don't care!" I tried to push Fane aside though I knew he only wanted to help me. "This is cruel! T-this, this is barbaric!"

Jeers came from all directions.

Fane saw that I was going to speak again and covered my mouth with his hands. His eyes darted left and right over the frenzied mob. I had to rip my own eyes away from Onitneir to even begin to understand what Fane was trying to say to me.

Don't interfere.

"But why can't we stop them from cannibalizing their young?"

Anera and Astral had come back from their latest mission very sad. We had provided aid to a drought-ridden planet and they'd been invited to partake in local traditions. While they didn't give every detail. It was enough for us to understand.

"Sometimes, the outer universe asks for our help. Sometimes, we're able to help. Other times, their laws don't let us or their leaders are too proud. We cannot change their minds. It's wrong to impose our own "enlightened" ideas on other sentient beings. They will not thank us for it. We may be able to force them, but free will is something we must not supersede."

"But Sae's mom could make it so they want to be civilized."

"Yes darling, but more than anyone else, the Raajali must have limits. Listen Sae." Anera scooted over so she was sitting closer to me. "Raajali must know the rules and follow those rules. Having such power as the Empress does, she must never interfere with the final power that eludes your family. The power of an individual's choices."

"Don't worry. I always follow the rules."

"There will come a day were it won't be so easy."

Today was that day.

Onitneir produced the paperwork the girl had signed. She had agreed to be tortured with no limitations for five days and five nights. She would be kept medically alive until the final night where she'd be raffled off to be beheaded, but before that could happen, she still had until midnight to be tortured. This was a state sanctioned murder. Anyone who dissented could be fined and imprisoned until the conclusion of the event.

He then asked if Fane or I dissented.

And we said nothing.

That was when Onitneir began the torture anew.

Fane looked away, burying his face into his shoulder. I couldn't look away as her two remaining eyes were ripped out by a primitive pair of forceps, as more people volunteered to violate her on stage, and as the crowd cheered them on.

Children vied for the prized souvenir of one of her eyes. Molten glass was poured into the holes in her arms and, once cooled, was ripped out again, tearing her muscles into pieces. For the finale, they hoisted her upside down between two posts, took a two-handed saw blade and began to cut her in half. They stopped when they reached mid-waist, leaving the blade embedded.

She was still alive.

Onitneir announced that she would be left there until morning for anyone who wanted to give their final thanks to their queen. He stepped off the platform to thunderous applause. I stood there, unmoving as the crowd dispersed. Fane tried to pull me away, but it was useless. I stared at the mangled meat that was the remains of a person. A living person.

I could hear her heartbeat, artificially kept pumping by some marvel of modern medicine. They'd cauterized almost all of her wounds and so it would take a few more hours for her to die of blood loss—I could take her back with me somehow. Get Esme to heal her somehow even though she was mad at me. I could help her live somehow.

It would be the first time I ever killed.

I stopped her heart and turned away.

Fane and I slipped quietly back into Nileanna's house.

Did she know what kind of monster she had raised in her house? Was I certain I wouldn't commit murder a second time tonight if I laid eyes on her grandson? All I knew was that Fane would not stop apologizing. After we were finally able to leave, Fane had bought intoxicants from almost every stall we passed. If only I could feel the seemingly blissful detachment that he could.

I was the only reason Fane was still moving.

It was the middle of the night and I could only hope that the others had gone to sleep. My argument with Esme seemed petty now. It was stupid to fight over something so inconsequential. I stopped walking long enough for Fane to decide if he was going to be sick and continued toward the guest wing once he signaled that he would not, at least for the moment.

"I love you Sae." Fane's head fell heavily on my shoulder.

"I love you too Fane." I sighed as a snore was my only response. Hopefully I could get him to his bed without further incident and find a quiet corner to cry in privacy. Fane, of course, was even more unwieldy now that he was entirely dead weight.

"Having fun pixie?"

Oh for the love of—

"Zarek. Could you please take Fane to his bed?" I tried to hand him off, but Zarek made no moves to take him from me. "Please, it's been a long night and—"

"A long night for you lovebirds maybe." He wasn't being serious but I wasn't in the mood for his jokes. I couldn't handle them right now. I didn't have the strength to pretend like everything was okay. Just once tonight, I needed someone to act reasonably.

"I don't appreciate whatever you're trying to insinuate."

"You know exactly what I'm insinuating."

"Fuck. You." I looked at him in the eyes as I said it. First time killing, first time cursing at someone, first times all around!

I towed Fane along with me as fast as I could and tried not to let myself be upset that Zarek was upset at me. Who cares? An innocent woman had died tonight, and I had killed her.

So what that I stayed out past a curfew no one had consulted me about!? I turned the corner and had to stop before I spiraled into a panic that I could not indulge in right now. Fane was asleep on my shoulder, and I had to get him safely to his room before I did something else ill-advised.

I shouldn't have snapped at Zarek like that. I shouldn't have left the others, especially without informing them, and I shouldn't have stayed out for so long. This was what I deserved for going out of bounds. It was what I deserved for being so stupid and reckless.

Fane's weight shifted and for a second I thought maybe he was sober enough to get himself to bed. Instead, I looked to see Zarek pulling him off me and I put up a momentary resistance, too tired to remember I'd just asked Zarek to take him.

"It's okay pixie, I've got him."

Tears came out of my eyes.

"Are you m-mad at me?" I let go of Fane.

"Shhh, no. Of course I'm not mad at you."

"I'm sorry. W-we should h-have come back sooner."

"You're tired aren't you sweetness?" His thumb swept across my check, stopping a tear from falling all the way down. "Go back to your room before I have to carry you too. I'll take care of our drunk idiot." He patted Fane on the back and got a grumble out of him. "See? I'll make sure he gets back. Get some of that sleep I keep telling you about. I promise it won't hurt you."

Minutes later, I walked inside to see Esme and Amie had taken the bed, so I curled up in on a chair and sat there, awake, for the rest of the night.

Chapter 20: Inheritances

The next morning, we all sat down to a quiet meal.

In the traditional fashion, we sat on the ground around a narrow ring on which rotated dozens of colorful dishes; all filled with delicacies. Using a long two-pronged utensil, one picked up a sliver of food from the dishes and slid the food down the length of the sticks into one's mouth. It was a cumbersome method of consumption to the untrained and the experienced alike.

My Sentinels were determined to pretend all was well.

Zarek had Fane propped up against him and was taking sips of some kind of caffeinated syrup that had come with the food; it was intensely bitter. Fane shoved food into his mouth without any of the enthusiasm he had last night.

"Fane. How close is Onitneir from the throne?" He stopped chewing. I stared at the dishes moving past me and waited for him to swallow his food. I tried one of the other syrups that came in tall glasses. It was very sour. I didn't like it.

"He's got three people in front of him. Nileanna's one." Fane threw down his utensil in disgust. "I forgot he—most of this branch was killed in the last civil war. He's basically what's left."

"That civil war was also between the Akon and the Dorj." The last thing I should be doing was involve myself in their political affairs. Isbul was a contender for the most powerful nation in the outer universe. Yet here I was with the third, fourth, and ninth successors to their government. "We should ask Nileanna for an answer. Even if she says no, it's better than staying any longer."

"I'll go with you," Fane volunteered. "She's never liked me, but I don't think she hates me either." He grabbed two of the remaining caffeine syrups and gulped them down before standing.

"Wait," I said as I saw Zarek about to stand. "I have to talk to Amie. Could you stay and keep Esme company?" Zarek raised his eyebrows but sat back down.

Amie barely held it in long enough to get to the end of the hall.

"Sae." I wasn't sure who Amie was more annoyed with, but it was giving her a visible headache. "You don't need to give Esme things because she wants them. Trust me, we shared a fucking womb and we both know she'll get over it!"

"Zarek is his own person." I said quietly "So is Esme. So am I. We can all make our own decisions and the last thing I want is for them to feel as if they have no options. If that means I take a few steps back? Then maybe it's the right choice."

Switching topics, I really did have something to talk to Amie about and summarized the news I'd seen this morning. There had been a triple homicide of high-ranking officials stationed at Rateer's border. All were Dorjs. An anti-war group had taken credit, but with the sudden suicide of one of Fane's uncles, it was clear the situation in Isbul was rapidly intensifying.

Amie and Fane, who both knew more about the conflict than I'd thought, started debating the consequences of the military being split between the two sides. So far, Rateer had not given the signal for formal warfare but their raids on the outer belt of Isbul's food production planets as well as a recent attack on a communication satellite may force the nation to declare war first.

"If cousin Tet's dead, that means I'm eighth in line." Fane grimaced. "That last thing I want is to get any closer. I'm not cut out for leadership."

"Aren't you the head of a profitable corporation?"

"Yeah, but I pay all of them to listen to me!"

"Can't you abdicate?" I asked as we neared Nileanna's quarters.

"No. I can appoint people to handle my affairs, but some dumb-fuck ancestor made it so the Akon line would have to die out before the throne goes to someone else." Fane rang the door and after speaking briefly with the servant who opened the door, we were ushered into the visiting chamber. An obviously distraught Nileanna soon joined us... along with her grandson

Fane went to comfort his aunt, but I couldn't stop looking at Onitneir, who didn't look at all displeased with his new position. The room temperature was dropping.

Onitneir's smirk faltered as he noticed my stare.

Frost was appearing on his eyelashes.

"What the fuck is your problem little girl?"

"Onitneir Akon! I know I taught you better than to speak that way to a guest." Nileanna huddled under her fur coat, tugging it higher on her shoulders. "Go and tell the servants to raise the heat, it's colder than usual for this hour of the day.

I tore my gaze away from her grandson so that he could stalk out of the room. It would do no good to antagonize him. It wouldn't bring anyone back. I sat down with the others while Fane explained to his aunt why we had come to see her.

"Are you so tired of my company already?"

Fane assured her that we weren't, but that we were also in a hurry. Nileanna countered that she would feel better if we stayed longer due to the recent deaths in the family. They went back and forth until Nileanna began losing her patience.

"Auntie, I understand why you want your family nearby, I truly do." I sat beside her and offered my hands. "But please understand that Fane is just trying to help me get home as well. If we could assist in any way, please let us know."

Nileanna still looked disgruntled, but she took my hands. "Dear child, I will try my best to expedite things, but with the gala I'm hosting, it isn't possible for me to get to it today. Especially as I need to arrange for memorial pieces."

"May I make a suggestion?"

"Will you turn that off?"

In lieu of replying, Fane made a rude hand gesture and kept watching the video. Amie, who hadn't even paused from her last-minute communication with vendors, sent him what I assumed was an even more vulgar sign with her hands.

Where had she learned that?

Fane scoffed and they both looked up to grin at each other.

It was now late afternoon, and we had a good hour left before the beginning of the gala. Everything was running smoothly and ahead of schedule. The event would feature several musical performances throughout thirty courses of supper followed by a short ceremony to celebrate Nileanna and Onitneir's rise into the royal family. Guests had already begun to arrive to claim their rooms in the house before the party began. Two hundred guests had been summoned, many with short notice, to this now political event and many would stay overnight.

The worst part was Nileanna's personal request to me.

That I perform for her birthday.

A video of my singing in Solaris had surfaced on Isbulian channels. It was rapidly gaining popularity. It was the same one Fane was watching and while I was glad he found it so humorous, there was a slim chance Mother would connect the dots or recognize my voice, and then I might as well be dead. Because she would murder me. Then resurrect me. Then murder me again.

I walked into the fully equipped theatre to do a last-minute check. It was set in rich blues and bioluminescent coral had been cut and polished to adorn the walls and ceiling. With carefully swirled fabric patterns pinned by lanterns, it created quite a pretty aesthetic. The caterers were setting out elaborate table settings, and the performers had all arrived backstage.

Fane would be cohosting the event to give his aunt a night off for her birthday. We were all hoping that if we got her in a good enough mood, she would sign the ownership transfer papers without going through the entire inspection process.

Then we could finally leave.

There was an expected increase in noise level when I entered the backrooms. People were tuning their instruments, warming their voices, and pulling together their costumes ranging from the sedate to the flamboyant. There were racks of clothes shoved to one side and mirrors taken up by various entertainers painting their bodies. Someone was playing prerecorded music.

There was a crowd against the back wall who were beginning to block the main walkway; stagehands were forced to circumvent them as they ran back and forth.

I quickly spoke with the coordinator who assured me there would be no issues and that my own ensemble was placed in the left corner dressing room; a place now entirely blocked by the crowd. He must have realized it too and went to disperse people back to their designated places.

Zarek and Esme were at the center of the chaos. Esme was holding onto Zarek's arm and cheerfully chatting with one of the art illusionists. I averted my eyes and tried to get past without being seen, making my way to the dressing room.

The space inside was only slightly bigger than the average supply closet, but I was finally alone. I sat down on the small chair that had been provided and took a look in the mirror. Seeing this face as my reflection would never feel right.

Brown when you're sad.

I never thought I would miss my own body so much. At least when I felt inadequate, I knew I didn't look it on the outside. Sighing, I pinned up my dark brown hair and looked over the clothes I'd been provided. They were dark gray.

Somehow, that was the boiling point.

Ten minutes later, Amie slipped into my dressing room to give me a report before the gala began, but stopped in her tracks when she saw what I was wearing.

"Wow. That's a choice."

"Please tell me it looks okay."

I needed some positive validation here.

"It looks great." Amie had me twirl around. The dress was now bleached a lighter grey, but every tissue thin layer was ripped to shreds. I wasn't actually showing any skin, but it looked like I was. I'd torn the sleeves off entirely as well as any trace of decoration and it now had splatters of dark red all over.

"Let me fix your hair." Amie unpinned and curled every strand impeccably before ruffling it all around my head. The result was so disheveled that it could only be on purpose. I'd never looked so wild. Amie also insisted on painting my face, neck, and arms. I would never be beautiful in this disguise of mine, but at least no one could mistake me for pitiful.

Amie left to search for the memory while the house was empty.

There was only one more performance before me. I was just about to leave when the door opened and I turned to find the last person I wanted to speak to closing the door behind him.

"What do you want?"

Onitneir locked the door.

What was he doing? His emotions were all over the place. He leered unblinkingly at me and it made my skin creep. Onitneir was supposed to be with his aunt in the center box of the theater. I moved to the left when he made a sudden movement to the right.

"What is it about you?" He ran his fingers over the vanity table, tipping over several bottles and allowing them to shatter on the floor. The mixture of scents gathered together in a puddle; an almost visible perfume saturated the air. He kicked aside the chair that was in front of him and although it hadn't been any real obstacle between us, the clang it made falling over made me flinch.

He took that as an invitation to invade my personal space.

"Why do I want you?" He reached for my face.

I pushed Onitneir's hands away from me.

"I'm leaving. Don't follow me." My insides were all twisted up. The way he looked at me made me feel sick and angry. I was too ready to hurt him and I didn't want to hurt anybody. I had to remove myself before I acted impulsively.

What I was not prepared for was him grabbing the back of my dress. I had to stop before he ripped the fabric. The high platform on my shoes unbalanced me and when he grabbed a handful of my hair and yanked, I was unable to stop my momentum and landed hard against the ground.

He was on top of me. "You fucking asked for—"

I slammed him against the far wall and held him there. I had lost a shoe in the scuffle and had to remind myself not to crush him to death. Onitneir was screaming obscenities, and I had to stop the sound waves before they got too far.

Now where was my shoe?

The door opened again.

The forced entry broke the lock into pieces.

Zarek took in the scene in what seemed like a calm manner, but when he closed the door behind him, I caught a glimpse of his face unguarded. Oh no. I tried to get onto my feet but forgot I didn't have a shoe and almost tumbled back over.

"Zarek. Let's be reasonable." I braced myself against the wall.

He always managed to be present at the lowest points of my life and I couldn't even imagine what he thought of me anymore. My reflection in the corner of my eye caught my attention then. The pattern Amie had painted on my skin was marred by obvious hand prints. There was even one on my neck.

Unconsciously, I ducked to try and hide the mark.

There was a short, gravid pause.

"I'm going to show him every one of his organs." Zarek flipped a knife out of his sleeve and placed it on the vanity. "Before they're found scattered around the city." Another knife appeared out of nowhere and joined the first one. "Being eaten by scavengers." The long-jagged blade that was missing its partner was drawn from his coat. "And I think that sounds reasonable. Don't you?" He pulled out six scalpels, including a laser scalpel designed for brain surgery.

Onitneir started screaming for help.

"Zarek. I'm going to let him go."

"Before or after?"

"N-nothing happened."

"I didn't ask if anything happened, I'm simply in the mood."

I raised my head and just looked at him. Somewhere along the way, I had learned to trust him. I had found that I could argue with him without fear and that he was willing to listen to my thoughts without dismissing them outright. Zarek was the only one in my life who ever seemed confident that I could solve my own problems. There was so much in him I admired and I had hope he was starting to find things he admired about me.

Zarek acquiesced and nodded.

After I let Onitneir down, he stormed out without acknowledging either of us. Once he'd slammed the door behind him, I gave up on finding my other shoe in the wreckage and slipped the other one off as well. Barefoot, I checked the time.

"Did you need something Zarek? It's my cue."

Wordlessly, he dropped something into my hand. It was a specimen dish used in many different systems for storing biological organisms. The branching sample inside was almost fully transparent, but I recognized the pattern nevertheless.

"The slime mold," I said in awe. "it's transparent in light!"

"Nileanna has a glasshouse. I don't think she'll notice the—"

I hugged him and dashed away to make my cue.

On the way, I past the coordinator who frantically signaled that I was late. Normally I would find myself nervous from the rebuke, but I was too happy to give it a second thought. I felt like a soft cloud on a sunny day. Like the mist dancing on a field of meadow flowers. It was such a bad habit to form; to feel such glee over a small act done by another.

But it felt wonderful.

Applause turned into gasps and exclamations of shock. The audience did not know what to make of me and having seen how I looked in the mirror, who could blame them? The sound crew themselves did not start the preapproved music selection right away, but it didn't matter because I had other plans. A small sliver of anger lined my fluffy cloud and this was for her. The woman whose name I didn't know, but had sacrificed herself for nothing.

"You think.
There's anything.
More sadistic.
Than us.
You know there's no coming back from this

We paid with their bones laid down on the streets
Every day I take a look and draw a smile..."

I'd never sung anything like it. It was a post-revolution anthem of a fallen civilization. A quasi-punk genre whose popularity had been short-lived. It was rough, loud, and fast. The tempo pumped against the walls, music coming from all directions with no discernable origin. I stomped my bare foot to the bass and stopped the music all at once when the song ended. There was no real conclusion, but instead an abrupt end that was stylistic of its type.

The crowd, for all their titles and wealth, were no exception to how everyone in the outer universe seemed to react to me. They screamed and cheered and cried. There was almost a storming of the stage, but I held them back this time. I bowed and gave my thanks once some of the fervor died down.

I then wished Nileanna Akon a happy birthday.

A spotlight flashed onto their box.

And caught Onitneir committing yet another violent crime.

She was long dead, that much was evident from the gash across her throat to the mess of open flesh on her torso that Onitneir did not stop stabbing. Nileanna's blood was clearly slipping down the sides of her box to the one below, her tongue had been cut off.

Someone in the audience started screaming and Onitneir's head jerked up. He looked around wildly at the spotlight, all around the room at the panic-stricken faces of his peers, and then directly at me. Hatred twisted his face, he dropped the knife and fled.

Seconds.

That was how long I had to make a decision.

I ran for the nearest exit to get ahead of the mad dash and then, after a brief hesitation, sealed all of the doors to the theatre. Around the corner, Fane was speaking with a member of the staff for the post-supper plans and with one look at me, he dropped what he was doing and ran after me. I started calling for Amie at the top of my lungs, moving as quickly as I could to the section of the house where I knew she would be looking for the memory.

"Sae!" Amie came rushing out. "What's wrong!?"

Cira Kyrian came out right on Amie's heels, colliding into her.

"What are you doing here!?" Fane and I said at the same time.

"I'm not. Bye!" Cira blew a kiss at Amie before disappearing.

"I can explain—" Amie started but I stopped her.

We didn't have the time.

Amie elected to go detain Onitneir once she heard what I had to say and Fane and I went to Nileanna's room. It was locked. Why was it locked? Isbulian tradition would have the high-ranking rooms unlocked as a sign of strength.

Why did it have to be locked!?

"Fane, can you pick the lock?" I asked in desperation.

"Do I look like I know how to do that?"

"Can you please find Zarek? I'll try and find another way in." He rushed off to do as I asked. I tried the adjoining doors to see if there was any obvious way inside her room, but with no luck. Why couldn't I just be able to open locks like Mother did? I couldn't force it or I'd leave an obvious sign behind that her room had been broken into. It didn't take a genius to know that the authorities had to be on their way. We needed to leave before they showed up.

"Sae? Have you seen Zarek?" Esme appeared around the corner.

"Sorry, I'm looking for him too—actually, if you could open—"

"Why are you looking for him?" Esme narrowed her eyes and came up to join me. "I thought we agreed that you'd let me have him. He and I talked all today about going home for a while and letting you go on with Amie or whatever."

"Did he—nevermind. Can you please open this door?"

"Why should I!? Were you with him!? Is that why he left me!?"

"Onitneir killed Nileanna. We have other things to—"

"Why aren't we leaving then!? Sometimes I have no idea what goes on in your head. Can't you think about anybody but—"

"Please just open the door!"

I wasn't interested in their relationship right now!

"Allow me."

The door slid open and I quickly thanked Zarek before running to where I saw Nileanna come out of her office. It was immaculately well organized and it took no time at all for me to find what I was looking for. It only took one look at her handwriting and signature to produce a flawless forgery. I manually carbon-dated the ink to a few days before her extremely public death; my old interest in historical cryptology now aiding me in committing felony crimes.

I whispered a fervent apology to her soul and to the universe itself as I used both her official seal and marker.

Fane whistled when I gave him the papers and asked if it needed any other authentication besides his sign-off. He reminded me that a release of funds to her chosen banking partners would speed up the process and so I made up one of those as well. I felt no guilt in taking from the inheritance that would undoubtedly go to Onitneir now that Nileanna was out of his way. There was a chance that the estate would be broken after the circumstances of her death, but it wasn't a guarantee.

This would be a much better use of her money.

She had no security cameras to speak of as it was her opinion that they were invasive and a frivolous expense. So I had to hope that my own meticulous nature would be enough to cover our tracks.

I was doing one final sweep before Esme's raised voice had us running back to the hall.

"I thought you said you would consider it!"

"I did. The answer's still no."

"But why not?" Esme started crying.

"Did you get what you needed?" Zarek asked and I nodded.

Feeling a tap against my wards, I realized the authorities had arrived. They were trying to break into the theatre. I ran toward that direction and hoped that Amie had found Onitneir before he could get very far. I could feel her running toward me and once she was in view, I relaxed.

"Esme? why are you crying again!?" Amie was dragging Onitneir with her and he was even bloodier than the last time I'd seen him. His own blue blood was spurting out of his nose now and mixing with his aunt's. Apparently he'd stupidly chosen to resist capture.

Esme refused to answer... I think she was giving us the silent treatment. It had seemed harmless enough, even funny when we were kids but now...

"I found this on him." Amie pulled out the memory and tossed it to Zarek. Once the memory was absorbed, we had a furious, but quiet debate on what to do with Onitneir. He was sure to tell the authorities about us but as far as he knew, we were just Fane's eccentric friends who left as soon as tragedy struck.

It shouldn't be a problem.

"Onitneir, why did you murder Nileanna?"

"I killed her for fun." He smiled at me.

His teeth were stained blue.

He was telling the truth, and it was astoundingly callous. His grandmother had raised him, given him every privilege and advantage in the universe and in return he showed no remorse for her death. In fact, he kept on smiling as if this were all just a little game of pretend. I tried one last time.

"Nileanna is dead, Onitneir. Don't you understand that?"

"It was so fun to kill her. So much fun!"

There was something deeply wrong with him. The cadence of his voice had changed. The look in his eyes. It sent a cold shiver down my spine. He repeated over and over that it had been so much fun to take a knife and plunge it into her flesh. To see her entrails leaking on his shoes and how much fun it would have been to decapitate her if he'd had more time.

Amie held him at arms lengths, disgusted beyond belief.

"My vote goes to throwing him off the roof."

"Seconded." Fane looked ready to vomit again.

"We need to turn him over to the authorities." I quickly reminded everyone that there were laws here. Archaic ones perhaps but it was not our place to decide what happened to him.

Another few seconds of bickering and Amie gave up the idea of committing a homicide. As we neared the main staircase where the authorities were gathered, trying to pry open the theatre doors, Amie motioned next move and I approved.

She tossed Onitneir down the stairs at the same time I released the panicked mob from the theater. He was tied from hand to foot and there was no way for him to elude anyone. Just to make sure, I waited an extra second until one of the constables grabbed him.

Then we made a run for it.

It took another half an hour before we finally found the slaves. We'd gone to the docking bay first to find Nileanna had already approved the sale. The guards had taken the money and fled; leaving the slaves to be sold at auction. Unlike in other ordinances where slaves underwent an examination between each exchange in ownership, this city allowed owners to sell the slaves in auction unchecked as long as they accepted their inability to control the price over each unit. There were only four auction houses in the city, but we had no way of knowing and were forced to check every one before we finally caught them at the last location.

It was the one closest to Nileanna's house, obviously.

The city buzzed with the scandal that had apparently shaken it to its foundations. The Akons had deep roots to this system and Nileanna had championed all the major charities in the area. So the shock of losing the last two members of this branch of the family was unbelievable. Fane was closely following the live updates and informing us once in a while of the news as Onitneir was taken into custody and witnesses were giving testimonies.

The auction house was the first place, in our time on this planet, that was properly lit. Instead of the blue tint of the sunlamps of the city, the warehouse was illuminated by stark white light coming from the ceiling, walls, and floor. It was in a silent auction style with rows upon rows of naked slaves. Each had a countdown above their heads telling buyers how much time they had left to bid. They also all held screens with additional information on display such as birthplace, past owners, weight, age, species, etc. for the public to view at their leisure.

I could barely walk the length of this demeaning display to get to the managing offices on the other side. Fane and Zarek accompanied me with Amie volunteering to stay behind and wait with Esme. Our paperwork was heavily scrutinized, but as one of the signers was with us, Fane Akon, they had no choice but to accept what was written there.

Over the next twenty business days all slaves previously under Nileanna Akon's purview would be freed and given enough funding to establish themselves where they wished within reason as well as a monetary gift to restart their lives. Funds would be withdrawn without limit to ensure their medical and physical needs were met. This act would be done in celebration of her rise to the royal family, despite the short length in which she had to enjoy her new status.

The legalities were laid out over the fifteen pages that I'd carefully created and, as Onitneir would be in no position to argue; there was little likelihood of an inquiry into this unusually generous arrangement. The auction house would get a cut for ensuring that Nileanna wishes were fulfilled, but I couldn't help that unless I took care of the arrangements myself.

When we finally exited the building, Fane pulled us all aside to show us the latest local news alerts.

He explained that this system had always been particularly regressive. More arcane laws were kept and as such, punishments for crimes were much more punitive in nature than other jurisdictions. With such overwhelming evidence against him, Onitneir had very few legal options left. Especially as he had violated multiple Class A felonies. Separate charges of serial murders, the murder of a family member for inheritance, the murder of an official royal family member, and the crime of being in possession of over one hundred units of Nitro Venom.

I looked sharply over at Zarek, who didn't seem at all concerned that the image they showed of the drugs in question, exactly matched the vial that he'd put in his coat just a few days ago. Looking further into the matter, it seemed there was no way for him to escape punishment.

So Onitneir Akon had taken a plea deal.

He was to be branded as a slave.

"That's way too fast!" I said once I finished reading the reports. "It hasn't even been a day. There's no way Onitneir would confess that soon and no reputable justice system would be able to convict him this quickly. Where did the serial charges come from?"

"He has a record." Fane sighed, "Nileanna bailed him out every time, but they were bound to get him eventually. This time, no one was able to stop them from searching the house. Onitneir apparently kept a sick little hobby in the basement. Please don't make me elaborate."

"But this means he's lost his citizenship. He can't inherit!"

"Which means... you're looking at the sixth in line. Oh fuck no." Fane flapped his hands and arms around in stress, "Please tell me this isn't fucking happening!"

"Fane. Fane! What is that!?" I caught one of his arms to make him look at the identifying photo they'd taken of Onitneir. Without his clothes, he was even thinner than expected, but on his forearm was an intricate tattoo in black ink.

"That's just his succession mark, we all have one."

"By 'we' do you mean the Akons? Do you have one?"

"Yeah, sure. It's on the back of my hip."

"Let me see it."

"What? Why!?"

"I have a really good reason. Please let me see it?"

"Fine! Fine! But the rest of you have to turn around."

"What? You afraid we'll be titillated at the sight of your magnificent ass?"

"It is magnificent but fuck you Zarek. Turn around."

Once they all turned around, Fane quickly flashed me the back of his hip and that was all it took for me to be absolutely certain. I had seen it before.

"Oh, wrinkle snaps."

"Are you sure you saw it?" Fane asked for the umpteenth time.

Amie, who was trying to concentrate, shushed him.

The labyrinth of ice stretched out in all directions before us. Its echoing song was even louder in the absence of a screaming storm. Night glazed these passages with a threatening coat and pockets that seemed never-ending. The temperature was even colder than our last sojourn into these caves, the wind cutting through regardless of direction or lack of discernable origin.

How could a person survive in these conditions alone?

We proceeded with the expectation that something was bound to go wrong. Amie had equipped both Fane and Esme with additional gear. Zarek pulled out what looked like a cybernetic skeleton of a hand. It wrapped itself around Zarek's wrist and fingers and the joints glowed a dim yellow.

"How many weapons do you have!?" Amie demanded.

"Oh are we sharing? I should have brought cookies."

No more words were spoken for a while. The trail lend us deeper underground until we could no longer see our breath. Even so, I was glad that we were dressed for the cold this time around and more prepared for what could be awaiting us.

"Sae, I need to talk to you." Amie held me back and waved for the others to keep walking. To my surprise, she also put a small sound barrier between us and them. Esme, once she realized that Amie really meant just us two, looked ready to cry all over again.

"This is about Cira?" I asked once Esme turned back around.

"Yes." Amie's feelings were jumbled, which was a sign in and of itself. Whatever she was grappling with, it made it difficult for her to say anything. She had to correct our course a few times before she could tell me what happened.

"Kyrian showed up and she... she apologized to me."

Not what I was expecting to hear, but the idea that Cira would regret some of her actions wasn't too far of a stretch. Ever since this scheme led us to Amie's parents and my grandfather, I'd been wondering what Cira's motives really were. A personal grudge against Zarek could still be possible, but it couldn't be the reason we were dragged into this. The longer we were outside and undiscovered, the less it seemed like she was trying to trap us.

"She said she hates her father. That he's evil."

"Lyxan Kyrian?" What did I know about him? He'd expanded his territory substantially after consolidating power in Rateer where clans were known to fight for dominance. He had to be in his old age by now, but other than the odd statement he'd make once in a while after taking over a system, not much else was known about him. Cira was his only accredited child.

"Cira said she has to do what he says, but that she was sorry."

"Did she tell you why she has to do what he says?"

"No. But she said Zarek is under the same coercion."

"... Did Cira say anything else?"

Amie hesitated before shaking her head.

"We need to confront Zarek. Get him to tell us what he knows."

"I'm not against it, but he won't tell us if he doesn't want to."

"Sae. You can just make him talk."

I knew that. I just didn't want to.

"I can also earn his trust and then ask him outright."

"You need to think rationally." Amie urged me. "That man—"

"Zarek hasn't done anything to us." I knew she was right.

"Sae. He may have gotten close to you because of who you are."

And there was the crux of the matter.

Once Amie saw that I wasn't about to answer, she went to check that we were still on the right path. I kept my distance from the others as we neared our destination. This area was close to the one Amie, Zarek, and I had crawled out of the river from. So we'd been trespassing inside his territory in a way, which would explain why we'd been followed in the first place.

On one hand, I was extremely busy with my thoughts to notice the light Amie held in front cast a shadow of me that was oddly misshapen. On the other hand, I had to stop being so preoccupied that I didn't notice my surroundings.

It happened very quickly. A hood was thrown over my head and I was picked up like a rag doll and swiftly carried away. The reasons for why I didn't struggle, free myself, or alert the others was that I was pretty sure I knew who was kidnapping me and they had taken great care to not do anything that may hurt the average person.

Also, it distracted me from having to think about Zarek.

After a few minutes where it felt like he was scaling a cliffside and sliding down ice shelfs, he slowed down and I was placed gently on a furry surface. When I didn't move or speak, he was courteous enough to remove the hood.

The man looked the same as when I'd last seen him. A thick coat of animal fur protected his body from the elements and his hair grew in a wild tangle all over his head and in a thick beard covering the lower half of his face. Despite looking like he hadn't bathed in a decade; his smell was not overtly offensive. Mostly he smelled of roasted meats and smoke. His gloves and furry boots looked as if they'd been mended dozens of times before.

"Where did you find fuel to burn?" In fact, the small chamber I found myself in had a clever little fireplace in the corner that warmed up the whole space.

The man dug into a small bag he'd tied around his waist and pulled out a clump the size of my fist. After examining it, I discovered it was made of an accumulation of partially decayed organic materials that had been dried into a lump. He was burning peat.

"That's clever. My name is Sae, what's your name?"

"You sing." His voice was scratchy and clearly seldom used.

"I'm not singing. Do you hear me singing?" I asked curiously.

"You sing. Like ice." He stepped forward and that was when I realized his eyes weren't just pale, they were blind. Yet despite his questionable lack of vision, he'd seemed so surefooted that he must be able to "see" somehow. The small amount of bare skin on his face was darker than the shade of blue Nileanna's had been, but it was close enough to ask the question.

"Do you know who the Akons are? Who Nileanna Akon is?"

I found myself at the end of Zarek's missing blade.

"I'm going to guess you do know. Nileanna is dead and Onitneir can't bother you anymore. I'm not here because of them. Can you tell me what happened and why you're out here?"

"Why do you sing?" He didn't lower the blade.

"I don't know. I might be putting out some kind of frequency and maybe that's what you're hearing?" It wasn't outside the realm of possibility. "But I'm here for a reason. I think you're in danger and need help." Trying to send out calming thoughts, I didn't move just in case he saw that as an act of aggression.

"They didn't like me." Lowering the knife, he sat down on the other end of what was probably his bed and began sharpening. When I saw he wasn't going to elaborate, I took a moment to observe him. He seemed very thoughtful in his own way.

"Your family? Why didn't they like you?"

Considering what a horrible person Onitneir had turned out to be, what could this man possibly have done that was worse? As an answer, he tugged on a strand of his hair and it didn't take long for a horrible thought to occur to me.

"Were you born with white hair?"

His silence all but confirmed it.

White hair, ever since Aristae's time, had become synonymous with the Raajali. Many cultures whose hair went white with age were often obliged to dye it. Many cultures, in more archaic times, hunted those with albinism. Species had gone extinct in the outer universe because of their naturally occurring hair color by those who sought our Light. Many believed it was a sign of a true Elysian bloodline. Only a few thousand of the original Elysians had survived the initial war millions of years ago.

All who laid claim to those roots had never left.

"I'm sorry. They must have treated you so unfairly."

He shrugged. "Only Onitneir was cruel."

"Why are you out here? Can you tell me?"

"My father died. They wanted to kill me. I escaped."

"Did you have anyone who helped you? Are you alone?"

"Nomads. They come every summer. Took care of me."

"Why stay here?"

He just shook his head and continued to sharpen the blade.

"You can come with me and my friends if you want. We can heal your eyes and keep you safe. You can trust me. One of your cousins, his name is Fane, is traveling with us too. He can confirm you're entitled to the Akon name and you can file to get an inheritance from Nileanna's estate. I know it wouldn't make up for anything, but I don't think you should stay here."

"Where are you going?" Good question.

"We're traveling and then going back to my home."

"Is your home... warm?"

"Much warmer than it is here."

A few minutes later, Amie and the others caught up and found us sipping on some of Omere's—that was his name—homebrewed tea. He was showing me various tools and items while I gave my opinion on whether it would be useful for the road.

Omere didn't seem at all phased by the variety of weapons being pointed in his direction and asked me through a hand gesture if I wanted more tea. I nodded and quickly explained to the others that he had agreed to come with us.

"You didn't say anything about taking him with us!" Esme had not put down her weapon. "Isn't Fane enough for you!?"

"We think the Akons are being targeted and not by the Dorj."

Fane, after the crown prince had been killed, looked into how the other, more obscure branches were also disappearing at an accelerated rate. The situation was dire, and that no news outlet had yet to report on the string of deaths was sobering.

It wasn't my place to interfere... but...

"I want to keep Fane and Omere with us for a while until we find out what's going on." I shook my head to tell Omere that a large, hollow tusk was not practical to bring along with us and watched as he tossed it aside.

"What about majority rules?" Esme demanded. "I don't want him to come!"

"Let me see the mark." Fane moved past the others but Omere had Zarek's knife up at Fane's face before he could get too close.

"I see you found more than one lost thing today, pixie." Zarek sat down next to me and what seemed like an adequate space for two or even three people proved insufficient to prevent his arm from brushing mine. "Is that tea any good?"

Before I could answer, he took it and drank from my cup.

"Omere, could you let Fane take a look at the mark? He's the cousin I was telling you about remember?"

My voice was too high-pitched, and Esme noticed.

Omere obliged. He pulled the neck of his coat down to show the marking in its entirety. Fane, still facing the sharp end of the weapon, didn't need more than a glance before he confirmed that it was real. "I've never even heard of you. Was your birth registered?"

He acted like he didn't hear, which visibly annoyed Fane.

"I don't know Sae. What if he's just Onitneir part two?"

Omere and Fane, for whatever reason, took an instant dislike to each other. They glared at one other, although Omere couldn't really aim his eyes directly at Fane's, and a low growl escaped him as he finally lowered the blade.

Amie sighed. "I guess we're already in too deep."

"If you want him to come Sae," Fane agreed.

We all turned to Zarek, except for Omere who held up a large peat block for me to inspect. When I gave the negative, he threw it unceremoniously into a corner with the rest of his rejected things."

"Can I trade you for that one?" Zarek said, pulled out a curved, single-edged blade. With a twirl of his hand the handle extended into a pole arm. It was almost as tall as Omere, but he caught it out of the air when Zarek tossed it toward him.

In silence, he tested the balance and weight and Omere seemed to approve as he tossed the first knife back.

"That is one fine edge." Zarek whistled as he tested it against his thumb. "And he plays my favorite game. He can stay." The weapon disappeared into his coat, undoubtably joining its twin.

"Throwing things is your favorite game?" I asked curiously.

"Only until someone gets hurt." He offered me my cup back.

Esme looked around at all of us before she stormed out of the room, her hands white-knuckled at her sides. We could hear her stomping her feet, kicking things and making little screaming sounds in the other room.

After a few seconds, Amie sighed again and went after her sister.

Omere, not giving a damn that people were rampaging through the rest of his house, held up a what looked like the skull of a large *caniformia* of some kind. It was festooned with decorative tassels and feathers in a slapdash pattern, the teeth were all still attached.

I just pointed to the reject pile.

Zarek poured me more tea.

Chapter 21: Old Lessons

It was the beginning of our second week in the jungle.

This planet was a penal colony of sorts. It was a far-flung quadrant of Isbul that revolved around a young star and whose plant life thrived upon thousands of hydrothermal vents. Gravity was slightly lower than average, but the humidity levels higher. Storms here had the unfortunate habit of appearing with little to no notice and sentient life was limited to the occasional reptilian and fish. We had yet to come across any of the residents on this world.

The other day, I had stood in the storm to see if I could accurately create meteorological grid models of this planet's climate, all of which were so different from what I was used to at home. I had gone up above the canopy where the jungle spread out in all directions. Undisturbed by any major geological features, the rain that came down was warm and salty.

Having studied chemosynthetic flora and fauna before, I spent a lot of my time on my hands and knees, trying to see how the root systems of the trees interlocked with one another and touching all of the fuzzy, sticky, and thorny components of a plant that I could find. The sulfur components that some plants excreted seemed to be acting in a symbiotic manner with a vast layer of fungus that spread around in thick clumps underneath the first few centimeters of top soil.

Almost everything in this jungle was saturated in blush, the canopy filtering the light into an ethereal pink glow. It was absolutely riveting. So far, I'd filled four notebooks with my observations and was happy to take a short pause from our travels; though I knew some of my friends disagreed.

"Aggghhh!" Looking up, I watched my Sentinel throw down the map I'd made her in frustration.

Amie in particular was having a difficult week.

She was having trouble pinpointing which direction this particular memory was. Amie had tried her best to describe what she was feeling, but I couldn't find a thing out of place.

We had spent the first few days walking around in circles until somebody got brave enough to mention it to her face; and Esme hadn't exactly been very tactful about it.

In fact, Esme hasn't been very tactful of anything lately. All of us knew at this point that she was extremely uncomfortable here. None of us had ever had to suffer from heat this high and humid; I couldn't feel it myself but it must have been awful.

I offered to make her some ice but my efforts to regain our former friendship were rejected at every turn.

I wish Esme would at least speak to me.

Fane, having been woken up from his nap by Amie's cursing, just raised his head and asked if it was time for lunch. They started squabbling, but I suspected Amie enjoyed reprimanding him. It was a similar relationship to the one she shared with her younger brothers, whom I knew she missed dreadfully. I turned my attention back to the nest, but in my peripheral vision I could see Zarek striding into the clearing and heading our way.

Esme intercepted him.

For the past week, I'd successfully avoided being caught alone with him. Either I was with Amie discussing our next move or I was acting as a diplomatic buffer between Fane and Omere. The latter of whom I was trying to repair his ocular nerves and retinas without Esme's help.

Amie didn't have the anatomical knowledge or medical training to approach the procedure. So, until we could locate a doctor or professional who could help, I was going to try.

Taking on Zarek's advice, I tried not to try too hard. Yet my attempts to downscale kept failing. If I tried to manipulate anything on a small scale, it exploded or crumpled or collapsed into a mass so dense it threatened to become a black hole. My matter to energy and energy to matter experiments went exactly as they did when I was a child. Anything smaller than a ten-meter cubic sample refused to listen to me and I couldn't understand why.

That night, we set up camp on a springy, moss-covered tree. It's truck curved into a bowl like shape about halfway up to the canopy, most likely to collect rainwater. We simply removed the few centimeters of water, relocated any lingering organisms, and found a perfectly soft place to stop for the evening.

Taking out the stones I'd collected over the past few days, I settled in to teach Omere the remainder of the Elysian alphabet. Elysian was considered the universal language as all of the outer universe used it during interstellar business and travel. The alphabet was also used in nearly all formal and public education programs, regardless of the language being taught.

There were one hundred unique letters in my native language and Omere was getting to the point where he could identify each one through touch. He exceeded all my expectations as a student and was meticulous in his studies. He rarely asked a question, but then again, he still preferred not to speak at all. I wondered if I should've taken the time to teach him an established sign language, but he was clearly able to get his point across when he wanted to. So, we'd stick with the written for now.

After we reviewed the alphabet, he made an unexpected request.

"You want me to cut your hair?"

With a nod, he handed me a knife.

"I've never cut anyone's hair, do you mind if I get Amie to help?"

Half an hour later, Amie made some final adjustments and we stepped back to view our work. Omere had asked to be clean shaven, like Zarek and Fane were, but also that we not cut his hair too short. After untangling his wild mane of hair, I'd focused on shaving his face while Amie tackled the cutting.

It was quite fun to groom someone else. Amie had settled on braiding his hair back and tying the braids together into a loose tail, resulting in a style that still suited Omere's serious demeanor. All in all, he looked much less matted and years younger. In fact, though fully matured, he seemed to be even younger than we were.

"Fuck. You made him cuter than me!" Fane whistled as he came over for a look. Impressed, he pulled out a small hand mirror so Omere could see for himself.

"How does it feel?" I asked as he patted his new braids.

Self-consciously, he rubbed at his smooth chin. "Less hot."

"You look very handsome," I reassured him when he looked to me. Now that his hair was no longer hiding his face, I could finally see the resemblance to Nileanna. Although instead of the brittle slenderness that his aunt and Onitneir had possessed, Omere's narrow bone structure was hardened by years of surviving in a hostile environment. Lean muscle filled out his shoulders and he looked quite beautiful in a way. His newly revealed ears were tapered back farther than his aunt's and the long tips visibly twitched as they processed unexpected sounds.

"Burrow?" Omere asked me once Amie went back to her maps.

"Yes, now should be as good of a time as any." After I called out to Amie to tell her where we were going, she just lifted her hand in a distracted shooing motion. Earlier this morning, I had found an oddly shaped hole at the edges of a bubbling pond and had sensed an entire family of amphibians asleep not too far down. It either meant they were in hibernation or that they were nocturnal in nature. Omere and I slinked silently through the jungle canopy and were careful not to disturb anything as we found a decent sized patch of scrub to hide in.

Soon after, we heard the sound of creatures approaching the mouth of the burrow and peeked through the leaves just in time for the amphibians to turn back. The grouping of tails quickly retreated into their hideaway and I couldn't blame them. Seeing who was out on a stroll, I wish I hadn't left the nest tonight too.

I was not going to eavesdrop.

It would be immature of me.

I covered my ears with my hands and got a confused glance from Omere in return for my troubles. If it were possible to somehow leave the bushes without further indignity, I would have done so.

Why did Esme have to talk loud enough for me to hear through my hands and sleeves?

Desperately, I tried to ignore her. I really did.

"You do remember my letters! I knew it! Do you remember writing to me? I loved hearing about all your adventures. They're the reason I wanted to leave home! I was obsessed with each and every one and I know you put your heart into writing to me!"

"I remember a few, they were unsigned. You're saying you—"

"Of course! How else would I know if I didn't write them?"

"Of course. I greatly enjoyed your vivid descriptions, in the classical sense, of naked singularities in charged-parity symmetry." His tone was neutral. Entirely bland. "Your insight into coogs particles was so funny, I laughed for days."

I had never written about anything regarding coogs particles.

"Of course! Coogs particles! I knew you would like that joke!"

Physics was never Esme's strongest subject.

There was no such thing as coogs particles.

"... Did you keep the letters I sent you?"

"Maybe a few! If you came home with me, I could show you around and you could help me search my room to find them."

Even I could hear the flirtation in her words.

My insides tangled viciously.

Esme was lying.

She was lying about something that had been so important to me. I hadn't even told her that all the letters were gone. I gave up on covering my ears and instead pressed my hands to my chest, trying to alleviate the pressure I felt trying to burst through my rib cage.

Omere, sensing that something was wrong, stood up.

I focused on keeping silent while Esme peppered Omere with questions about why he was out here, had he been following them, what he'd heard, but Omere said nothing. Eventually Esme tried to convince Zarek to go with her and when that proved futile, she went back alone.

"Nice haircut."

"Thanks."

I wasn't sure what Zarek was waiting for, but he seemed just as content as Omere to let the silence rest. It was so quiet we actually did get to see the amphibians slowly come out and dive, one by one, into the bubbling pond. They were thin and wispy, with what seemed like overly large heads in contrast with their bulk. It wasn't until the last one dived in after its neighbors that Zarek finally turned to go back. I thought I was in the clear.

"So, did you keep any of my letters, pixie?"

Omere waited for another minute before he too left.

I remained where I was.

Zarek remembered the letters; he suspected I wrote them; and I didn't want to hide from him anymore. I could explain everything and hope that it didn't matter. That it wouldn't matter to Zarek what my name was... if I were anyone else, I would have risked it.

"Sae? Are you out here?"

Amie had come looking for me.

I stuck my hand out of the thicket and waved.

"Why are you in a bush?"

"Because I've lost all control of my life."

I let her grab my hand and help me out. She looked just as wired as I felt. Both of us were restless and agitated from our inability to move forward. If only I could feel what Amie was feeling, I could help. If only I could share what I was feeling...

"When we were kids, you used to race competitively. I remember the day you couldn't anymore; you wanted me to try but I was too busy to play." I could see she did remember and pointed south. "I'll give you a two-minute head start out of a ten-kilometer sprint."

She didn't wait for me to finish the sentence. I waited exactly two hundred seconds before I went after her. The ground was bumpy and filled with obstacles that made the run even more thrilling. By the eighth kilometer, we were weaving past one another through the jungle brush. In the second half of the ninth, Amie surprised me with a reserve burst of speed. She wouldn't be pleased if I let her win however, so I sprinted past just in time to finish first.

"Shit." Amie gasped as she sucked in air. "No wonder you were banned! I think I pulled my damn—"

"I'm falling in love with Zarek," I blurted out.

Amie straightened up and listened as it all came falling out.

How nothing seemed certain anymore. How badly I wanted Zarek to have come back for me because he cared about me and not about who I was. How Esme had lied about the letters and how much it hurt that she had and how scared I was that I might have inadvertently done the same to all of us. I was still carrying around the slime mold that he'd given me because I couldn't seem to control myself anymore. I couldn't stop thinking about what Esme had said and how she could be right; I was going to make Zarek miserable. Just like my father.

When I finally forced myself to close my mouth and stop talking, Amie didn't say anything right away. She went and sat on an overgrown root, motioning for me to join her while plucking a seed pod out of her hair—I moved to help her.

"When we were growing up, mom said you'd be my best friend." Amie turned so that she could look at me. "It was hard to see it sometimes but now... you've changed."

"I don't want to change because of anybody."

"Trust me. I get it. My dad changed his whole life to be with Mom and they're different when they're together. I've seen how scary they can be to other people. That's how I saw you. Scary. You're a lot more mortal when he's around."

"But I'm not mortal. How can he like me for myself?"

Amie snorted. "Then explain why he's like a tuning fork that goes off every time you're less than ten meters away. Look, I'm still suspicious. That man for sure knows something, but I'm not against the idea. Whatever you decide, I'm with you."

"Thank you." I reached out and hesitantly offered a hug.

Amie was surprised but accepted just the same. Esme had always been the physically affectionate one. Growing up, she'd always acted as a middleman between Amie and me. I had thought we had too little to say to each other. Now I realized I should have reached out sooner and taken the time.

There was something else I wanted to try before we went back.

I'd never been able to share my Light with my Sentinels. The last time we'd attempted the energy conversion, I had tried to take a single thread and it had stabbed them. Like a needle with a grudge, Amie had called it. This time, I tried to reach for something with smooth surfaces and a wide surface area. I held out the simmering warmth and Amie met me halfway. I didn't try to push. I let her to take it in at her own pace until Amie glowed with my Light.

"No wonder you don't need to sleep." Amie laughed.

"If you let it sink in a bit more, you'll probably stop glowing."

"Are you telling me your default is to glow in the dark?"

"Technically, I would glow in the daytime too."

We were giddy with success. There were many things her parents could do when linked to the Empress and we'd have to experiment to see if we could replicate them. As we headed back, we spoke enthusiastically about what she could try first and our next move now that she could pinpoint the memory.

"Sae?" Amie said as she put out the remainder of the lights.

"Hmm?" I went and placed an extra blanket over Fane.

"Thanks for finally trusting me."

The next morning, we were awoken by screaming.

Amie, and for some reason Omere, threw themselves in my direction. They would have collided if I didn't raise a soft barrier and thus it took me an extra second to register who was screaming and why people were trying to get in front of me.

Esme was loudly mumbling under her breath now.

She was tossing things left and right and once in a while a shriek of fury escaped her when she didn't find what she was looking for. Fane, seeing what had dared to wake him up, flopped back down again. Valiantly, he pulled a blanket over his head and tried to fall back asleep despite the noise.

"Esme! What in Elysia are you doing!?" Amie grabbed her arm.

"My bag! It's gone! It was just here and now it's gone!"

It did indeed look as if some of our things were missing. Now, we had put up detection barriers and it was unlikely that they failed; but what was more surprising is that Amie, Omere, Zarek, and I had all slept through the ransacking of our camp.

That is, until a fist-sized reptilian scurried out of another bag with one of Fane's gloves in its mouth.

"I thought you put up the barriers last night!"

"It was your turn." Amie shot back at Esme.

"But you always check when you get back, don't blame me!"

"Okay! Okay! Just let me try something." Amie took a deep breath and moved her hand from left to right over that area of our camp. Footprints and skin traces glowed and spread out into a trail that led into the jungle. That was a new one, but Esme didn't notice. She leaped out of the tree as soon as the tracks appeared and ran full tilt without waiting for any of us.

"Can we please wait until later to follow her?" Fane groaned.

"No." Amie yanked the blanket off of him.

Twenty minutes later, we found Esme battering her fists against an energy field covering a massive doorway. The light on the inside was a dark red and the structure itself was made of a stone that had long molded over. Besides the gaping maw of the doorway, there were no other visible entry points. It was large, but its true size was hidden under mounds of dirt and plant life.

"Esme! Calm down!" Amie grabbed before she could try again.

"But the tracks lead in there! Sae! Do something!"

Upon closer examination, I could identify thirty-eight people inside and several lifeforms that were about the right size to be our thief. My concern was there was likely a good reason for those people to be in a prison inside a planet meant to be a prison. If I did something on my own, there was a good chance I'd break the barrier somehow or even trigger an alarm.

I convened with Amie on a strategy and once we found a workable solution, I made sure to keep my reserves open for her, just in case. She thinned the barrier over a space big enough for us to walk through. Once we retrieved our things, Amie would be able to neatly reseal it behind us.

This time, Esme noticed her sister's newly discovered skills. "How did you do that?" She demanded once we were done. Amie gave her a pointed look, her eyes going to the others. "I'll tell you later."

"Whatever!" Esme ran ahead again without waiting for us.

Fane groaned. "Can we not follow her and just wait here?"

"Suck it Akon." Amie took the lead.

The inside of the prison could fool one to believe that it was abandoned. While the exterior of the building was crafted out of stone, the inside was sealed in a dense metal that was oxidizing in patches here and there. The air was hot and stale. The floor was one large drainage grate that hovered over a pit so deep that we couldn't see the bottom. While I knew I could always catch myself and the others in a fall, it was unnerving nevertheless to put your weight on a surface with no visible supports.

The red lighting coming from the center of the cavernous ceiling did nothing to dispel one's anxieties. I could hear people shuffling in the cells that lined this place. All of them were sealed behind visible barriers tinged, predictably so, in dark crimson. There wasn't much room to maneuver as a large swath of space in the middle was left open to the pit below.

In the first cell we past, the prisoner inside was dead.

His body was being feasted on by larger versions of the reptile we'd just seen. Their heads whipped up as they caught our movement; their maws slick with chunky gore. When we made no move towards them, they returned to their meal with renewed gusto.

How did they keep these prisoners alive at all?

This planet was where many convicts were sent to for serious crimes, but they were allowed to roam freely and were presumably able to take care of themselves. Trapped in here, there was no detectable system to feed them or dispose of—

A giant with bulging muscles and only one arm rammed themselves against the barrier of their cell, shaking the grate below our feet. They possessed a plated forehead that looked like it had been cracked straight down the center in the past, but it didn't seem to pain them as they rammed it against the barrier again.

Screaming the entire time.

"You motherfucking shit sniffing fuck!" It bellowed before ramming the barrier again. "Let me out so I can rip out your throat you bastard! Let me out! Zarek! Let me out!"

As soon as they yelled his name, all of the other cells erupted into a caterwauling display of rage. The grates rumbled under the assault of dozens of people throwing themselves into the walls and floor. Some begging, but most threatening to do terrible things to Zarek's wellbeing if released.

I looked to Zarek, hoping that he knew what we should do, but he didn't make eye contact with me. He didn't have any expression at all. It was as if Zarek couldn't hear them. He certainly didn't respond to the multitude of disgusting things aimed in his direction.

Amie was in a defensive position, but didn't know where to turn. I left Omere's side, seeing that he was preoccupied in covering his ears from the racket and walked up to where Zarek was leaning against a pillar.

He stared off into the distance.

"Zarek?" He wouldn't respond to me.

Something sharp was rising inside me, scraping against the inside of my organs. I couldn't hear myself think with all this screaming. I felt repulsed by the explicit threats being hurled in our direction and I couldn't take much more of it. I whirled around.

"Shut up!"

I shouldn't have yelled. The force of it physically knocked them back and the silence that followed was unnatural. Amie had to nudge Fane and Omere away from the edge of the grate, just to make sure they didn't accidently fall and awkwardly just shrugged her shoulders at me.

An explanation was due here.

"Zarek, I—" I was left speechless when he picked up my hand and placed a kiss against my palm. Empress help me. Why did he have to look at me that way?

"Fierce little thing, aren't you?" He murmured against my hand.

"Hi guys! Am I interrupting anything!?" Esme popped up out of nowhere and I jumped back from Zarek, which in retrospect sent an obviously wrong message.

There was a brief second I thought she might physically get between Zarek and I, but the moment passed. She did seem much happier now that she had her things back and chatted endlessly beside Zarek as we retraced our steps back to the exit. Her earlier agitation now a distant memory, she was nearly hopping with renewed cheer; her speech moving a million kilometers an hour.

We were only steps from the exit when I heard someone call my name. It was very faint but unmistakable.

"Am I the only one who heard that?" Amie shook her head, trying to make me keep going. Then we heard it again. The voice was a familiar one. I couldn't not go and investigate. "Esme, keep the others safe. Amie, I think we should go back and investigate."

When Zarek moved to follow us, I stopped him.

"You need backup, pixie." He said gently.

Hearing this, Omere slid up to my other side and while he didn't look pleased about it, Zarek allowed it.

He, Fane, and Esme left the prison to wait for us.

It didn't take long to see who it was. In the back right of the prison, in a cell of her own and dressed in the same bloody clothes, was Leah Dorj.

"Sae!" she cried in relief. "Please let me out of here!"

"What are you doing here!?" Amie blocked me from view.

"I promise that I don't deserve to be in here. Please!"

"Did Cira put you in there?"

Leah hesitated, but shook her head no.

"She's not lying," I pointed out, but Amie wasn't satisfied.

"Why are you in there? Why should we let you out?"

"Please. Rayde must be so worried! I can't tell you why I'm here. I can't tell you. I can't!" Leah sobbed. "I thought I was done. I thought he wouldn't have any use for me after Dorj. If you leave me, I'll never get out!" She beat her hands against the barrier.

"Who is he?" Amie doubled down.

"Is it Lyxan Kyrian? Cira's father? Your father?" I slipped around Amie and knelt down across from Leah. She looked so young. She couldn't have reached her majority yet and it was heartbreaking to feel her raw fear and desperation.

"I can't, I can't." She shook her head violently. "I can't say."

"Who can tell us? Can Cira tell us? Can Zarek?"

Fear dilated her eyes into wide chasms and her shoulders heaved like she was going to be sick. She just shook her head, over and over.□"Please. Let me out." She whispered. "I promise I will never do you or anyone you love harm. I just need a chance. Please." She wouldn't answer any of our questions after that, she just kept repeating please over and over again.

Amie pulled me away and Leah's pleas became hysterical. She only quieted when she saw that we weren't going but a few meters away. "Sae. Everything in me is telling me we can't let her out." Amie must have seen my disagreement because she cursed under her breath. "We can't take her with us. Fane, fine. Omere, I gave in. But this time? It's too dangerous."

I needed a moment to think. I shook Amie's grip off my arm and went back to Leah. She was now genuflecting on her hands and elbows, her forehead touching the ground, and her hands clenched tightly together. Logically, there was nothing that Leah could do against me. She could not harm me in any capacity and did not have the means to lie to me.

"Why did you kill prime Minister Dorj?" I asked her.

"I was told to, but I didn't want to." She was telling the truth.

"Why did you do it? Couldn't you have said no?" Leah shook her head. "What do you plan to do after I let you go? Where are you going to go?"

"I can't tell you but I promise I won't hurt anybody." Leah's head touched the ground again. "I swear I just want to save myself."

It would have to be enough.

I let Leah Kyrian out.

Leah hugged me tightly, sobbing into my shoulder, thanking me, promising me that she would repay the favor someday. For a brief moment, I wondered if her words should be taken more seriously. Fate had a funny way with the Raajali and promises.

When we finally emerged from the prison and sealed the entrance behind us, Leah shrank back to huddle behind me. It was evident she did know Zarek and that he knew her. He didn't try to move any closer, but Leah cowered anyway.

"Leah," he said curtly in greeting.

"Zarek." Leah's voice shook over the syllables.

"Did you finally piss off Cira enough to get locked in there?"

"No. Goodbye."

Leah looked over her shoulder more than a few times as she quickly ran off into the jungle. There was a part of me that wanted to follow her, but the fear that she'd shown toward Zarek changed my mind. Leah, whatever her business was, likely had nothing to do with me. Zarek's secrets on the other hand, were starting to feel as if they had everything to do with me.

Chapter 22: Civilizations

The more we wandered, the less distance we traveled.

What should have been a leisurely stroll to the location Amie marked on the map turned into hours of walking. Amie and Fane began to squabble over our direction as Amie insisted that she hadn't changed it at all, but Fane was adamant that we had changed it at least a few times. I thought we'd walked in a perfectly straight line, but Omere agreed with Fane for once, which did give us pause. To resolve the matter, Zarek carved a cross into a nearby tree.

It only took us ten minutes to walk by it again.

"That's impossible!" Amie slapped her hand against the carving as if she could somehow wipe it off the truck of the tree. "It doesn't even look like that same tree!" She pointed out the curve of the tree and I had to say that she was right.

The tree was shaped differently.

"I don't feel anything." I closed my eyes and tried every method I knew of to see if anything was being distorted and I went as far out as the upper atmosphere, but there was nothing. "I can't find anything. Zarek do you feel anything?"

"No, but I know when I'm being played." Zarek picked up a pebble from the ground and threw it so hard that it made an audible zip through the air. It only took a few minutes, but the surprising part wasn't that it came back, but that it came back from three different directions. The pebbles crashed into each other in mid-air and crumbled back to the ground.

"But there's nothing here that could explain that." I knelt down and dug my fingers into the ground. I couldn't fight something if I didn't know what I was fighting. I flinched when Zarek knelt down and put one of his hands over mine. I hadn't been expecting it, but I pushed aside my own feelings and dug deeply into the basic building blocks of this world.

I felt the sweltering pressure under the surface layer being relieved by the hydrothermal vents. I felt the changing weather systems rise and fall, the feeling of multiplying new life being formed and the rot that was already piling on top the jungle floor. I smelled the sulfur and the salt, the tang of metal deposits, and the bitterness of life pushing forward on this developing world.

There was something... something utterly void of sensation.

I felt Amie put her hand on my shoulder and I let her see what I could see, a great big patch of nothing that loomed right in front of us. It had no clear shape or color and all attempts to touch it directly past right through. I opened my eyes and let go of the ground. Sitting back on my knees, I saw that Amie and Zarek were both as confused as I was. Whatever it was, it was unique.

"Well? What's going on!?" Esme snapped, in a bad mood.

"There's something that's not there. Right here." Amie waved her arms in that general direction, and I was half expecting something to happen, but nothing did. "And every time we get near it, we're right back where we started."

"It's possible it's another plane all together," Zarek mused.

"But artificial planes are exceedingly rare!" I took Omere's stones out and began to lay out the probability functions. A place or idea that were self-containing interpretations of reality that only existed within the confines of the plane. There were certain fields and topics of cosmology that were hidden to all but the Empress of Elysia, but that didn't stop scientists from hypothesizing. Any remaining areas of observation had been collapsed eons ago within Elysia.

It could be this phenomenon was natural, but such areas and concepts had a bad habit of consuming any nearby mass or energy, expanding their size rapidly. The fact it was stable in size would indicate it was artificial or at least fed by a large power source. What that source was, one can begin to infer through quantum dispersive differential equations and analytic number—

"Sae! Hey! Enough with the lecture!" Esme clapped her hands in front of me, snapping me out of my thoughts. One look at my friends' faces and I knew I had been talking whilst thinking again. It was embarrassing. I had annoyed Esme and had not done anything productive to help the situation.

Now was not the time to go off on an endless tangent.

"Right. Sorry. Um, Amie if you want to try to match frequencies with the plane, we can hold it and try to push me inside. It will likely be easier to leave than it is to get in. It shouldn't take more than a few minutes, I'll try and get back as soon as possible. I read about the sequence, but I think taking a field approach—"

"You're not going in there." Zarek interrupted me.

"I understand your apprehension, but I think I can—"

"This isn't jaunting off to the star system next door, pixie and it isn't worth the particle decay."

"... But you still don't remember me. Do you?"

"It doesn't matter." He said softly, "You're not going in there."

"Yes I am. Amie get ready to bungee me because it's happening."

"Oh like hell you are! She can't be dumb enough to listen to—"

"I am standing right here. Please don't insult Amie's intelli—"

"Actually, I'm calling her a genius because she isn't doing it."

"Then I can do it on my own. Just watch me."

"If you think I'm going to just let—"

I ran off. There was no possible way he could reach me before I got myself inside. I threw down my bag and sprinted, thinking that if I timed it right, I could be back before they worried too much.

I'd have to apologize to the others for not discussing it fully with them, but at least I'd have the memory. This one was so heavily guarded that it had to be his memories of me. It had to be.

Quickly, I gathered the energy that would take me a sidestep out of plane zero of the material universe.

It might have been a good idea after all to do this alone. The practice of such an act was complex and possibly unforgiving. I was just at the threshold when I felt him grab my hand. I couldn't twist to look and it was too late to reverse my trajectory. I threw back the shielding to cover both myself and my stowaway as we plummeted through the layers of shifting particles and kaleidoscopes of exploding atoms into a great unknown.

My mouth tasted awful and for the first time in my life I experienced what it felt like to have an under-moisturized throat. I sat up and looked around at a jungle that looked exactly like the one we had just left behind. Except it was blue.

The light filtering through the canopy was still pink, but the ground, trees, and undergrowth were all a frosty azure.

Zarek was in one piece as far as I could tell. I had never gotten good results with my Light when dealing with other people and this undertaking had been dangerous enough without the added factor. He was still holding onto my hand and no amount of tugging proved successful in gaining my appendage back. It was quiet here. Not even the wind made an effort to stir.

"Hello?" I finally whispered, giving up on getting my hand free. "Zarek? You need to wake up now." I shook him gently on the shoulder and then the world rolled over a few times before I found myself on the ground.

I held still, both wrists trapped above my head, staring up at him as he woke up all the way. He released my hands and I scooted back until I was no longer trapped underneath him.

"You're an Elysian. Aren't you, pixie?"

My heart stopped for a beat.

"Yes. I am."

"Full-blooded?"

"Yes." It wasn't a lie to affirm it.

"Can all Elysians do what you just did? Can Amie or Esme?"

"No. My innate gifts rare." Extremely, tremendously rare.

"There's more, isn't there?" Neither of us really expected me to answer. "Do I already know? Will I remember?"

"There aren't that many left to find, you should know soon."

He stood and held out his hand to help me up. What confused me was that he kept a hold on it even as we began to walk. Without looking at me, he explained that it was a good precaution to take against being separated here. Neither of us knew what to expect and it would be better for us to not wander away from the other.

I accepted it as a logical step.

We didn't have any time to prepare ourselves.

The entire landscape stretched and flew past us all in one, blurry stripe. It was as if we were the only things on solid ground and everything else was painted film being run past our eyes. Trees and other objects in the landscape that should have smashed into us flew to either side instead. Any attempt to stop it was futile. Faster the landscape flew until everything around us was nothing but for an impression of speed and light.

Zarek grabbed onto me, and I grabbed onto him as the dizzying array spun and then, all at once, snapped to a dead stop.

I found myself face-to-face with him, my arms around his neck and my feet clear off the ground. His arm held me firmly around my waist and the other behind my upper legs and it felt... good.

He put me down quickly and gently and I had to remember to lock my knees before I made a fool of myself. My entire body felt like I'd walked through a solar flare. I started to look around for something, anything to take my mind off of matters that were not important right not and should not be a distraction.

Zarek did the same and we spent an awkward few seconds not looking at each other until, mercifully, a doorway appeared in front of us and a person walked out.

Now, our current setting was an empty room that looked like the inside of a large gemstone. It protruded outwards in the center of the walls, bulging out, but the ceiling and floor were smooth and flat. Our reflections could be viewed from a hundred different angles of the carved surfaces, and everything was bathed in a gentle pink glow despite any obvious light source.

The person who entered was really very similar in appearance to the room with ivory skin and no hair. They looked like a child, but the forced smile on her face aged her. She wore trailing grey robes that looked as if the fabric was simply draped over her shoulders and then tied by the rope around her middle.

Her bright pink eyes were unnervingly dilated.

"Leave." The voice that came out of their child-like stature was deep and vicious. A venomous bite hidden under the façade of a flower. I could read nothing from her. I couldn't hear her heartbeat or the blood that had to be pumping through her veins.. I couldn't see her thoughts. I couldn't feel her. Just like this plane had been from the outside, it was like she wasn't there.

"I'm sorry for trespassing. We're just looking for a—"

"I know what you're looking for. Leave before I kill you."

My instincts were on edge.

The longer I looked at her, the more I felt like I had met her before somehow. I remembered every face I ever come across, even the nursemaids who I had spent brief periods with as an infant; but I couldn't match this face with any that I'd seen before.

So why did it feel so unnerving to look straight at her?

I had seen plenty of intelligent lifeforms and facial features of all kinds. Most dominant species were bipedal, but beyond that one moniker, the universe was a diverse place.

There was no reason to find it so hard to look at her.

Then she moved and both Zarek and I involuntarily flinched. It hadn't been natural. It was like she had sputtered, phased out of place. Zarek had his hand on my shoulder and I could feel the tension in his fingers. The room itself crackled around us, as if responding to our discomfort.

"One. Last. Chance." Her smile was too wide. Her head too swollen for her tiny frame and her eyes too large. "Leave."

"We're going." Zarek's hand on my arm tightened.

"I don't think—" I began to say and then never got the chance.

Zarek yanked me aside as the girl's arm whipped forward and what was her hand crashed through the wall behind me. The hand whipped back and to my horror was now a monstrosity of pivoting sharp edges with shards of the wall embedded deeply into the skin-colored surface. Zarek had one arm around me and the other plunged into his coat, looking for a weapon that apparently wasn't on him anymore because they were all floating around the melting candle that was her main body.

The doorway she'd come through was suddenly sealed and so was any entry point that we may have come through.

The air blurred around us.

"Looking for these!?" The blades spun and raced toward us, somehow piercing the barrier I created between, but still stopping before reaching us. How was that possible? There was no way those knives should have gotten as far as they had. I flinched when several of the smaller projectiles exploded on impact, the sound ricocheting all over the shifting room.

"Were you carrying explosives?" I asked Zarek in disbelief.

"Well, it wasn't ever a problem before now."

Gravity was flipped and turned on its side. If it wasn't for Zarek holding onto me, I would have gone flying. He'd dug his fingers into the floor that was now the wall and kept us both from sliding right into the person trying to kill us. She walked on the vertical surface and suddenly the wall itself was on fire. Zarek was forced to let go and I created a floor for him to keep his footing.

Pain seared my shoulder as I felt what seemed like teeth bite into me. I cried out and saw that I was bleeding, only it had to be an illusion because there was nothing that could pierce me like that. The invisible teeth felt like they were going to rip my entire arm off and I shoved back with all the might only to have the room dissolve around us and the world spin as the force of my influence boosted us out into open air. The teeth lost their grip.

I cried out again as Zarek was putting too much pressure on my shoulder and we both hit another flat surface only to see the girl, now only half flesh and bone, diving at us. Zarek rolled us to the right just in time to keep from being crushed. I pushed away from him and slammed what I knew was near one hundred thousand kilograms of pressure per square centimeter in all directions around us. It blasted the visible form of this creature away and yet I could feel something battering at me from all angles.

What was this feeling!?

My shoulder no longer bled, but the pain felt so real. My body theoretically regenerated faster than could be expected of a mortal being, but I'd never been in a situation that could actually hurt me. So what was this sensation if it wasn't pain?

I tried to manipulate the fabric of time around Zarek and I to give myself time to think. I wasn't supposed to, but this was an emergency and I didn't know what else to do, but the moment I took my attention away, the universe exploded in an anti-matter matter explosion that blew Zarek and I apart. I contained the reaction and found myself dodging the crazed being in close quarters as they tried their absolute best to cut me with that looked like overgrown claws growing out of their whiplike arms. Their speed and dexterity was incredible to keep up with me.

They were laughing and I could not think of what I should do while holding down the anti-matter explosion and keeping Zarek from falling into a never-ending space of this plane of reality. I had no idea how the physics worked in here and I could not collapse the plane without the danger of Zarek being injured. I had to go on the offense. I didn't have a choice.

I collapsed the matter in the center of the being's body into a mass so dense that no particle could escape. I did it so often by mistake that it was almost second nature to stop the process, but this time I let it grow. I vanished and reappeared floating next to Zarek, who had been knocked unconscious by the initial force of the antimatter blast before I could contain it. It amazed me that he was still physically okay after such an incident, but it reinforced the idea that some part of all this was just an elaborate illusion.

I reached for him, but was slammed back into a ground that hadn't been there just seconds before and found myself blinded. I thrashed in panic before I broke through the sphere of darkness that enveloped my head. There was no time for me to recover and I had to get out of the way of the arc of energy that sliced through the place where I once sat.

Combat was not something an Heir ever learned in their classes and I could now see what a huge gap in my education that decision had created. I bent the light coming from what I assumed was the sun inside this place and split the entire place in half. Everything that I could see was rendered straight down cleanly in the middle.

A roar of pain that shook the ground told me I had hit something, but I was not going to take the time to look at what.

"Zarek!?" Where did he go? I had just left him here! "Zarek!"

I should have kept him close to me, where did he go? I couldn't protect him if I didn't know where he was! Panicking, I did not feel any better when the ground starting to thrash about violently. Zarek couldn't have been in any condition to go that far.

"Zarek! Where are you!?"

Come here you little bitch!

Oh no. Terror tasted just as horrible as dry did. Where was he!? Did she have him? I stood my ground, but my hands were shaking again. The ground in front of me burst open and out came enormous wings feathered in an array of stunning pink hues... she was beautiful. She was ethereal.

She was a Ryunaga.

An enormous being who dwarfed Mio in size, meaning she was older than the Empress' companion and thus even more deadly.

Had the Raajali ever fought the Ryunaga?

I did not want to be the first one to test it.

I didn't think I was allowed to hurt a Naga.

I didn't think she was going to give me much of a choice.

My brain automatically rejected the idea of doing anything that could possibly endanger a member of a species already so close to extinction. I couldn't do this.

I couldn't hurt Yuki's people.

She screamed and out came a wave of highly charged electromagnetic radiation and plasma. Before I could counter, both the Naga and the radiation were flung to the side where splattering plasma accidently burned one of her legs.

"Zarek!" I appeared at his side and braced him against me. He'd burned up too much of his own reserves. He was bleeding from several puncture wounds and was not steady on his feet. "Sit down.

I promise I'll get us out of this." The mere fact that he was still upright was a feat in and of itself. "Zarek please. Please stop."

"Sae. Get back." Zarek's dark eyes glowed eerily.

The next moment, I had to let go of Zarek in order to keep the Naga from tearing him apart on a subatomic level. She was focused on me and I could feel the strain against my Light as I forced her back. The landscape around us dissolved into a stomach-turning, battering quagmire of consciousness.

I may not have known before how I stacked up, but apparently the Raajali had at least a slight edge. I began to close in the space around her, finally getting a grip on the range of her abilities. She may be powerful, but ultimately she was no match.

Unexpectedly, Zarek's hand grazed my arm and I felt a jolt.

He collapsed next to me and it turned my attention for a split second. Just long enough for her to escape. In the instant that I felt her break free, I didn't think about it; I simply threw myself on top of him; knowing whatever she was going to do would certainly kill Zarek, but just might not kill me.

Oh please let it not kill either of us.

Lashing out blindly, I had no idea what I was doing, but knowing that I needed to do something to protect us. In the seconds that ticked by, I heard her screaming, but not in pain. It was an anguished screaming that chilled me in a way that Omere's home world had no hope of replicating. In those seconds, our surroundings stabilized and no other attacks came our way.

Hoping that I hadn't done too much damage to him, I scrambled off of Zarek, but to my astonishment, there were no longer any visible wounds. What in the universe's name?

I could hear his steady heartbeat and his breathing was normal. So, after a brief hesitation, I went to go check in on the woman that had been so deadest on harming us.

She was struggling with all her might. We both knew at this point it was useless but she made no effort to stop her frenzied actions. In her panic she tore some of her feathers and they littered the ground. I couldn't get very close before she spotted me and her struggle grew even more frantic. I kept her enclosed, but I didn't get too close. Trying my very best, my efforts to ease her panic and pain did nothing. I couldn't do anything if she fought against me.

"Let me help you! Please!" I beseeched her.

Gruesome murderer of children! Her cries echoed in this plane from all directions. *Enemy of my blood! Why do you seek to kill the very vestiges of us!? Wasn't the first genocide of my people enough to sate your bloodlust!? How dare you speak to me! I will rip your spine from your body! I will curse your child to die in your womb and only then will you feel what I have felt!*

Her ranting was heartbreaking.

There was a glint of madness in her gaze that I didn't know Ryunaga could obtain and although I listened to her; there was something else about her that demanded my attention.

I had encountered this sensation only once before.

"You're expecting?"

She let out a cry so anguished it broke the sound barrier.

Finding myself in the position of holding back her explosive rage, there was little I could do for the next few minutes as she exhausted herself. My face felt tingly when she finally stopped smashing against the bubble I'd put around her.

I'd never been able to use so much of my strength before and found it to be quite an agreeable sensation. I stepped closer to her knowing she watched my every move; her body was heaving from her rabid efforts to escape my hold.

I was drawn to her midsection, where all of her species possessed an underbelly pouch. They held their eggs there. Yuki used her small pocket to keep trinkets and snacks in, but I knew that this woman held young inside... and they felt wrong.

They weren't alive.

Judging by the size, they felt to me about the size Yuki's egg had been when we'd met. From what I knew of Naga physiology, their young didn't hatch until conditions were ideal for them to be born. Their eggs were virtually indestructible and appeared in groupings ranging from one to five. Although it was rare, depending on the bloodline some Naga gave live birth.

The right thing to do would be to find Zarek's memory and leave her alone. She obviously didn't want my help and many of the things she said troubled me. The Ryunaga and the Raajali had always been at peace, but ancient Elysians had held a distrust of them due to their abandonment of us in our time of need.

We had mended that rift when the Second Emperor, Taiyo Raajali, became the companion of Illi, the first of their kind to be raised in our family. Ever since, a Naga had always sat beside an Empress, as an equal and friend.

Before the plague, most had lived within the Empress' jurisdiction, but they were not, in any way, under the Empress' rule. Though we coexisted, they had long kept their own councils and their own secrets. Meaning that, by the time my grandmother discovered they were dying out, it had been too late.

Liashimi Raajali had found both cure and immunization when her companion, Saar, had fallen ill. As the Empress, she had given it to the Naga only weeks after Saar's death, but we had no way of knowing how many it had saved. Ever since the tragedy, their society had vanished and all communication had ceased. Mother and I had no idea how many had died.

It was commonly believed that not many had survived.

I felt a stirring then, unlike anything I'd ever known.

This field trip was turning out to be quite the... my brain seemed to soften into fluff the more I tried to anchor my thoughts.

I stretched out both my hands and didn't think to question why she was allowing me so close. My disguise fell away and while I didn't intend it, my skin blazed with light. I could see every vane and barb that shaped each feather. The wisps of down and the curvature that assisted her in flight. Here was a kinship I achingly missed. The knowledge of an existence so far and above the spectrum of life that makes one so uniquely alone. I felt each of her blood vessels, the shape of every atom convalescing to form an inheritor of the most ancient creation in the universe. I felt the eons that had passed, virtually unchanged. I looked and I saw the fever, the pain that could only form after millennia of suffering.

I plunged my hands into the plumage in front of me.

There was a surge of light and then...

Nothing but darkness.

I jerked upwards out from my unconsciousness and immediately regretted sitting up so fast. There was a slow roll of instability laid over my every nerve. Having never known what it felt like to be nauseous, I now assumed it was what I was feeling. How did one stop feeling sick from movement and sound?

Disregarding my discomfort, I looked around wildly at the vast amount of soft bedding floating atop a sea of soft pink clouds and found no immediate danger. Had I dreamed it all? I found Zarek right next to me, still very much asleep.

You're awake. Acceptable. Now leave.

Springing to my feet, the world spun around a few times before it finally decided to settle around me.

It was her; she poked her head up from the edge of the bedding and with one flutter of her wings, landed gracefully in front of me. With all that had happened, we naturally spent an initial few seconds eyeing each other suspiciously until something else caught my attention.

"They're alive!?"

I ran forward in excitement, only for her wing to come down and stop me. I had to blow the errant feathers out of my mouth before apologizing. I knew better than to get into someone's personal space like that without permission.

"Are you feeling alright?" I asked.

She snorted and began preening her wings.

You Raajali think you're so wonderful.

I was trusting her not to bite me again and turned my back to check on Zarek. Although I could see the tears in his clothing, he seemed perfectly unharmed.

Somehow, I had healed him and something else as well.

Even from this distance, I heard the six heartbeats behind me.

My name is Cor. Are you the elder or the younger?

"I'm Saekonari Raajali, the Heir. Nice to meet you."

The feeling is not mutual. Cor settled down on her side, keeping both eyes on me as I moved around Zarek and made sure he was all in one piece. Despite her relaxed form, she was unable to keep her silence for long. *Stop that. You're making me ill just watching. Your mate is alive isn't he? So leave before I decide otherwise.*

"He is not my mate." I put down Zarek's arm and took a few seconds to gather up my thoughts. "Did you mean what you said before?" I walked over to Cor and sat down next to her neck. She allowed it. "You think my family had something to do with the Plague? That somehow we're to blame?"

I always suspected so. Cor scraped the bedding with a claw, opening a small window. I found myself awestruck, looking onto what was once a great metropolis. Dreamlike, they swooped and flew through a crystalline structure so fragile one wondered if it would melt under a warm night's sky. Suspended in open space, the central dome shone with the light of a thousand colors.

Children raced through the columns and open aired edifices, disturbing the peace of several elders. I saw their libraries, their gardens, and I felt the numbing pain of grief when it all rotted away. Black bones were all that was left on their homes and streets. From tip to tail, some of the older Naga left a carcass spanning fifty meters or more. The children less than one.

My city was gone in a matter of weeks. My entire family in mere days. My friends perished. My children dead inside me. The window disappeared into the wind. *Now tell me. How could this be without your power over life and death?*

I was still processing what I had just witnessed.

I had never seen so many, not in our records and certainly not in real life. I knew that they were myths to many civilizations, but to me, they had always been a part of my life. Yuki had always been a part of my life. I had never questioned that perhaps she could have been there. When they all disappeared.

"What do you mean by power over life and death?"

I said what I meant. Cor didn't sound angry, just tired. *The Raajali may deny it, but she gave my people a priceless gift. The first of you. Blood of your blood. She freed us from being the watchers, the observers of this universe. The arbiters of balance and the harbingers of light and dark.*

It was readily apparent who she spoke of.

Aristae. Whose name and face I held. She who had scarified herself and her life to serve our people. She who'd held the universe in her hands. Who was long gone and who couldn't answer my damn questions like a decent person.

"There may have been some gaps in my education."

Hmmm... are you still in your infancy?

"No. I'm young, but considered fully grown."

Then why do you have a training mark on you?

"A what?" What in the universe was a training seal?

I held still as Cor lowered her head and turned slightly, allowing her to blow a cool breath over my body. A white ring appeared around my neck. I could see it in my reflection in her eye. I tried to grab at it, but my fingers went right through. I was collared. Like a slave. I could feel myself panicking and I scratched my skin trying to somehow grab this thing. Scrabbling, grasping, it wouldn't come off! Why wouldn't it come off!? Had it always been there!? Why had I never known it was there!? How do I get it off of me!?

Calm down! Cor snapped at me.

I gave up trying to get at it and just hugged my knees to my chest. I started going over the four thousand nation capitals of the outer universe, starting with the sector adjacent to the upper right quadrant of the universe and making my way to the lower left.

A neurotic Raajali. Hilarious. Cor snickered.

"I don't appreciate the commentary. Please keep it to yourself."

If I'm not mistaken in who placed it. You can't remove it yourself.

"What do I do? What does it do? Why is it on me?"

We place them on hatchlings when they grow strong too soon. I never thought the Raajali did the same. You all seem to be born with the skill to control yourselves.

"I struggle with smaller projects, but I've never lost control."

Cor seemed intrigued. *It can't possibly be inhibiting you. You wouldn't have gotten in here if it was or have brought my children back to me. You would never have been able to fight me or heal my mind the way you had.*

"Is that what I did?" I placed my palm against her cheek.

Don't get conceited. You Raajali are always in danger of hubris.

"And Naga have always been known for their modesty and humility." Cor actually laughed at my humor this time.

I think she was warming up to me.

We sat in the peaceful quiet and Cor allowed me to lean against her feathered neck. Mio and Yuki were scaled, so I'd never experienced such a soft hide on a Naga. I had so many questions that I wanted to ask but at the same time, I was starting to think that Cor would not be the one to answer them. I would have to ask the person who chose to keep me ignorant.

"Cor? Will you please take the mark off of me?"

I knew Mother had placed this collar on me.

She had neglected to tell me key components of my past and now I suspected her of far worse crimes. There was a child that screamed in me. Who was trying to close her eyes and ears against anything that suggested the Empress was at fault. That she had lied. That she had treated me unfairly in any way.

Mother was the most compassionate, loving woman in the universe. She only wanted what was best for me. How dare I suspect her? She had raised me and taught me everything I had ever known about fulfilling my role with honor and kindness. Mother would never do anything to hurt me on purpose... unconsciously, I reached up to rub at my cold, wet cheek.

The Empress could do no wrong. It was impossible.

Whatever Cor thought on the matter, she kept it to herself.

Ordinarily, I do not interfere with parenting choices of others... but I will make this exception. Once. Do not come back and ask for more favors. I have my own hatchlings to raise now. Cor warned before she gently blew another breath over me that smelled of flowers and warm grass.

I could feel tears prickling my eyes as mother's influence was lifted. I could no longer deny that it had been affecting me. Weight I'd never noticed rolled off my shoulders and from around my neck. I fumbled into my pockets until I found one of the stones I placed there and when it lifted off my hand with ease, I cried.

I felt so scared in that moment. So relieved.

There hadn't been anything wrong with me. There was never anything wrong with me. The stone flew in a perfect circle over my palm faster and faster until I couldn't stand it anymore and let it fall apart into dust. Dust that I could easily make fly into the breeze and spell out my name.

"Thank you. Thank you!" I hugged her tightly around her neck.

Cor did not seemed moved in any way by my gratitude.

Enough. Go pick up your mate and get out.

She pushed me away from her, more gently than her tone would imply, and I quickly did as I was told.

I was just about to leave Cor to her home and her children, apologizing for barging in without an invitation, when I remembered the memory. We still needed to look for it!

Once I came to my senses, I found it lodged in my pouch. Cor said, irritated at the delay in our departure. She had put it near our unconscious bodies and it had been absorbed.

Good enough for me.

I got back into my disguise and sidestepped out of Cor's home.

Chapter 23: Reckonings

The sinuous, gyrating bodies hypnotized the eye. Bodies shimmering with moondust, slick from oils, or provocatively patterned ink danced behind the transparent walls of the tower. Hundreds of species, of all sizes, genders and ages, stacked one on top of the other in individual pods. A spiral walkway dominated the center of this structure and slowly it moved to transport customers and gawkers alike up and down this display of recreational enticement.

Having found myself a spot right against the railing of the walkway, I was content to let the slow pace guide us upwards into the central district of the city. I tried not to stare at any one being too long, but I couldn't hide my fascination with their trade and lifestyle. One of the smaller women waved at me with half her face hidden under a veil and I waved back.

"I can't believe you're so into this." Amie hadn't given up on her quest to keep people from bumping into me, but at least she'd settled into quasi-discretion about it. Another person dared to invade our space, but shrank back when she glared at them.

"Mostly I wonder about their socioeconomic backgrounds, but their motivations to enter prostitution and why they continue generation after generation is just as interesting. Oh and where they get their clothing! Or what their daily schedules look like!" Prostitution was technically filed under manual labor in Elysia's employment bureau, but it was an outdated practice replaced by artificial or reality enhancing activities. Individuals could go through training and safety seminars to gain and renew a license to practice, yet very few chose to do so.

Here, each pod in the central tower was owned and operated independently. They often were passed down several times before being sold off. Simply possessing an active pod gave the owner a basic income from the state. I watched the green glow of a pod turn black when a model was selected for services and I speculated if I could convince Amie to let me purchase time; just for a few minutes with one of them; and ask a few questions...

Maybe more than a few.

"We need to get back." Amie pulled up her hood and so did I. Facial recognition in this city was strict and the others were borrowing the faces of citizens we'd seen in the past few days. My face was already one without a discernable record, but taking precautions was always a wise decision.

It was a slow shuffle back to the run-down hostel we'd found. Our choices in lodging had been limited with an unconscious man in tow; no questions were asked and they still accepted physical currency; that was all that had mattered to us.

Amie stifled a sound of disgust as a large insect unraveled itself and scurried across our path on a thousand legs.

Zarek hadn't woken up since our face-to-face encounter with Cor. Between the physical stress and whatever damage plane stepping may have caused, I was simply happy that he was alive.

All of his vital signs were normal.

We were letting him sleep but if he didn't wake up at all tonight, we'd discuss waking him up ourselves tomorrow morning.

A small whimper caught my attention.

I saw a little girl crying over a bundle of blankets; they were huddled in the mouth of an alleyway and the girl had no shoes. Was it a baby that she held? I broke away from Amie's side with a murmur and had just begun to crouch down beside her when a barrel of a weapon was pointed at me. I froze.

Amie had the boy disarmed and on the ground in the next second, causing the girl to drop the blankets containing nothing at all and scream in a dialect that revealed her nationality. She moved to kick at Amie, which was a very bad idea.

I grabbed her and reached into my coat.

Both children stopped struggling when they realized I held money. Amie got off the boy, who grabbed the offering. They tumbled over themselves to get away before we could do or say anything else. Their territory had been taken over by almost a decade ago now. Their people were refugees and almost none of them ever made it to the Elysian border.

This was also why I wasn't allowed to carry much money.

I knew it was stupid and it didn't help anyone to overcome the systemic issues that plagued the outer universe. That didn't mean I should hoard the resources others desperately needed.

I tried to keep my eyes forward from then on, but once we got within three streets lengths of the hostel, we heard Esme's distinctive screaming and sprinted the rest of the way back.

We took a hairpin turn and headed for the covered passageway that was the entrance to our temporary shelter when we almost crashed into Zarek.

He looked more disheveled than I'd ever seen him. His shirt buttons were out of alignment and his coat only half on.

He kept his gaze level to a space above my head, not bothering to acknowledge or even make eye contact with either of us. Before we could ask him what in the Empress' name was going on, he swiftly passed us and stormed out of sight.

What was happening?

Stunned, I had to choose between following him or following Amie toward her sister's clear distress. I chose the latter. Something told me he needed a moment and Esme needed to stop screaming before she gained the attention of the entire neighborhood.

Fane and Omere were making a heroic effort to hold her back. Fane was trying to muffle her, but then she bit his fingers and caused him to howl in pain. He already had a bloody nose and Omere was sporting several scratches that hadn't been there when we'd left. Just before she grabbed Omere's arm in a hold designed to break it, they saw Amie and leaped out of the way so that she could tackle Esme out of the courtyard and back into our rooms.

"Close the fucking door!" Amie yelled at Fane, who complied immediately. Our last glimpse was Amie telling at Esme to be quiet and Esme pushing at her face, trying to leverage her twin off as she babbled something about Zarek and a misunderstanding.

I locked down the sound coming from the room and a hush fell as everyone around us stopped their excited chatter.

After a second or two, the crowd dispersed and I was left with two very pissed off, injured friends.

Omere's braids had come loose in the scuffle.

Quickly, I healed Fane's cut lip and nose and checked for any damaged bones. I also made sure Omere was comfortable with me disinfecting and closing his cuts before doing so. Their injuries were superficial but the ones on their pride were much deeper.

"She's crazy." Fane told me as soon as his nose was aligned.

Omere agreed, but I didn't want to take my attention away from their wounds to answer right away. Lastly, I slipped the blood off their skin and clothes and only then did I say anything.

"What happened?"

I had Omere sit down so I could tidy his braids.

"She went into the room where Zarek was sleeping and closed the door. Two minutes later Zarek was up and out of that room half-dressed like something stung him in the ass." Fane sat on my other side on the bench, rolling one of his shoulders back and forth. I would have to check it for any strained muscles. "Zarek was pissed. Esme kept trying to grab him and he shoved her hands off and that made her go completely nuts! She started throwing things! Then this genius," gesturing toward Omere, who didn't deem it important enough to react "thought it was a good idea to hold her back from throwing something else and then I had to help him so that he didn't get his ass kicked by that rampaging bitch!"

"Did Zarek say anything at all? Were they arguing?"

Omere seemed like he wanted to say something to me, but no matter how long I waited, he couldn't properly express what it was. I eased the strain in Fane's shoulder and tried to defend Esme as best as I could. This trip had changed us all and while she had acted rashly, it didn't mean she wouldn't feel bad about it later. I wanted to make sure there was room for her in case she wanted to make amends. Esme had always been so supportive and caring. It wa s difficult for me to reconcile that image of her with the screaming, crazed woman I'd just seen.

Eventually, Fane got tired of waiting and went to look for dinner and for a while, it was just Omere and I sitting in the small courtyard. As I was going over some basic syntax structures, I was simultaneously trying to explain to him why we were here specifically. Omere didn't seem to totally understand how or why Zarek was missing some of his memory.

Speaking of the dead, Zarek scared Omere by stepping off the raised monorail tracks above us and landing neatly in front of us. I suppose he hadn't been able to see the rails above our heads and it seemed like Zarek had appeared out of thin air. Somewhere along the way Zarek had found a mask to hide his face, revealing his familiarity with the recognition technology here.

Omere bared his teeth and hissed in annoyance at Zarek's antics.

"Back at you." Zarek said flippantly before sitting down next to me. Without further pleasantries, he pulled up his mask to address me, causing a fluttering sensation in my chest. "I still don't remember you. Should I be concerned for my health?"

"There's only three more," I explained quietly. "Only three."

"Ulisirach isn't the most friendly place to visit, pixie."

He was right. We had left Isbul behind to a nation that bordered it and Elysia. It was a thin, stretched out line of systems that was well known for their xenophobic policies and iron-fisted approach to governance. As a result of those polices and their lax legal system, Ulisirach had entrenched a large, permanent oligarchy and a highly militaristic, authoritarian government. This city we found ourselves in was the very capital of Ulisirach itself, Neo Uxar.

"I know this isn't what we expected, but it's just three more."

"I don't think my curiosity will hold out." Zarek caught my chin and tilted my face up to look at him. "The pieces I'm missing. You're in all of them somehow. We need to talk."

I knew he was right.

I nodded in agreement. It was past time for us to sit down and listen to what the other had to say. So much had happened in so little time. It was enough. It would have to be enough. I'd long thought carefully about how I would word things, how I would reveal myself, the tone I'd use, what I would do if he didn't believe me, and what I would do if he did.

However, our conversation was fated to be postponed yet again.

Amie opened the door and dragged Esme outside.

As soon as Esme saw Zarek, she tried to break free of Amie's grip but failed. Zarek stood up from the bench, his posture immediately defensive; but Omere, with his wariness of Esme at an all-time high, slid to hide behind me slightly.

"Esme has something to say." Amie's hold on her sister held.

"Not in front of everybody!" Esme cried. "Amie! This isn't fair! At least give us some privacy!"

"No." Zarek stopped me. "This is as private as I want it to get."

"Zarek! Please!" Esme's face already flushed from crying, grew alarmingly red as she cried more. "I swear this is all a misunderstanding! Just listen to me! Please!"

"I'm listening just fine from right here." He said simply.

"No! Sae! Go inside right now and take Amie with you!"

Everyone looked at me then.

Oh I really didn't like this. Amie and Omere would go inside with me if I asked them but... I looked up at him and without a word, I knew Zarek wanted me to stay. He was uncomfortable, but he also wouldn't ask it of me himself.

"I'm sorry Esme, I promise we'll try to not get involved, but I think we should stay for this conversation. Just in case things get out of hand and—"

"No! No! No! No! NO! NO! NO!" Esme emphasized her words by raising her voice with each syllable. I had to step in to keep her voice from carrying. The last thing we needed was a bigger audience. "How could you do this to me Sae!?"

She only sobbed harder and Empress, it felt like she had done nothing else since we'd begun this journey.

"Esme!" Amie raised her voice. "Just get this over with!"

"Zarek I know you love me just like I love you!" Esme tried to lunge forward and Amie had to wrap both arms around her midsection to stop her. "Zarek! I know you feel it too! We're meant to be together and I know you want me! I love you! More than anything! I know you know it too! We're perfect together! No one can love you like I can! Tell them! Tell them we're in love!"

There was more. A lot more.

No one said a word as Esme continued repeating the same refrain that she loved him, he loved her, and they were together. The longer it went on, the louder Esme's volume until Omere couldn't take it anymore and put his hands over his poor ears. There didn't seem to be an end in sight to Esme's tirade.

Zarek finally lost his patience.

"I don't love you."

"I don't even like you." Zarek just kept going when Esme tried to say more, his words holding no room for an argument. "I actually barely tolerate you. So let's stop this before we all expire of secondhand psychosis."

Esme's eyes were so wide, I was afraid they'd fall out.

Amie was blindsided by her twin's elbow slamming into her face and her legs being swept out from under her the next second. Free, Esme threw herself at Zarek. I think at first she was trying to kiss him, but Zarek held Esme back as far away from her goal as physically possible. So she switched to screaming at him and beating her fists on anything she could reach.

"THIS IS BECAUSE OF HER ISN'T IT!?"

Esme kept screaming.

Over and over again.

This was too much. I grabbed Esme's arm before she could hit him again and I felt her other fist slam against my temple. I heard a sharp crack signifying that Esme may have just broken some bones. Before she could realize what she had done or do it again, I was suddenly wrenched out of her reach and was half in Zarek's arms with Omere holding onto my legs. Omere was snarling and I tried to pat his shoulder to assure him that I was fine.

"You hit Sae!" Amie had her twin pinned face down on the ground, her weight pressed down to immobilize Esme's limbs.

I don't think I'd ever seen Amie so angry in my entire life.

I'd also never heard her scream like that until now.

"You fucking hit Sae! Do you understand that Esme!? Do you know what the fuck you just did!? What the fuck is wrong with you!" Amie forcibly rolled her over and pinned her shoulders so that Esme was forced to look at her. "I don't fucking care if you think she's going to murder you! You! Do! Not! Hit! Sae!" She shook Esme so violently I was afraid she'd do actual damage.

Amie was crying. They started screaming at each other. Neither of them gave the other a centimeter to escape. Their combined screams tore at everything we thought was sacred. A cut over Amie's eye was bleeding. Esme's nose must have been damaged when she hit the ground, because it too bled. They were close to blows. They were essentially already there are Esme tried to scratch at Amie's face. Esme struggled viciously to throw her sister off of her and this was the first time in our lives that Amie had ever been able to successfully grapple her sister.

"You never gave a crap about me! It's always Sae!"

"Who the fuck are you because you can't be my—"

"I deserve to be happy! You're always so mean to me!"

"You fucking hit her in the face! How could you—"

"It wasn't my fault! Why are you blaming me!?"

"Stop! Esme just stop! You swore to protect her! You—"

"She's always the fucking victim! Oh poor perfect Sae!"

I pulled Amie off Esme, but they continued to scream at each other—I really, really didn't want to do this to them.

"I order both of you to cut it out! Stop. Now."

Their sentences stopped, but Esme screamed in inconsolable rage for at least another ten seconds before falling silent. Letting go of Esme; I pulled Amie further back so that she was no longer putting weight on her sister's legs. They were both a mess, Esme especially so. Her hair had twisted itself into a tangle, her curls caked with mud and other substances from the ground. Her nails had blood under them and I quickly looked back at Zarek, seeing for the first time that his arms were marked in the scuffle. Those scratches chilled me to the bone.

Esme looked at all of us, pieces of hair stuck to her face. Sometime during this whole event, it had started raining and we were all getting drenched. I didn't know what to say to reach her. Her pupils were blown wide as she looked from one face to the next, clearly looking for sympathy. In that moment, more than anything, I wanted to give her that understanding.

At the very least I wanted to try.

Amie tried to hold me back but I shook my head no.

Crouching down, I tried to show her things would be alright.

"Esme, let's go inside okay? We can get you cleaned up and—"

"This is all *your fault*!"

I flinched at the ugly vitriol in her voice.

"Esme. I'm trying to help. You're angry. I get it. Please—"

"I fucking *hate* you!"

She turned and sprinted wildly into the rain.

No one tried to follow her.

Esme's words resonated for far longer than it took for us to finally go inside. How long ago did we start to feel relief at her absence? Should Amie and I have gone after her? Did she even want us to? I kept playing over her words in my mind.

I love you!

Zarek, you're mine!

We're meant to be together!

I love you! More than anything or anyone!

The words had frightened me. They tread inside, swirling to the rhythm of a dissonant drum. Was that how love sounded? What it looked like? Numbly, I fixed the cut above Amie's eye and some of the other scratch marks she'd accumulated. It took quite a blow to injure a Sentinel, but apparently they could hurt each other just fine. They usually healed so fast.

These wounds were an exception.

Amie and I sat on one end of the small gathering space and Omere and Zarek sat on the other side. Omere seemed somewhat wary of Amie now as well, but I hoped it was a temporary shock rather than a lasting impression.

I disinfected the tools of the small health kit stored in one of the washrooms carefully and made sure Amie had no more injuries before moving to where Omere and Zarek sat.

It was better if I manually aided.

It gave my hands something to do.

"Your cuts are gone." I placed the kit off to the side. Zarek allowed me to stretch out his arm to examine his forearms and hands. Nothing. Not a single scratch left on him. Now this was evidence of a much more developed regeneration speed than I'd first given him credit for. It had only been minutes, but not even scars remained. "Should I even bother to clean your arms?"

"I'm at your mercy, pixie."

His smile made my heart leap.

"Hey! Anyone home!?" Fane came inside with an armful of bags. "I brought dinner!" He dropped the food on the table the moment he saw our faces. "What happened? Why does it smell like wax bandages in here?"

Amie explained in a monotone, her head in her hands.□

"So that's it right?" Fane said once she finished. "She's out."

"What do you mean out!?" Amie snapped. "Nobody's out!"

"She attacked all of us today! Every single one of us! She's crazy!"

"She's not crazy! You don't know her! We grew up with her—"

"She's crazy," Omere responded before Fane could. "Sick."

"We'll talk to her." I didn't know what we'd say but that wasn't the point. She wasn't acting like herself. She needed her friends. "Esme's hurting, she—"

"Don't talk to her alone, pixie."

Zarek's hand gently brushed against the side of my head, where Esme had broken her fingers trying to hit me. There was no mark, but that didn't seem to matter to anyone.

I felt myself begin to tremble when he finally dropped his hand.

"I'm fine. Really. And I don't plan on confronting Esme alone."

"I say send her home." Fane argued, "She doesn't even want to be here! Why are you letting her walk all over us!?"

Amie's response would go unspoken as Esme entered the room.

"You don't have to send me anywhere. Fuck all of you!"

Esme viciously shoved Fane, who just got out of her way; behind her back, he looked around at us as if to emphasize his point.

Esme went straight into our rooms where she proceeded to toss her things in seemingly random directions. With her hair still matted and blood running down her face and neck, she did look as if she was sick... was she thinner?

She muttered under her breath in bursts of ferocity as she shoved items one after another into her pack. She was still so angry.

The others didn't bother to pretend they cared.

Amie just turned to me imploringly and, knowing I couldn't just ignore the issue, we went to stand in the doorway. At first, we tried to wait until she felt ready to say something—which was seemingly never going to happen.

"Esme, what are you doing?" I tried to ask softly.

"Oh Esme what are you doing?" she mimicked in falsetto. "We all want you gone anyway, but I want you to feel bad about it because I'm so fucking perfect!"

"I'm not trying to make you feel bad Esme, I just—"

"I'm not trying to make you feel bad Esme!" She ran a brush roughly through her hair, ripping out long strands. "I'm just showing everyone how much better I am than you! Because I'm a Raajali, I'm perfect, I'm going to be Empress one day!"

"Esme!" Esme danced around her twin, laughing now as she put me between them. "Esme what do you think you're doing!? What the fuck is going on with you!?" Amie cried.

"Did you know she's been lying to you!? The entire time!" Esme dodged Amie's arms and threw Fane in front of her so that they collided. "That entire time she's been hiding it because she doesn't care about you! You hear me Zarek!? She doesn't give a fuck about you! Or anyone else but herself! This is all just a little game to her! An itty-bitty little game to Saekonari Ra—"

"Stop talking."

Esme's mouth closed and she slowly turned to look at me.

"Aww! Look at you! Look who finally grew a shiny new spine."

The way she laughed.

The way she looked at me now.

When had her eyes stopped being kind?

How long had it been since she'd spoken to either of us with affection? Had being in the outer universe really changed her so much? Or had Amie and I gotten used to placating her whenever she grew the least bit upset?

Her loathing dripped stains, saturating our memories in hate.

"Esme, I think it's best if you went home early."

"Of course! Your will is my command!"

Nothing else was said. I opened the door for her back to her own room. A magnificently cozy nest of jewel colors and filled to the brim with memories. My first night out of the nursery, Esme had snuck me inside to eat sweets with her after bedtime. Mother had caught me of course, but Esme had always welcomed me back with open arms. Esme had always shared her toys with me, chatted endlessly whenever I tried to help her in her studies even when I refused to let her copy mine. She and Amie had always been there.

Constant and forever.

"By the way." Esme grabbed my arm and leaned in to whisper into my ear. "I was the one who told the Empress about your stupid letters. I was sick of seeing you go behind everyone's back and then pretend you were some perfect fucking princess." Her nail pierced the skin on my shoulder and drew a drop of blood. Apparently she could hurt me if she really meant to.

Her glee numbed me to the core.

"You're the one who spread those rumors."

"Who the fuck else do you think did it?" Esme laughed.

Esme blew a kiss at Zarek before stepping through.

She didn't stop to say goodbye to her sister.

Esme wouldn't even look at her.

Amie just put her hand over her mouth and turned away once I closed the tunnel. Her shoulders were shaking. No one spoke, waiting to see who would be the one to break the silence.

"Amie, do you need—"

My remaining Sentinel shook her head and went to the temporary room she once shared with her sister. I couldn't do anything else for her tonight, that much was clear.

Now, left with the shards of my deceit, I knew this couldn't wait any longer. It had become unbearable.

"Zarek, I'd like to talk to you. Please."

"I'm sure you do." He stood and headed for the door.

Omere tried to follow but Fane pushed him right back down by his shoulders. "Come on you idiot, even you can't be that dense."

"I'm backup," I heard Omere answer from behind me.

"Not this time. Trust me, you do not want to go with them."

If anything else was said, I didn't get to hear it.

There was no perfect place to have this conversation.

At least according to Zarek. He'd been going so fast for the past half an hour I was starting to think he was trying to lose me. Later, I would have to ask him if he'd been to Neo Uxar before. He dove through streets that appeared out of nowhere, scaled buildings with ease, and vaulted over rooftops like he did it every day. He was too fast for the average eye to track.

Twice I almost lost him.

The first was when he'd grabbed the connecting hinge of a monorail compartment, and I had to double back to leap onto the moving tram. It shook so violently under my feet that I had to roll a few times to stop my momentum. That thing could not be up to code. The second time was when he'd slipped through a night market laid out in the worst possible place for one. I was forced to duck under the arms of merchants who carried things on their heads and shoulders and still almost lost the trail when he ducked into a door and out of a six-story window. It was only after we'd reached edge of the rooftops did he stop.

Neither of us were out of breath.

This building was built on the edge of a precipice. From here, one could look down into the mountain valley this city had been built on top of. A mixture of their unique atmospheric conditions and polluted air spread a permanent blanket of smog over the terrain and while the day was far from over, residents here enjoyed an extended period of darkness. Fiber optics was the lighting of choice. As a result, the city and the fog glowed a radiant green.

It was just beginning to rain again.

"Was that some kind of test?"

"No. It's a demonstration."

"A demonstration of what?"

In lieu of an answer, Zarek took a small device and slapped it against the wall of the building behind him. When it engaged, I could hear it humming at an infrequent pace. Though I didn't recognize it, I assumed it blocked any possible sound from escaping.

I knew it was now or never again.

So I told him everything.

I told him about how we'd met, our letters, when he came back to the palace and how I'd asked him to show me the universe. I explained what I suspected about Cira and what we knew of the situation as a whole. I talked about how Cira had led us to my grandfather and the Esholittes. I even told him about meeting Cor and everything that happened after he'd passed out.

The more I spoke, the easier it became. My rationale for holding back for so long seemed inconsequential now that everything was coming out in the open. I apologized for not telling him earlier. I apologized for lying by omission. I apologized for not trusting him. It was an act that liberated me from the claustrophobic birdcage of anxiety and lies I'd built for myself.

When I fell quiet, the only sound was the rain pouring down.

"So you are Saekonari Raajali."

"Yes."

"You broke universal law coming out here."

"Yes."

"And you did it because I was kind to you."

"...Yes."

The sound barrier shattered.

I was shoved to the ground by a person dressed entirely in black. The cowl of his clothing went all the way down their face with the pattern of an animal sewn with fiber optic lights. They had a weapon and it was pointed at my face. It was chaos as dozens of them swarmed up the sides of the building. Zarek and I were quickly encircled on all sides. I grabbed the person's head, ignoring the blast that bounced off my shoulder and threw them off of me. Acting hastily, I appeared at Zarek's side but would have taken a tumble if he didn't catch me.

"I told you if you ever came back to my city, I'd kill you Zarek!"

One of them stepped forward and pulled the hood back on their head. He was horrifically disfigured; the skin on his head seemed to have melted and then cooled on his skull. His teeth were rotting and visible through several holes in his cheeks.

"I fucking warned you!" He screamed. "I'll kill you, asshole and your bitch too!"

"Watch closely." Zarek whispered in my ear before he appeared behind the small man. With one hand he picked them off their feet and threw them headfirst over the edge of the building and the cliff below. His screaming could still be heard as Zarek grabbed the arm of the nearest man and ripped it off of his body.

This wasn't a fight.

This was a massacre.

In the end, more than half of them fled after watching how their team members had been dealt with. All of his weapons had been taken by Cor, I realized, that was why he fought unarmed. No matter how many there were, none of them were able to hinder the personification of death that Zarek had donned.

Half of them rushed him all at once while others stood back to shoot from a distance. Zarek quietly and systematically ripped them to pieces with his bare hands.

There was so much blood everywhere that it was impossible to tell if any of Zarek's own was dripping off him. Bodies littered the ground with limbs in all sorts of unnatural positions. Zarek kicked one out of the way as he walked toward me.

I knew what he expected of me, seeing his bloody hands and the splatters that had even reached halfway up my own legs. But I refused to do anything but stand my ground.

He stopped, a hair's length from me.

Any closer and he'd risk staining my clothes.

"Was that your demonstration?" I asked, my voice scratchy.

"Do you think this is a joke? Go back home."

"They attacked you first. I know what you're trying to do."

"Saekonari. You don't belong out here."

"I don't care. I like it out here. W-with you."

"For fuck's sake!" He all but exploded. "I have maimed and killed more people than I could keep track of. I have done unspeakable things. My hands are literally stained with blood. What part of this appeals to you!? I'm nothing below my skin. You may like my face, but there is nothing inside for you, pixie. What part of me would ever be for you!?" He'd grabbed me during the course of this outburst and once he stopped talking, Zarek jolted back, as if he hadn't planned on touching me at all. He'd left bloody handprints on my upper arms and shoulders.

The sight of me now turned his eyes flat and... panicked.

I slowly took back his hands. The blood smeared lightly on my fingers before it all dropped to the ground and his hands were cleaned of any residue. Zarek had never once tried to shield me from who he was; he treated me like his equal.

He'd always trusted me to make my own decisions.

Eventually, I had to learn to trust myself too.

"You gave me my first kiss. I know you don't remember, but I do." I gently intertwined my fingers with his. In this form, his hands were so much larger than mine. "You treated me like a person when my father passed and not just as the Heir. You wrote to me pages and pages for years, reminding me my best friend was out there somewhere in the universe. Thinking of me. You made me laugh. You asked me what I wanted and when I didn't know, you never made me feel badly for it—"

"I don't know what the fuck you're talking about."

"You. I'm talking about you." I stepped closer, trying to make him look at me. "You said you were going to show me the universe and now I've seen quite a bit of it I'd never thought I'd see. I told you I'd find your memories. I told you I'd help find your sister. I'm telling you now, even if you say no part of you is meant for me... that I'm right here. That every piece of me is—"

"Your taste in men is terrible."

He pulled away from me and I let him.

"Did they deserve it? Tell me the truth."

"Who knows? Maybe. Probably."

"You don't scare me, Zarek."

"Thanks for the help, pixie."

After everything I'd laid out on the table, this was a reaction that I had not prepared for. Accusations, disbelief, mockery, anger, every other scenario would have been preferrable to this one. "Zarek!" I called out after him, walking at a fast clip to keep up with him as he jumped from one roof to the next. He didn't reply. "So, you're just going to leave? Is that all you have to say?"

"That's it. Have a nice eternity."

An eternity. Why had I never thought of it?

An eternity without his humor, his teasing, his willingness to listen to me speak about obscure insects and the carpentry styles of the pre-avant era. Never having him try to read what I was reading, only upside down. Without him pulling me from my daydreaming and being the first person I'd see. Forever without him playing with my hair and trying to feed me when I least expected it; without the chance to try and make him happy no matter who I really was.

I could make him happy.

"You once told me you'd give me anything I wanted!" I stopped following him. "But that I needed to tell you what that was!" I wouldn't chase after him when he didn't want me to. I didn't even know if he could still hear me through the downpour. "And I never told you what I really wanted because all I ever wanted was you! So I'm telling you n-now."

My voice failed me.

"I want you." I whispered.

That was the best that I could do.

I'd seen what Esme had done in the name of love today and I couldn't walk the same path. Zarek wouldn't turn around this time. He wouldn't come back for me. I turned away then, so I didn't have to watch him leave.

I nearly yelped when I found him right behind me.

My words had certainly conjured a response.

I just hadn't expected it to be anger.

"You don't know what you're saying."

"Yes I do. I k-know exactly what I'm saying."

"You don't know where I've been. What I—"

"You seem to think that matters to me."

"Trust me. You don't want my hands on you."

"Yes, I do! I—" I did not think that one through.

My mind and body were rioting. I tried to read Zarek's expression, but I couldn't tell if he was going to strangle me or if he thought I was joking. Maybe he couldn't tell either because he also seemed at a loss for words. Finally, after what felt like an eternity, he took a step toward me.

"Pixie. Tell me to go away."

There was something different in the way he stalked after me. Inexplicitly, I found myself retreating back until I hit a wall of an adjacent building. As soon as my shoulders hit the flat surface, Zarek paused, giving me the space to escape to either side. As the seconds ticked by, neither of us moved.

He snapped first.

Or maybe I did.

What did it matter? Zarek hands were all around me and mine held on to him for dear life. He gave me one more chance. One second of hesitation to change my mind. One last pause that I decisively threw away before plummeting headfirst into madness.

This was nothing like the soft, sweet kiss he'd stolen when we were children. This was a rapture of heat so scorching I felt a hot lick of pleasure everywhere he touched me.

Zarek pulled me against him roughly, my hands tugging at the front of his clothing. I was no longer standing, but I couldn't be certain as I'd lost all feeling in my legs. He pressed me back against the building behind me and it was like I'd swallowed the stars. I whimpered; heat that bloomed from the depths of my abdomen made me want to struggle against him.

I wanted him to devour me.

"Sweetness, hold on, easy…"

He pulled away ever so slightly to try and calm me, but I was not having it. Frustratingly, he was able to hold me back from getting any sort of leverage.

With a flick of my fingers I slammed down wards that would hopefully stop any number of detection technologies. I wasn't in my right mind but who cared if I was discovered!? Who cared when this was what I wanted?

Right now.

I turned back into myself. My feet touched the ground and I instantly reclaimed his mouth. Yes. Finally. He'd looked absolutely flummoxed when I turned back, but the moment my body hit his, it was like we'd never been apart.

No longer could I tell where my body ended and his began. Everywhere his hands slid left a searing trail behind. One cradled my neck, the other liquifying my spine through my clothes. I shamelessly trembled against him. I marveled at the things Zarek knew to do with his mouth.

He nibbled on my bottom lip and teased me until I would have done anything he asked. Some of his ministrations were so light they barely whispered across my mouth and others were so shocking, so dark and ardent that it was all I could do to keep upright. Every little movement patient and testing.

I was gasping when he broke away again.

Zarek let his head drop onto my shoulder as I slowly came back to myself. The fact that he was also struggling to regulate his breathing was the only thing keeping me from melting into a puddle. I turned my head to try and look at Zarek, but then did something else completely impulsive and gently nuzzled him near where his ear met his jaw. That got his attention.

Zarek groaned, his arms tightening around me.

"Sae. You're killing me."

"Does this mean you'll stay?" I asked tentatively.

He took a step back and really looked at me. A second or two was all it took for that look in Zarek's eyes to return and he gave me a few more hard, breathtaking kisses before he let go of me. My mouth felt swollen and I reached up to touch them lightly with my fingertips... I quickly stopped when I saw he was watching me do it. Zarek actually did look quite pained.

"Saekonari. I seem to have a problem saying no to you."

As I digested that, I couldn't help but steal another kiss.

"You can kiss me whenever you want if you stay."

"See, now you're just playing dirty." He placed his forehead gently against my own. The shaky laughter in Zarek's words had hope blooming bright and bold.

"No, but I'm afraid this is. I'm falling in love with you."

Something flashed in his eyes, was he wary of me now? I knew it wasn't the best time to tell him, after everything that had happened today with Esme, but I had used similar rationale to keep other secrets from him. I wanted him to know where I stood. I wanted to be honest with him so that maybe he would be honest with me. There were so many things I wanted now.

Zarek started to say something, but I stopped him.

"I didn't tell you to make you do anything or say something you don't mean. I just wanted to tell you." In my real body, I was only a few centimeters shorter than Zarek and I could easily brush a kiss against his cheek. "I don't believe you'll break me, but being with me comes with its own pitfalls. Think about it. I'll answer any question you ask and we'll reevaluate at a later date."

"We'll reevaluate at a later date." He repeated back to me slowly.

"Reflection before major decision-making is vital for successful outcomes. I'm very good at it. I can help."

Zarek started to laugh. He hauled me against him again and buried his face into my hair. I could still hear him snickering but had no time to get annoyed as he kissed me once more, wiping all rational thought out of mind. He continued to drag his mouth down the side of my neck until I made an especially strange noise at a spot he'd found and started to squirm.

"I thought we agreed you'd think more about this before you—"

"We agreed that I can kiss you whenever and wherever I want."

"What do you mean wherever? I didn't agree to that!"

"Yes you did. It's extremely vital to my reflection time."

"I was thinking more like a list of pros and cons..."

"As you can see, I'm working on the pros."

"... You're making fun of me again. Aren't you?"

"Shhh, sweetness I'm thinking, don't interrupt."

Chapter 24: Calculations

Breaking into the Ulisirach royal citadel would be no small undertaking. So many of their former leaders had been assassinated by outsiders that it was considered one of the most secure fortresses in the outer universe. The ruling clans had long held a reputation for ruthlessness, cruelty, and acute paranoia.

Their current sovereign was the dowager Ikki Ulys. A woman who I had met once before and had left quite the impression.

Years ago, she and her eldest son, Woltarie Ulys, had come to petition Mother on returning over ten million of their citizens after they had fled across the border to avoid military conscription.

They had been severe in both dress and manner.

No adornments marred the pressed military uniforms they'd worn. Woltarie, though only a child himself at the time, had been the spitting image of his mother.

They were known to be an aggressive species, but under the Empress' gaze, they had proven unable to rise to the challenge.

Woltarie and I had taken a walk during their meeting.

I had tried to make conversation.

All he'd done was stare.

In the end, Mother had refused their request. Citing our laws, anyone who made it into our borders and swore under our name gained the full protection of Elysia and the Empress herself. They had no recourse but to return to their homes without their former statesmen. In the war to follow, they would triumph; but not as easily as one would have predicted.

Ikki Ulys undoubtably held a grudge.

"Woltarie's temper is said to be much less explosive than his mother's." I brought up everything I knew of him. He'd recently reached the age where he was eligible to kill his mother and take over Ulisirach. It was the expected outcome if he didn't want his siblings to beat him to the punch. He would then need to produce an heir before his nieces and nephews reached the age to kill him. Once he accomplished both tasks, he would be able to execute anyone who threatened him... it was a wonder that anything got done with their current system.

"It's not like we can just walk up and ask him to let us search the citadel." I muttered. According to the new channels, Ikki and Woltarie were both in house at the moment. Ikki's other four sons were not. We could find nothing on her daughter but as the princess had recently given birth, her reclusiveness wasn't unusual-

.

It was a quiet time of year. Their legislative term was over and an unseasonably hot summer had driven many out of the city itself.

Amie and I were going over possible strategies for infiltrating the citadel. From what we already knew, if even a small touch of our presence was caught by a sensor it would cause a dozen alarms to trip. Every entrance was designed to identify intruders. No one was allowed inside until they were searched thoroughly for weapons and even then, you couldn't get close to the first gate without a blood trace set on you. It wore off after a few days, but there was no way I wasn't about to let any one of us take that risk.

A blood trace killed you if they decided you were a threat.

"We could wait to see if anyone leaves with it,"

"I don't think Cira plans to make this that easy, maybe if we—"

Zarek had snuck up behind me and wrapped his arms around me, his head resting on my left shoulder. It was one thing to sneak back inside together in the middle of the night and quite another to face him in the light of day... actually it was still barely dawn. He should have slept for a least another half an hour.

Had Amie and I been too loud? Did we wake him?

What was I just talking about right now?

Zarek reached out and tapped the map in front of us. Amie had made a model of the citadel, sketching out a rough estimate of the walls and floors looked like inside. It had taken her all night to do so, but keeping busy was her way of coping with the reality that Esme had left us behind.

"The curvature of the towers is off. There's an underground bunker that pitches them closer at the bottom than at the top. Like pincers." Catching Amie's less than pleased scowl at both being corrected and being corrected at such an early hour, he added, "you're welcome."

"Sae. Are you sure you're happy with... this?" Amie waved her hand vaguely at the both of us.

"Yes." I was so absurdly pleased I couldn't even pretend otherwise. Turning my head slightly to look at Zarek, an inexplicable wave of joy swept through me. So consumed by own fears, I hadn't given a thought to what this would be like.

How wonderful this would feel.

Impulsively, I brushed a soft kiss against his cheek.

Zarek abruptly stood and turned away.

Had I done something wrong?

"He's blushing." Amie sounded absolutely gleeful.

"I've been called worse." Zarek came around to sit next to me and he proceeded to pick out what he saw as glaring flaws in Amie's drafts. While she may have been feeling prickly this morning, Amie still took detailed notes of everything.

The more Zarek spoke, the more obvious it became.

"You've been inside, haven't you?" I laughed.

"The general public is forbidden from entering the grounds."

"But you're not the general public," Amie said caustically.

"Thank you. See pixie, I knew she would come around."

I did my best to hide my smile but ultimately it was a futile effort.

"Sae. Are you *absolutely* sure you don't want me to shoot him?"

The next few days flew by. My friends settled into a surprisingly harmonious dynamic as we plotted to get in and out of the citadel without detection. Their technology was outdated but layered. There were only six points of entry for the entire complex and all of them were heavily guarded. Any attempt to enter underground or in the air would trigger an immediate lockdown.

A vast field surrounded the main buildings, pitted with generations of land mines, elaborate traps, and kill-on-detection grids. These fields were again surrounded by walls designed to be unscalable and virtually indestructible. If we used too much at any moment, they'd be able to triangulate our location. The probability of injury was high, which was why the more we learned about this endeavor, the more I believed it would be best if I went alone.

Logically, I knew it was safer and quicker. At the same time, there was no way I would be able to convince the others and it felt wrong to blindside them. So the day before we set our plan in motion, my mind let open the floodgates and swamped me with all the things that could go wrong for my friends and a hundred different scenarios that ended badly.

Just as I was calculating how likely it would be for Fane to accidentally catch himself on fire, I found myself buried under my own coat. Someone pulled me up and I was deftly maneuvered into the garment by Zarek.

A cowl was drawn over my nose. It smelled like him.

"Where are we going?" I asked as he pulled me out the door.

"For a walk." He said before covering both our faces.

It was a cold night. Ice had formed on all the windows and created a thick, yet clear layer over the ground. Was the silence between us awkward? I couldn't tell. It was the first time we'd been alone since the other night and nothing had really changed except for a few casual points of contact here and there. Zarek was always the one to initiate and it wasn't very fair of me. He just flustered me to the point where I didn't think to respond right away.

I would work on it, I told myself. Starting right now.

Our hands were ungloved, so I reached out and intertwined our fingers. He stopped walking... I took a peek up at him to see if this was okay and the next moment I found myself jogging to keep up with his long strides.

He turned the corner and pulled me into the shadows of a narrow alleyway, ripping off my mask and lifting me off my feet.

Pleasure sunk into my bones and simmered under my skin. Every tantalizing stoke of his mouth I felt all over; never had I ever been so aware of my physical form. He was achingly gentle with me. Responsive to every quaking nerve of my...

A sharp clang brought us to our senses.

It was a very large species of vermin, with an outstandingly blunt snout, that had fallen off of a ledge and was now rummaging around the ground for sustenance. Zarek looked so disgruntled by the interruption I had to stifle a laugh.

He noticed anyway.

"So, you think this is funny, do you?" He laughed too.

"That depends. Was this your idea of a walk?"

"You're more devious than you look pixie. You led us both astray." To my disappointment, he put me back on my feet and handed me my mask. It must have shown on my face because he muttered under his breath, "universe help me, I only have so much self-control." He put the mask on my face himself and pretended to scold me. "Now behave. Or you'll never see the surprise."

Knowing better than to ask what the surprise was, I followed him through a myriad of back streets until he finally slipped into what looked like an abandoned storeroom and a place no one had been inside of for years. Maybe if you looked past the thick layer of dust and grime... no it was still just as decrepit as one would expect a condemned building to be.

I turned to ask Zarek why we'd stopped here, but he was gone.

Where did he go? I was standing in what seemed like the only door. I heard a knocking noise from above and that was when I knew. There was an open-air duct more than halfway up the ceiling. That was where he'd went. I didn't trust that the dust was just for show and floated up until I could peer through the duct.

It wasn't nearly large enough to crawl through.

A hand appeared out of nowhere and pulled me right through the wall. Not into the vent, but simply through what looked like solid bricks. Hidden behind a remarkable force field; one could see out clearly as if the barrier was glass, but the other side was obscured from seeing in. The loft itself was spotless but sparse with only a few benches lined up against the far wall.

Zarek moved about the loft, tracing his fingers in a complex pattern until panels glowed on both the left and right walls.

They folded inwards and back to reveal their contents.

My eyes widened.

It was an arsenal.

Weapons of all shapes and sizes were holstered, stacked, and stored here. The metals were gleaming and the variety teetered on the wrong side of legal. Having only a fraction of the weapons training that Amie and Esme had received, I had no hope of identifying everything. There was an entire garrison of knives; some of them looked more ceremonial than practical. I knew there were at least twenty types of incendiary devices and I couldn't begin to catalogue the firearms.

"Was this the surprise?" I said quietly, walking over to him.

"Ignore the excessive paraphernalia," Zarek actually looked quite sheepish, "this is what I wanted to show you." He handed me a shabby, but well-loved notebook. There were only a few pages inside that weren't ripped out, but on each one of those crumpled sheets were sketches of a little girl. She couldn't have matured past her toddler years, but she was gorgeous.

"Alexi... she looks so happy. Did you draw these?"

"I didn't have any pictures, but I do have a lot of memories."

"What was she like? Was she anything like you?"

"Thank the Empress, no." He laughed. "She was like starlight. Warm and impossibly cheerful."

The significance of his actions didn't escape me. Secretly, one of my fears had been that he would hold back. That Zarek would never truly trust me to love him and know him. I took off my coat, folded it, and placed the sketches carefully on top of it on the nearest bench. Turning back into myself, it felt like the most natural thing in the universe to walk into his arms.

"When were you separated?" I wanted to understand.

"We were kids. I was six, she was a little over three."

"None of this is your fault. You know that, don't you?" I didn't question his silence. My hand went up to his cheek and my heart tumbled as Zarek ever so slightly tilted his head to rest against my palm. "Will you tell me what happened?"

"Lyxan Kyrian offered us a life." Zarek hesitated, cautiously choosing his next words. "I had little choice but to agree. He swore Alexi would be educated and taken care of, but he never said anything about his plans to make sure I'd do whatever he wanted. I haven't seen Alexi since. There's a chance she's dead. A good chance she died that day."

"Did you ever ask him why he did all those things?"

"I couldn't. He had Alexi. So I became his favorite doll."

"What does that mean? What did he make you do, Zarek?"

He just held me and while I didn't have much practice hugging another person, no part of me felt at odds with his body. Like I'd been waiting my whole life to be right where I was.

"I don't want to tell you, pixie." He finally sighed, his face still buried against my hair. "I'm not proud of it."

"Fane once mentioned to me you worked as a freelancer."

"Whatever Fane told you; he was putting it nicely. I wasn't lying to you when I said I've done unspeakable things. War crimes. Torture. I've wiped out personal hit lists and taken down people who will never stop looking for me. Want to know why they tried to kill me a few days ago? It's because I offed their last leader and presented her head to Ikki Ulys."

"You're still trying to scare me. It's not working."

"It should. I was starting to think I could make it happen. You and I." Zarek's nose brushed against mine and somehow it felt just as intimate as kissing. "That we could get this done, find Alexi, and leave it all behind. But you are the last person in the universe who could disappear with me."

"You were thinking that about me?" I whispered.

"Sweetness, you've been driving me mad for years."

"We've only been out here for a few months, not years."

"I have a feeling. That when I remember, it'll be years."

"We could still try running away, but I think Amie would actually kill you." I was glad Zarek found my humor funny, many people never seemed to know if I was joking or not. After his laughter died down, I made a promise to him.

"After this is all over, we'll find her."

Quantum tunneling was a tricky skill to master. Difficult to pass through on your own and much more dangerous when taking another person. It was also so energy demanding that the average person would never attempt it. There were a thousand better ways to travel and simpler methods to go unnoticed. Of course, the citadel was not your average case of breaking and entering.

Whereas the Empress was the ultimate security for Elysia with sweeping, omnipresent capabilities, the Ulys had to rely on every other method to secure their fortress.

By all accounts they had been thorough.

Fane and Omere had been argued down to keep back unless a worst-case scenario occurred, but they seemed much happier about it when they saw what we had to cover ourselves with.

Before we'd left Zarek's cache yesterday, he'd restocked on what he called "essentials"; including a thick, slimy paste made from the mucus of some rare parasite in the Parwawa galaxy. According to him, it stung like hell and itched like a motherfucker, but it was our best chance at not being detected.

I had to trust that it would be worth it because it was disgusting.

Now the three of us were waiting, a few meters from the outer wall, for the scanning net around the citadel to change its frequency. The pattern changed at random intervals, but it gave us a fraction of a second to get through the perimeter and far enough away from the wall on the other side to prevent tripping an alarm. Once inside, we needed to keep to a cardinal rule. Assume that all objects and surroundings were wired and the only safe thing to manipulate was ourselves.

I had to be precise with my calculations. Any misstep on my part was bound to reveal us all. I had to keep our bodies from being seen while allowing us to pass through the wall and keep my Light tightly wrapped enough to not to be detected. Warping particles like this damaged the average individual if done too many times in a short time period. So this was an experiment I hadn't been able to practice... and one I'd only ever done on inanimate objects.

"Five seconds." Amie counted us down. Three. Two. One.

We sprinted forward. The change to our bodies at a subatomic level slid us through the solid mass, our bodies taking on a subtle buzzing feeling before we were slammed back out and on the other side of the wall. Even knowing that the wall was over a meter thick hadn't prepared me for the claustrophobic sensation of every atom in my body being squeezed.

Reconstructing our bodies was much easier than the deconstructing and in the last third of the second we had to get away from the wall, Zarek reenforced the soles of our shoes to hover slightly over the ground.

We paused. If our attempt failed, we could expect the consequences to be instantaneous.

Nothing happened. Thank the Empress.

Now came the difficult part. There was no way for us to open doors ourselves without raising our chances of being caught. We would have to follow Amie's lead to get as close to the memory as we could and then grab it before teleporting away. After we left, it didn't matter if we were traced on this planet because we would grab Fane and Omere and leave immediately. This meant following individuals as they walked through the various levels of security. It would be best if we could find someone of sufficient status, but a stray guard would work just as well.

Carefully, we made our way across the vast field.

As we got closer, I was reminded of the Elysian palace. People were rushing from place to place just like the University and Shipyard students back home. I should have expected there to be plenty of people, no matter the Ulys' reputation. We wouldn't have trouble finding someone to follow, but we now faced the issue of blending into a crowd without bumping into anyone.

Walking in a single file line, we made our way to the main gate where people were being checked for active blood traces. Only we could see each other, but it made me nervous to slip past the double lines of guards standing by. If their work description said anything about glowering at people, they were doing a great job.

Within minutes, we entered the citadel.

The two towers that comprised the citadel were identical mirrors of each other that soared into the sky like blades sticking out of the earth. The interior walls inside the central hall were carved in the neo-brutalist fashion, stone pointing inwards every few centimeters in a style that looked as if you could impale a thousand souls upon their needle-sharp edges. The room was massive and yet barely any sound bounced off the stone walls.

No one here spoke above a whisper.

"There's too many people in here." Zarek was forced to move away from us, out of the way of a group that abruptly changed direction. Amie and I rushed back to his side once they had passed. It was a bad idea to get separated in here. We had no way of contacting each other if the worst happened.

"We can see that." Amie barely avoided a group of school-aged children. Their miniature military school uniforms were adorable.

"No. There shouldn't be this many and no children at all."

Before Amie or I could question him further, a sharp and distinctive voice came booming from the center of the hall. An image of queen Ikki Ulys sitting on a throne comprised of black stone appeared in larger-than-life format.

She wore her formal military clothing once again. Only her hair had changed from when I saw her last. It was now a short cap of grey hair that ended right under her ears. Soon she would have to dye her hair to stop it from becoming white.

"Welcome. The final counsel will be held tomorrow. Tonight I invite the shogunate and their families to supper. Please follow all instructions that had been delivered to your rooms. Thank you." The image dissipated and as soon as it did, activity resumed around us, voices and faces only slightly more animated than they had been. High emotion was frowned upon here.

There was only one reason why the shogunate would be here and I could see that Zarek understood as well. Ulisirach, although it bordered Elysia on one side, was a thin, stretched out conglomerate of brutally conquered galaxies. Each district was ruled over by a family who wielded absolute power within their territory. Plagued by endless threats over the many eons, their shoguns famously did not play well with each other. The only time they ever spoke as a unified front was on matters of interstellar conflict.

This was the worst possible time to be caught here.

We'd broken into a shogunate summit.

No one would be able to leave the citadel until it was over.

I grabbed Amie's hand and we weaved our way through the crowd to a largely unoccupied corner of the room. After explaining the situation, Amie wanted all of us to leave now, but it wasn't possible. This was the only time when certain safety precautions were taken. With the queen, her family, and the entire shogunate in residence, the citadel was covered by a suicide pact.

If anything or anyone tried to leave before this was over, it was possible all of the blood traces would activate. I refused to hurt innocent people just because of a miscalculation.

The shogunate had their successors stay in their home territories, but they had brought guards, servants, their spouses and other children. We were not going to risk murdering an entire generation of Ulisirach's ruling class, much less all the innocent employees and staff in the building.

No matter if my identity was revealed or not.

We would have to wait until tomorrow morning. The shogunate would meet in the middle of the night. By dawn, they should be finished with whatever discussion they were having and the pact would be lowered soon after.

We just had to find the memory and keep hidden until then.

If only it were that simple. Getting out of the citadel's central hall was easy enough, but the passageways were built to confuse potential invaders and our progress was as grindingly slow as harvesting oaxano beans as we ducked and dodged hordes of people. The ceilings were too low to float above the crowds and guards lined the walls so that it was impossible to keep to them.

Amie pointed to an archway up ahead that seemed to lead into a more open space and we changed our trajectory to flow into the current of people headed in that direction. Just as I slipped past the guard on the lefthand corner to head in Amie and Zarek's direction, A woman came crashing through one of the closed doors right in front of my nose. Her traditional weapon slashed at bystanders before piercing the wall that she too collided into. Another woman, an adolescent really, leaped out into the hall with her own weapon gleaming with blood.

Instant chaos.

Guards converged on the two woman, shoving and throwing people out of their way. Servants and other miscellaneous staff were no more courteous to each other as they tried to get away from the scene. Objects went flying in the disarray. The most jarring part was how all of this was happening in relative silence, as if everyone as afraid of being caught making any noise at all. I wasn't sure if it was a cultural oddity or an official part of their protocol; all I was certain about was that I had misplaced my friends.

Zarek and Amie were nowhere to be seen.

Within minutes, I was completely lost.

I had found my way back to the correct archway, but there was no sign of them. Our plan if any one of us got separated was to leave the grounds. Now I found myself stranded, alone, in hostile territory with no backup plan. The repercussions of being caught inside the citadel unauthorized during a summit would tarnish my name for at least ten generations of Ulisirach rulers. Mother might actually lock me away forever for such an egregious—

A naked baby ambled past as I panicked over my impending doom. Wait... what?

It was a little boy, who was not yet convinced that walking was the way to go. He half crawled; half shuffled past me with no clear guardian in sight. If I remembered my international cultural relations classes correctly, Ulisirach preferred their children locked away until they reached an age where their military training could begin. Even before they could walk and talk, I was at least sure that they also preferred their infants clothed.

The baby was now reaching up to pull at a very sharp art piece.

Barely clearing the wreckage, I pulled him out and up before he could feel what it was like to be hit in the head prematurely for his culture. I'd never been around an unsupervised baby before. There were certain times in my life where I blessed a maternity ward of newborns and babies were sometimes presented to me formally, but I'd never held one in my life.

The baby was laughing at his sudden ability to fly. I hastily put him down and then had to pick him back up when he started crying. I didn't cry as a baby. I remember Amie's little brothers crying sometimes but they were never far from a loving relative who knew what to do with them.

"Shhh, it's okay little one. Um, do you like songs?"

I softly sang a little nursery tune about the follies of setting out into the open ocean without only a river stone for company and to my relief he stopped crying. I started to look around again for a place to put him... and there was a man staring through me at the musical floating baby.

I stopped singing and slowly put the baby down.

This was bad. I dove out of the way as the man quickly came forward to pick the baby back up. Maybe he wouldn't suspect anything? There had to be cases of especially gifted infants who manifested abilities at a young age.

Floating wasn't even that hard to do!

Please think it was just a gifted baby.

"Come out whoever you are. Before I raise the alarm."

No, no, no, no, no. Please don't do that.

I put him and the baby to sleep, catching them before they toppled over and propped them up against the corner. I was still in trouble. I couldn't make them sleep until tomorrow morning; it would be too suspicious even if no one found them. Whoever this man was, he would be missed and the baby would most definitely be noticed as gone sooner rather than later.

"There!" I almost jumped out of my skin at the guard who pointed right at me. Looking down at my arms to check if I was still invisible was almost my downfall as I barely got out of the way in time. The guards surrounded the man and baby.

The baby was pulled away and, to my horror, they started to ruthlessly beat the unconscious man who did not wake up because I had been the one to make him sleep. I woke him up but that did nothing to remedy the situation.

All at once they started whispering over each other as the man tried his best to cover his vital organs. There was quite a bit of jargon thrown in by the guards that was incomprehensible to me, but the man was urgently saying that he just found the prince wandering about. He had nothing to do with it and had just happened upon him. The guards didn't believe him.

Kidnapping an underage member of the royal family, no matter the circumstances, meant execution.

Empress help me.

That baby was Hisoe Ulys, only grandson of queen Ikki and offspring of her only daughter Riasphone. There were no other royal family members that young. It wasn't like I'd ever seen a picture of him, but somehow this was all my fault.

The guards split into two parties. One hopefully was bringing the baby back to his mother and the second roughly dragging the struggling, innocent man away. It amazed me that he could be so quiet in his desperate bid to escape.

I couldn't let this happen to him.

I followed the guards deep down into the citadel. While light reached upper floors through strategically placed windows the size of small coins, the architect gave no such consideration for the space most likely designated as the dungeons. The walls here were lined with doors so narrow that even in my current form I would be hard pressed to fit inside of. None of my education had ever touched upon what these passageways would be for.

After many twists and turns, we came to a place where the doors all stood wide open to reveal spaces barely large enough to be called a closet. Now the man was screaming. They broke the fingers on his left hand before shoving him inside of one of the closets. A door slid closed and severed the tip of his foot. If he was still screaming, no sound could be heard anymore.

This was a prison. The guards kicked at the severed toes and laughed, one quipping about how they would need to call the slaves down a few days early. I could feel my insides twisting at their casual sadistic jokes.

Was this legal in Ulisirach?

Who else was locked away down here?

The wiser choice would have been to follow the guards back up.

Layers of security fell behind them and I had very little opportunity left to keep myself from causing a security breach. Examining the small closet with the bloody puddle in front, I saw many of the same security measures found all over the citadel.

There was only one obvious way of getting him out. I penetrated through the charged metal with my hand, grabbing the fabric of his shirt and pulled his particles through just as I had tunneled my friends through the outer wall. The security barriers here had far fewer layer of detection to worry about.

If I were to guess, it was because only the dead were kept here.

The man was still screaming and I physically muffled him. His screaming got worse when I reattached his toes, but that was his own fault for distracting me.

Once he saw his foot whole again, his eyes widened and he fell silent. Not moving from the ground, he gulped in air like it was in short supply. Perhaps it was and I just didn't notice... no the air was normal. It was just him.

"Why didn't you say anything to the guards about me?"

"No one would believe me. Crazy's worse than criminal."

"Do you have clearance? Can you get me back upstairs?"

"I would feel better if I could see you."

"I just saved you from being suffocated in a closet!"

Apparently, obstinacy was endemic to his species. For almost a full ten minutes he sat right where he was and closed his eyes and ears to me. Amie and Zarek were likely tearing the place apart by now looking for me and I needed to get back

I made myself visible to him.

It was a good thing I'd picked a very ambiguous appearance.

"What species are you?" He demanded.

"That is information irrelevant to the situation."

"How did you get me out of there without being killed?"

"Also irrelevant. Let's go. I can make both of us invisible."

"Are you here to harm Woltarie Ulys? Or any of the—"

"What? No. This has nothing to do with any of the Ulys."

"Why else would you be here? What are you doing here?"

"I'm trying to help a friend. I'm not going to harm anyone."

Something I said must have gotten through to him because he finally stood up and lowered the first few levels of security barriers.

I kept to my word and made him undetectable to the naked eye. Once we reached a floor where there were other people I tried to leave him, but he insisted that I take him all the way back to where he's supposed to be. Both because I'd put him through so much and because he was jumpier than water on hot steel, I agreed to escort him back.

We made our way up a passageway that seemed only in use by other maintenance workers. He must be staff of some kind. I hope I hadn't done irreparable damage to his life.

Despite his current clinginess, he seemed like a nice person.

Nowhere we went did I see Amie or Zarek.

Finally, he peered out through a door before motioning for me to follow. The door itself disappeared back into the wall once we exited into the room and he let out a sigh of relief. "Can you make me corporeal again? It's safe here." I didn't point out the fact that he was still corporeal, I just did as he said, and he reappeared again. There were a few scuff marks on him and now that I had the chance to really look at him, his fingers were still broken. So I fixed them.

"How did you do that?" He opened and closed his hands, awed that even his scratches were gone. "Not even the queen's physician can mend bones that quickly and she's a tier-one medic."

I was going to assume that it meant she had some iota of power in her species or bloodline.

Elysians only became more powerful with time. Immigrants and refugees would only begin to develop once their families had been incorporated for generations or by intermarrying. Not many Elysians ever left the borders, even temporarily. Some species in the outer universe possessed gifts independently, but they were so coveted by other nations, most were driven into the Empress' care anyway. It wasn't fair, but having spent some time outside, I could see why they might have found it too dangerous to stay.

It was dangerous for anyone without protection out here.

"I'm leaving you now. I have to find my friends."

"There are more of you here?" he whispered. "It's not safe. This is the worst time to visit the citadel in years. You should bring them here. You shouldn't be wandering around. You shouldn't have come at all. What in the universe were you thinking?"

"We didn't know about the summit until we were already here."

"That's because it was supposed to be a secret!"

"No one told us! I have to go find them."

"Ione, who are you talking to?"

Chapter 25: Successions

I was beginning to think I had the worst timing in the universe.

Woltarie Ulys strode into the room, looking exactly like the portrait his mother had sent to me of their entire family. She had four other sons of unifying age and two of them were back home right now. His mother's accompanying note heavily implied that she was willing to sacrifice any number of her children even if it meant they served in a harem. The fact that no Empress or Heir had ever maintained a harem hadn't seemed to bother her one bit.

"My new friend!" Ione said without a single qualm.

I now regretted taking him out of his cell. He tried to get me to say something, but I was no longer willing to entertain his requests. I didn't care if he did look crazy.

"I swear she's right here somewhere." He waved his arms around and I just stepped out of reach. "She saved me earlier. I know you told me Ikki was looking for any excuse to get rid of me, but I didn't think she'd do anything until after the summit."

"Did they hurt you!?" Woltarie demanded, lowering his voice.

"I'm alright my darling. All in one piece, just how you like me." He started waving his arms again and I was forced to circle around.

"She's still here. I know it!"

"Are you sure they didn't do anything to you?"

Ione was suddenly on the ground, convulsing.

He was almost foaming at the mouth, shaking uncontrollably as Woltarie tried to pick him off of the ground. Shocked at his sudden downturn of health, I picked up his hand and tried again to see what could be hurting him but as soon as I did, Ione stopped convulsing. He seized my hand, grinning in triumph.

I had been tricked.

"See I told you she was there!" Ione crowed.

Woltarie grabbed Ione and tried to move him away, but he refused to let go of me. The result was Woltarie picking him up and then staring at Ione's hand because he was holding onto something that wasn't there. He responded by pointing at me and saying something that sounded like a convoluted way of coughing. Apparently whatever that was, he was angry it didn't work.

The crown prince then reached out and grabbed my wrist. He tried pulling on what looked like thin air and when I didn't move, he dug in his heels and tried again. I didn't move.

"I command you to reveal yourself." He snapped and that was when I knew this had gone too far. I couldn't do anything to make them let go without tripping an alarm. Both of them had to have layers of protection, especially Woltarie. Any sign of resistance would end badly for me. I couldn't risk it.

Zarek and Amie were still missing.

So I reappeared and stepped down to the floor.

"Who are you?" Woltarie demanded, lowering his voice.

"Um... I'm Amie." I should have practiced that.

They did not believe me.

"Tell me why I shouldn't arrest you."

Charming. He must be well-liked.

"I just saved Ione from a painful demise. You're welcome." Zarek was apparently rubbing off on me.

As an answer, the man did something unexpected.

Woltarie Ulys raised his arm and shot me.

The blast came from what I now knew was a prosthetic hand. It burned the front of my clothing and left a gaping hole in the fabric. Ione's startled cry died out once he saw that I was unharmed.

I should have felt frightened by the blatant display of violence. Instead, I was angry he'd ruined my only coat.

"Answer the question."

I would not.

"Ione, what color are her eyes?"

"Dark brown, like Daryinyan cinnamon..."

I could guess my eyes were no longer brown.

Of all the times for someone to notice—he couldn't think it was me. His family was known to be paranoid, but it would be absolute lunacy for the Heir to be here.

"Ione. Wait in the other room."

The universe was awake today, careless in its infinite step.

"You didn't change your voice. It's too distinctive."

"Thank you for the advice. I'll take it under consideration."

He wanted to say more. It was all over his face despite his efforts to seem disinterested. Slowly, he offered me his hand and I met him halfway to meet the formal sign of respect. Honestly, this was going better than I could have ever hoped for.

"He's my only real friend." He said roughly. "I owe you his life."

"It's alright. I'm sure you would have found him yourself."

"Why are you here? Tell me and I can help you." Now that was a statement I could not trust no matter if it came off as truth.

"It's better if we both pretend this never happened."

Woltarie was scared. Terrified even. He walked over to the corner where a small shelf slid open. Ulisirachs preferred synthetic food over organic, it was much easier to maintain adequate nutrient levels that way. But instead of using the device for its intended purposes; he cracked open a hidden space behind the shelf and brought out a bright red bottle, its contents still sealed.

He broke the seal and breathed in the smoke from the bottle. Then he looked at me again. "You're still here."

I had to remind myself that responding with witticism would not help matters. Instead, I moved to leave through the same door Ione and I had come through. I'd wasted enough time here and couldn't be sure how long until Woltarie changed his mind.

"Wait!" Ione burst into the room completely transformed.

I had to do a double take to realize it was him. He was dressed in traditional women's clothing for Ulisirach. By design, it was an outfit designed especially for a woman of the royal harem. A long, dark green wig was beautifully studded with gems and Ione's face was expertly painted and veiled.

I'd seen this woman before.

"You waved at me the other night!" I realized, excited all over again. "At the center tower in the neon weeds."

"Oops." She giggled. "I still dance sometimes when my sister wants a night off."

"Do you prefer one over the other?"

I needed to leave, but this was fascinating.

"I'm a gynandromorph sweetie, so it doesn't matter to me."

I had so many questions, but no time to ask them.

"If Woltarie ever comes to visit my home world, go with him. I have to find my friends, but you look absolutely beautiful."

Ione hugged me, her perfume wrapping me in a spicy cloud. "Tarie are you sure we can't keep her? I think I love her!"

"Let her go Ione, she makes everyone feel that way."

I threw a sharp glance at him, but Ulys' attention was all on Ione, whose face paint had been smeared by her veil. Slipping out, I found my way back to the maintenance corridor to resume my search for Amie and Zarek. It wasn't like anyone could see them I reasoned, so the probability that they had also been caught was low, and if they had found the memory we could find a quiet corner and just wait the Ulisirachs and summit out.

That was when the alarm went off.

People rushed to their designated locations for a security breach. I had limited options if I was to evade detection in the next few minutes. There were only a few locations that would be left unscanned and I could guess where the closest one would be. Knowing that this could only end badly but needing time to think, I followed the lines of soldiers with black trim on their sleeves down the twisted halls and straight into queen Ikki's bedchamber.

Ikki Ulys was a woman with a cruel past and a reputation for instability. She was known to turn on those most loyal to her and richly reward those who pleased her. Once I was inside the room, I found a nice spot out of her way to stay until the security clearance passed. The queen arrived moments after her guards cleared the room and she was visibly twitchy.

Rumors abounded that she had gotten even more paranoid as of late, but nothing could have prepared me for the mumbling wreck who entered. It was a display of weakness that I would never have expected to see. The guards stood as still and quiet as statues, but her other attendants crowded around her, their whispered words of comfort falling on deaf ears.

"Why tonight?" The queen chewed on the jewelry on her fingers "The shogunate will never believe this wasn't orchestrated... Kyrian will murder us all in our beds... declare war on us all... he's crazy, they're all crazy! I'm the only one who... Woltarie thinks he's ready to take me... that runt was never fit to be born..."

She spoke a dialect of a language that was virtually extinct and that I was unlucky enough to have learned for the linguistically complex suffixes. It may have been gobbledygook to the others, but it was reckless nonetheless.

Then again who was I to judge her for thinking out loud?

The more I listened, the more convoluted her speech became. By now, the security scan must have been completed but there was no sign that the queen was going to stop talking to herself anytime soon. She seemed to believe Rateer was going to forcibly take Isbul, Ulisirach, Hitea, and the Oon Alliance all in preparation to go to war with Elysia. Those four nations held considerable territory. Even if Rateer was able to defeat all of them, Kyrian could never hold it. It was almost six percent of the outer universe. It would take centuries, millennia of sustained military action, and no nation that large had ever been united under one rule.

Except for the Empress.

Elysia was over half of the known universe. Not only did we have infinite resources to draw upon, but there was no way to get into Elysia if Mother chose to close the borders. It would stop even me from being able to return home. An Empress could vanish worlds; stuff the stars and obliterate an entire civilization from existence... just like the Ryunaga had suffered.

They didn't stand a chance even if they did try it.

During the end of the Sixth Empress' reign, she had closed the borders as the entire universe raged in the last of the major interstellar wars. That war had leveled so many advanced civilizations to ruins that the next Empress spent much of her reign preserving and restoring those dying nations back to life. Territory had swelled under the Seventh Empress as people chose to live under her rule rather than align themselves with cultures that had self-destructed.

Elysia had not seen war since Aristae's time.

Twenty-three million years ago.

What would our response be to such an unprecedented event?

A guard whose tactical uniform was torn from his right side entered the room then. It wasn't obvious from his stoic demeanor, but he was badly hurt. Blood had soaked his garments, and he was unable to open one of his eyes.

He knelt down and waited to be addressed.

"Did you catch them!? Are they traitors or invaders?"

"We caught the girl and recommend immediate execution."

"I commanded you to bring them to me alive and you kill all but one girl!?" The queen hissed, her brow twisted in rage.

"She was alone and neutralized half our forces, my queen."

The color leeched from her face. Her body became so stiff a flower petal may have had more physical integrity.

"Gather the shogunate. Bring her to me."

They had Amie. I had no choice but to follow them.

Following the queen revealed the true nature of the citadel. While all others would find the winding passageways unyielding with their secrets, the walls and floors fell out from before the queen. Wherever she went, the citadel bent around her.

It was truly an inventive design.

Our journey ended at the doors of the inner shrine. While the religion affiliated with the shrine had long been discarded, many of the same superstitions still plagued their culture. It was one of the few sacred objects of their culture and it was believed that to tell a lie within would curse your descendants.

Here was the only room in the citadel crafted entirely from wood. Hundreds of different species of trees were sourced to create this chamber, and no outsider had ever been welcome within its doors. The striped wood inside was mesmerizing. Until now, I thought this would be one of the places I would never get to see.

Whoever had alerted the shogunate had been efficient for all of them were seated at their ancestral positions along two sides of the triangular room. At the center point, opposite the door, Woltarie and Riasphone Ulys sat on the floor on either side of their mother's throne. It was odd to me that everyone but Ikki sat on the ground. The guards dispersed to surround the shogunate along the walls and I slid forward to Woltarie's side.

"My friend was caught," I whispered and, to his credit, he barely twitched a muscle at my voice materializing next to him. "I need to help her. I'm sorry."

"There's nothing you can do." His lips didn't move, impressive.

"If you want to repay me for Ione, then now is the time."

Amie was dragged inside of a net burning with energy currents. That didn't stop her from breaking the arm of one of the people carrying her inside. Not one of the guards surrounding her was uninjured, but I could see that Amie was getting tired. If the collapsed staircases, gaping holes, and gorges on the central hall hadn't been enough, she'd suffered several serious wounds.

Alarms went off again as she lashed out again and almost severed the arms of several of the soldiers who held on to her. She was dropped to the floor, and I could see that Amie was in too much pain to get to her feet right away. She knelt before the shogunate, panting. The guards did surround her, but they did not look keen on continuing their efforts to stop her.

It didn't matter if I healed her now because the alarms were already going off. Whatever I triggered would just be attributed to Amie. So, I healed the wounds I could see, eased the headache that was hounding her, and replenished her blood supply as well as I could. I needed to take additional medical courses when I got home now that I could work on other people. Amie and I also had to work on energy transference from a distance. There was no way for her to access my reserves from there. Amie stilled as she felt her wounds closing. Even the bruising on her face was fading.

Amie knew I was here.

She knew I wouldn't let anything happen to her.

Ikki Ulys must have taken her stillness as acquiesce.

She nodded for her guards to part ways to allow for a direct appraisal of Amie. They glared at each other in open hostility. The shogunate whispered among themselves, but otherwise, there was no sound in the chamber.

"Who are you? How dare you defile my halls with your blood?"

"You mean their blood." Amie spat. "Nice security by the way."

One of the guards moved to hit her with the butt of their weapon and Amie dislocated their knee. The other guards looked to their queen for instruction, but Ikki would not give them any. As it was, they just decided to shuffle a few centimeters away.

Smart of them.

Amie remained silent throughout the questioning. I realized that the words Woltarie had used earlier were some kind of trigger for forcing the blood trace to activate and when it didn't, the shogunate became even more outraged. How could anyone have made it into the citadel during a summit without the blood trace? How could Amie have concealed herself so thoroughly?

If Amie could just get dragged out of here, we could escape. It wouldn't be easy to get to the memory once we did, but at least we would be able to regroup once out from under queen Ikki's eye.

Just hold on a little bit longer.

The lights went out.

In the darkness, Zarek jumped down from the room's center beam and ripped the net entrapping Amie open. The guard closest to them blindly struck out with his ceremonial spear and Zarek casually broke it in half. Silently he took out one leg of any guard who got too close. Their screams of pain finally caused the other guards to break into a disorderly mess.

The sentries along the walls were rushing to calm the shogunate, the queen was screaming for order, and Woltarie surprised me by leaping in front of me, blocking my path to my friends. He couldn't exactly know where I was, but his hand closed around my arm nevertheless.

"Woltarie, those are my friends and I need to get to them, let go."

He had stepped off the dais, so it was still possible to whisper to him. Zarek's head snapped up and turned toward my direction as I spoke. More guards converged on them. Then, from the far side of the room, one of the shoguns began to scream.

Her skin was melting, exposed limbs were smoking from some kind of chemical reaction. It was airborne. I lunged forward and hit my nose against a new force field, one that surrounded the dais. Woltarie had turned around and was beating on the clear surface. Looking back at his mother, Ikki was smiling. Only she, her daughter, and I were safe inside this containment chamber.

The guards that hadn't been immobilized by Zarek were now running for the doors. Such paper-thin panels should never have held up to the stress they were now being put under.

The shoguns were in a wild stampede to either help the guards or plead with the queen to spare them.

Faced with another impossible situation, I acted.

I broke the containment chamber, and the shoguns tumbled like stones over each other at the queen's feet. I pushed the colorless, odorless gas back and found the hidden venting system that was being pumped out of. It was too late for four people who had been unlucky enough to be directly under it, but I did my best to heal the burns and corroded limbs of those left alive.

"Where are you!?" Amie was looking wildly around for me. I made myself visible and she nearly knocked Zarek over on her way to get to me. "Are you hurt!?" She looked at me all over herself without waiting for an answer and it wasn't until Amie was satisfied did she let Zarek near me. It was then that my attention was ripped away to a horrific sight.

Ikki Ulys, a strange weapon in hand, was driving it downwards as her son turned away to try and address the room.

If she killed him, she could blame this day on his corpse.

I turned away from Zarek to stop her. The queen flew backwards into the wall, cracking the wood from the force of my will before I could think to temper it. The weapon was dropped to the floor and the shogunate changed their minds from trying to escape to rallying around the queen. Half of the lights were starting to flicker back on as they tried to pry her from the wall. Her daughter had tumbled sideways off her seat and was silently watching from afar

"Are you alright!?" I asked him, "Did you see what happened?

"I saw enough." Woltarie's face like stone. "I—"

He was cut off by his mother's wrathful cry.

The queen's face scrunched into itself with hate.

"I know this power. I know this fear!" There was blood pouring down the side of her face. I had to remember to ease the pressure on the queen before I crushed her. Her eyes swept across the room and judging by the rage that now emanated from her, it was over.

Queen Ikki knew.

It couldn't get any worse.

"Deletii Mirona Corias Arget Raajali! How dare you infiltrate my house?" I rescinded my statement.

Her assumption that the Empress herself had violated interstellar law was so much worse. If I wasn't holding her against the wall, I think she would have killed the nearest person to her. The instant she accused me of being my mother, the room exploded into panic. People were falling to their hands and knees in front of us, people were grabbing at their queen and others again tried to flee. Amie was trying her best to keep them off of me.

"I knew this day would come! The Empire is here to purge us!"

"There's no need to shout! I can explain if you just give me a—"

"The Empress will wipe us from this universe, desecrate our worlds, and bathe in our entrails!"

Gross. People were screaming over each other now. shoguns were pressing themselves against the walls, guards were begging for their lives. Why was I even bothering to argue with her!? What should I do!? She had tried to kill her successor. It wasn't unheard of in their culture but I'd never heard of it being done in public. I put a bubble around her head so that she could rave all she wanted to and, making a decision, I turned to Woltarie.

"My friends and I have done damage to your home and people. I formally apologize for our intrusion. What do you want us to do now?" His eyes flickered down at me ever briefly at my words before he looked over at his mother.

He seemed to swiftly come to a decision himself.

"Let the queen down but leave her muzzled." I did so.

"Silence!" His voice carried over the assembly and miraculously the room went dead quiet. Even his sister stopped crying, startled by his raised voice. Woltarie seemed like the type not to yell often and I could see his subjects were mostly just shocked rather than cowed. It was an excellent display of his temperament.

Then he did something so out of bounds it was ingenious.

He offered me a military salute, saved for only the most ceremonial of occasions and while his next words were meant for those gathered around us, his eyes told me to play along. "Saekonari Raajali, your acceptance of my invitation honors me. I apologize for this unseemly disarray at your formal introduction and at the disgraceful behavior of the shogunate in your presence."

Brilliant.

I wanted to applaud his subterfuge.

As an alternative method of saying bravo, I turned back into myself and raised the illusion of a formal outfit suitable for an unprecedented state visit. With my coat destroyed, it was as good a solution as any. I now towered over the Ulisirachs, who shrank back at my changed appearance.

"Apology accepted," I said with a straight face. "Your hospitality has been exemplary up to this point and we, in return, will overlook the minor mishandling of Amythesia Esholitte. Rest assured this misunderstanding will not impact our future relations in any way. Will supper be served soon?"

He almost blew it with a smile then, but simply offered his arm.

I forced the doors to the inner shrine to open and as the alarms blared behind us. No one moved as Woltarie and I walked out at a leisurely pace. I could see them shrinking back from Amie, who glared at everyone; but if I had to guess, Zarek was still hidden.

"Are they really going to go along with your narrative?"

Woltarie Ulys almost smiled again.

"They have to, or they lose face in front of the Heir of Elysia."

Supper with the shogunate and their families was so tense that one could light a match on the air we breathed. Their spouses, children, and other entourage members had no prior warning a Raajali would be in attendance and more than a few had formally withdrawn from the occasion as soon as I entered the room. If it wouldn't be literal suicide to leave the grounds, I'm sure many would have done so. Woltarie and I spoke about his military background and various historical wars significant to his culture throughout the first few table settings.

Later, I hoped to discuss what had happened in the inner shrine, but now was not the time to speculate on what had occurred. If I hadn't stopped the gas, everyone save the queen and her daughter would have perished in agony. Woltarie's mother had tried to kill him, but he had not been fazed. Their family dynamic was one that I could not comprehend.

How could anyone turn on their children or parents so easily?

No one else spoke. Woltarie had introduced me to all those who shared the table, but it was their duty to engage me in conversation, not the other way around. His sister was also seated at our table and tried her best to look stoic. It would not do for her to fall to pieces twice in one night.

Amie and Zarek were standing behind me and I desperately wanted to make sure that they were okay, but this was a critical moment. I could not make a single mistake. I was in my own body; representing myself and my people; and I could not waste this opportunity to better integrate myself with the Ulisirachs. Ever since I had left home, it seemed like changes were gaining speed around us and I wanted to understand. All of the things I'd learned in the outer universe would not let me rest and maintaining an open mind could only benefit me.

"There are hairs in here," I commented, stirring the cold broth.

"It's not hair but thinly sliced skin drafts." Woltarie said blandly.

"And I'm sure they are a delicacy." I tried it out of curiosity but was just putting my spoon down, appetite gone, when his sister passed out of her chair. Her face was turning an alarming color.

She was struggling to breathe.\

Whatever was wrong with her, if I didn't fix it, would be blamed on me. Anything out of the ordinary would be blamed on me and there was already too much that had happened tonight. Others who had rushed to provide aid kept their distance once they saw that I was doing the same.

Riasphone Ulys' heartbeat was irregular. Her vital signs were equally erratic, and I wasn't sure what was wrong with her. I cleared the table with a flick of my fingers and her body rose to lie on top of it. There were people around me who were yelling again. Riasphone was in pain. "Woltarie, why would your sister be in pain? Does she have some kind of chronic disorder?"

"No, but she never fully recovered from childbirth—"

"She's been fucking poisoned is what's wrong with her."

Amie pried open the princess' mouth as her announcement took hold on the rest of the room. The queen was incensed, and people were now trying to pull her off of the table and away from us. Amie took care of them and after that display, no one else tried to get near the girl.

"Amie, what do I need to do?" Amie scowled down at Riasphone like she was an idiot for taking poison in the first place, but quickly explained to me how to purge her systems and replenish her blood with untainted cells.

As I worked on her, yet another interruption barged in.

"What now?" Woltarie muttered beside me.

It was Ione being dragged into the room. Since the last I'd seen her, she had been beaten to a pulp. A man who was dressed as a shogun, but had not been present at in the inner shine, came in screaming assassination.

Expressionless, he fell to his knees in front of the queen.

"You know, I just remembered why I don't come here anymore." Despite his careless comment, Zarek took one look at me and must have seen how torn I was between Riasphone and Ione because he took over her care with a motion; as if to say that he had her, allowing me to follow after Woltarie.

The guards stepped back the moment they saw me coming; Woltarie got there first and had to scoot over so I could get to her. The usually stoic Ulisirachs were whispering freely amongst each other, many of them sounded suspiciously delighted. I knelt down beside Ione while keeping one ear on the conversation between the shogun and the queen.

Ione's bones were a mess. It was good that she was unconscious. I numbed his pain before knitting everything back together as best as I could. She had internal damage that would need to be looked over later on by a medical professional, but he would live. Ione's facial swelling went down and as the people around me became oddly quiet, I looked up to see them all looking at me in fear. I knew that doing this was out of the norm in and of itself. This might be the first time some of these people ever saw the universe manipulated in this way.

Behind me, the shogun was making a convincing case that Ione had been the one poisoning Riasphone Ulys for months. That as part of her harem, Ione had the opportunity to tamper with her meals and her motivation was she was jealous of Riasphone's relationship with her older brother.

Apparently, it was no secret that Woltarie and Ione were friends.

People just didn't like it. Those judgmental bastards.

I stood up from Ione, whose nose I was still reconstructing and faced the shogun and queen Ikki. The man hadn't noticed me yet, it was the only explanation for his high-pitched screaming once his eyes found me. "Queen Ikki. he's lying to you. He knows Ione didn't do anything."

"Oh? And you know this for a fact do you!?"

"Yes. I can show you his last few days if that would help."

"No one but my personal soldiers are allowed to view the citadel's footage."

"I don't need them." I drew up a large window in between the shogun and the queen. There were basic equations for the fabric of time space and how one would go about observing them without triggering the observer effect or creating paradoxical variants. While this wasn't my first experience, it was so obviously their first time witnessing such a procedure.

I was showing the Ulisirachs too much of my Light, but I was not going to let them frame Ione of murdering a royal family member. From what little time I had spent with her, I had seen his love for the Ulys and their nation.

She had nothing to do with this.

All was silent as we watched the shogun being given instructions by queen Ikki to blame Riasphone's death on Ione and to plant the evidence in Woltarie's room. An investigation would uncover the evidence and mar his name.

With her son dead, no one would contest it.

The numerous attempts to rid herself of her eldest son, her only daughter, and Ione today had failed. What a shame for a notoriously cunning woman.

I closed the window. We all knew she would not be punished by their laws, but it was the height of humiliation for her to be caught murdering her family. It was an accepted custom only if it was never revealed who did it or how.

Even worse, queen Ikki had been caught in public.

Hatred flowed from the queen as the silence grew. She could not accuse me of fabricating the evidence. I was the Heir of Elysia, it was worse to insult me. She could not spin the narrative with so many witnesses to her plotting.

She could do nothing to harm me at all.

So, she simply stood and swept out of the room, taking most of the people with her. Eager to flee from me, there were very few who stayed, and most were servants who had no choice.

I brought Ione to lay on the table with Riasphone and carefully examined them once again.

"Your Eternal Grace. May I make a request?"

I nodded, too preoccupied to see that Woltarie had knelt down.

Amie had to nudge me to get me to look and for a Ulys to kneel down on one knee, it had to be serious. I kept one hand on Riasphone's arm while I listened to her older brother. It wasn't the easiest request for me to fulfill, but I could not refuse. Not only because I liked Woltarie, but because I saw him as a suitable leader for his people. He was kinder and his integrity not nearly as compromised as his mother's. Ulisirach could do far worse.

The first step was waking my patients from their slumber.

It took a few more adjustments on Ione's organs and bones, but they were able to walk on their own now.

Woltarie then took us to a private room where we wouldn't have to hear the alarms go off all over the citadel.

I thought for a moment of what was the best strategy before making a path back home. Hopefully, Mother wasn't watching this particular part of the palace; yet a few seconds was all it took to see my timing was again not ideal.

My grandfather, former Emperor Kelex Raajali, apparently slept naked and I would never be able to forget it.

I had to yell his name several times before he finally responded.

"Saekonari?" Groggily he pulled his sheets up, thank the Empress, and took a few seconds to stretch before he looked my way again. It was midday back at the palace and he looked not at all abashed at his nap or nakedness.

Allusi were not known for being self-conscious.

"Hello." I still wasn't used to having another family member. "Um, would you be willing to help a few friends of mine get settled in the palace until I return? They've requested political asylum. If you'd rather, I could talk to Anera instead."

"Nah, they're busy these days." He started looking around the room. "Let me find my pants and I'll show them around."

I averted my eyes as he got up from his bed and went to look for clothing. There were just some things I didn't want permanently stored in my brain, thank you.

"Amie, can you take Riasphone to pick up her son?"

The princess started crying, her body racked with sobs.

"Oh! I'm sorry. What's wrong?" I didn't have anything she could use as a tissue. Her emotional fragility was extremely out of character for her species and to see her cry twice in one day was considered quite disgraceful to her entire culture.

Woltarie spoke over his sister as she continued to cry.

"Hisoe Ulys went missing today, and was found dead."

My body went cold.

I had just seen him. I had picked up that adorable baby and hadn't given a thought to him since. I'd believed he was in safe hands. How could this have happened? Why didn't I feel something wrong? Quietly, I explained to them what I had seen earlier with Ione backing up my story. Riasphone stopped crying, her face growing so gray that I worried her blood was being stopped from flowing into her head. After I finished my explanation, neither sibling commented.

Ione and Riasphone stepped through to where Kelex took charge of them. He then reached out to squeeze my shoulders affectionately. "Come see me when you get back." He told me before yawning. "Everything's fine on this end, even if Leti's throwing her daily hissy fit. Are you almost finished?" I nodded. "Good. I forgot how blasted boring it is here without Shimi."

I closed the rift. "Woltarie? What will you do now?"

"What I must. The pact will end at dawn, don't linger here."

"We won't. Thank you for what you did for me."

I offered him my palm but instead of giving me the usual motion for farewell, he kissed my hand. It was a shockingly intimate gesture for both the occasion and the person.

"Hey Ulys." Zarek put a hand on Woltarie's shoulder.

Not the most respectful thing you could do to a stranger in Ulisirach. Woltarie let go of my hand and they stared each other down for a moment, Woltarie looking defensive and Zarek smiling, seemingly without a care in the world.

"What are you doing here?"

So Zarek had kept hidden until now.

"I'm always invited to the good parties."

Before Woltarie could absorb that outlandish statement, Zarek took out something from his coat and held it in front of Woltarie's nose. "Do you know what this is? I happened upon it. Just lying on the ground. Asking to be rescued."

It was that weapon Ikki had tried to murder her son with. It was so black it absorbed light and was an unusual shape for a weapon. It was not in their culture's traditional style at all, and the texture had a ghostly quality to it.

I hadn't realized Zarek had taken it.

"No." Woltarie was lying and both Zarek and I knew it.

"Woltarie, what is it? Why don't you want us to know?"

"It's none of your concern."

He tried to take it, but Zarek didn't give it up.

"It's Ryunaga bone." Zarek answered for him "It's Illegal to be in possession of or traded for any reason."

It was what!?

Woltarie started to say something, but he stopped once he got a look at my face. That weapon was made from Naga bone. Their species took the disposal of their bodies seriously. Their remains were destroyed entirely, like the Raajali, and scattered into open space or into the nearest star. It sickened me to think that one of their bodies had been used for something so grotesque. I held out my hand and Zarek gave it to me. It took no more than a fraction of a second to render it to dust.

"Woltarie. You should go."

Whatever he had to say to me, I didn't want to hear it.

Turning on his heel, he left us. The sound of alarms hit our ears in the brief moment the door was opened, the door closed with a quiet finality, and we were finally left alone.

I went directly to Amie and offered my reserves.

She assured me that she was okay, so I turned to Zarek.

"Are you alright?" I couldn't resist and touched his cheek, trying to see if he was hurt. Zarek stood absolutely still during the quick examination, but when I was about to let go, he laid his hand over my own and turned his head ever so slightly to rest his lips against my fingers. "I'm glad to see you're feeling alright." I tried to pretend I wasn't affected but without a single word, this man had eroded away my composure. "Now we just need to find—"

"We already found it, It was in the nursery."

Amie sounded about as regretful as I felt.

My throat tightened up at the unfairness of it all.

"Good, that's good. I'm glad. We should go."

"Amie. Turn around." Zarek pulled me against him.

"Oh for the love of—" Amie quickly looked the other way.

Would kissing him always feel this way? As if all the space between the skies had been created only to lead to this. I could barely hear the words he whispered against my mouth between each one, "Saekonari, I remember... everything about you that kept me awake at night... every time I wished you would never look away from me... every time I wanted you..."

I could feel tears prickling my eyes.

"Now that you know, do you still..."

"Sae. Every part of you. Calls out to me."

We were smiling like idiots.

I kissed him again.

"Hey! You two! I am still here!"

Chapter 26: Sacrileges

On the outskirts of the Oon Alliance, one could be fooled to believe that a post-warp society had never taken root. Unlike other aligned powers, the Alliance was laid out in satellite territories with no major capital or shared language. Their system came as close to an absolute capitalistic society than any other. To be a citizen, all one had to do was renounce citizenship elsewhere.

Architecturally, from our perspective, it was a model city of early eighth era deco. All curves and dramatic dips built completely out of white and grey composite materials. No dust or dirt could remain inside due to their air circulation system and as a planned settlement, the streets and buildings all curved around each other in a practical manner. Artificial plant life everywhere.

The only real authority were the regulators who were trained for the profession from a very young age.

Not that many laws existed for them to enforce.

This hollowed out shell of a moon charading as a legitimate trading post was infested with illegal transactions, corrupt tax havens, and crime ridden pockets of apathy.

All accomplished under a false veneer of order.

Yet in this labyrinth was Zarek's second to last memory.

What was the goal behind all of this? Cira, if she was telling the truth, had been coerced. She had dragged us from one end of the outer universe to the other; forcing me to become involved with matters that no Heir should have ever gotten involved with. If her father was at the root of all of this, he'd arranged that I'd witnessed several high-profile events changing the course of several nations and had finally succeeded in having my identity revealed.

The evidence was irrefutable.

Why hadn't I thought to check for cameras?

Who would have known being spiteful against me would matter more to queen Ikki than revealing their sacred conference room?

Every news site in the universe was playing the footage of the inner shrine. Of a nondescript girl turning into the Heir of Elysia. Wild speculation of my performances in Solaris and Nileanna's house abounded. So far, neither Isbul or Ulisirach had sent an official statement on the matter but that didn't mean there weren't people calling on Mother for an explanation.

"Will you miss me after my mother gets her hands on me?" I half-joked, looking up at the massive screen projecting my own face. It was no longer safe for me to go around looking like either of those girls, but I had decided against changing my appearance again. Opting to just keep on a mask wherever I went, I regretted my recklessness now. I could have made any number of choices that wouldn't have exposed me, but there was no use in looking back.

"I'll visit your grave every day." Zarek said solemnly, before slipping past my guard and putting food in my mouth.

"Mmph!" I dodged his next attempt to feed me. "You don't have to—I don't really need to eat." Yet I somehow found myself with more food in my mouth. This one was sweet. There was a hint of tartness, but mostly it melted into a luxurious cream.

Mmmm.

"Oh, thank the Empress, you're finally back!" Fane drew our attention to Amie and Omere, returning up a stairwell to the rooftop. Amie pulled down her hood and by her scowl I knew they hadn't found it. Once again, it was moving faster than Amie could discreetly navigate the city.

At least Omere seemed happy about the walk.

I had restored much of his sight in the last few days, a feat that had involved Fane looking up a dozen additional medical texts and a lot of patience. He didn't have full vision yet, but I was sure Omere's eyes would continue to restructure themselves and heal over the coming days.

If not, we'd try again once we were back home.

"I can't stand them anymore Amie." Fane hung on her arm.

Amie just rolled her eyes before reaching out to fiddle with Fane's implant, which he allowed even though he was still griping about common decency and public displays of affection. She projected all of the major news channels all at once and it only took a few seconds to see why. All of them were broadcasting the same topic and this time it wasn't about me.

Rateer had invaded Hitea's home system.

Their military, stationed at the border to intercept Rateerian forces, was blindsided and there was no response from the Hitean president or his cabinet as of yet. Their head admiral was expected to ask for formal intervention from the Empress any day now as the body count grew.

They wouldn't get it.

Elysia had long set the precedent to never engage with the wars of other nations no matter the circumstances. Once, I may have believed that it was the right thing to do. Neutrality in all matters; that it was the right decision to never provide military aid and the business of the outer universe was none of our concern.

As long as Elysia was safe, everything was fine.

Did I still believe it?

"Amie, shut it off." She did so. "We need to find the memory and get back home. I need to talk to my grandfather. I need to talk to Mother." I tried to recall if Elysia even had an information network of any kind stationed in the outer universe. I knew there was a treaty from the seventh Empress' time that banned the use of state sponsored espionage. We had signed it, as did all other developed countries in the outer universe. Something told me we followed rules no one else bothered to adhere to.

Gunshots splintered the air.

I reacted before I knew what my body was doing. I tucked and rolled away from the edge of the rooftop in similar fashion to what Zarek did beside me. It was only once we'd rejoined the others did I see the volley was in no way related to us.

They were coming from below; pedestrians were fleeing from the two groups shooting at each other in the middle of the street. One group wore the regulator uniform, the other was wearing uniforms of the Rateerian army.

It didn't help that the majority of the regulators were in training. I knew the Alliance enlisted young but I hadn't know just how young. I couldn't leave them and pulled the children away from where they huddled behind their superiors to the base of the building we stood upon. It was all I could do right now.

"We need to get away from here." I put on my diffraction mask and headed for the stairwell. This was not the time to get in the middle of yet another nation's struggles. The Oon Alliance may technically be a sovereign nation, but without Hitea acting as a buffer it was only a matter of time before this region was destabilized. It was more dangerous than ever for me to be out here.

Omere was walking in the wrong direction.

He was squinting his newly minted eyes, his ears twitched forward just a bit. "What's wrong?" I asked him, trying to see what he was looking at. He made a noncommittal noise and pointed across the square and down at a small group of people on a balcony.

They were watching the riot below from what I could tell.

The one in front looked uncannily like…

"Oh you have got to be kidding me." Fane pulled up a small lense from his implant that enhanced the vision on his right eye. It didn't take more than a few seconds for him to report. "That's Edjeridi Akon. His grandmother was just sworn in, he's second in the succession line now, maybe first."

"So should we warn him?"

Amie pulled both Omere and I back from the edge.

Fane stilled. Without answering, he swore a profane word and would have run off if Zarek didn't grab him. "Let go! I swear to the fucking Empress I will rip that dickhead's eyes out and feed them to him if it's the last thing I ever do in this—"

I didn't blame Fane for his overreaction. I'd seen him too.

The lithe man with green eyes, standing next to Edjeridi.

Dylis stood at attention while Edjeridi said something to him. Before I could try and listen in, Dylis bowed out and went inside the building. Fane was still shouting profanities; but there was no way to tell if his shouts were getting anywhere with the amount of noise surrounding the square.

We were still calming him when an explosion rocked the moon.

It came from the upper units; a plume of corrosive chemicals and smoke rapidly filling the air, flames shot out in all directions from above. The centripetal force of the trading post pulled the fire inwards, setting off a string of explosives in rapid sequence. Deafening shockwaves sent debris falling in arches. Large chunks of infrastructure rained down on the city's heart, crushing everything in their efforts to punch another hole through the moon.

The outer shell had been breached.

This trading post was going to fall into pieces.

Units stacked irregularly in towers of geodesic domes were already far from stable. Alarms blared as I sealed the structure and held the crumbling halves together. I couldn't weld the pieces fast enough. This moon had passed one too many lenient inspections.

I tried to reenforce sections, but I would have to pull energy from their star to create new materials out of thin air. A full rebuild would draw far too much attention. I would have to hold it until we finished what we set out to do.

"We need to run!"

Fane resisted against Amie and Zarek's efforts to drag him along. Was he still trying to get to Dylis? There was a good chance he was dead and buried under the rubble by now. I had deflected larger pieces away from the thickest of the crowds, but I couldn't save everyone without drawing attention.

The building Dylis was in was about to collapse.

"Don't make me knock you out Fane!" Amie moved to pry him off the doorframe and Fane almost hurt himself trying to throw them off. "Stop it Akon!"

"I can't just leave him!" Fane blurted out. "I can't leave Dylis!"

"Oh yes you can! Screw him!" Amie pried his fingers off.

"No! Let go! I need to get Dylis!" Fane desperately refused.

Solar nymphs, we didn't have time for this.

"Amie go with Fane and get Dylis!" There were other explosives that hadn't gone off yet. I could taste their metallic shells trying to blow up other parts of this moon clear off. "We'll regroup inside the crust in fifteen minutes. Amie if you can't find Dylis in under five, knock Fane out and drag him back."

I looked at Fane's mutinous face as I said the last part.

He swallowed hard but nodded his assent.

Zarek let Fane go, Amie grabbed his hand, and they disappeared. That left the three of us to get off of this building before it too collapsed. Omere and Zarek donned their masks, and we set out for the place no authority figures would set foot in willingly and a location I'd been dying to see.

This black market's black market.

The only one of us who knew how to find it was Zarek, but Amie could find me no matter where I was. He'd described the winding passageways in detail earlier when I expressed interest.

The tunnels used to be transport hubs for the original ore mining operation. Carved into the outermost layer, they'd been abandoned decades ago due to a growing risk of exposure to open space. Nicknamed the crust, it was now used for activities the regulators couldn't outright ignore.

I couldn't wait to see them.

On our way out into the crust, the number of people who stared as we passed decreased and the number of doors increased. Everything was white but for doors that possessed windows of a frosted polymer. There was a single strip of lights down the center of the passageways that were more broken than functioning. They stretched on endlessly in an open grid pattern.

It wasn't at all what I'd built up in my head.

At a certain point, Zarek took his mask and hood off and had Omere and I do the same. "We're almost there. Try to look like you could kill someone."

I wasn't sure if he meant it, but I tried.

"Never mind. Omere look like you're going to kill someone. Pixie, stay close and don't look at anyone." He placed his hand at my back and that little spark of warmth made me jump on contact. Zarek must have felt my response because he leaned down to whisper in my ear. "Now you've done it. My reputation will be in shreds. Your flirting is just insidious... and effective."

"Omere can hear you," I blushed regardless. "Why whisper?"

My answer was a featherlight kiss and him pulling my hood down to cover more of my face. A few more turns were taken before we walked through a wall into a bustling business; a food service establishment if the smell indicated anything. The loud chatter almost ceased once we entered and took a few moments to build back up. I heard a snippet of conversation here and there about the recent explosions, but I didn't dare raise my head.

I knew they were staring at me.

All throughout this trip I reined myself in with a tight leash, but now I was holding together this entire moon. Zarek and Omere could feel it too even if they hadn't brought it up yet. There was a chance that someone would even be able to identify the feeling, but that chance was a slim one. The walk across the open space and up the staircase felt like decades passing.

Zarek opened one of the doors on the third floor and interrupted what looked like an intense discussion. I don't know what Zarek did to make them leave, but they left quickly. Inside the room was a table low to the ground, a keypad embedded into it.

"You're holding this place together aren't you?"

I nodded at the question and went to go inspect the keypad. It didn't just have the ten basic symbols for Elysian numbers, on its face were over a hundred random number symbols that varied from modern to ancient.

"What happens if I touch it?" I knelt down to get a closer look.

"If you put in the wrong code, the room will try to off us." Zarek sat down next to me and gently pulled my hood back. "All kinds of deals are struck in these rooms. For specific services and goods, you punch in a reception number and are referred to their catalogue." Why was he looking at me like that?

Zarek seemed to be searching for something.

"What is it? Do I have something on my face?"

"How do you feel pixie? Do you need anything?"

"Because of the moon breaking up? I can actually hold it together indefinitely, but I was thinking it would be more practical to send an anonymous letter for this colony to evacuate by a certain date and then slowly release the shell to show signs of visible stress. That way, the citizens would take the warning seriously.

Now whether it would be more impactful coming through on a journalistic approach or one that involves the head regulator is the real question. It would be a riskier endeavor to involve the regulators especially if they don't agree with my suggestions—I'm sorry, this can't be interesting to listen to. I'm perfectly fine."

I was a nervous wreck by the end of my tangent.

I should have just answered the damn question, was that so hard to do? To my befuddlement, instead of saying anything right away, Zarek tugged at me until I was leaning against him.

I could hear his heartbeat.

Omere, fully absorbed in one of the short story books we'd gotten him, didn't care what we did.

"Don't apologize." Zarek said quietly. "I love hearing you talk."

Oh. It was the first time I'd ever heard him say that word in relation to me. I was blushing so much I was afraid I might set the room on fire. Mother had always scolded me for ranting.

The urge to apologize for speaking out of turn was always present whenever I opened my mouth.

Esme especially got annoyed whenever I talked too much.

The door opened and I bolted upright.

"If your fat ass would just hurry the fuck up!"

"Excuse you! I'm the one carrying your deadbeat boyfriend!"

"Dylis is not my boyfriend anymore! But watch his head!" Fane was too late in his warning and Dylis' head bashed into the door frame. Amie, looking more than fed up, let him fall on Fane, who tried his best to have his ex-boyfriend fall the rest of the way to the floor gracefully. Ultimately, he failed and they both landed in a heap next to Omere, who ignored them.

Fane held on a little too long before moving Dylis away.

"He has a bad concussion," I said after examining Dylis. "I don't feel comfortable working on his brain, but I can wake him up."

I waited for Fane to nod before I did so.

Dylis came to with a start, but then his eyes closed again. A low groan told me I should have thought to ease his pain beforehand. I did so then but just enough so that he could focus, I didn't want him to think the damage wasn't there.

He briefly met my gaze before looking away.

The person he chose to speak to was not Fane, but Zarek.

"How did you find me Deutreax?"

Why use Zarek's middle name?

"I didn't. He did." Zarek nodded at Omere, who was still reading and not responding to his name.

"And who the hell is he supposed to be?"

"Oh, you didn't know? He's Fane's new boyfriend."

Omere didn't even look up from his book.

He was joking of course, but Dylis flinched as Zarek hit a nerve.

"If that's all. I'll take my leave." No one moved as he headed for the door, all of us looking at Fane except for Omere, who was trying to silently sound out a particularly long word.

Fane didn't say anything at first. His fists were so tightly clenched I was afraid he'd draw blood.

Finally Fane overcame his pride and said a few quiet words.

"Dylis, why did you do it? How could you?"

He didn't stop walking away.

He wasn't planning on answering Fane's questions at all.

Unfortunately for him, Amie had decided otherwise. She had taken one look at Fane's heartbroken face and was up before Dylis could open the door. Amie slammed her hand on the surface of the panel and very obviously locked and sealed it. Her fingers crackled over the metal in a clear and poignant threat.

"Sit down before I make you." She glared at him and far more courageous men have cowered when Amie decided to be mean. Dylis was no exception and sat back down, albeit he still refused to look in Fane's direction.

In fact he refused to look at any of us.

"Dylis. Just tell me why." Fane reiterated.

"For the money obviously. Why else?"

"We had plenty of money! That can't be why!"

"Yes that's why! I never loved you anyway."

"He's lying," I said when Fane turned to me, tears leaking out.

"Don't try and spare his feelings!" Dylis snapped, "Why else would I tolerate his vain, needy ass? He's always been loaded and dumb as dirt—" His voice cracked, but Dylis kept going. "He was impossible to live with you know! He snores and always wears my new clothes before I get the chance. He always remembers to bring me my favorite tea in the morning and waters my plants for me when I forget..." Dylis suddenly got a very confused look on his face. "Fanelius always screams at the wrong part of a scary film, but he never lets go of my hand—"

Amie's shielding was stripped from the room and Zarek was suddenly dragging Dylis up and out toward the door. His shoes scraped against the floor as he fought for purchase, Zarek's grip almost lifting him off the ground. Fane and Amie shouted at his back for him to stop and I had to clamber onto the table to get in front of them. "Zarek! What are you doing!?"

"I'll explain later." He shoved Dylis out of the room. "The nearest exit is up the stairs, last door on the right. Don't think until you get back to your post."

"My post?" I heard Dylis repeat before Zarek shut the door.

"What the fuck was that!?"

Fane tried to shove Zarek out of the way and failed.

Zarek looked right at me and there was a fear that I'd never seen in his eyes. "Did he know who you are?" Zarek asked and when I hesitated his face grew dark. "Omere I hope you've been paying attention in our quality time together because you're upgrading." Zarek threw an object at him that wrapped around Omere's forearm under his clothes and created a visible energy field between his fingers. "We need to leave. Right now."

"Zarek, what's going on?" I saw Omere putting away his book. "Why is Omere taking orders from you? Why won't you answer me?" I didn't dodge his hand when he reached for me, but I also didn't move when he tried to move me.

"Tell me what's going on." I said softly.

"Is Sae in danger?" Amie was now ostensibly taking Zarek's word as gospel because she immediately took his side when he nodded. "Sae. We need to leave. I don't know if lover boy's exaggerating, but I don't think he is." She started tugging at me too. "You better tell us what the hell you've gotten us into." Amie managed to drag me forward a bit. "Or I will—"

I watched Zarek pull Fane and Amie down in slow motion.

Turning, I caught the tail end of a blinding burst of light and heat. It was only a last second adjustment that kept my clothes from being melted off me. Scorch marks marred the once pristine white walls and once the light subsided, a little blinking blue light caught my attention. The table was completely untouched by the display and on top of it, several of the numbers on the keypad were blinking. I must have accidentally stepped on some of them.

Thankfully, Omere, the only one of us sitting down, was fine.

"Zarek get out of my way! I'm going after Dylis! Let go of me!"

"Fane, he's too far gone. He'll snap out of it and he won't—"

"What the fuck!? What are you talking about!? Zarek let go!"

There was a small screen projected above the keypad that wasn't there before. It was encoded, but not well. I recognized the patterns from my linguistical logic courses. Amie was pulling at me again, but I shook her off and got on my knees to reread the words my eyes refused to believe were correct.

I must be decoding it incorrectly somehow.

SHIPMENT #304-088 [PAYMENT UPON ARRIVAL]
RYUNAGA BLOOD TYPE K NEGATIVE – 200 GRAMS
RYUNAGA OSTEOCYTE CELLS – 500 GRAMS
RYUNAGA ARTICULAR CARTILAGE – 10 GRAMS
RYUNAGA DORSAL KERATIN – 800 GRAMS
RYUNAGA MEDULLA SPINALIS – .00005 GRAMS

□There might not have been any blood left in my face. Amie was still pulling at me and instead of resisting, I read out the message to her. She stopped trying to move me by the end of the second line. "This is signed by Cira Kyrian. Just a few hours ago." I stood up slowly and looked at Zarek. "Did you k-know about this? Is that how you recognized the weapon in the citadel?"

He didn't automatically deny it.

I let him hold Yuki. Yuki adored him. He had slipped her little snacks and toys when we were children, she'd fallen asleep on his lap, and Zarek had been alone with her just a few months ago. I think I was actually going to be sick. In the background, I could hear Omere quietly ask Amie what a Ryunaga was.

"Zarek. Please say something."

Zarek finally let go of Fane and came to sink one of his hands into my hair. He touched his forehead to mine and I couldn't help but respond. I couldn't help but reject all implications of everything I'd seen. It couldn't be.

I couldn't love him if he'd done this. It was a line that I didn't know existed, but one that threatened everything.

"I need you to trust me Sae." I wanted to. So badly. "Let me take you home." Why couldn't he tell me the truth now? "I'll tell you. I swear. Just not here."

My gut was telling me no. This wasn't right.

"I do trust you." Taking a deep breath, I pulled back to that I could look up at him. "But trust goes both ways Zarek. Tell me what's going on. Be honest with—"

The door fractured inwards by a blast that hit Fane dead center in the back. Tranquilizing gas canisters were thrown. I immediately reversed their trajectory and sent them soaring back out. With no time for finesse, I shoved the crowd of armed men back and sent some of them flying from the force.

It was an entire platoon of regulators.

Amie threw up a barrier between the regulators and us as they open fired. Dozens of them were flooding into the business below, their weaponry clearly not set to incapacitate, but kill. Their standard issue phasers were no match for some of the hidden weaponry I saw being pulled out, but their sheer numbers were threatening to overrun this establishment.

Amie turned the barrier opaque to give us breathing room.

Whoever was in charge of bribing the local district regulation authority had either wasted their money or had been killed and I didn't have time to take in the full situation. I had to piece together Fane's body or he would be dead in minutes.

Why did I never think to take more advanced medical training? It was all I could do to keep his blood circulating properly and oxygen levels steady. Sealing the wounds and exposed arteries kept him from bleeding out, but from what little I did know about this level of physical damage, I needed organic matter to rebuild his organs. Where would I find—I saw one of the regulator's head blown clean off their shoulders—no, I couldn't do it.

Instead, I took a calming breath and accelerated Fane's cells to multiply the necessary components. It was a good thing he'd eaten a large meal today as I did what I could to make those cells turn into compatible replacements for his body. Slowly, I rebuilt his lungs and other organs that had been singed or damaged. I had to be careful of where I was taking materials from and how quickly I was transforming cells to weave together his body, but it was working.

What I should have done was map out his anatomy before he got hurt. This would be far more intuitive if I fully understood the layout of Fane's body.

"Fane's heart has five chambers." Zarek advised me, nudging my left hand which was busy regulating Fane's blood and oxygen. He took over the task for me in the next minute so that I could focus on reestablishing the arteries supplying Fane's digestive system.

"We are still going to talk about it. Just so you know."

"You are the most terrifying thing in the universe."

Terrifying? "I'm not try to hurt you Zarek."

"I didn't say you were." His voice got a bit rougher as we finished matching the skin tone and began to pump blood through the new organs and veins. "Saekonari. I have never taken a step where I could fall, but you. You tempt me off the edge." Both of our hands rested right above Fane's heartbeat, strong and steady again. "You underestimate yourself, pixie. I..."

Fane's eyes were open. I checked for pain, but everything seemed to be in working order. Once he saw that Zarek and I had noticed him, he pretended to play dead again. "Don't mind me, go on, I'm dying to know what follows "You tempt me off the edge—ow!" Zarek had struck him in the upper arm. Fane laughed as he was hauled onto his feet. "Hey! Be gentle with me! It isn't my fault you decided to have a chat over my messed-up body."

"Sae! Get us out of here!" Amie said once she saw Fane standing.

"We can't just leave! This entire place might fall apart!"

"And I still need to get Dylis!" Fane yelled over everyone.

Amie looked like she wanted to say she didn't care, but this moon had over twenty million people living inside of it. Neither of us could conceive of letting such a disaster happen. Amie and I tried to brainstorm on how to best alert the colony without also revealing my identity again, but we didn't have many options. We didn't know who planted the explosives and we also couldn't reasonably say that the colony was falling apart without letting it fall apart. The regulators were still shooting people, and I now understood they were not here to enforce the law.

Another explosion rocked the floor. Amie pushed out the barrier forward, forcing the crowd to move or be smushed.

We could now look over the railing, but nothing made any sense.

The ground below had turned into a warzone in our absence. Tables and chairs were broken, bent, and tossed aside, the once sterile atmosphere was now a mess of bodies and equipment with a liquid spurting out of a nearby containment unit.

There were a few people sitting on the ground in a circle of regulators, but Dylis was the one holding a weapon to their heads. They didn't look like the friendliest of people, but that didn't excuse the fact that they seemed to be the only people left alive. Whatever the cause of this raid, it didn't justify an extermination.

The ones closest to the center were those children I'd seen earlier, the regulators in training. None of them had received medical treatment since the last I'd seen them and all of them had what looked like explosives strapped to their necks.

Some of the younger ones were crying.

Of all the people who could have walked in at that moment.

It had to be Edjeridi Akon.

The crowd below parted to let him through. Accompanying him was an older woman, with steel gray hair and eyes that perfectly matched her uniform. Her face seemed weathered and cruel beyond her years. Edjeridi gestured grandly at the scene before them, ranting that he'd found the culprits who'd tried to destroy the colony. He was lying. Why did so many people in the outer universe lie? Didn't it get exhausting having to remember them all?

He was wearing a shiny pendant that caught the light.

I had seen that material before.

Leaping over the railing and through Amie's barrier was not the hard part. Ignoring my friends shouting after me was also not it. The hard part was leashing my anger enough to not injure the regulators who tried to get in my way.

They were not who I was angry with.

Cor had almost torn me apart in her rage. She had loved her children and her people so much that the grief had almost destroyed her. Now I would have to act in her stead and I started to understand the anger that had driven her to blindly lash out. The fury that hadn't cared about collateral damage.

The regulators fell unconscious as they rushed at me and, so help me, they were not going to wake up until we left this Empress forsaken place. It didn't take a heightened intelligence to see what was happening to their coworkers and those who remained awake shrank back as I passed.

"Where did you get that necklace?" It flew toward my hand and Edjeridi was almost strangled trying to keep up with it. "Do you know what this is?" I broke the chain with one hand and let it fall to the floor, creating a small burst of dust once it made impact, the particles rising unnaturally around me.

"Who are you!? Let me—"

"Answer my question. Now."

"No! I don't know what it is—"

"Edjeridi Akon. You are *lying*."

I pinned him against the far fall, causing a flood of excuses, threats, and profanities to fall out of his mouth. Uncaring, I turned to face the woman who had come in with him.

The pins on her collar meant she was in command here.

"Did you know he was wearing Naga bones?" My anger only worsened as she backed away from me. "Did you know the Empress holds public tribunals for being found in possession of any part of Ryunaga?" I was getting sick of looking at their handling of children and forced all of the bombs to detonate within an enclosed space. As soon as they stopped reacting, I let the debris fall harmlessly to the ground. "Did you know your colony was colluding with Rateer in this act of despoliation and just what the Empress would do if she ever found out?"

I raised my hand, palm side up and closed my fist. When I took hold of Edjeridi's pendent, I had felt a pulse of recognition.

All around us, the moon trembled. In that moment, I could feel every soul that had once been held within these pieces of their former bodies. They crashed through the crust, through containment fields and storage facilities. Through walls and floors they shot through to spin around me. Only trace amounts held here and there, but together they were almost the weight of baby barely a decade old. They glowed ever so slightly, and I knew by the fear in their eyes that so too did I.

"How dare you allow this atrocity to take place!?"

"Hey! Hey!" Fane and Omere got in between me and them. "Calm down!" Fane hissed at me when there was an entire room of people complicit with this disgusting practice. I didn't care what they were using their bodies for.

Like the Raajali, the Naga were of a primordial order.

"The Naga are of the primordial order," I repeated it until it looked like the words sank in. "It would not be an exaggeration to say that these pieces of their bodies are *cursed*. No one knows what would happen if that order was broken."

The pieces around me crumbled into nothingness. I swept the room of all that remained and sent it whirling out into open space. Amie and Zarek were talking into my ears, but I was still too furious to listen to them. "How would all of you like to be taken apart and sold to the lowest bidder? Hmm?"

I took a step toward them and they all flinched.

Empress I was so tired of them all.

"This colony is going to fall apart in one week. One hundred hours because I am the one holding it together." I wasn't about to hurt anyone. My anger was already turning into grief, and I had a limited amount of time before I would most likely fall apart. "I suggest you evacuate before then." I hesitated but gave one more directive. "Let those people and the children go. Edjeridi was lying about the explosives. You can ask him why later."

"I'm not lying!" He screamed behind me, still lying.

I was this close to muting him. Forever.

I let him down.

He was first in line to the Isbulian throne. I would know where to find him later. Just as he turned to leave the room with as much dignity as he could, his head was blasted off his shoulders.

We whirled around to see Dylis with the literal smoking gun.

Edjeridi's body fell to the ground with a jarring thud.

"He did this to me." Dylis turned the barrel under his chin.

"No!" Fane tackled him, but it was already too late.

The blast went clean through Dylis' skull and shot his grey matter into the air behind them. The children started screaming, but Fane was louder than them all.

"Sae!" Fane howled, he was trying to hold the head together and it wasn't working. One look told me it was far too complex matter for me to safely operate on. Fane saw the look on my face and started begging me. "Sae please! Please don't let him die! Please! Sae! I can't watch him die! Sae!"

He started bawling and I couldn't bear to tell him no.

Amie saw where this was going.

"Everyone back up!" She ordered and was obeyed.

There was only one place that could guarantee Dylis' recovery and that was the medical facilities at the Academy. So, once again, I folded the space between the two locations and as soon as the other side was established we had a room full of curious staff members peering back at us.

"I'm transferring a patient who most likely requires a partial to full cerebral reconstruction. Please stand by." Questions were pelted at me and several medical professionals actually stepped through to see what was going on. They converged on Dylis as I stabilized his body and lifted it off the ground.

Once they had him contained, some looked about in confusion.

It was unlikely any of them had ever been outside the borders. It struck me just how guileless my people looked compared to those who lived in the outer universe. Did Amie and I look like that? They'd probably never been somewhere that was so dirty. Some of them tried to rush to others who were obviously injured, but Amie just redirected them to Dylis.

One of them asked for an emergency contact or next of kin.

"Fane, you should go with them." I nudged him toward the bright lights of the Academy's medical wards and he looked truly torn. "We'll catch up with you soon. It's okay. The other side is the medical facilities of the Academy, ask for Kelex. They'll find him."

"I can't just ask for your grandfather!" He said in a hushed voice.

"I promise you that you can." It took another minute more of convincing, during which Amie kept any more of our people from walking through and he finally gave in and went after Dylis, answering questions as he went.

He gave Amie one last hug before stepping through.

Amie's hugged him fiercely in return.

I closed the rift. Now to deal with the rest of them.

"Ninety-nine hours and ninety-four minutes left to evacuate."

Finally, the older woman took over and started mobilizing her people. I woke up the ones I'd knocked out and stopped others from taking the children. These children had most likely been sold into training by their families, but even without the injuries from today, it was clear they were not well-cared for. I left them with Amie on guard for the moment.

Zarek was speaking to the few people the regulators had let live. The room quickly emptied, and I was about to go see if they needed anything, when I was stopped by the regulators' superior.

She had an especially pinched expression on her face.

It surprised me when some of the children broke ranks and ran to her. Her hands went to stroke their heads. She never looked away from me, but something gentled in her face. "They have implants attached to their cervical vertebrae. They're difficult to get out without harming them, but I suspect they won't be a problem for you, Saekonari Raajali."

"Do you oversee their care? What are the implants for?"

"I do not, and the implants are designed for corrective behavioral therapy. Rebellious members are punished through them, and they can kill or paralyze any dissidents from the neck down. Barbaric compared to how children are treated in Elysia isn't it?"

Yes. It was.

"Let me see." I knelt down and offered my hand to the little boy hiding behind her. He followed my directive so quickly that I wanted to hurt whoever had hurt him. The edges of the implant were beginning to dig into the bone, but it was easily isolated, and I removed it quickly.

The boy felt the back of his neck in wonder when I showed him the device. I quickly went around and removed them all. The last one was an older girl. Her implant was more dug in than the others, but I was able to remove hers as well and crushed all of them in my hand. The children were silent as I did so, but more than one of them began to cry.

"Can you remove mine?"

Her request was so quiet, I questioned whether I heard it at all.

I stood up and locked eyes with the head regulator.

She looked just as, if not more tired as I felt.

"Should I trust you? Can I trust you with these children?"

"Yes." She held out her foot. "My name is Glaci Polov."

Glaci Polov was not lying to me.

I lifted my own foot and tapped the side of our boots together. It was a basic sign of friendliness and after all that had happened, it made me smile.

Her implant was much harder to deal with than the children's were. It had years to embed itself into the bone and I could see that there was a good chance of paralyzing her anyway if I moved it or took it out. I explained this all to her quietly as well as how I was going to deactivate the implant instead. It was going to stay in her body, but as a souvenir rather than a menace.

"I didn't know about the Ryunaga." She was still telling the truth. "Will you let me take the children? I swear I will ensure no harm comes to them."

After I saw them off, I was suddenly faced with six strangers who did not know the meaning of personal space. Zarek had taken care of their more serious wounds, but I could see he left some of the scars behind for some reason.

They all just stared at me. People stared at me all the time; I was basically used to it; but usually they didn't do it so... openly.

"I don't know. She doesn't seem like his type."

"She's in disguise, idiot. Haven't you seen those public releases?"

"I have. And she's way out of Deutreax's league."

"Ha! Like that ever fucking stops him!"

"Shut up you fucking morons. She's standing right there!"

"I'm just saying! What else does he have beside a pretty face?"

I looked over at Zarek, who looked both amused and appalled at the same time. Putting on a neutral face, he clapped his hands together and interrupted their arguing. "Great job people. You've made yourselves, and more importantly me, look bad." He placed a quick kiss on the top of my head, which surprised a blush out of me and sent these strange people into fits of some kind. They hooted and shouted in a manner reminiscent of howler evifauna.

"They mean well." Zarek whispered before introducing me.

"Sae. This is Ali, Joo, Reaper, Kenna, Quark, and Finny."

"Dammit! I told you not to call me that anymore Deutreax."

"So sorry." He was not sorry. "I meant fuzzy spider boy."

After they calmed Finny down, he explain in detail that he had taken on his wife's family's ancestral name that honored a large araneae creature from their home world. He pulled up a picture and while it did look quite ferocious...

It was also quite fuzzy.

Amie was not pleased when we found out exactly how they knew each other—they were smugglers.

Some freelanced on the side, but assured us that they had nothing to do with Naga. Since it was true, I was no reason not to like them. They were a charming group who didn't treat Zarek any differently than how they treated each other. It was refreshing to meet people that weren't afraid of him by default. They gave us their blessing, which came in the form of ragging on Zarek pitilessly, and told me to call them if I ever needed anything.

After their departure, I felt like I'd been tossed in a cyclone.

I looked up at Zarek, who had become apprehensive now that his friends had left our group alone. It wasn't a coincidence his friends had been here and had been spared. If Kyrian was after his friends... we still had two memories left to find. I knew he wanted to take me home and I wanted to keep going. I wanted to talk now and he wasn't ready. So we'd compromise.

We'd find the memories now and talk later.

Chapter 27: Ambitions

The colony was in a panic.

My name was being thrown about in every doorway and on every street. Mass evacuation plans were a foundational part of any respectable colony, but I would just have to hope that it was still true of ones in the outer universe.

People pushed and shoved onto public transportation platforms. Children were secured to their parents and the elderly and sick were being transported by specialized pods. So far, no one stopped us from following Amie across the rooftops.

Once in a while, we came across an official who was being airlifted, but even then the regulators ignored us.

The piers where we found ourselves were open to space and held back the vacuum through three separate control fields. Ships were incoming and many were anchored outside the ports to wait their turn. Tucked away against the side of the piers near the top was a massive transport ship and that was where Amie led us.

She tried to see if she could get the memory out without having to go in, but she couldn't. We'd tried before with similar results, so no one expected much.

Strangely, this ship was one of the only ones that wasn't being bombarded by residents trying to get on the first seats out of the colony. It was squat, rectangular, and obviously designated for transporting cargo; but there were others with the same appearance, all of which had people scrambling to board them.

Only a few privately employed guards stood watch.

"I'll take the ones on the left," Amie muttered and all of a sudden Omere and Zarek moved to the right of me. I stopped walking. Were we going to resort to violence again? I knew I'd thrown subtlety under a collision generator by confronting Edjeridi, but these people hadn't done anything to us.

They were just going about their regular work day.

"How about we just ask them instead?" I suggested hopefully.

It took a bit more convincing, but they relented with the caveat that Amie was the one who asked, not me. We still had masks on, but none of the guards called for us to remove them. The three of them politely listened to what Amie had to say, nodding along. This was going much better than we could have hoped for.

They even waited for her to finish before speaking.

"If you get on, you can't get off until you get there."

"That's fine." Amie agreed, taking out the money to bribe them. "We just want to get off the moon and can find our own way."

"No exceptions. We can't let you off. There's no extra rations."

"We'll manage." Amie said firmly. "We can handle ourselves."

"We're not supposed to let anyone else on." That said, the guards collectively shrugged, took our money, and stood aside.

And just like that we were allowed to step on the boarding incline that would bring us to the ship's main entrance. "Thank you!" I waved back to the guards once we were on the ramp but for some reason, they found my appreciation uproariously funny.

The door closed the second all of us were inside, cutting off their off-putting laughter and dropping us into complete darkness. I was about to pull up a light source when thick metal walls slammed down between me and everyone else. I heard Omere and Amie shouting my name before the box jerked me to my left with an obnoxious screech. I was unexpectedly slammed to a stop and could barely orient myself before the floor fell out from underneath me.

A thick gas of some kind was filling up the space and it tasted very much like a potent coating of sedatives. Were my friends also being sedated? What kind of cargo ship was this!? I pushed the gas upwards to look closer at the box I was trapped in. It was completely smooth on all sides and was an industrial grey. I touched one of the walls and I felt a substantial amount of energy pushing back against my fingers. What in the universe was going on?

I pulled my hand back and crumpled the box to the ground. Once the metal was compressed down, I found myself in yet another box, this time with a highly charged grid on one side that led to a dark hallway. I peered out and saw that the entire hallway was lined with similar grids. At this point the gas was leaking into the hall, so I melted the vent closed before stepping out.

The grid tickled a bit as I went through, light bending around my form before snapping back into shape once I'd passed.

This wasn't a cargo ship.

It was a prisoner transport vessel.

When I got home, I needed to look up the outer universe's latest incarceration rates.

I walked quietly by all of the cells and each one contained an unconscious and manacled criminal; all of whom sported a variety of prison uniforms. Where was this ship going to that it had prisoners from Hitea, Ulisirach, Isbul, Tertii, Wonox, U.F.O. Yiter, and a few others I couldn't instantly identify? It was highly unusual for one nation to extradite so many prisoners and the colony we had just left was nowhere near any facility that could house them.

I heard footsteps up ahead.

Thank the Empress the others were okay. I hurried to meet them and just as I was about to call out to them, the group turned the corner in front of me.

They screamed when they saw me.

In a flurry of white robes, they turned and ran.

"Wait!" I ran to catch up, but they wouldn't stop running even though it was painfully clear that they could not outrun me. "I'm not a criminal! I'm just on this ship to look for something and I'm not going to do anything to you! I promise!"

Another white-robed person came running through a doorway to see what all the fuss was about, and their fellow apostles almost knocked them over in the rush to hide behind them.

Was this their leader?

They were small, about as short as my disguise was.

"Hello. How did you get out of your cell?" she asked calmly.

At least, I think I was talking to a woman. Most of her face and head were covered by her clothes, even her eyes were hidden behind a mesh veil. Not many cultures veiled so completely anymore.

Only her hands were uncovered and she offered one to me.

"I know it's improbable, but I'm not a criminal. I'm just here to look for something." I grasped her hand and was met with a firm and confident grip.

"I do think I believe her." She told the others. "Go on your rounds, if anything happens, remember to call me. Also, be considerate of the ones sleeping and try not to scream so much, alright?" Her light scolding was infused with humor but deflated the others regardless. They hurried off to do whatever it was that they were doing before I interrupted them.

"I'm AJ, can you tell me your name?"

She waved me into her tiny office.

"I'm sorry for scaring your fellow apostles. My name is Sae."

"Don't worry too much, this is their first assignment you see. I'm not an apostle myself, but I agreed to be their guide for this trip." AJ cleared her small desk piled with papers and offered me her chair, which I declined.

"May I ask what it is you're looking for?"

"Actually, I boarded this ship with three friends. Is it possible for you to help me find them? We were separated just a few moments ago so they can't be far."

I quickly explained what happened after we boarded the ship.

"That's horrible. I'll need to report them to the regulator's district office, even if I know nothing will be done to discipline them." She straightened out some of her papers, clearly outraged. "You shouldn't have been allowed to enter through that door. I wish I could have stayed to help with the evacuation, then I could deliver the letter myself, but this ship is on an ironclad schedule."

"Where is this ship going? We didn't think to ask."

AJ stilled. Slowly, she put her papers down.

"We're going to Invicta."

Invicta... Invicta... no, I had never heard of it before.

"Is it a newly established planetary system or penal satellite of some kind?" I guessed with much misplaced faith. "Perhaps a program specializing in rehabilitation? I did find it strange the prisoners on board seem to come from a range of nationalities. Is this a new collective initiative of some kind?"

"Oh, that sounds wonderful!" AJ went to grab a star chart from the corner. "Regrettably it's none of the above."

The projection expanded on the desk once laid flat and whirled to show an empty stretch of the universe. "Invicta is right here." Her finger pointed to the dead center of that space. There was nothing marked there. It was just an expanse of universe between Hitea and Yiter. The nearest star was over 5,000 light-years away.

"Invicta's existence is not recognized by any nation," AJ explained. "It used to be a labor camp for political detainees. They would mine for radioactive ores on the rare asteroids found in that section. A few centuries ago, a collision with a rogue planetary object and the largest asteroid made the area extremely unstable. Those poor people were abandoned by their home worlds. Later, it was discovered that a settlement had survived. It's been used as a dumping ground ever since."

"A dumping ground? For sentient beings!? That's illegal!"

"It's actually only illegal in Elysia, where the law in enforceable."

AJ softly closed the door to her office. What did it say about me that I now tensed at such a normal act? At home, I would have never seen it as anything but what it was.

Was AJ yet another threat?

"I really need to look for my friends. It was nice meeting you."

She blocked my path to the door.

"You're Saekonari Raajali. Aren't you?"

So my mask did nothing to hide my identity anymore.

Looking back, I should have given her a fake name but the last time I tried giving one, they didn't believe me anyway. "Yes. I don't want any trouble and I really would like to leave now—"

"Would you be willing to give the Empress my appeals for the reopening of external aid channels?" she blurted out. AJ went around me back to her desk where she pulled out several universal serial bulbs shaped like imaginative animation characters.

"There was an interstellar incident during the Tenth Empress' reign where several Elysian citizens were injured during a kidnapping attempt on route to providing medical aid to the Tzeong galaxy. After that incident and following the apathetic response from the outer nations, Elysia shut down their exterior aid projects to reassess the safety of participants. An abrupt acceptance of fourteen major galaxies to your six and eight hundredth quadrants caused the reassessment to never be completed." She had to stop to take a breath before she continued.

"I have hundreds of signed affidavits as well as a list of potential partners and locations willing to open certain sectors to Elysian volunteers and resources with minimal negotiations. Currently, there is no public option in asking for the Empress' intervention.

There are statements from the border checkpoints here who are willing to compromise in exchange for monetary compensation as well as several developing economies who would be thrilled to offer their goods and services if the Empress is willing to bypass the ITA and exchange directly with them."

AJ was talking so fast I was afraid she was going to pass out.

"I know these aren't very official looking!" She waved nervously at the colorful display. "But I can assure you that I am very serious in this proposal, and I am at her Eternal Majesty's beck and call for any questions or suggestions or anything she or you may need to start the process. I know this isn't the customary manner to approach the Raajali and I'm sure you are extremely busy with a countless number of issues—"

She stopped when I held up my hand.

I took off my diffraction mask and placed it down on the desk.

Lifting one of the bulbs, I took a moment to scan the information inside it. It was quite the project if the other dockets were anything like the one I held. We had a long history of providing aid, but only at the behest of another sovereign nation. Otherwise, we kept to our cardinal rule of noninterference. If a person crossed the border, they were instantly eligible for both asylum and citizenship, but we could not do anything to help the families they left behind. If a particular region or system wanted help, it often had to be approved by a higher bureaucracy such as the Interstellar Trade Association or the outer council itself.

Only then were our resources distributed to them.

This would involve direct dealings with Elysia.

It would involve interference from Mother and I.

Something I'd learned very recently was not a desirable outcome to the outer universe or the outer council.

"Tell me AJ, why do you think Elysia should get involved?"

"Should I be diplomatic, or may I say what I honestly think?"

"The truth."

AJ still hesitated.

"Whatever you say won't change my mind."

"Well, then I think the Empress can and should do more for the outer universe. Even if it isn't the best thing for your people." AJ paused, but when I didn't react she continued. "Your people have everything. It isn't a crime, and it isn't your fault at all. The outer universe is flawed in a way that Elysia has never had to grapple with, but your people will lose nothing by accepting the terms other nations want to impose on your aid. You have all of the cards. You can afford your principles. It shouldn't matter if we are imperfect. We share the same existence. We deserve to know the same justice and happiness that Elysians have never gone without."

During her impassioned speech, her hood became disheveled and AJ readjusted self-consciously as she waited for my response.

I didn't make her wait long.

No matter if the Empress disapproved or not, it was time I carved my own path and made my own decisions.

"AJ, I'm going to make you a promise. I am going to draw up a formal proposal and give this to my mother, but I doubt she'll find it very convincing. It goes against eons of precedent." She made a soft noise, one that struck right to the heart. "Instead, I'm going to take this project on personally. I may not have the reach and power that the Empress has, but I agree with you. I would be honored to work with you and your contacts. Will you come to Elysia if I ask?"

"Yes! Yes! Of course! Thank you! Oh my Empress, thank you!" She rocked back and forth on her toes, almost hopping with excitement. Her happiness was contagious and it struck me then that AJ couldn't be as old as I first estimated. I didn't want to accidentally ask an invasive question, however, so I simply stood by quietly while she packed away all of the necessary documentation and handed it over to me in a little fabric pouch.

After I tucked it securely in my coat, I decided I might as well ask her if she'd seen the memory. Remarkably, once I described it to her, AJ produced it from one of her endless stacks of files. As I took it, I again noticed how each one of these memories felt so different from one another. Even after all the practice she'd gotten, Amie still had a hard time pinpointing each one. Also, now that I had it hand, I found myself reluctant to leave my new friend.

As if sensing my thoughts, while handing me her keys, her hands squeezing mine in reassurance. "This is a key that you can use to get to all of the other sections of the ship. We're at the helm and if you follow this hallway, you can—"

An ear-piercing alarm went off.

The lights all along the hallway were cast into a sickly flashing yellow pattern and we could hear prisoners from around the ship awaken and start to scream at being caged. Apostles came running from all sides and AJ hastily called out her goodbyes before she turned away to lead her flock elsewhere. I felt very protective of her, not just because I needed her help in the project, and placed a thin layer of protection over her and the other apostles.

I couldn't think over the alarm, so I muted it and that was when I heard a crash. Guessing my friends were mostly likely in that direction, I went that way.

They must have been at the other end of the ship because it took three passes with the key before I finally ran into them trying to break through the next door. I had to flatten myself to the ground to avoid the large piece of metal being flung over my head.

"Sae!" Amie rushed over to check me for injuries but I didn't know why she bothered anymore because she never found them. "Are you alright!? Those damn guards are going to eat dirt if I ever fucking run into them again!" She brushed imaginary dust off my clothes while I assured her that I was entirely in one piece and that I had found the memory.

"Have you seen Omere?" Amie asked me.

Zarek plucked the memory from my hand.

"No, but I ran into some really helpful—what's wrong?"

All of the color had drained from Zarek's face.

He ignored my question entirely.

"Amie. Take Sae home. Now."

What in the Empress' name?

"What the fuck? Why?"

Even Amie was perturbed at his sudden shift in behavior.

"You were right. This was a trap. Sae needs to leave."

"Zarek, we're so close. We only have one more—"

"No!" He snapped. "Are you that desperate for me?"

I flinched at the unexpected insult, making Amie even more angry. "Amie, it's okay," I said before she could say anything.

Compromise was important in all interpersonal relationships. A concession on my part would not hurt me. It stung my pride a bit, but Zarek was first and foremost worried about me. "I'll find Omere and we'll go home ahead of you. I'll give Amie enough reserves to get you both back when you find the last one."

"I'm not going back to the Empire, pixie."

"I'm sorry? I think I heard you wrong."

"I'm going alone. Take both of them back."

Uh-huh. I thought about it for a second.

"No. Zarek, can we please talk about—"

"Esme was right. You are selfish."

Amie lost her shit.

He didn't say anything as she yelled at him. Zarek just looked down at her, not at all concerned that it was the most callous possible thing he could have said to me. If I had been alone, I may have just curled into a little ball like I'd done as a child. Just hide away and wait until the universe righted itself again. I stared up at him... until I realized he wouldn't look at me.

"Amie. Move."

Her head jerked back to look at me, but then, she moved.

I counted to ten.

"Zarek. Please, just tell me what's wrong."

"Why is there always something wrong with me?"

"Because you keep acting like there's a problem."

"You're my problem. I never asked for your help."

"Stop trying to pick a fight with me. I don't care what it is."

"I can't believe I thought I could make this work. You—"

"Stop deflecting and just tell me what is going on!"

"I don't want you! Is that so hard to understand!?"

"It wouldn't be if you weren't lying to me!"

At that point, I was floating so I could argue with Zarek face-to-face because I was tired of looking so far up at him and he grabbed my upper arms. In the next heartbeat, Zarek pinned me against the nearest wall and I could see Amie barely restraining herself from interfering.

Even though I was the one pushing him.

I knew it. He knew it. And I didn't care.

We stared at each other until I saw something break in his eyes.

Instantly, my anger shriveled away.

Empress, what was wrong?

"Zarek? What is it? Why are you acting like this? I promise I—"

"I was the one. It was me."

"You were what Zarek?"

"I was the one who was going to give you to Kyrian. Is that what you want to hear?" He let go of me and I was too shocked to keep hold of him. "That I just needed to gain your trust enough to fuck you and leave you with that monster. Is that what you want to know? He told me to go and get you for him and it didn't even take more than a few weeks to convince you! How about that I was going to drug the twins in their sleep and dump them in the—"

Amie pulled her weapon on Zarek for the first time in months.

He just held up his hands and stepped back from me.

Amie motioned for me to go back the way I came.

I didn't move.

I was still processing really.

"Sae, go. We'll find Omere and—hey! Sae!"

A few tears leaked from my eyes and onto Zarek's shoulder. I knew he was trying so hard to push me away, but all I could do was hold on tighter. Was he always in so much pain? I couldn't fathom it. No matter how much it had hurt me to listen to the truth, it must have been so much worse to have to say it. I felt his whole body shudder before his arms finally went around me. If I had known all along, would I have been so eager to help him?

If I had known everything I did now and that I would fall in love with this man, I would have done it all over again.

"Sweetness, didn't you hear a word I just said?"

"Did you think I was going to let you go so e-easily?"

"Shhh, see? I made you cry again."

"Would you still give me to Kyrian?"

He kissed me so gently that a few more tears fell from my eyes. There was no part of me left that doubted him. I knew there were dark places Zarek wanted to keep from me, but none of them mattered more to me than he did.

"The universe would fall before I let him have you."

"*Ahem.* Ahem! Ahem, hem, hem!"

Amie made several other coughing noises before Zarek reluctantly let me go enough for us to look at her.

Somehow, we'd ended up on the ground with Zarek braced against the wall and me securely being held against him.

"Are we done here?" Amie still looked peeved.

We had to stop doing this in front of Amie. Eventually she'd resort to something more direct like dropping something on his head and that was not something I wanted to witness. Zarek helped me up to my feet and the easiest way I knew to preempt an awkward silence was to insert a sense of purpose.

"Let's go find Omere and then we can—"

"Wait." Amie's hand shot out to stop Zarek.

"Why are you going around doing Kyrian's dirty work?" Amie didn't sound accusing, but the underlying message was there. "What's he got on you? Why would you agree to go into Elysian space, kidnap the *Heir of Elysia,* and hand her over to some asshole with a colonizing fetish?"

"Because I was going to trade her for Alexi."

Chapter 28: Hard Truths

It all made sense now.

Amie looked from him to me and then back at Zarek.

"Is that supposed to mean something to me?" Then Amie remembered. "That fuck all chick Cira was raving about!?" Her hands twitched like she was considering strangulation. "If you tell me she's your girlfriend or some crap I—"

"Alexi Deutreax is my little sister," Zarek said quietly.

That knocked the fight out of her. Amie looked to me for confirmation and once I nodded, she made an aggravated noise reminiscent of a failing engine bay.

She took the lead without addressing either of us again and just kept muttering loudly under her breath as she walked away. "The next time he fucking... and says something like that... I'm going to... then shoot him in the ass."

Amie aggressively kicked pieces of debris out of her way.

Like chastised children, we followed her at a safe distance.

Amie put to sleep any of the prisoners who called out to us as we passed them. Several threatened us, but most begged for leniency. Hopefully, the universe would be merciful in preserving its equilibrium. I was not part of their justice system, and I had no right to play judge to these people. Nevertheless, after even a vague description of their final destination, I empathized with them. How many were innocent? It was better if I didn't know.

"Is Deutreax your lineage name?"

"It was my mother's, I think."

"Where did Trace come in?"

"It was what my mother would tell everyone. Trace is a common name. Found in a few different cultures. I use it for work." Zarek was struggling to talk to me. I could see it in every cautious pause before he spoke and it melted my heart.

"Help me!" One of them had waited until Amie had passed to lunge at the grid of his cell, it was burning him, but he just kept his face pressed against it. "Please! Help me! I don't deserve to go to Invicta! I have a sick mother! She can't—"

Amie put him to sleep.

He was lying, but that didn't mean he deserved Amie's disgust.

"It's official. I never want to visit the outer universe ever again."

"It hasn't been that bad, we've seen some amazing things."

"Sae, sometimes I really have no idea what goes on in your head."

A strangled noise had both of us looking back to see Zarek holding the man Amie had just put to sleep up off the ground by his collar. "What did you just say?" Zarek was choking him too hard for him to answer.

"Zarek!" He dropped the man at my shocked exclamation.

"What did you just say?" he repeated, no remorse for the man's fear. How quickly the warmth in his eyes died out; smothered under a ruthless, angry storm. Crouching down, Zarek was no less menacing as evidenced by the man cowering back into his cell.

"I-I have a sick mother. She needs me—"

"Before that. Think harder."

"I don't deserve to go to Invicta?"

The man's head slouched to one side, forced back into sleep.

"Where's the last memory?"

"Ship's headed right at it," Amie confirmed.

"Sae, I need to talk to you. Alone."

Every word sounded forced and... wrong.

Not even Amie had the heart to question him right now.

She nodded to me and went off to look for Omere on her own.

"I know a place we can talk."

It felt as if I'd scaled a wall to find a labyrinth. Every moment a chance to misstep and the only way forward was if Zarek was willing to navigate it with me.

"I met some apostles on my way to find you." I spoke not to fill the quiet, but to try to lighten whatever shadows were following him. "Their guide has a small office that we can talk inside of. I don't think she'll mind letting us borrow it. I quite liked her, and she had done some groundbreaking work on a project to reopen Elysian external aid channels. She gave me her contact information and I'm planning on meeting her again once I get back home."

Knocking on the door, we waited a few seconds, but no one answered. The door itself was unlocked and I opened it to reveal that, in the short time since I'd last been inside, AJ had organized her things. Most of the file drawers were neatly folded back into the walls. All that was left was her desk and chair, both of which were bolted into the ground to prevent them from being jostled during travel. The ship must be close to the drop-off by now.

We entered and it didn't feel right to have whatever this conversation was hidden under a façade. So I sealed the room, triple-checked for surveillance technology, and turned back into myself. In all that time, Zarek did not say a single word. Not knowing exactly what he expected, I sat on the desk facing him and tucked one of my knees under my chin.

"You always did that when we were kids."

"I like to think in this position," I didn't think he'd remember such a small detail, "but would you rather I sit in the chair?"

I succeeded in making him smile, even if it was a small one. "What do you see in me, Saekonari? No, don't answer. It was rhetorical." Zarek sat gingerly on the other end of the desk.

He'd never been so hesitant with me.

"I was going to kill my sister when she was born." He shot a glance at me... did Zarek expect me to condemn him? I had seen how much he loved her. It must have seemed like impossible odds. "My mother died bringing her into the universe. She was just another mouth to feed when I could barely take care of myself."

"Your mother, she couldn't afford medical care?"

It was all I could think to ask.

"Alexi was born on Invicta."

At first, my mind attempted to veto the notion entirely.

The idea that children could be born or raised in such a place. Children were not easily born to Elysians. Heirs had been born quickly before, but the average skewed into the hundreds of thousands of years before successful conception... and they could only ever have one. Abuse statistics in Elysia were nonzero, but only just. Unclaimed or unaccompanied orphans were even rarer.

"You want to know about my father." He read my face all too well. "My mother didn't know so I don't. She whored for as long as I knew her. Alexi and I are likely half-siblings. Too many clients to tell." He smiled grimly at me. "You can say she tried her best and she did. But I was an angry, selfish kid who thought she was pathetic. Brainless. Spineless. Worthless."

"When she died, you were only three. You were just a baby."

"I grew faster than most species. You were a prodigy by six months old. Would you have called yourself a baby at three?"

No I wouldn't. I had been preparing every waking moment to be allowed out of the nursery. I remembered long periods of isolation followed by bursts of frazzled panic whenever someone other than my tutors came to see me. Even then, I had always been afraid of someone reporting a failure to Mother.

"Why did you let Alexi live?"

"I didn't know why exactly." The more Zarek spoke, the less halting his speech. "I was at the bottom of the food chain and so was she. We were far too pretty. We covered ourselves with filth so foul, people thought twice about touching us. Even then, we had to keep Alexi's hair short and her face covered. Almost every day I maimed or killed for food. Alexi would wait for me, not knowing if I'd come back or if that was the day I'd abandon her. No one was going to help us. We lived in a sewer pit. Sometimes, our fingers would freeze and crack from cold—"

He broke off as my shoulder bumped against his.

I'd slowly moved so that we were touching. I wanted to cry for him, at the unfairness of it all, but that was not what Zarek needed from me. Zarek believed if he told me enough, he'd scare me away; his questioning gaze searching me for any signs of revulsion or rejection. Deliberately, I intertwined our fingertips and elicited a tremor from him. I could never be disgusted by him.

He took a ragged breath before continuing.

"I raised her because she was the only good I'd ever seen. Alexi smiled every day. She never cried. She made me want out. I barely remembered the universe before Invicta. Alexi knew nothing, but she deserved more than dying in an Empress-forsaken hellhole."

"So did you Zarek."

"... One day, an inspector came to Invicta with a kill-on-sight order. I didn't know what the hell they were looking for, but it was our only chance to escape. We were caught and Alexi was shot. I barely felt any pain at all, I was so fucking angry. I ended up being thrown into a holding cell with Alexi. Every bone in my body must have been broken that day, but I regenerate faster than most. It's how I kept alive. I couldn't move from the agony, Alexi wasn't waking up, and that's when Kyrian walked in."

"You don't want us to go to Invicta." I said outloud what he was trying to ask. "That's why you're telling me this."

"I told myself I would never go back." He said with noticeable difficulty. "I don't care if I have to gag you and drag you back to Elysia. I can't let you—"

"Zarek Deutreax Trace. Let's go home."

He was left momentarily speechless at my words.

"Really." Saying he was skeptical was putting it lightly.

"Really. We can make other arrangements once we get back, okay?" I was no longer so afraid of Mother's reaction if we went to the Academy together. "You can see our neurologists and we'll see if they can help. Whatever you want, I'm in no rush." I picked up his hand and shyly nestled my cheek against his palm. "Nothing you can say can change how I feel, Zarek" I said quietly. "I—"

I heard Amie yelling and a loud banging sound coming from the door. I quickly lowered the seal around the room to see what was going on, but then the door slammed open on its own and my friends almost fell over once it did.

"I told you she's fine!" Amie snapped. "They're busy!"

Omere stubbornly held onto the door frame.

"It's okay!" I assured them both, looking at Zarek for confirmation. "We're done for now I think."

Amie let go and Omere made his way over to me, confusion all over his face. Oh yes, this was likely the first time he'd seen my real form. I'd told him I wore a disguise, but he must have interpreted it in a more figurative sense. He picked up my braid and compared it to his own hair. Not a perfect match, his still had greyish undertones, but he seemed happy about it.

"You still sing." He hugged me around the waist.

I patted his head absentmindedly. He'd gotten more affectionate after observing Zarek and I physically interacting. I found it very sweet that he seemed to view us as family. Amie closed the door and I explained quickly that we were going to go home now rather than going to get the last memory in Invicta.

I didn't give much of a reason, but Amie accepted it.

"The ship's ejecting the cells right now. We should hurry."

Was Omere sniffing me? He was.

"You smell different." He lifted my coat to look inside.

"Omere!" I laughed and pushed him back a bit. "Ask first."

"Sorry." Contrite, he handed me back AJ's pouch.

I was just about to place it back inside my coat when my eyes landed on a little embroidered flower, right under the clasp... my mind flashed back to the moment when AJ had been adjusting her hood and a small patch of hair was briefly visible above her forehead... no... I turned to Zarek and placed one hand on his chin, moving his head from one side to the other to see it in the light. Flashes of dark blue appeared... but her hair had been lighter...

She had been petite, tiny in stature.

They didn't sound anything alike...

"Zarek. Say my name." His eyes widened a bit.

"Should we leave—" I shushed Amie without looking away.

"Sae?" I knew I was too close to him, but I needed to be sure.

"Say my full name. It's important." I let go of his face.

"Saekonari Raajali." I could see Zarek was flustered.

Any other time, I would have found flustering him delightful, but I had heard it. The ever so slight cadence on the vowels that I was sure I had heard from only one other person... her entire face had been covered. I had assumed for cultural or religious purposes but what if it was because of something else entirely?

Alexi was born on Invicta.

Why would she ever go back?

"Zarek can I see Alexi's handkerchief?"

Even to my own ears, I sounded off.

Wordlessly, he reached into his coat for the small square of fabric. I didn't know what to say or how to tell him. So, I just laid the two items down; their embroidered flowers side by side on the desk.

Both were missing two petals in the same spot. It never occurred to me the flaw might have been a deliberate choice.

Zarek didn't move a muscle as I tried to explain my suspicions that I met Alexi and that she had been the one to pitch the project to reinstate Elysian external aid. I grew more nervous when he didn't respond her plans about guiding the apostles to Invicta and even pulled out her contact information for when she got back from their mission. I ended with the fact that she was most likely already there because I'd really liked her and put protections on her I couldn't find onboard anymore.

"Alexi is on Invicta."

I gave Amie a quick glance and she quietly pulled Omere out of the room. "We can pull her off-world and back here." I'd wrapped a marginal amount of protection around her. Amie could find her. "We don't have to go there."

"Alexi hates being teleported. She'll fight back."

"It doesn't matter if she does. I can get her here."

"Sae. I don't know if she remembers me." This was a much deeper issue than just getting to her, I realized. I stepped between his legs and put my hands on his shoulders.

Eventually he tore his gaze away to look at me.

"She's alive." It was a lot to come to terms with.

"We can go get her." He looked shellshocked. "I'll go with you." I couldn't stand the desolation in his eyes. "She knows me and I think I know her. Your sister is a brilliant, intelligent, extraordinarily kind person. She was like starlight, just like you said."

"I don't want to see you there. I'll go alone."

"I told you I was going to help you find her."

"And you did. Universe help me. You found her."

"You're not going alone. We can go. Together."

CHAPTER 29: CONFESSIONS

Invicta's sky was empty.

Hovering in a dense interplanetary dust cloud with no nearby stars, it was my very first time looking up at and seeing nothing but darkness above me. The universe was still there I told myself, but nothing could shake the feeling we'd stepped beyond it. There was so much noise. Why had I assumed it would be quiet? My gut told me no one was supposed to be here of all places.

The air was toxic. Our diffraction masks filtered it, but somehow it remained foul to the taste. I had sent all of our possessions back home, even our weapons. It was one of the many conditions that Zarek had placed on accompanying him. Amie and Omere had both been horrified by his insistence that we went unarmed, but in the end, they refused to be left behind.

"It'll only make them excited." Zarek said as explanation.

We'd aged our clothing and strategically ripped at seams and hems. Amie had asked why they couldn't just use a cover, but Zarek said something then that made her stop asking questions. "If they realize. They'll kill us to get to you."

It also meant that I had to go as myself. No hiding under an alias.

Zarek then raided the ship for a confusing agglomeration of items. Engine sludge, dirt from the small hydroponics kit Alexi kept in her walls, industrial cleaners, and it wasn't until I saw him come back from the small lavatory with the decontaminated remains of pre-recycled waste product did his intentions become clear to me. I looked away as he mixed it all together.

It was the worst smelling thing I had ever been faced with, but when Zarek, one of the most fastidious men I'd ever known, started smearing it over his hands and arms so did I. Amie and Omere watched for a few moments, speechless.

Omere was turning green.

"We need more shit," Zarek said once we were covered top to bottom in grime. His voice had gone flat. "We're too clean."

"We're too clean!?" Amie said in disbelief, her eyes already watering from the smell. "It's not possible to be less clean!"

"Your ears aren't covered." Zarek shot back. "And it's obvious that this is new dirt. Old dirt stains your skin into peeling layers of grunge and infected sores. I'd make you take off your shoes if I didn't think your dainty feet would give us away..." Zarek's words trailed off as his eyes flickered to me... "Fuck."

Amie looked at me too and said the same thing.

"I tried my best," My hair did not want to be dirt colored. It gleamed brightly despite working the sludge over every strand. "I'll tie it back under my hood. I'll be fine. Really, I don't think—"

"Do we have more clothes?" Zarek asked Amie desperately.

"Don't look at me!" She scoffed. "I have no ass or tits, give her some of your fucking clothes if you're so worried!"

After layering several more layers of grubby clothes on, I felt like I was being smothered inside a plush toy. Zarek and Amie looked at me up and down and neither of them looked happy.

"New plan. Kill anyone who approaches her."

Amie and Omere both nodded.

Alexi was in a densely populated area of Invicta. When I showed Zarek exactly where his demeanor grew even more forbidding. He showed me another spot that was less busy, but as close as we could get without attracting undue attention.

Now, I knew that he had not exaggerated.

We were too clean.

Rivers of biowaste streaked through this claustrophobic mess of scrap metal and garbage. It fell in sludgy chunks off of unstable roofs and was smeared over every visible surface. It was so dark that we had to equip Omere with one of the optoelectronic devices we'd found in Alexi's office. It smelled so horrible that Amie had gagged uncontrollably when we first arrived.

Zarek had warned us, but it was all she could do to retch out her guts in silence. I had the luxury of not having to breathe.

My friends did not.

After Amie regained control of her body, Zarek stalked off at a stride that could only be called reckless. Gaping holes that served as doorways yawned in the filth. The splashing of thick fluids around our shoes soon soaked through the fabric wrapping our legs and the fumes flooding these narrow paths almost seemed like a physical touch. A clawing, cloying, living miasma. Every exposed particle of my body itched in a way I'd never known. A sudden burst of movement to my right made me squeak.

Whatever it was, it had mutated into a horrific blob of too many limbs and teeth. Before it could reach me, Zarek ripped out one of its tusks and used it to kill the thing where it stood. A liquid even more putrid than the layer of moisture around our legs spurted out of its wound. Its death cry was haunting.

He didn't give us any time to react. Zarek grabbed my arm and yanked me forward at a brutal pace. People appeared out of nowhere around us. Mangled and unnaturally thin. Their bloated stomachs and jutting bones crashed into one another as they reached for the thing Zarek had just killed.

What were they... they were going to eat it.

I watched as teeth ripped into the still thrashing body; no matter that it was covered in open sores. A person screamed as their shoulder was bitten into and torn off their body by someone hungry enough to try it. I wanted to scream as their sign of weakness caused the mob to turn on them. Their brittle bones cracked with stomach-turning fragility as they were pinned down and drowned under a few centimeters of excrement and urine.

Several smaller figures raced after us to offer things that I had no translation for, but that made Amie push Omere and I to go faster. What were they saying? Were they children? They didn't sound like children, they sounded like they were drugged and beyond reason. One of them offered to graphically kill the others for our entertainment. My blood ran cold.

Zarek forced me to keep my eyes to the front and keep walking. Their slurs got quieter as we lost them until they were nothing but echoes. Those echoes kept me shaking for a long time.

More than once, we were forced to squeeze ourselves through openings that were studded with hidden dangers. Piles of intravenous needles. Trenches designed to trap the unknowing in bubbling vats of sewage. Lines of flesh melting acids or industrial byproducts. Zarek steered through all of them with heartbreaking confidence. Only once did he slip, and his hand was sliced open by a spring-loaded shard of glass. "Fuck!" he swore with an agitated fury I'd never seen from him.

"Zarek," I dared to whisper. "I'm here. It's alright."

"I should have never let you see this." Zarek sounded livid. "The fuck was I thinking. Bring you to this shithole stain of a—" He proceeded to say more than a few words that I had no definition for, but I didn't think they were good ones.

He was raging. I grabbed his uninjured hand.

I didn't think I could hold it together if we both fell apart.

A new wave of screaming shattered Zarek's tirade and snapped him to his senses. He pushed all of us down into hovel slimy with yet another horrible smelling substance. Crouching low to the ground, we watched in silence as the screaming came closer. It was one of the prisoners who'd just recently been delivered here. He had only shreds left of his Yiterian uniform.

Blood poured from where they had castrated him.

He screamed for mercy. For help. They chased after him, singing vulgar rhymes of brutal acts and referencing his sawed-off genitalia. Which was being held aloft by one of his tormentors at the front of the mob. They were tossing handfuls of some unknown pellet at him. They stuck to his skin like leeches and nothing he did got them off his skin. He just kept screaming

"Initiation day. He should have rolled around in the shit if he wanted to live." Zarek muttered.

His voice was so cold I wanted to cry.

This was where he grew up. In this screaming pit of hunger and filth and violence. All I could think of was how I yearned to leave my nice, clean palace where boredom was the only threat available.

The pellets had dug into the man's flesh. Fungus was forming under his skin, growing and breaking through his bones to release more pellets from their spores. His dying screams were overtaken by the sound of his lungs being filled with mycelium and bursting through his rib cage. They tore him apart, scrambling to pick up the pellets and feast on his mangled corpse. The fungus soaked up the blood splatters until they were engorged with juice and eaten.

Zarek tried to block our view of the carnage, making it so that he was the only one who needed to keep watch... here, in this place knee-deep in filth, I knew I would never fall in love with anyone else. Even now, Zarek's arm protectively stretched out the length of the entrance; his other hand on Omere's shoulder to reassure him that nothing was going to happen. No matter what Zarek thought, he was a miracle. He'd fought bitterly to survive in a universe that relentlessly tried to beat him down.

He'd been forced to serve monster after monster.

All I could see was how badly Zarek wanted to protect those he loved. How often he check on me. How hesitant he was with me at times and how reluctant he was to ever let me go. I saw a soul marred, but whole under a weight that should have broken him.

I was overwhelmed by my emotions, unquestionably magnified by adrenaline. "Zarek." I leaned forward to whisper. "I love you."

His head turned my way so fast he almost fell over. This entire time I hadn't seen how tense he was, but now I could feel the air around him settle. The wrath that he'd been wearing as a second skin dissipated just enough that, regardless of our diffraction masks, I could see the calm wash over him. "I love you, Zarek." I said it again, more at ease with the words.

"You have the worst timing in the universe."

"I know."

Once the parade of new visitors and their welcome parties past, I held onto Zarek's hand as we walked on. It got louder around us, but we didn't run into another soul for a long time. As we walked uphill, the slick ground grew sticky from dried-up residues, the rivers of waste turning into mere rivets. We would hear screaming in the distance. The cries of the damned. Constantly. There was always someone screaming and very rarely from fear. How could anyone live with the screaming?

The smell was getting worse. It shouldn't have been possible, but even without breathing, I could feel the noxious molecules coating the inside of my nostrils. The higher we climbed through the shacks and vacant hovels of this garbage heap, the more unbearable it became. Black insects swarmed here, so thickly you almost couldn't see through them in the darkness. They made a maddening buzz and a revolting sound when they flew into your clothes. Onto your skin.

At one point, the ground under one of Amie's feet caved in and released a burst of rancid air so putrid that Amie began to gag silently again. She yanked her leg out from the hole and what looked like rotting entrails came with it. It was a body. Barely covered by a thin layer of grime. This was the reason for the smell. Why hadn't I seen it before? Looking around, there were body parts sticking out of all the ground and walls. In the piles and towers; openly rotting. The flies swarmed into the open pit Amie had created, filling the chest cavity.

"Don't help." Zarek stopped Omere and Amie glared bloody murder at him. "You'll survive," he said in a measured, clipped voice. "He might not if he gets near you. This is the plague district. Almost no one is desperate enough to eat these."

"How much further is this girl?"

Amie didn't even bother to clean her leg.

"Not much further," Zarek and I said at the same time.

I blinked; how did he know? I thought I'd been guiding him.

In this last stretch, his hand gripped mine with almost bruising pressure. Every squelching step brought us even deeper into the abyss as the garbage above our heads piled up.

At least no one would recognize me now.

Omere tripped rounding one of the narrow corners and I caught him, my other hand sinking into the wall of muck that was both disturbingly warm and solid... was that what I thought it was? Zarek tugged at me to keep moving, but instead, I fought against my instinct to stop touching things and wiped my hand downwards across the flat surface. It was.

Elysian runes.

Elysia had stopped using these in the second era after we standardized our alphabet. They were only used in record-keeping and certain ceremonies. What was it doing all the way out here? Amie saw it too. It said *We serve but one fate. One universe. One...*

The rest was hidden under the garbage.

My skin was crawling.

A loud disturbance from nearby had me turning my back to the mystery. This was neither the time nor place to be distracted. Before we could get very far, the reason for the disturbance fell from up high. A naked girl, her limbs bent and stapled into unnatural positions splattered us with her blood once she hit the ground. Whoever she was, she had been tortured for days.

A twitching of her lower body told us that she was alive, barely, but it was the gruesome grin she sported on her soon-to-be death mask that was truly disturbing.

We stepped around her.

Doubling back more than once, we slipped through places that I was sure were not made for fully grown adults to crawl through. Unable to keep from touching wet and slimy surfaces, we endured. Finally, Zarek motioned for me to take Omere's hand and we jumped into an open pit of sewage.

Emerging a second later, I felt like I would never be clean again.

There was a ledge here that one had to fully submerge oneself to find. And while the ledge itself was also covered with garbage, there was also one sight that was actually familiar to me. A large taxidermied animal, standing on its hind legs. With long ears, a pointed snout, patchy fur, and a wide smile carved into its face.

I'd seen it before.

No wonder he'd known where we were going.

"I'm gonna kill him." Amie groaned from where she dry heaved.

Zarek pulled something from inside the animal's head. It was a handful of dried roots that looked like they'd been there for centuries. He handed one of each of us and started chewing on the ones left in his hand. We followed suit and mercifully, the smell became almost bearable.

"I don't even want to know." Amie spat out the empty husk.

He was stalling. Scanning the waste like something was going to pop out at any second, I felt like he wished something would. So

I took his hand again. "I can go talk to her alone if you want." I ruined it by trying to touch foreheads and instead bumping our masks together. Hard.

"No, it's okay." Zarek said ruefully. "I needed the concussion."

Omere was still holding onto my other hand. He had been stoic throughout this whole ordeal and while he knew we were trying to find Zarek's sister, he had gone through all of this just to stay with us. I squeezed his hand and hoped Omere wasn't regretting his choices too much.

"It's here." Zarek pushed the taxidermied doll and it swiveled on a surprisingly well-oiled anchor. Nothing but more darkness awaited us below. "There's a ladder about three meters down that has its top rungs broken off." The hole was so small that he had to raise his arms over his head to slide through. I adjusted my eyes so that I could see his outline. He gave the signal for me to hop down next. I thought it wouldn't be a problem and it wouldn't have been if I wasn't so genetically disadvantaged for it.

My face heated up once I realized the issue.

"Amie! Stop laughing and help me take these layers off!"

"Do not take those layers off!" Zarek hissed from below.

"Do you have another solution you want to share!?"

Silence. Yes, this was such constructive feedback.

Amie helped me to untuck and take off most of my outer layers. The difference between the "new" dirt I had plastered against my arms and the old dirt that was staining my exposed hands was stark. Eventually we gave up trying to take the layers off one by one and she just yanked them all off. Now in nothing but my undershirt, I was able to squeeze myself through. Zarek had braced his legs against the ladder's rungs and caught me on my way down.

That one brief second of contact was shocking.

As soon as I got my footing, Zarek let go and we both looked away from each other as if we both didn't have full face coverage behind our masks. I climbed down and watched as Zarek caught Omere and then Amie. As soon as we were all inside, Zarek pulled on a rope and the entrance slid shut. We were now sealed inside what looked like the ruins of a giant ship. There was barely any room to maneuver on the ground, but besides the thick layer of dust this was the nicest place we'd seen yet on Invicta.

It was luxurious in comparison.

"Why couldn't we just appear in here!? What's wrong with you!" Amie was clearly not happy. About any of this.

"You can't." Zarek said grimly. "Not in or out. Go ahead, try it."

A few seconds passed.

Just in case we couldn't get back in, I refused to try it too.

There was only one route from here and we all had to stoop down to go through it. The floor, for the very first time, was dry. Once or twice, we had to shimmy over and under large piles of debris, but this portion of the trip proved to be both uneventful and much more sanitary.

A light winked into focus ahead of us.

As we came closer, I saw that it was a piece of string floating above a container of oil. An old-fashioned light source I'd never seen before. It sat on a relatively level hunk of metal and was oddly soothing in its own way. After everything we'd seen, the warm light it cast was like a balm to our frayed nerves.

We were still outside the circle of light, but you could easily tell this was a main intersection with four more tunnels branching off.

I felt Zarek freeze and then heard it myself.

Footsteps were coming down one of the other tunnels.

We waited, not daring to breath as a figure dressed all in white walked toward us from a peripheral direction, but the closer they came, the more I was certain they weren't Alexi.

"It isn't her," I whispered to the others.

It must be one of the apostles I'd hadn't met before.

She walked with a pronounced limp. Her age was carved deeply into her face and she chewed something in her mouth that revealed missing teeth. She was too thin, but something told me that she was in no way feeble. Scars traveled up and down her bare arms. The white clothes the apostles wore didn't suit her war battered appearance at all. In fact, they only underlined the glint in her eyes and the impression that she could be dangerous if provoked.

Zarek stepped into the light just as she did and didn't move a muscle when a rusty knife flew past his head and dug itself into the wall behind him. Zarek reached up and pulled off his diffraction mask just as she was about to throw another. The recognition flooding her face was the only reason I didn't jump out after him. She looked like she was going to faint.

She raised a trembling, spindly finger up to point at him.

"You little brat! You owe me money!"

"Good to see you too Mallee."

"Don't you try and bat your ridiculously overgrown eyelashes at me! Good to see you Mallee, I should have beaten you when I had the chance!" She gripped. "I should have drowned you in the upper pits but did I? No!" She was raising her voice, and I walked up next to Zarek in hopes of making her stop.

I took his hand and pulled off my own mask.

"Empress' mercy." She did lower her voice, but not by much.

"Hello. I'm Sae." I cleared my throat, but she just gaped at me, her eyes popping out of their sockets. "We were hoping to see Alexi. Do you know where she is?"

She didn't answer.

"Your name is Mallee isn't it?"

"Yes! Yes! I am so sorry Your Eternal Grace!"

She was bowing now. On the ground.

"Don't stop her, pixie," Zarek said when I moved forward to do just that. "This is the only time I'll get to enjoy this." Mallee's head snapped up and I do think that if I hadn't been standing right there, she would have thrown another knife.

"You haven't changed one bit you arrogant little shit! You let me think you were dead! I come back one day and there's parts everywhere!" She got to her feet with the help of her cane. "After everything I've fucking done for you—"

"Let's not exaggerate. You didn't do anything without a price."

She didn't argue further.

Her eyes fell to where our hands met, and I felt an unexpected pulse of fear coming from her before she turned away. At first, I'd thought their interaction was simple banter, but the undertow was much more hostile than it seemed. Zarek had kept his tone light, but he had no affection whatsoever for the woman. He also didn't move to stop her as she hobbled away.

What had gone on between them?

"Alexi should be this way." I pointed to the tunnel opposite the one we'd come from. Zarek nodded and let me take the lead, never letting go of my hand. Amie and Omere followed, but for some reason, I could feel Amie glowering at our backs. I didn't want to start another fight and tried to ignore her, but Zarek's remaining supply of tolerance was low.

"If you have something to say. Say it."

"You shouldn't have treated her like that."

We were still walking and only I saw his reaction.

A flash of pain in his eyes before they fell flat and dull.

"Amie," I said without turning around, "please drop it."

"Why should I!?" Amie's volume was raised. "It's obvious she took care of them when they were kids! He had years to help her get out and he just left her here. It's not right!" I tried to make her stop, but Amie was dead set on saying her piece.

She had been left in the dark to draw her own conclusions and no matter how wrong they were, I couldn't correct her without betraying Zarek's confidence.

"Why aren't you fucking saying anything?" Amie demanded. "Did she raise your little sister and now you're mad about it? Huh? Did you lie about Kyrian and you just left her here too!? What the fuck are you trying to—"

I physically pushed my hand against her mouth until I'd backed her against the wall. This was the very first time I'd ever laid a finger on Amie, but we both knew who was stronger. Just like how she knew better than to throw unfounded accusations at anyone, much less a man who'd done nothing to warrant them.

"Amythesia Esholitte I am ashamed of you." Amie tried to yank my hand off her face, but to no avail. "I know you're sick of being here and you're angry, but I need you to get a grip. Do you understand what I am saying? You didn't have to come. If you don't want me to send you back home. Then. Stop. Talking."

She nodded her head and I let her go.

"You know, I always wondered how naïve Elysians had to be."

Zarek leaned against the wall, his dark eyes reflecting the light of the flame behind us. I found myself nervous when he acted this nonchalantly. No matter how deceptively relaxed he seemed, it always ended badly for the person on the other end of his ire.

"Did you know," Zarek said in a hushed tone, his eyes boring through us, "that not everyone in the universe likes eating a fully grown steak?" He got even quieter. "Some people prefer to butcher their livestock younger. Some would even call it a delicacy. Especially when they're so easy to chew, pretty and... desperate."

Huh?

Zarek held out his hand to me and I took it, not understanding why he would talk about eating at a time like this. He saw my confusion and his expression instantly softened. "I'll explain later."

His thumb gently stroked the back of my hand as if I were the one needing comfort.

"I was wrong." Amie choked from behind me. "I'm sorry."

Surprised at her abrupt reversal, I turned to find her staring at the ground. Zarek just nodded his head slightly, never looking away from me, and we went on without another word from Amie. I wanted to ask somebody to explain the metaphor to me because it was obviously a metaphor... right?

I looked back a few times, but never once caught Amie's eye.

Most of this ship was completely impassable due to large pieces of debris blocking the tunnels off. Some of the collapse seemed recent. There was a chance that, depending on how old this structure was, the entire place might cave in if disturbed too much. Hundreds of tons of garbage sat atop this shell and the likelihood of it seeping inside this safe harbor was high.

Someone was humming.

Sweet and low, it coated the walls with serenity and filled the air with melancholic emotion. Up ahead, we could see light filtering out from one of the doors on the left. A slender shadow walked briskly from one side to the other, carrying something in her arms.

I walked ahead to knock on the wall, not wanting to startle her.

Alexi turned, her body still covered head to toe in apostle white.

But I would know those eyes, now unveiled, anywhere.

The shape, the arch, the fathomless darkness filled with life. They were Zarek's eyes and they stared back at me in wide surprise before crinkling in the corners like his did every time Zarek smiled. She was holding an infant, who she efficiently tucked away into one of the many cribs lining the walls and almost skipped her way toward me, graceful and lithe on her feet.

"Saekonari! What are you doing here?" She held out her hands to me despite my repulsive condition. "Goodness, did you come from above ground? Did you have a question for me? I'd invite you inside, but the nursery isn't the best place for a chat right now. I just got them all down for a nap." She took one last distracted look around before she closed the curtain acting as a door and dimmed the lights. "Oh, you brought your friends! Hello! I'm AJ."

She held out her hand to Zarek, who just stared down at it.

Unperturbed by the slight, she dropped her hand and kept an ongoing stream of cheerful chatter as she led us to a small chamber equipped with three sterilizing units. "We just got these installed a few months ago and our power supply is a bit fickle," Alexi tapped a few buttons on a control dial and hummed in satisfaction as it lit up, "but it seems to be working fine today."

"Thank the Empress." Amie immediately took the first one.

Omere took the second after I explained what it was.

"I think I can find some spare clothes, let me check with the others..." Her hands moved as she tried to eye our measurements, but even when she stretched up her arm she barely reached the height of my shoulder. Much less Zarek's.

"I'll see what I can find, be right back!"

"She doesn't know who I am," I'd never seen him so unraveled before. "Maybe I should leave her alone."

Zarek cogitated as I pulled him into the third sterilizer.

"Or we could just explain to her who you are." I untied my braid and ran my fingers through it to separate the strands. Sludge was being vaporized off of me, but the larger chunks would have to be broken up manually if I wanted it to be done quicker.

Zarek took over the task and, knowing he liked to think while working on something, I relinquished my hair over to him. "What if she blames me?" He sighed, reaching the last of the larger clumps and lifting the heavy locks so the sterilizer could reach the back of my neck and shoulders.

"Well then we'll have to change her mind." I tried to sound firm and confident. "Also, I think she suspects."

"How do you know?" I ran my fingers through his hair, trying to make sure I didn't drag my nails too hard against his scalp.

He held very still as I did so, which helped.

"I saw her looking at you as if she were trying to figure out if she knew your face. Also, I think some of her questions were aimed at trying to make you say something to her." I kicked my boots off and pulled down my trousers, which were a lost cause by now. I was left in my underwear and camisole, which were thin enough that the sterilizer should reach the skin.

"Sae, should I step out?"

His voice sounded strained for some reason.

"Hmm? No, it's fine. I've shared communal baths with Amie's brothers before. Unless you're uncomfortable with nudity—" He made a strange noise in his throat. "—alright... well, I wasn't planning on undressing entirely, just enough to make sure the sterilizer gets everywhere."

The moment I said everywhere, Zarek's eyes slowly traveled the length of my body and back up again and I was suddenly not as comfortable with the idea. This did not feel at all like bathing with the Esholittes. I should have gone with Amie.

It was much smaller than it looked from the outside.

Zarek placed one hand on the wall behind me.

Leaning toward me, he was much too close now.

I almost shivered despite the hot air around us.

"Actually, I'm quite interested in your cultural norms." A grin began to slowly stretch across his face. "Nudity did you say?"

"You really don't have to," I assured him quickly, "If you're uncomfortable—"

"Perfectly comfortable. Eager even." He said without an ounce of self-consciousness as I struggled to maintain eye contact. "Do I strip now or do you help?"

"I think I'm clean! I'll just leave you to it."

I dashed out before he could say anything else, his low laughter at my hasty retreat doing nothing to calm my charged nerves. I was so distracted I almost ran right into Alexi, who was semi-buried under the mountain of white clothes she held in her arms.

I dropped my old clothes and helped her get her burden to a nearby table, her veils now slightly out of place.

"Thank you." She wrinkled her nose at the pile. "I'm sorry it's all so monochrome, the apostles don't wear any other color but they're baggy! So at least they should fit alright but let me know if they don't and I'll see what I can do."

"They're much appreciated. Actually, if you have a moment, we were hoping to speak to you about a private matter."

"Of course! My office is just down the hall to the left. I'll leave the door open, so take your time—" She turned and ran face-first right into Omere, who'd also chosen to strip to his undershorts in the sterilizer with soiled clothes in hand.

She was knocked over, her veils slipping down.

Empress have mercy.

No one would think a sibling of Zarek's would be lacking in physical attributes, but now I could see what justified covering her head entirely. What was blue-black on Zarek's head was a deep, rich sapphire on hers, all in a riot of curls that glowed in the faintest of light. Her features were flawless—precisely, beautifully carved into an achingly vulnerable face.

Obviously in a panic, she struggled to wrap the fabric more securely around her face and head. When Omere reached out to help her, she flinched. He didn't notice and deftly wrapped the veils securely over all of Alexi's hair before taking the other and wrapping it over the entirety of her face.

Obviously pleased with his work, Omere walked around her without a word and started looking through the clothing she'd brought in, leaving her sitting on the ground.

Alexi pulled the fabric down to uncover her eyes and peered back at Omere, who had found a suitable shirt. She seemed wary and just as before, I felt a kinship with her. I knew what it was like when people fell over themselves trying to help you. The exasperation of people using any excuse to get near you, even touch you. It was suffocating and I was glad to see Omere had no more use for appearances than he did for the too-small shoes he was trying on.

"Thank you," Alexi said cautiously.

Omere nodded, preoccupied with the shoe hooks.

Ten minutes later, we looked like we were attending Elysian coming of age ceremonies—clad in all white as we were—and broke into two groups. Amie and Omere to go scout out the rest of the bunker for the memory and Zarek and I to find Alexi's office.

"Please come in!" Alexi cheerfully called out, seeing us in the doorway. "I'm just finishing up the transfer paperwork for the next pickup." She gathered her work and set it aside. "This will be the biggest case we've ever accomplished. Twenty-six infants, all under their first year and in relative good health."

"Where did they come from? Where are they going?" I sat down in one of the chairs, so I wasn't looming over her.

I tugged at Zarek's sleeve until he sat down next to me.

"It's easy to buy or find babies abandoned on Invicta," Alexi explained matter-of-factly. "I partner with a few organizations, but there are only enough spots for me to come by once a year or so. The children are scattered, and I get regular updates on them." She was shooting glances at Zarek, who was doing an excellent job of not looking at her at the same time she looked at him.

"Most of them are never adopted and get contracted to work off their debts, once grown, to their nation state. Their futures are so much brighter once they're removed, especially for those who've been crippled or are the product of addicted parents."

"Have you ever considered taking them across the border?"

"I would love to." Her eyes lit up. "But crossing into Elysia would mean taking the risk of being shot down by the outer universe's border control. We've been discouraged from asking official channels to take children there, but I do have some mock ups!"

Alexi and I were too easily absorbed into the topic. It took her getting up to rummage through her files for me to remember why we were here. I turned to Zarek, hoping he wasn't too put out, but found that he was smiling at me and not at all bothered by my monopoly of Alexi's attention.

He leaned forward and gently swept my hair behind my ear.

"I should have known you and Alexi would love each other."

At the sound of her name, Alexi's files slipped out of her hands and the files scattered to the ground.

Zarek and I stood up, which was not the right move as it just made her back up against the wall behind her desk. We slowly sat back down and tried to look unthreatening.

"How do you know my name?" She asked calmly. "Who are you? Are you really Saekonari?"

"Yes, I am." I turned to look at Zarek.

Now would be a good time for him to explain.

"My name is Zarek Deutreax Trace." He was trying to seem harmless again but Alexi didn't look like she believed him. "I'm looking for my younger sister. We were separated when she was three. Her name was Alexi."

Where did she pull that out from? It was quite the firearm and Alexi looked very capable of using it. "There was no separation. My brother died when I was three years old." She said softly. "I don't know how you tricked Saekonari into finding me, but I can assure you I am much less gullible."

"Is that what Kyrian told you? That I died?"

"Is he who you're after? I have no idea where he might be."

"I'm looking for my sister. Who I wasn't sure was alive until—"

"I haven't spoken to Kyrian in years."

"I don't care where that bastard is." Zarek stood back up, circumventing the desk. He stopped short of arm's length to give her room to shoot him if she decided to. "Look at me, Lexi. Don't you recognize me? Remember me?"

She shook her head vigorously.

"I don't know who you are, but I—"

"I'm looking for my little sister. Who told me she'd teach me how to read when we got out because we both knew you were the brains of the family. Who asked me what her mother's name was when I almost forgot. Our mother's name was Jacqueline, which is where I'm guessing you got AJ from. My little sister hummed to help me sleep because she can't sing worth a damn. She had a horrible habit of trying to raise vermin instead of eating it."

A soft sound escaped Alexi, and she lowered her weapon.

Zarek tsked at her.

"Didn't I teach you to never lower your weapon in a fight?"

Alexi must have missed that lesson, because she dropped the firearm. Zarek easily caught the weapon before it could hit the ground. He placed it carefully on the desk and seemed very much at a loss for how to approach her now.

"Can I hug you!?"

Zarek barely had the time to nod before she did so.

Should I leave? I mouthed at him as soon as I caught his eye.

I don't know! He mouthed back, looking a bit overwhelmed.

Just as I was going to get up and leave anyway, Alexi pulled back and motioned for her brother to let her go. She went rummaging around her desk, and when Zarek offered her a handkerchief, it caused another flash flood of tears.

"I can't believe you kept this." Instead of using it, she pulled off her veils to mop up her face as I went to go close the door. "Thank you," Alexi sniffled "I wasn't thinking." She wiped her nose and even that was adorable.

"Has your life been good Alexi?" Zarek asked her gently.

"Yes. The universe is bigger and more beautiful than I could have ever dreamed. I have so much I want to tell you!" Alexi laughed through her tears, and just as quickly she turned shy. "What about you Zarek? Has your life been good too?"

His gaze flickered to me and my heart skipped a beat.

"Better than anything I could have hoped for." He wiped away a few of Alexi's tears. "Did Kyrian do anything? Was he kind?"

"No, Kyrian never gave me a second look but I hated the way he treated everyone else." Alexi then held out her hands to me and when I came closer, she threw her arms around me too.

"Thank you for helping my brother." I stroked her curls, feeling some of her tears soak into my clothes. "How did he convince you?" Alexi asked, still hugging me. "I know he's tenacious, but he's not the most tactful or persuasive—"

"I think I'm offended." Zarek laughed.

Alexi made a face at him.

"We were already traveling together when he told me about you." I gave an abridged summary of the past few months and the more I spoke, the more surprised she looked. When I finished, she tugged at Zarek until he bent down.

"You told me you would never fall in love!"

It wasn't really a whisper.

"Don't mind her." Zarek covered her mouth before she could say more. "I dropped her on her head one too many times. She was sadly never the same. It's unfair really that I inherited all the beauty and brains in the family."

"Oh my good Empress, you really do love her!"

Chapter 30: Memories

Alexi was hesitant at first to return with us, but enthusiastically agreed once I extended the invitation to the babies. After being assured that small amounts of my Light wouldn't be detectable from the outside, I performed a routine health check on them. Several of the infants had genetic disorders and birth defects, some I could handle myself but the majority would have to be seen by professionals back home. They were also all undernourished, which I quickly and easily remedied.

"I wish I inherited my mother's gifts," Alexi said wistfully.

"AJ?" A few apostles stood awkwardly in the doorway.

Alexi put down the infant she held and went to speak to them.

I was very glad I'd followed Alexi's lead to cover my entire head and face from view. There was no telling what these already jumpy people would do if they found out I was standing in front of them.

It was better to keep them in the dark.

"I'm sorry, but I really must insist that you stay on this level. The ground becomes more unstable the lower you go." Alexi held up her hand when they began to argue. "I know how important your research is to you, but no study is worth risking your lives."

They looked categorically crestfallen but nodded their assent.

"Excuse me, I don't mean to interrupt," I came up and the apostles took a moment to tear their gaze away from Alexi. "I just wanted to thank you for the spare clothes. What is your research about? Perhaps I can be of some help."

"It's a sensitive topic." One of the older ones said apologetically at the same time, one of the others said, "We're trying to find the—ow!" He was slapped in both shoulders by those next to him.

Before things could escalate, Amie pushed passed them, Omere right on her heels. "We have a problem. C'mon."

This time the apostles got out of her way.

They and Alexi decided to follow us to the end of one of the unused sections. It was easy to see why this part of the ship was blocked off, I could hear the metal creaking with every step we took. Exposed wiring and mechanical parts were rusted over into unrecognizable shapes. Taking in every detail, I calculated the possible costs involved with retrieval and historical preservation.

"Did you always live down here?" I asked Zarek quietly.

"Only the last few months. I found it by accident and besides the occasional skeleton, no one ever bothered us down here. Alexi must have shown Mallee how to find it." Zarek and I ducked under the dented ceiling. "She's never been good at keeping secrets."

Amie walked to where the wreckage collapsed the passageway and rapped her knuckles smartly against it. "The last memory is behind all of this. There's an open space on the other side."

She finally noticed the apostles and glared at the ones who tried to get a closer look; they very quickly backed off.

"I know you're all curious." Alexi gathered them together to scold them, "But this is a private matter for our guests and has nothing to do with your research. Not to mention, it's almost time for your daily meditations, isn't it?" She shooed them away and while some looked mutinous, they left.

We waited until the apostles cleared the immediate area.

"Let me see." I placed my hand against the ship's walls.

From behind me, I heard Alexi complimenting Omere's braids and him saying thank you. I heard Amie's foot tapping against the ground impatiently and the apostles gathering in another part of the ship. As the layout and shape of this place unfolded before me, one thought raced forward in my mind.

This ship was Elysian and it was ancient.

Several examples of Elysia's original fleet remained in hermetically sealed storage alongside many other artifacts of the Raajali. I had written about the breakthroughs in engineering Eun-hye Raajali had made in preparing to retake the home world and establish our borders. This ship was built very much identical to those stealth ships, but on a much larger scale.

What was this place?

I couldn't think of a single incident that would have resulted in this ship being so far away from home. The configuration was such that it could sustain quite a sizable colony. It reminded me of ships used by nomadic tribes in the outer universe to live generationally, but it couldn't have survived existing for over twenty-three million years. Yes, there were signs of aging and decay but nothing that could be more than a few millennia old.

I felt like I was being watched and I let go of the walls.

"I want to see what's on the other side." I told the others. I wasn't entirely positive of what I was seeing and I didn't want to recklessly leap into any conclusions before I was certain.

For all I knew, an Empress of the past could have sent this ship outside on purpose for covert reasons or it could just be a very good forgery. I'd never seen this model even in history books. If I'd learned anything from this trip outside, it was that doubt in moderation was not cynical, but healthy. I'd be risking detection, but this seemed too important to wait.

Amie nodded and started putting up sound barriers. I put up a few more lights into the air to illuminate the area and reinforced the floor in all directions just in case. Something that I found particularly alarming was that this ship was partially carved from living stone. No civilization used nonsynthetic materials to build ships if they could help it. They were too heavy and, as a general rule, unable to withstand the extremes of open space.

I approached the wreckage and seeing that most of it was structural to the ceiling, it would be better to lift rather than push. Taking every precaution, I began checking for stress points. Just as I was calculating the approximate weight and area, Omere came up and held my hand.

"Hmm? What is it, Omere?"

He shrugged but looked agitated.

Omere would tell me in his own time if it was important, so I just let him hold my hand for support. Seeing that Amie was done, I wrapped my Light over this entire section and raised the wreckage to form an open archway to the other side. As the pieces settled into their new places, dust rose around our ankles and settled as Zarek kept the air around us clean. What I expected to find was darkness on the other side as opposed to the light that now flooded out

.

No. It couldn't be.

I walked quickly through to the other side, hoping that it was not what I thought it was. Amie slammed into me when I stopped, but I barely registered it as my eyes took in the scene before me.

Oh, good and gracious Empress.

The walls were inlaid with the same jewel that the palace throne room was carved from. One that produced and bounced its own ultraviolet light inside their crystalline structure. They were endemic to the home world. They grew brighter with age, but it took millions of years of being left undisturbed for the gem to turn this blinding. The columns of gemstones arched upwards in the perfectly round room to form the dorm. In the center was a pedestal about a one hundred and fifty centimeters tall.

On top sat a little black cloth bag.

Surrounding the pedestal was a floor overrun with skeletons.

Somebody behind us screamed.

We whipped around just in time to stop a horde of apostles from entering. They were weeping, praying, and speaking gibberish as they tried to shove us out of their way. One of them pushed Alexi over and that was the wrong move.

Zarek shoved them back through the archway with one snap of his fingers, no longer entertaining their attempts to get to the holy place, or at least that was what I thought they were saying. He gave his sister a hand up before turning back to deal with them. The apostles were back on their feet, but none of them accounted for the fact that Zarek was still angry.

"Wait." I grabbed his arm and Zarek stopped.

I needed to talk to them.

I pulled off the veils that covered my head.

The moment my white hair was uncovered, they stopped running toward us. By the time I'd pulled the veils off my face, four were crying and all of them had their heads dropped down to the ground. I could hear them start to pray.

Why did people think we liked that?

"Um, could you please stand?"

The man closest to us almost hurt himself getting up too fast.

He spoke first.

"Eternal Majesty Nicaristae I am so honored to be in your presence! The apostles and I have prepared accolades in preparation for such an event! Please excuse us for being unaware of your holy visit to us mortals!" He was sobbing and I was more uncomfortable than I'd ever been in my life. "We are unworthy! We are unworthy to see your perfection in the flesh! We—"

"Please stop." I underestimated how awful this would be. Not to mention embarrassing. "Is there perhaps a representative who can speak for you?" It took a bit more coaxing before I found an apostle who was not awed beyond reason.

"Eternal Majesty Nicaristae! How may I be of service you!?"

"My name is Saekonari. No one calls me Nicaristae. And Eternal Majesty refers only to the Empress." I grabbed them before they could throw themselves on the ground again. "Please don't do that. No one in Elysia does that."

He met my eyes and disturbingly, he started reaching for my face.

"I'd rather you didn't..." His eyes completely glazed over.

I let go of him and tried to take a few steps back, but he followed.

One moment he was reaching.

The next he was jumping at me.

Zarek was there in an instant, grabbing the man's wrist and applying pressure in such a way that the glazed-over look in his eyes shattered and he screamed. Zarek let go of him and the man curled up on the ground, gasping for breath.

"She said no," Zarek growled low in his throat.

"Let me try something." I touched Zarek's shoulder, noting how rigidly he stood. He helped me wrap my head back in the veils, using a thin layer to obscure my eyes as well. I knelt down to get to the level that the apostle was cowering on and waited until they felt safe enough to look at me.

Thankfully, his eyes didn't glaze over again.

"Earlier, I heard that you were trying to find something for your research. Why did you come here? What are you looking for and why are you looking for it?"

"The apostles have always searched for the One's temple."

"You mean Aristae, don't you? Aristae's Temple doesn't exist."

"Yes, it does!" He insisted. "It's here! We finally found it!"

"Aristae is not in there. She died a long time ago."

One of the older men on the ground actually raised his head to disagree with me. "The One *disappeared* before she had reached adulthood! There is no evidence to say she *died*. Her temple will be found in the days leading to her resurrection! She will unite the universe in her glorious return! She will reward those loyal to the Raajali with everlasting happiness and peace!"

The others joined in with varying levels of fantastical dogma. Aristae's Temple was where the chosen would ascend to join her in a euphoric plane of existence! Aristae was destined to reincarnate, despite none of them actually believing that she'd died, into the new heir. Me. That my birth led credence to their doctrines and that the Empress was sure to come at any moment to announce the coming of the One. They explained that I must be feeling the truth to their words and the anticipation of the One's soul must be confusing me. On and on they went.

"What is it that you expect to find in there?"

"The soul of Aristae! When the body and soul of the one meet, she shall be reborn. She shall create a new era devoid of suffering and pain! Her Light is one so great that her reach shall finally encompass all others in this universe. The Empresses shall finally take their rightful place and we shall bear witness!"

"Are you saying she'll take my body?" I interrupted again because it was clear they would not stop. "Is that what you believe?"

"Yes! It is truly an honor! my congratulations!"

"What happens to my soul?"

"What?"

Apparently, they had no ready answer for me.

As they looked to each other, I felt something truly horrid stir inside. I was so angry. Angry at them for seeing me as some sort of empty vessel for their delusions. Angry at Mother for keeping me ignorant. Angry at Elysia for not stepping in as the outer universe struggled right outside our doors.

Angry at myself for everything else.

It rose up to strangle me all at once.

I got to my feet and my anger was causing the apostles to inch away from me. I just couldn't seem to feel as sorry as I usually did for scaring them. What a misguided group these people were.

I felt a soft pressure around my waist, Zarek's lips brushed against my temple and like ice water on a white-hot surface, my anger bounced and sizzled out. I sighed as he hugged me a bit closer. "You ruined my perfectly good temper."

"How dare you touch Nicaristae so cavalierly!"

That was it.

I silenced all of them.

"Here is what I'm going to do," I told the apostles once I had them all upright. I pulled them into a single file line, their feet lifted off the ground. "I am going to take you all with me into the room you want to call Aristae's Temple. You are going to see for yourselves that she is not there and you are going to swear to me that you will never reveal this day, or anything related to this day to anyone ever. You will not do or say anything. Understand?"

I waited until they agreed and one by one, a ring formed around their wrists and sealed their vows. I nodded at Amie, and she took custody of the apostles as we reentered the room.

Omere took my hand again and behind me, I could hear Alexi and Zarek whispering to each other.

"How come you never looked this happy when I was bossy?"

"She makes it look good. You don't."

Coming back into the room the second time, the feeling that I was being watched grew. I had Amie line the apostles along the wall and keep them there while we looked closer at the room's occupants. There were forty-two full skeletons in total. All of them fully intact. There was no evidence that they'd rotted where they lay and no signs of trauma that may have caused their deaths. Everything in this room was spotlessly clean. Even the ground beneath the skeletons held no dust.

I covered everyone in a thin layer of air that would insulate both us and the room from being cross-contaminated. No matter what I found in here, I would want to send actual experts someday. If this ship really was of Elysian origin, it was a priceless, missing piece of our history. Despite my trepidations, I was thrilled.

Their clothes were unmistakably Elysian, but a few of the bodies had the skeletal structure of another species entirely. The fabric I dated to be only a few thousand years at most. The style echoed my family and Esholitte's ceremonial robes, but they were off in a way I found uncanny. Various decorations adorned their bones, gleaming as if they'd been polished just the day before, and they were positioned implying they'd all died the same way.

Facing the pedestal and that little black bag.

I circled around it, narrating all of my findings out loud for posterity's sake in the recording devices Alexi had produced and put off getting too close to it. There was a meter-wide circle around the pedestal. It was carved from the same gem that decorated the walls of the room and nothing about it was inherently threatening. I could see that whatever was inside was tiny.

It didn't stop me from feeling uneasy about it all.

"Note the time as I proceed to open the artifact."

I'd done all of the tests that I could think of to see if this was a trap and I couldn't postpone forever. I reached out to touch the pouch, but as my fingertips grazed the fabric, my ears filled with a hundred voices all blending together.

She didn't love you! I thought this obsession—

It's not a fucking obsession! Just because she was too fucking good for me!? I loved her! She would have loved me too if it weren't for everyone else telling her lies about me! Everyone thought she was so fucking perfect! She was so fucking perfect! They treated me like shit and for what!? I deserve—

Please, for your own sake! Forget about her!

Don't tell me what to fucking do! Fuck you all!

He's dangerous. We need to get rid of him. Before it's too late.

He shouldn't even be here in the first place.

He wouldn't take no for an answer. He never has.

This is all her fucking fault! I should have known they had it out for her just like they had it out for me! Why couldn't they just let me talk to her!? Wasn't I fucking good enough for her!? Didn't I do everything to show her that nobody loved her more than I did!? She wouldn't even give me a chance! All I wanted was a chance and they couldn't even give me that!"

He's unstable. He'll kill us all in our sleep.

We need to contact home.

The voices vanished just as I lifted the pouch and opened the thin drawstrings. I stared blankly inside of it for a few heartbeats, not believing what I was seeing. I slowly looked up at the apostles who were watching me with wide, hungry eyes.

And tipped the bag over, shaking it to show that it was empty.

As Alexi tried to calm them from their silent violent struggling, I palmed the memory that had been inside the pouch and discreetly passed it over to Zarek so the apostles wouldn't see.

He just raised an eyebrow at me, his eyes laughing as the memory crumpled to nothing between our fingers.

I waited until the apostles settled down before releasing them.

"This isn't Aristae's temple! We have to continue the search!"

"How could this not be Aristae's temple!?"

"Nicaristae herself appeared!"

"This is simply further proof that we are on the holy path!"

"We must have missed something in our research!"

"We need to regroup!"

They eagerly headed for the door; their belief entirely unshaken. They invited me along, but I just waved them on. Interacting with them had been exhausting. Amie and I joined together one last time to check if there were any more memories left and found none. Zarek tried to see if there were any obvious gaps in his recollection, but found nothing particularly glaring.

As soon as we got home, I would need to have a talk with Mother. Universe help me.

"We're done!" I beamed up at Zarek. "We can go home!"

I allowed myself feel giddy with relief, actually letting out a helpless laugh as Zarek pulled me up against him and spun me around and off my feet. He grinned down at me, his smile making me feel like starlight myself.

That was when it all came crashing down.

Chapter 31: Absolutions

The apostles were dead.

Their bodies vaporized by close range disruptors illegal in most nations. It was only Amie's quick reflexes that stopped the next volley from entering the room. Zarek pulled me to the ground and out of the line of sight. Alexi had managed to shove both herself and Omere out of the way. It happened so fast that I hadn't been able to identify the threat. Amie collapsed the tunnel I'd made earlier, crushing whoever was trying to attack us.

A massive explosion rocked the ground below our feet and just as I thought the ship would settle, another sequence of bombardments blew open the top of the ship. I stopped the collapsing ceiling from crushing us just as I felt the ship beneath us cracking from the stress. The gemstones and mosaics were falling off of the walls, the support beams buckling. A sharp shard sliced the back of Alexi's leg open but at least I could be assured she healed just as quickly as her brother.

The stench was even more horrible than I remembered. I held up not only pieces of the ship's hull, but hundreds of meters of layered garbage and sewage. It now all poured down in in a never-ending torrent over our heads.

"Everyone get closer!" I shouted, "I'll get us out of here!"

"We can't leave the children!" Alexi yelled as she wrapped her leg in her veils. "They won't survive on their own!"

Aster belts, she was right. Whatever was causing this place to collapse wasn't physically on Invicta and I had to stretch my senses to realize that this entire floating deathtrap was surrounded by a legion of Rateerian ships.

What were they doing all the way out here!?

They were indiscriminately blasting at the surface and only a few hits were penetrating deep enough to get to us. Yet, it wouldn't be long until Invicta completely fell apart. I could hear the inhabitants above, furious at being exterminated from the face of their universe, and truly felt conflicted on whether I should help them. I didn't have much time to decide.

"I'll take us to the children, but we need to go now!"

Too many sources of stress were bearing down on us.

We needed to move.

The collapsed tunnel was blasted open and I had to quickly sweep them aside before the pieces hit my friends. The soldiers on the other side of the debris did not wear Rateerian uniforms and none of them carried regulation weapons.

It meant this wasn't a state sanctioned attack or that Kyrian was trying to make it look like it he hadn't approved this.

Omere and Alexi were directly in the line of fire. I threw out an absorption field to protect both of them, but my attention was then forced back to the situation above our heads. Rateerian ships were converging over us and taking advantage of the weak spot they'd created where the ship's hull had caved in.

The concentrated strike caused the entire place to lurch under our feet and I almost lost my balance. If I didn't somehow stop their attempts to destroy this place, we wouldn't be able to get to the children. Some of them were on external life supports and we would need time to stabilize them before transport.

I tried to stop their weapons from firing, but instead caused an explosion on three of the ships. I didn't want to hurt anyone! They kept firing even before I let them go. I didn't know what to do!

I needed time to think!

I didn't have any sort of training for this!

"An electromagnetic pulse can take out their ships long enough to distract them." Zarek's calm voice drew me out of my panic. He took over the protections around our friends, allowing me to pull all my attention into keeping this ship together and creating a wide electromagnetic net to push outwards from Invicta.

All but a few of the ships were hit and stalled.

"It won't slow them down for long. If you can find their engine rooms..." Zarek stood at my back and gave me detailed instructions on how to sabotage their power cores without harming their life support system that were wired into a secondary source.

It was finicky but it was working.

At the same time, he was moving the protections so that our friends could make their way over to us as quickly as they could. Amie was busy pulling down the nonstructural elements of the ship to block the soldiers trying to blast their way through and Alexi was still limping from the deep cut on her leg. Omere held her up, kicking skeletons out of her way.

Omere and Alexi had almost reached us when something large shattered Zarek's force fields and caused a shockwave so brutal it knocked us all to the ground. Zarek rolled both of us to the ground and threw out his arm to raise a heavy layer of shielding around Omere and his sister.

A violent change in pressure created a second shockwave that crackled against Zarek's efforts, but even worse was that I could see Amie take on the blast full force. Weapons mounted on armored drones were the source. At least five that I could see. Amie was knocked off her feet and into the far wall. Shrapnel peppered her left arm and shoulder, her blood cascading down that side of her head and blinding her in one eye. I threw my Light recklessly to her, but I could see that rather than healing her, my panicked attempts were harming rather than helping.

I could see the soldiers aiming right for Amie and at us. I was holding up the ship from collapse while preventing us from being crushed under the tons of filth that threatened at any moment to leak through. I was still trying to disable another power core but it was taking too long to finesse each one. I was panicking and my mind went blank as they fired at Amie again.

The room filled with billowing black smoke.

Every weapon within a radius of one light year melted into molten pools, burning anyone who held or stood next to them. The room burst outwards and crushed soldiers against the falling rubble that I'd let go of.

Explosions rocked every single ship within one light year.

I'd been too concerned about hurting them and look where it had gotten me. I could not afford to worry about them while those I loved were in danger. This had gone on long enough. I swept the floor clean of obstacles and debris, sending it flying out of my way as I ran toward Amie. Already apologizing to her over and over in my head for letting things get this far.

With my senses thrown wide, I could feel reinforcements warping into this sector. If Kyrian thought he was going to get to me now he was sorely mistaken. Zarek had taken his sister from Omere and the two of them sprinted after me. I'd let the mess of the world above us gush down to seal the space around our bubble, no longer caring if the soldiers drowned in the sewage.

I stopped in my tracks, shocked at the picture before me.

Cira Kyrian had appeared and she'd used her own body to take the brunt of the blast. The entire back of her body was an open wound, both of her legs had suffered enough damage that I wasn't sure if one of them could be kept instead of amputated. A quick glance told me that there was no major organ left untouched by blunt force trauma. Cira's scorched spine was almost fully visible. Her brain was most likely suffering from severe hemorrhaging. She was only barely alive and wouldn't be for much longer. She didn't have a chance if I didn't intervene.

She trafficked in a Naga's dismemberment, bought and sold their bodies as if they were common commodities. I could not forgive her for it. Cira Kyrian deserved everything that was happening to her. She'd done this to us.

She'd endangered us all over and over.

But she'd protected Amie.

Amie, who'd I thought hated Cira the most, was frantically trying to stop the blood from gushing and her body from seizing while only being able to use one of her arms. With no formal medical training and still heavily injured herself, Amie looked up at me, a desperation I'd never seen clouding her violet eyes.

Please. Amie's lips formed the words, no sound coming out. Each syllable weighed down by unspeakable emotion. *Please, Sae.*

"I can try to shore up as much blood as I can." Zarek said, "Between the two of us, it wouldn't be impossible..."

He waited to see how I would respond.

Amie was cradling Cira's body, covered in the blood of a woman who'd been complicit in so much harm to the universe.

Amie had never asked me for anything before.

"I need you to move back." I hovered Cira's body off the ground and supplied the necessary chemical components to her brain manually while I reassessed the damage. Zarek and I knelt on either side of her ravaged body, and he kept her from losing any more blood while simultaneously collecting and cleaning Cira's blood cells off of the ground and all around us.

"Take from my reserves and keep the barrier stable around us." Amie nodded and we pretended not to hear her tears and muffled sobs. I took note of it and then shoved it aside. "Zarek. I want to send Alexi and Omere ahead to get the infants ready to transport. Do you think it's a bad idea?"

I spoke just softly enough so the others couldn't hear me.

"It's a good idea." But he didn't like it. "I can't let her get hurt."

"And I won't let them get hurt." I met Zarek's gaze, Cira's skin cells rapidly multiplying under my hands. Even with both of us working on her body, she'd suffered too much physical damage for us to move her unless I froze the time around us. It would be a step that I didn't think I could do, even for Amie.

The list of things that could go wrong was too long. Alexi was the only person who knew which technologies and treatments the children needed to be able to survive transport. Omere would follow her direction with no questions asked.

I had come to care for both of them. Deeply.

Which is why this decision had to be made by all of us.

Zarek explained the plan to Alexi and Omere and they both agreed immediately. There were no signs of these intruders on that end of the ship. Their focus was centered on this room and on us. If we could keep them distracted long enough we could get Cira to a workable condition and grab Omere, Alexi, and the children in the instant it would take to get back to Elysia.

I had to exchange one of my priorities for another, feeling that the reinforcements were now blasting down deeply into Invicta to reach the ship. This place was going to be destroyed before Elysian archeologists would ever get the chance to study it, but the lives of my friends were far more important to me.

So, I let go of my hold on most of this crumbling world.

The moment I reined in my Light to protect only this room and the area I'd sent Omere and Alexi was the moment that this world fell apart. I watched hundreds, thousands of people thrashing around our little bubble, clawing at their fellow sentients to try and survive. Their lives taken before my eyes.

Their last breaths were filled with excrement and misery and there I sat, in the middle of it all, repairing the body of my enemy while their lives were extinguished in the darkness.

It was all I could do to keep the Rateerian ships at bay and my shaking hands occupied on creating and knitting together pieces of veins, muscles, and skin. My entire focus was to bring this woman back from the death and every second that passed I only felt her soul slipping out of my reach.

Her heart stopped beating and I forced it back alive. Her brain wanted to dose itself with death chemicals and I delayed the inevitable. Her body was giving up on her but if I could only save her than this would have all been for something tangible. I needed her to breathe. I needed her to live!

When I restarted Cira's heart for the fifth time, Zarek tried to dissuade me. "She's not going to make it. We need to go." He grabbed my hands.

"No!" I started shaking. I was once again covered in filth and blood and I couldn't stand it if I watched another person die today. I had hurt so many people. I needed to save one. I still had questions for her. She still had so much to answer for! I threw my Light down into Cira's body, no longer caring where it went or if I was following proper medical guidelines.

I could no longer hear her soul.

A searing glow flooded from my hands. I felt my Light burst like the sun over the horizon. A warmth that was achingly familiar filled my body and beckoned to the souls that barely clung to life. It was not only Cira's that I felt, but thousands of lives that had ended prematurely around me. Thousands of people who were touched by my Light, and just as abruptly, I felt my own body collapse beside Cira, whose wounds were gone and whose eyes were open.

I sat up of my own volition just as Zarek appeared to pull me away from Cira and frantically checked me all over to see if I was hurt. He was shaking. I was shaking. I had never done anything like that before. No that wasn't true. I had done it before and Cor's words once again echoed in my head.

How could this happen without your power over life and death?

Zarek was holding me to him, whispering unintelligible words against my hair, calming and flustering me all at the same time. "You scared the ever-living shit out of me." He held back just a bit to look me over a few more times before pulling me tight against him. He was so warm and solid that I couldn't help but cling.

Whatever else he whispered was lost on me; however, as I watched Amie slap Cira across the face and then put up absolutely no resistance when Cira pulled her down for a hard, needy kiss.

Now that, I did not see coming.

Zarek lifted his head once I poked him in his shoulder a few times and he barely reacted at all to seeing them rolling on the ground, each seemingly trying to outdo the other on how aggressively they could kiss.

"At least they won't take it out on me anymore." He grumbled.

Another shockwave boomed above us and made the two of them come to their senses. I went over and checked Cira's body, amazed there didn't seem to be a single thing out of place. Amie had draped her own cloak over her so she wasn't naked, but a closer examination found not a single mark left on her skin.

"Are you feeling alright?" I asked her quietly.

"Better than I ever have." She said sincerely. "Thank you."

"I did it for Amie. You don't have to thank me, Cira."

"But I do have to apologize. For a lot of things."

In that, we agreed. I checked Cira for weapons or communications devices and had the cloak wrap itself securely around her, binding her head to foot. Cira struggled, but I wasn't letting her get away. An apology was just not enough to make up for the damage she had done. The crimes she'd committed. Amie was biting her lip hard and I knew this wasn't going to be easy for her.

On one hand, I'd just seen what Cira meant to my Sentinel. On the other, Amie had a sense of justice even more rigid than mine.

As we appeared inside the nursery, I let the section we'd left behind fall away.

"What are you doing here?" Zarek grabbed his sister and pulled her away from Mallee, the baby that Alexi was about to hand off to her was jostled and began to cry.

Omere was busy moving the breathing apparatuses, his hands full, and was taken by surprise by Mallee's knife.

Omere lashed out at being pinned to the wall by the blade in the shoulder, but his struggles only succeeded in twisting the knife in deeper. The pain only seemed to make him angrier but he was forced to stop moving or have his jugular sliced open by another knife Mallee held in her white-knuckled hands.

"Mallee what are you doing!?" Alexi yelled. "Stop it! Let him go!"

"She's the fucking snitch who told Kyrian you were here!"

Amie had to stop a second knife from hitting Cira.

I forced Mallee away from Omere and into the far wall.

Rushing forward, I eased his pain and healed him as quickly as I could, pulling the knife out swiftly to minimize damage. Omere grunted his thanks and would have thrown Mallee's knife after her if I hadn't stopped him. She wasn't worth any of our time. I didn't know exactly how she'd hurt Zarek, but I did know that she'd just attacked Omere with no provocation.

"Forget about her. Are all the children ready?"

"All of the children are ready," Alexi confirmed.

"Alexi you can't leave me here! After all I've done for you!" Mallee screamed. "You told me this was the last time and that you wouldn't leave me behind this time! You swore you would get me out of this festering shithole! Alexi! Help me!"

She wouldn't stop screaming for Alexi to help her.

Alexi was pale, but she didn't once look Mallee's way as she gathered the infants together for me.

She made one final request before we left.

"I need to take care of her." Alexi nodded at Mallee, who instantly switched from screaming to crowing in triumph.

"I told her I'd get her out of her life here after this last pickup. She fulfilled her end of the bargain," Alexi said simply and Zarek nodded his assent, forcing me to allow Alexi to do as she pleased even if neither of us liked it.

I let Mallee down from the wall and she rushed forward to embrace Alexi. Her grin was almost ghoulish as it stretched her face wide. Alexi pulled something small out of a pocket in her trousers just as Mallee ran into arm's length.

And shot her clean in between the eyes.

Mallee fell over, dead on impact.

"That was for my brother."

She shot Mallee once more through the back of her head.

"And that was for Omere." Alexi smoothly slid the weapon back into what we now knew was a small thigh holster. She smiled serenely as she stepped over Mallee's corpse. Just like her brother, her face showed no remorse for those who wronged her.

"I thought you loved Mallee." Zarek said, dazed.

"When I was a baby, maybe. But I wasn't stupid Zarek. I knew." Alexi said fiercely. "I needed a contact here for the children, but I never forgot what she did to you. I never forgave her. I was never going to let her loose on the universe."

That day, I learned Alexi's eyes burned just as brightly as Zarek's.

Taking a moment to calm myself, I opened one last rift and assisted Alexi in transferring the children over to a very familiar place. A place that signaled true safety.

Aristae's tower lay on the other side.

A dormant piece of me felt it calling. Of course, I would never choose another fate than the one waiting for me back home. No matter what came, I had responsibilities and too many people who depended on me.

It was simply time to return to them.

Zarek reached for my hand, and I met him halfway.

This was only the beginning.

Our departure signaled the destruction of an aberration in the universe. A place that would not be missed by any who knew of it, even those inhabitants who called it home. The futility of the sacrifices made in that blink of spacetime would surely come back to haunt me someday. As I stepped back into my rightful place, I could hear the universe take in a breath.

All who could feel its pulse held their breath along with it.

About the Author

Having never thought she'd get this far, she'll be equally surprised if anyone actually reads these biographies hidden behind rarely turned pages. What could you want to know about a turtle? Favorite season? Winter. Hobbies? Yes, absolutely. Favorite herbs? Mint and Shiso. Spritfarer and Stardew Valley are her comfort videogames of choice. What mushroom is she wearing? *Lactarius Indigo* or Indigo Milk Cap. Her best writing is done between the hours of 1:00am to 6:00am.

Tea or coffee? Tea.

A lifelong love for Bradbury, Butler, and Star Trek inspired this story. Guilty pleasures of star-crossed romances and secret rendezvouses centers its soul. When not attempting to write with a giant pencil, she's checking in on James Webb or collecting banned books for her home library. She also acts as tech support for her old tortoise grandfather; who doesn't entirely understand, but fully supports her secret ambition of getting a physical copy of her work to the moon.

For extras, news, and more, visit A.D.Aelin.com

www.ingramcontent.com/pod-product-compliance
Lightning Source LLC
Chambersburg PA
CBHW060811120726
47909CB00006B/1876